DARKNESS FAIR

ALSO BY RACHEL A. MARKS

Darkness Brutal
(Book One of the Dark Cycle)

Winter Rose
(novella)

DARKNESS FAIR

BOOK TWO OF THE DARK CYCLE

RACHEL A. MARKS

SKYSCAPE

SKYSCAPE

Text copyright © 2016 Rachel A. Marks
All rights reserved.

Published by Skyscape, New York

www.apub.com

Amazon, the Amazon logo, and Skyscape are trademarks of Amazon.com, Inc., or its affiliates.

ISBN-13: 9781503950290
ISBN-10: 1503950298

Cover design by Cliff Nielsen

Printed in the United States of America

For my daddy, who taught me how to see.

Darkness brutal, darkness fair
steals a heart
with bell and book
and candle mark.

Even as I rise
I fall
apart
because of what it took,
clawing into home and hearth.

Bought by Darkness, lost to Light.
Love defiled
seeds child of night.

She seeks salvation in the stone
and lies among the brine alone,
her grave
a nest
of thorn and bone.

Darkness fair, Darkness savage,
at last atonement for my soul.
With Love so pure
it shields from night
when son will fall in sacrifice.

~ scribbled on a church bulletin, stuffed into Mom's grimoire ~

Hey Demon Dork,

I know that you're reading this and feeling betrayed. A sister isn't supposed to hurt her brother like I'm about to hurt you.

You know now what I am—you know that my humanity isn't real. Your determination, your goodness, isn't going to save me. But that's not your fault. Hopefully, by giving myself to them I can at least save one of us for a little while. Maybe wherever I am now I can stand in the doorway and hold them back. But you need to hear me. Don't come find me! Don't try and save me anymore. It's too late.

The Darkness knows you're in the wrong place, the wrong time. It'll do whatever it needs to make you surrender to them.

But that can't happen. You can't be brave, Aidan.

I will see you again, I will, but for now this letter will be my voice, my way of telling you what's next. Don't throw it away. Don't, for any reason, burn it. I'll find a way to write again.

Soon,
Ava

~ A note tucked away, waiting to be found ~

ONE

Aidan

I never would've come on this job if I'd known it involved a demon. But last night during the briefing, Sid acted like it didn't even involve anything paranormal.

"Probably just a human thing," he said. "We can wave a little smoke, give the client a prayer or two, maybe one of Holly's happy cookies, and the nice lady will be feeling better in no time."

Not exactly. Standing here looking at the client's massive living room that's piled to the ceiling with stuff, I can tell this won't be as easy as appeasing a grumpy five-year-old.

"You should've brought Connor," I mumble to Sid as I survey the mess around us. The *thing* is here somewhere. I can smell its rotten-egg ass even over the stale air and must coming from the clutter. Mountains of junk rim the walls and cover almost every inch of what looks like a very expensive marble floor. "I can't believe you dragged me here."

It's my first time on a job site since everything went to hell four weeks ago—literally. I've tried to stay out of the paranormal stuff; I need to know more about my Awakening and my new powers before I run headlong into crazy again. Not to mention that I need to focus my energy and abilities on figuring out how to bring my sister, Ava, back to me, not on helping random strangers. So instead of going out on jobs, I've spent most of my time at the LA Paranormal house, trying to figure out what I can do to fix Ava's sleeping state and wake her back up. I visit her body in the beach cave by my great-grandmother's house every day, looking for her spirit, looking for some sort of change in her, but that's about it for my excursions. Eric, my supposed guardian angel, appears to be in the wind. And all he left me for guidance was a vague journal. No help at all.

If Sid heard my complaint about being here on the job, he isn't acting like it. He's just smiling his salesman smile and listening intently to the large woman in the silk muumuu on the leather couch as she tells him how her cat tried to eat her last week. She looks young, midthirties. Too young to be wearing a muumuu and living in this filthy place. A bit of bandage peeks out from under her flowery sleeve. There's an angry-looking scratch on her neck, too. She ended up in the ER with twelve stitches from the attack.

"Fluffy keeps leaving dead mice lying around, dead rats, even floppy gophers," she says, her face wrinkling with disgust. "Dead all-sorts-a-stuff everywhere. It's starting to stink no matter which room I sit in, and I can't take it anymore. I can't seem to escape it. And then this happened." She motions to the scratches on her neck.

I smell the death, but the odor is layered with the putrid stink from rotten food, moldy boxes stacked end to end, and piles of clothes mixed with God-knows-what. Not to mention the sulfur wafting around from whatever demon is hiding in this place. How can this woman tell one gross thing from another?

Sid crunches his way over some debris to sit beside the client on the five inches of couch space still available.

"You rest easy," he says as he pats her broad shoulder. "My boy, Aidan here, will take care of anything that's gone wrong." He

motions toward where I'm standing by a stack of magazines and
DVDs, and the woman looks at me for the first time since Sid and
I walked through the door.

Her eyes grow a little when she studies my face, my hair, her
gaze taking in the markings on my hand and arm for a few seconds
longer than normal.

I really should be used to the staring by now. Ever since my
"change," or whatever we're calling it, strangers seem to think I'm
either something to marvel at . . . or something to fear. It makes me
wonder what they're sensing. Just one of the reasons I like staying
at the house and leaving the jobs to the others.

She gives me a half smile, half grimace, her lips tightening over
her teeth, then she turns back to Sid. "I'm not sure what else I can
do. I'll pay you whatever you want, just please, fix Fluffy. He's all
I have left now." Her voice shakes a little and she points to something near her foot that looks like a plastic box. No, a cat carrier. I
hadn't noticed it among the piles of clutter.

Something moves inside the carrier. A shadow. The cat? A hiss
emerges, like an answer, and the smell of sulfur billows out even
thicker.

A shiver runs through me.

Sid leans on his cane and stands up from his spot beside the
woman as he runs a hand over his bald head. Then he hesitates,
like he smells it, too. He steps back, studying the carrier, then looks
sideways at me, a question on his face.

Could the cat be possessed?

Or maybe the cat isn't a *cat*.

"So, Ms. Bentley." Sid clears his throat. "How long have you
had, um, the, um . . . Fluffy?" He tries to move back toward me,
but stumbles over a box marked *As Seen on TV*, before steadying
himself on a nearby coatrack—his arm tangles in the strap of one
of the very large bras hanging from the hook. He doesn't seem to

notice, though; his eyes still haven't left the small cat carrier at the client's feet.

"He was a neighborhood stray," she says, sounding deflated. "I took him in a month ago, shortly after . . . after my mother died. She hated cats, so I was never able to have one. And Fluffy was such a sweet thing." Her eyes glisten with growing sadness.

She puckers her lips like she's holding something in. Finally, she says, "Until a few days ago, he was all cuddles and smooches."

Well, now Fluffy is all talons and teeth.

"Very sorry." Sid finishes making his way over to me and pats me on the shoulder, very fatherly-like. "Aidan will need to look at the, uh, the . . . your Fluffy."

I turn to him. "Will I?"

He nods. "The show must go on, my boy."

Really? Must it?

Didn't Shakespeare say we're all actors on the stage of life, or something? Well, Sid takes that notion very seriously. The twenty-four-year-old time-traveling magician from the Babylonian court is always playing some part or another to fit the game.

He nudges me again and whispers sideways, "I know you've been wanting to jump back in, so here you go. Just see what you can accomplish. It's in a cage and all that." He waves his arm as if he's just explained how to go about this.

I glare at him and shake my head. "You're an ass."

He lets out a fake laugh and gives the client a look like, *Aren't teenagers impossible?* "It's a preliminary test, Aidan. So we know what we're dealing with."

I sigh. As much as I don't want anything to do with this job, I need to start figuring out my power. It feels like it's growing, every day, bigger and louder, like a ringing in my ears. It's pushing now, this weird urgency, making me itch to . . . well, kill. It's terrifying.

I need to get these new urges under control. And if I want to kill a demon again so badly, why not give it a whirl?

I'm wearing my amulet, so if a corporeal demon is in that carrier instead of a cat, then it won't see me. However, if the demon is *possessing* the cat, using the cat's eyes to see, then I'm about to be discovered.

I take a deep breath and step closer to get a look. Following the boss's orders.

Ms. Bentley leans toward her innocent Fluffy.

I crouch down to get a clearer view, avoiding the trash at my feet.

The cat hisses and its plastic carrier jerks and clangs. But the thing's not looking at me, it's more like it's sensing danger, its hackles rising. And then I see tiny horns beside the ears, and thorn-like protrusions on its back through grey-striped fur. Its eyes dart around the room—eyes like light reflecting off a pool of oil. Its teeth are shiny silver.

Not an actual cat. An actual corporeal demon. Check.

This lady is lucky all the thing did was set her up with a few stitches. It could've scratched off her face entirely.

Prickles work over my skin as I stare at the thing. Corporeal demons are somehow less disgusting than the ones I see on the other side of the Veil. The ones that manage to get called up by witches and cross over to the physical plane are always trying to masquerade as something they're not, and sometimes they suck at it—like Fluffy here, a cat with horns. Yes, they're still creepy, just not as creepy as when they're full monty in their spiritual form.

Looking at it makes the strange new urges in my gut stir, reminding me that I'm a killer now. Officially.

"Thank you, ma'am," I say, quickly standing, itching to run but not wanting to scare the woman more.

I stumble back to Sid's side and say under my breath, "We're done here."

"What sort of help will you be if you leave?" Ms. Bentley rests a hand on the carrier, as if comforting the demon inside. "We need help."

A corporeal demon as a pet. That's definitely new. I wonder how she hasn't noticed Fluffy's oddities. I mean, horns? Come on.

Maybe the fumes from the rotting crap in the house have messed with her head.

Sid clears his throat and waves an arm as if trying to keep her calm with hand gestures. "It's all right, Ms. Bentley. It's merely that your cat may be possessed and in need of an exorcism."

I turn and gape at him, wondering why he'd spit that out right now.

She gasps and clutches her muumuu to her chest with a meaty fist.

I nudge Sid. "But my boss and I should maybe discuss it and get back to you." Sid's reading this all wrong. Not surprising, since the guy is slowly losing his senses from staying too long in this time. But I'm not a fan of him blurting out made-up shit to the clients before we've agreed on what shit can be said out loud.

"I'm paying you to fix this now!" she says. "I can't leave poor Fluffy in a cage forever."

"We'll call you," I say, shoving Sid toward the door before he can say anything else stupid.

Sid trips over a karaoke machine and nearly dives into the wall headfirst. But somehow he looks graceful about it, with his thin limbs and delicate fingers reaching out like a dancer's. "Don't let it out of the cage. We'll call you tonight," he says, righting himself effortlessly with his cane. "And we'll try to get help here in the morning. Just, please, keep it locked up until then."

She stands, watching us maneuver our way out of the living room. "One more day!" she hollers with a catch in her voice before the door closes behind us, leaving us on the porch.

I need a shower.

TWO

Aidan

Once we're a few yards from the house, I turn on Sid. "You knew there'd be a demon on this job, didn't you?"

"I was unsure." He shrugs. "But I did have my suspicions," as if he's actually remorseful about snowing me.

I shake my head, pissed.

"You need to begin working again, Aidan. It's important."

"You keep saying that, but you have no idea what's going on."

"True," he concedes. "But neither do you. Wouldn't you like to discover the truth of who and what you're becoming?"

I'm not sure. Can this new version of me help me save Ava? Can it save the people I care about now?

I know the answer to the second question. This part I'm meant to play may not help me with Ava, but it can likely help me save *other* people. And it'd be selfish to think I have a right to keep something like that to myself. Even if it does scare the shit out of me.

"Listen," I say. "I get it. I needed to come into the world again. I need to figure all this stuff out, everything that I can do."

His eyes light up a little, thinking he's won, but he has the decency not to smile in satisfaction.

"But," I add, pointing my finger in his face. "If I'm going to help on jobs again, don't spout off like a dipshit before asking me what I see."

He nods, and pats his legs and arms like he's brushing off dirt as we walk to the car. "Yes, yes, but what the client believes is irrelevant. And it's obvious that the cat is possessed. A fool can see that."

Obviously not, since the cat *isn't* possessed. I sigh and walk to the driver's side. Sid's as blind as a bat.

"So," he continues, plucking hair from his shirt with a frown, "we'll give the client one more night to live in her *situation*, then we'll call her in the morning, letting her know, regrettably, it may cost a little more because of the complex ritual we'll have to perform." He winks at me and stands at the passenger side of the Camaro, waiting for me to unlock the doors.

"Seriously. You should be in prison. It's not a possessed cat, Sid."

He pauses. "What?"

"It's a demon, not a cat."

He glances back at the house. "Not a cat?"

"It had horns. It's not a cat."

"Interesting."

I open the driver's side door but hesitate before getting in. What if the demon decides to kill the woman before we can get back? The thing seemed to feel my presence, sensed I was a threat. It could be spooked now.

"We'll have to kill it," I say. "But I'm fairly sure the client won't be thrilled that we're eviscerating her kitty. We need to figure out a way to get rid of it without her knowing." Getting sued for killing a woman's cat is nothing compared to leaving something like this undone, knowingly abandoning a person in a deadly situation, but it would be great if we could avoid both.

Sid pauses for a second before responding, maybe deciding whether the money is worth it or not. "When we come back tomorrow, we'll convince her that the cat is dangerous. Maybe explain that it's a monster?"

"Or I could come back later tonight and finish this when the client's asleep," I say. "Kara and Connor can help me break in. The client will never know what happened."

Sid shakes his head. "What if you get caught? No. We can't take that chance. We should just leave it." He frowns at the house, his mind ticking away, obviously not sure about his decision. Then his eyes widen. "Actually we could fix this right now." He comes around to the driver's side of the Camaro. "Do you have a dagger?"

I nod. It's tucked into the waist of my jeans. I always have one with me. Iron or silver. Sid's bought me several of them in different sizes. The one I have right now is the smallest: a five-inch iron blade.

"Get it ready," he says. "I'll tell Ms. Bentley that you have to take the cat out to the yard, near the trees, to do the spell, then I'll wait with her in the house while you . . . dispose of it. You can say it ran off."

He heads for the door before I can mention that I think the plan is lame.

"Just make sure it scratches you up a bit," he whispers over his shoulder, "then we can threaten a countersuit if she starts talking about calling her lawyer because we lost her Fluffy."

"Great," I say as I follow. "I'll be sure to let the thing chew on me before cutting off its head." Sid knocks on the door, and I add, "You have a takeout menu stuck to your pants."

He turns in a circle, looking for the Chester's Chicken propaganda that's trying to hitch a ride on his pinstripe suit. He plucks it off and tosses it aside, then rights himself just as the client opens the door. I stand back as he explains—*lies*—about our plan, saying we'll cleanse the cat of the demon inside its furry body, and that it'll be painless and quick. The client's excitement is a glow around her as she waves us back in.

"Why don't you make me some tea?" Sid asks her as I maneuver my way to the cat carrier. "We'll let Aidan do what needs to be done." He nods for me to continue as he leads the client down a pathway through the junk mountains and into the kitchen, out of sight.

I hate being this close to a demon. The creature's energy is a damp chill against my skin. My new instinct screams to tear into the carrier and rip the thing to shreds, but I swallow the urgency and breathe. It's only a small demon, maybe twenty pounds, but its strength is more jungle than it is house cat. At least it's contained in something that I can carry.

Four weeks have passed since I killed my first demon. Sometimes I wonder if that night in the cave was actually real— did I seriously annihilate the wolflike monster that tore up my mother? The idea sends a wave of energy through me, my skin prickling with remembered adrenaline. I wish I could've done the same to the Heart-Keeper, but that thing is locked down in Sheol now, thanks to my mother's final sacrifice.

As if the demon in the room can sense what I want to do to it, it slams its body against the side of its cage with a bang, sending a crack across the plastic surface.

It's now or never. I grab the carrier handle and haul ass to the front door as the thing inside bucks and spits and hisses, its smell nearly unbearable now.

"Poor Fluffy," Muumuu-Lady moans from the kitchen.

I make it outside and down the walkway a bit before a claw breaks through the crate's side, snagging my forearm, leaving two long welts behind. My sue-worthy scratches.

Fire shoots up my arm from the strike, making me drop the carrier.

The box hops with the furious movement of the demon inside, and several more cracks form as the plastic bangs against the brick path in a frantic rhythm. The cracks become holes. The holes grow.

And the carrier bursts open like a hatched egg.

I pull my amulet over my head and toss it onto the walkway before I slide my dagger from the waist of my jeans; I *want* the thing to come at me, I can't deny it. I have no fear—or if I do, it's lost in the storm brewing inside me. My stomach swirls with a hundred sensations: anticipation, anxiety, readiness. Need. *So much need.* Because I *must* kill this thing. My brain screams with it. I knew a small taste of this four weeks ago in the cave, but this is so much stronger. The creature's smell, its dark energy . . . It's a warm meal calling out to me and I'm starving. It reminds me that I have power now. That I'm not as helpless as I always feel.

It also reminds me that I'm a murderer.

The first thing that emerges from the broken pieces of the carrier is a silver-furred paw, then overlong whiskers.

"*The light of Elohim surrounds me,*" I whisper as I move closer.

The surfacing ears fold back at my words.

"*The love of Elohim enfolds me,*" I say a little louder.

A hiss comes from the shadow of the cage and the reek of sulfur billows out.

"*Wherever I am Elohim is.*" I stand over the wreckage now, only a foot away. The force in me is nearly buckling my knees. "Get your furry ass out here, coward," I say through clenched teeth.

As if my words alone have power, the creature is yanked from the remnants of the carrier with a loud screech of claw scraping over plastic. The demon squints at the sunlight: cat features too pointy, eyes too large, and the thin overlong tail too much like a rat's.

My hand clutching the dagger sparks, catching fire. The flames fill my left palm and begin to burn a trail along the marked pattern on my wrist. Then the fire moves up, following the dark lines on my arm to settle in my chest where the design ends. Where the seal on my power is. And I have no choice now but to kill. The need propels me and I lunge. Fast. Faster than I ever moved before my rebirth, and before the thought can even settle I have a hold of its neck.

I yank it off the ground, its body contorting unnaturally, its back bending awkwardly as it latches its rear claws into my arm.

I barely feel the claws sink in, thanks to the tornado of this force inside me.

Words emerge from my lips, not in English, but in a demon tongue, "Shed this visage." It needs to be in its true form to be killed. It can't be hidden in glamour; the lie protects it. Eric's journal goes on and on for two dozen pages about these rules that I never knew. Never knew because it was always impossible to actually kill a demon. Or at least it was until I came along.

It screeches again in protest, "You are not my god, you cannot command me." Its throat vibrates against my clutching fingers, but its words mean nothing in the face of my power. Its fur melts away like heavy smoke, its black eyes grow even larger, teeth elongate. Its mouth turns almost humanlike. The thorns on its spine sink back into its thin pink flesh, and the torso grows, ribs ballooning out as if filling with air. As it transforms, the beast screams, "You are not my lord. You are King of Never, Prince of Mistake, and Liege of Time's Folly." Rage twists its already twisted features. "You shall bring Death among us, you shall bring her forth." And then its screech morphs into a cackle, grating at the inside of my skull. It digs its claws deeper and strains to reach me with its teeth, even as my fist tightens around its neck. "Death follows after you. She is your downfall—"

I shove the blade up into its ribcage, just under the sternum, stopping the torrent of lies.

The demon goes silent. Its expression of rage freezes and then shifts into shock. Its large, oily eyes fill with the reflection of the strange flames dancing over my marked arm. And then the fire pushes along the dagger handle and enters the beast.

Gold sparks surge from its mouth and eyes as its black blood spills out and fills my hand, coating my skin in its chill. And what once was flesh becomes coal, then dust, falling to the grass. Ash from a burnt-out shell.

My power stills and I stare down at my bleeding arm, at the ashes on my shoe, at the demon blood now turned to clay on my hand from the heat. I want to feel some form of remorse, but all I feel is elation. Satisfaction. And even though it's a demon I just killed, this death on my hands mingles with Lester's death, the memory of the demon's wide eyes becoming a soft brown as I plunged the blade into his very human neck, the black demon blood becoming red and sticky on my fingers, the smell of darkness becoming the smell of loss, so much loss. I shouldn't feel exhilaration, I shouldn't feel bliss. It's wrong. All wrong.

My knees buckle and I collapse onto the lawn. I heave air into my lungs, gasping, trying to gather my wits. And then I throw up on the grass. I stay like that for several minutes, on all fours, before I finally sit back and realize that steam is rising from my skin. I glance at the front door of the house, wondering how the demon's screams weren't loud enough to bring out Ms. Bentley, let alone the entire neighborhood.

I focus on my punctured arm again. It's coated in sticky smears of blood, but the bleeding appears to have stopped. And the wounds . . . there aren't any. All that remains are six small mounds of scar tissue, shaped like twisted stars.

The wounds have healed. Already.

My new body is obviously more . . . resilient. Wow. I knew it was stronger, and oddly in tune with nature—like the whole breathing underwater thing—and faster when it needs to be. I can even take a jog now without gasping like an eighty-year-old chain-smoker.

After considering my options, I stand on shaky legs, grab my amulet off the brick path, and make my way to the end of the driveway and down the quiet street. I pull my cell from my pocket and tap Sid's name to call him.

"Yes, this is LA Paranormal Investigative Agency," he answers in a formal tone. "No problem is too weird."

"Really, Sid, you still haven't programmed my number into your phone?"

"Oh, hello," he says, sounding chipper. He muffles the speaker, but I can hear him say to Ms. Bentley, "I need to take this. Please excuse me for just one second." After a few beats more he says, "Okay, I'm outside. What happened? Where are you?"

"I'm not sure the sight of me right now would be good for the lady. Just tell her that Fluffy got away and I'm chasing after it, or something. Then pick me up at the corner."

"Is it gone?"

I stare down at the demon's blood crusted on my dagger hand. "It's dead."

"Excellent!"

And then the line clicks. The bastard hung up on me.

THREE

Aidan

Once I get in the car—trading places so I can drive for him—Sid explains that the lady was "in a huff" about her innocent kitty running away. Not a huge shock. As long as she buys the story and doesn't sue us, I don't really care.

"You did well," Sid says, staring out the window as we drive out of the neighborhood and pass through the San Fernando Valley, heading back into the city. "And you say it just burned up?"

I take in a deep breath, wishing I didn't have to explain it all. It's confusing enough living through it; I'd rather not rehash the strange emotions. But he's right: we need to figure out how my new power works. Sooner rather than later.

"Yeah, and it was like . . ." I pause, unsure about saying too much.

"Like what?" His voice turns a bit more somber. Maybe he can tell it's all getting to me.

"It was like I *had* to kill it. Like I had no choice."

"I see. And this bothers you, not having control?"

I shake my head, surprised my answer is no. It should bother me, but it doesn't. "What scares me is how much I *wanted* to kill it."

He turns to look at me. "But it was a demon."

"I know." I sigh. "It's lame."

"No, Aidan." His voice turns gentle. "It's amazing. It means, even after everything, your heart is still pure."

Well, that's unlikely. I haven't totally explained to Sid everything that happened in the house that afternoon before my Awakening—haven't told him that it was me who killed . . . Lester. I just can't seem to say it out loud. Even though Sid can't see my soul, I don't want him to know that those cracks around my eye are there—the stain on the soul of every murderer. But he looks at me like he's aware anyway. Maybe his abilities to *see* aren't as faded as he likes us all to think.

We make it back to the house after an hour of freeway traffic on the 101.

As we pull into the driveway, my phone pings three times in my pocket. I wait until Sid's out of the car and walking toward his shed before I get it out. A new wave of guilt hits me.

Rebecca.

Coffee today? <3 Usual spot.

OMG, Samantha got tickets to see Hozier next
    week. You should come! :)

I know you can't, but I thought I'd ask. :(
    Still, u have to meet me for coffee. I have
    a surprise for you!

My heart beats a little harder looking at the three white bubbles on the screen.

"Damn." I'm supposed to meet her this afternoon in Santa Monica, but I've been going back and forth with myself, knowing I need to cancel. And now I'll just look like an ass, ditching her this late.

But what else is new.

She and I have hung out twice since she came back from Ireland. We met at the Coffee Bean in Santa Monica and talked about dumb things—about nothing, really. We took a walk along the boardwalk and watched the oddballs on Venice Beach, trying to guess what astrology signs people were. All simple and safe. There was no mention of demons or of the scar running along her arm. No mention of my sister. It was exactly what I needed. I didn't have to worry about her asking me how things were because she didn't want to talk about what had happened, either.

I wrote her emails when she was in Ireland, told her that I can see things, that she was being attacked by demons . . . so she knows more than she used to, but she still doesn't know everything. She doesn't know that I see her virgin soul, that I'm supernaturally bonded to Kara, or that she herself may be bonded to me as well—that she's one of these Lights that Sid's always talking about. Maybe the most vital one. Maybe she senses the link, though, like I do. Maybe she's aware of more than she's saying. There's this look in her eye when I leave her that seems almost panicked.

With everything that's been going on, and because I don't know how . . . I haven't told Kara that I've hung out with Rebecca.

I'm a bastard.

Not telling Kara feels like lying. And I don't lie. Today would be the third time I've seen Rebecca, the start of a regular thing, and I can't let that happen. If Kara finds out, she'll think I want something more from Rebecca.

And I don't. It's not about that at all. Kara is who I want—that's been very clear to me since before my Awakening. And it only became more clear afterward. It doesn't matter that things are PG between the two of us now, the surge of hungry energy tempered into something less consuming.

Last night Kara said that I was the first person she ever felt truly safe with. All I want is for that to be true, for her to be able to trust me, to be safe with me. But standing here, staring at the messages from Rebecca, at the crusted demon blood on my hands, a chill works through me. The horrible reality seems suddenly clear: this person I am now, the weight of this power I've been given, it's only going to bring pain in the end.

FOUR

Aidan

Jax and Holly are in the kitchen when I walk in the back door.

A piece of carrot flies at me from Jax's direction. "Hey, ass face," he says. He has a large knife in his hand—hopefully he's just chopping vegetables. His close-cut dark-brown hair is splotched on the sides with green dye from Holly trying to copy some style she found on Pinterest. Apparently it was supposed to look like leopard print. Instead it looks like an army of green Sharpies attacked his head.

"OMG," Holly says. "So glad you're home." She slides a casserole into the oven and closes the door. "The phone's been ringing off the hook, and there are three messages from panicked clients. It's become Ghost World War III out there today, and your girlfriend's no help. The queen was off galavanting yesterday morning when I needed help with that hospital video of hers, and now she's been upstairs hibernating all day today, like she's on vaycay or something. It's nearly four!" Holly's got her hair up in its usual ribbon-woven way. She added a few pink and green strands to the brown during the Great Hair Experiment. She's wearing neon-colored exercise clothes—which means she's probably going to be doing yoga up in her room later. Which is good because it keeps her calm. Ever since the stuff with Ava she's been more short fused than usual. We've all been on edge.

"And for some reason I'm helping cook dinner," Jax says with a long-suffering sigh, like he's been given the job of scrubbing the floor with a toothbrush. "I'm a sucker for this señorita's orders." He winks at Holly and brings his knife down on a carrot with a *whack*.

"You look very put out," I say.

Holly laughs drily and comes at him, pointing a piece of the celery in his face. "You keep your eyes on those carrots or I'll be making Jax-salad instead."

I raise my brow. "Better watch it, man. She'll spit in your eggs in the morning."

"If she wants her spit in my mouth, she should just let me kiss her already."

Holly whacks Jax over the head with her celery stick. "I'm suing for sexual harassment." Then she turns to me and says, "This is a hostile work environment." And she walks from the kitchen, flipping off Jax over her shoulder and yelling several inappropriate words in Spanish.

Jax chops another carrot, smiling. "She loves me."

I leave him to his work and head for the stairs. Finger is sitting on the couch, playing something on his Xbox with a lot of loud gunfire and screaming. I nod as I pass the archway, but he doesn't look up. He smiles, though, sensing me there. A wave of calm spills out of the room like a greeting, and I pause for a moment, breathing it in.

"Hey," Connor comes from the office. His blond hair is a mess and he looks like he's been sitting at a desk all day. He's still in the sweatpants and T-shirt he was wearing when he woke up and disappeared into the office before I left with Sid this morning. "Sid texted me with the update. I need your summary of the job." He taps a pen on a pad of paper he's holding. "I gotta get this paperwork done for the secondary release. In case she realizes somehow that you killed her damn cat."

"It was a demon."

"To her, it was a pet. We just need to get our ducks in a row or we'll be paying out everything we've earned from that Reese shoot to Crazy Hoarder Lady. Let's just hope she buys the 'Fluffy ran off' story."

"Okay, fine."

"Today."

I give him a look. "Seriously. I hear you." When he starts to walk away, I add, "Holly said Kara's still in her room. Is that right?" She had a headache last night. Hopefully she's not getting sick; the health insurance plan isn't too awesome for a ghost hunter. And the whole "off the grid" thing makes medical care even tougher.

"I wouldn't know," Connor says over his shoulder as he walks away. "I've been stuck in this damn office all day."

I head up the stairs and when I make it to the top landing I notice that Kara's door is cracked open. I was going to take a shower before checking on her, but the idea of her sleeping at this time of day is so odd. She's usually full of energy, running around, helping Connor, or looking for new sites to film and doing research on local history if she's not with Sid on a job.

I move closer to her room and try to feel for negative vibes or emotions, but I can't sense anything rising above the spells and protections on the house that muffle my abilities. Whatever's going on with her, it can't be too horrible.

"Kara?" I whisper through the door. I knock softly, in case she really is sick.

Several seconds pass without an answer. I push the door open and peek inside.

She's lying in her bed, facing away from me, sheets tangled around her bare legs. The afternoon sun shines across her in white beams, heating the room, making the space smell like her vanilla lotion, like warm cotton sheets. The scent fills my head, settling my nerves a little. I want to go to her, lie beside her and feel the peace of it all, until I'm dreaming.

But then my own smell catches up with me and I decide to take a shower first.

I turn to leave but my eyes catch something smeared across her pillowcase. Stepping closer, I see red-brown streaks on the blue sheet, near her head.

Not blood; I'm just being paranoid.

But as I lean closer the copper scent makes my body tense.

I panic, grabbing her, shifting her to face me. Her eyelids. Her cheeks. Her chin. They're coated in crimson. It's coming from her eyes.

Dread wraps around my throat like a noose, making it impossible to breathe, to think. I grip her arm tighter, "Kara, wake up," but she doesn't move. I touch her neck, feeling for a pulse, but my own heartbeat is too fierce in my skin, it's all I'm getting. A stampede of frantic thoughts fills every molecule. *She told me she had a headache. Why didn't I check in on her this morning before I went on the job with Sid? Why did I assume things were fine?*

"Kara!"

A moan slips through her lips and I breathe out in a rush of relief. She's alive.

She mumbles into her pillow. "What?" And then she grunts.

"Kara, wake up. Open your eyes."

She rolls a little closer and tries to open her eyes, but there's dried blood on her lashes, sticking them together. She lifts her hand to her face, groaning like a tired kid. "What the . . . ?" She finally gets her eyes open and squints at me through blood flakes and sleep. "You suck. Why're you waking me up?"

I stand and rush to the landing, yelling down to the first floor, "Holly, get Sid! Jax, bring me a wet rag! And hurry!" Then I go back to Kara's side.

She shushes me when I sit back down on the bed. "You're soooo loud."

"I'm loud because I'm freaking out, Kara. I need you to sit up."

She shakes her head, then hisses in pain. "God, who drugged me?"

"Tell me where it hurts."

"My brain is mad at me." Her words are slurred, making her sound drunk. Or hungover. But I was sitting with her last night on the porch until we both went off to bed. The only thing she drank was some iced tea.

And a hangover doesn't make your eyes bleed.

Jax comes in, holding a rag. "Dude, what am I, your servant now? Clean up your own mess." He hands me the damp cloth and then steps back, noticing the blood on Kara's face. "Whoa, what'd you do to her?"

"Nothing, dumbass. Did Holly go get Sid?"

He nods. After a pause he points at Kara and says, "Her eyes are bleeding," like I'm blind.

Kara jerks to attention at that. "Wha . . . ?" Her hands fly to her face again.

I glare at Jax. "Way to ease into it."

He shrugs, but there's concern in his expression. "Maybe I should go tell Sid to hurry it up." And then he's jetting out of the room and I hear his footsteps rushing down the stairs.

Kara's voice trembles when she asks, "Aidan, what's going on?"

"You've been up here all day. And you're . . . bleeding."

She licks her lips and rubs a few flakes of dried blood from her cheek. "What time is it?"

"Nearly four."

Her caked eyes widen. "In the *afternoon*?"

"How do you feel?"

"Like baked shit."

Sid appears in the doorway. "That's bad, I assume," he says. "Could you be more specific?" He grips his cane and taps it nervously on the floor.

"What's going on, Sid?" I ask. Is this something medical or something spiritual? "What could be doing this?"

Sid comes closer. "I'm not sure." He shoos me out of the way and takes my place on the side of the bed, settling in as he examines Kara. He feels her pulse, counting the beats as he stares at his watch. He runs a finger through the flakes of blood on her cheek, then rubs them with his thumb and brings them to his nose. He studies her eyes, and makes a sound in the back of his throat.

"What?" I ask, impatient.

"I have no idea what's going on."

"Perfect," Kara mutters.

Connor bursts in, he looks frantic as his eyes lock on Kara. "What happened? Are you all right? My God, you're bleeding."

"I'm *fine*," Kara says, trying to sound annoyed. But I can hear the fear in her voice and see it in the way she's gripping the edge of her shirt.

"She's not bleeding anymore," Sid says, trying to ease everyone's panic, even though I can see that he's trying to conceal his own worry, just like Kara.

Holly and Jax loiter in the doorway. Jax pipes in, "Maybe it's that stigmatism thing. She could be, like, turning into the Virgin Mary or something."

Holly rolls her eyes. "It's called *stigmata*, moron."

Jax raises his hands defensively. "Whatever you say, Queen Catholic."

I move to the door and shut it in their faces, blocking the two of them out as they begin bickering, then I turn back to Sid. "How do we figure out what this is?"

"We need to do something," Connor says, kneeling at Kara's side and taking her hand protectively, staring at Sid like this is all *his* fault. He's never liked the way Sid deals with Kara, but it all really comes back to me in the end. Anything Sid did to Kara, he did because of me.

Kara starts to sit up, clenching her jaw like the movement is causing her pain. "You boys better calm the hell down or I'm kicking you all out."

Sid glances over at me. "You should look at her soul, Aidan. Can you see it when you're in the house?"

My insides churn. I haven't looked at Kara's soul in weeks. Not since that night on the beach when we confronted the Heart-Keeper. It felt wrong after that somehow, because of everything we'd been through. Like I was spying on her. And seeing all those handprints on her shoulders, her chest, and that one bright-red one on her neck . . .

I can't bear to think of what those men did to her.

I look at her. "Is it okay if I try to see?" I'm not even sure I'll be able to. I've seen it in the house before, the first day I met her, but the wards are much stronger now, since Sid reinforced them after my Awakening.

"Yeah, sure," she says with a shrug. She's still pretending to be more relaxed than she really is.

"Just focus on the protection spells that are on the property first," Sid tells me. "Then pierce through them, like pulling back a curtain."

He makes it sound so easy.

I force myself to look at her and my pulse picks up. I let my inner walls fall and focus as hard as I can. Before I know it, every emotion in the room rushes at me, colliding and thickening the air. Well, I can sure feel *that*. I slow my breathing and try to sift through it.

Kara sits up more and leans against the wall behind her, her chin high, her muscles tense. She won't look at me, though. And I know that I won't be able to see her soul, not like this. We need to connect in some way if I'm going to sense her clearly over the muffle of the house.

"Can you focus on me?" I ask her, quietly.

She blinks up at me and blood flakes sprinkle onto her chest. Goose bumps rise on her arms and legs. She grips the sheet tighter to keep her hands from shaking. But she's Kara. Strong. Stronger than me.

And I feel her, the core of her. So I try to look. I sense the block on the house pressing at me, the energy that turns the air into cotton. It hugs me like a blanket I can't see through. I try what Sid suggested and move the thick coating aside in my mind, then push back at it.

There, it's working. The marks surface on Kara's skin, the image of her soul rising up. First and brightest is the red handprint on her throat, the reminder of her pain. Then the Chinese characters on the back of her neck; evidence of the curse her father placed on her when she was eleven. Each of the six characters is lit with her energy's blue glow. But something's different; the usual cerulean color of the light seems faded. And the other handprints on her arms and chest are fuzzy, blurred into grey smudges.

Maybe they're blurry because of the house, though. "I'm not sure if I'm seeing it right. But there's nothing bad, nothing new that I can see."

Kara releases her breath in a puff, like she was holding it in.

Sid is still frowning.

"I can look at it outside of the grounds," I say. "Some of it's kinda blurry."

"I don't want to drag her anywhere right now," Sid says, not looking satisfied in the least. "And I need to do some research." He leans over and kisses Kara's brow. "You need to rest."

Then he stands, waving for me and Connor to follow him. When we all get to the base of the staircase, he stops and whispers, "The blood is not a good sign."

"No kidding," I say, worry turning to anger. "This is why I hate casting magic. Nothing good ever comes of it."

Connor's just standing there, staring a hole through Sid's head.

"That magic has helped her, Aidan," Sid says. "You didn't see her when I found her. She was a shell of a girl, barely spoke. The spell I put on her has given her freedom. And it brought you both together—"

Connor steps forward, interrupting. "We should be taking her back to the doctor. This could be some sort of side effect from her concussion last month."

"Perhaps you should consult WebDoc," Sid says, absently.

"Be serious, Sid," I say. "If she's got a residual head injury, that's not a joke." My pulse speeds back up at the thought. I'm only good with the supernatural, I can't fix the natural; my abilities would be useless.

"I realize that," Sid says. "Perhaps one of us can call the doctor tomorrow to be safe. But I don't think that's what this is."

"What the hell else could it be?" Connor asks.

"I can't be sure, not yet." We just keep glaring at Sid, so he adds, "I believe the blood may be a signal that the spell I put on her in order to awaken your powers, Aidan—it could be . . . weakening. When I reversed the curse her father placed over her, things had the potential to fail. If that first curse was too strong, then my casting to flip it could have initially missed the mark, so to speak. And I do recall a stigmata-type manifestation being mentioned in the text as a possible sign of that." His posture sinks, making him seem smaller. "I thought any signs like this would have come earlier, but perhaps not . . . If I'm right, there must be a way to repair the damage."

"There better be," Connor says. "In the meantime, I'm not waiting to call the doctor." He turns and heads into the office.

"This is just great." I rub my temple to keep from grabbing Sid by the throat. I've told him again and again how lame his plan to awaken my power was, how his use of Kara was twisted and wrong. Ever since the beginning, his logic has been majorly sideways. And now, if Kara is sick because Sid fucked with her soul for the sake of my destiny . . .

"I'll fix it," Sid whispers, fear in his eyes. Fear of me, or for Kara, it doesn't matter, as long as it puts a fire under his ass.

"Yes, you will," I say through my teeth and head into the office after Connor.

FIVE

Aidan

When I get back to Kara's room, she's sitting at the edge of her bed, cleaning her cheeks with the wet rag Jax brought up.

Her gaze finds mine and my chest constricts. Vulnerability and fear linger right on the surface. I feel the fear inside me, too, but she can't know. I can't let her see that the terror nearly swallowed me whole the second I saw her so pale and bloody.

"How're you feeling?" I ask, sitting next to her. My memory flashes back to our kiss the first week that I got here, after Rebecca's party, the way we were both so desperate, so wrapped up in each other, even when I was fairly sure we didn't even *like* each other. I don't feel the buzz in my skin when we touch anymore—she was right, it faded soon after my Awakening. But I still want her. And not because of a spell or a curse, just because of my normal human heart.

She smirks at me. "Considering I was bleeding out of my eyes a little while ago, I feel surprisingly good." She leans over, poking me in the side with her elbow. "Don't look so glum, Mr. Frown. I'm fine."

"Very funny."

"What did Sid say? I know you guys had a secret meeting just now. Are you planning the funeral?"

"Stop it, Kara." Despite her mirth, my throat goes tight. I can't even . . .

"Man, this has you freaked. I really do feel fine, Aidan. Now that I'm fully awake, the headache is even fading a bit." She reaches out and turns my face toward her, then kisses the corner of my mouth. "I'm not going anywhere. I promise."

I nod because I can't speak. My mom, my sister, and now Kara. And it could all be due to me. Because I was born and the spiritual world tipped on its head.

But maybe she's right, maybe it's nothing. Maybe it'll be fine since she's feeling okay now. Connor reached the doctor who Sid uses for basic care, and he's coming over to check her out tomorrow.

I hold on to the hope that nothing else will happen and swallow the fear. Too many emotions today as it is, and I can't let the torrent take me. I can't let it win.

"So, tell me what Sid said." She moves away a little to look at me.

I clear my throat and hold her hand to help me feel more grounded. "Connor got you an appointment with Doctor Brander for tomorrow morning. And when we googled the symptoms—"

She interrupts, waving me off. "No, what did *Sid* say?"

I hesitate for a few seconds. "He's wondering if it's the counter spell he put on you to reverse your father's curse. It's possible that the protections could be slipping."

She blinks, her breath quickening. "Sid's spell might be failing?" I feel the pulse under her skin now. "Not totally, though, right? I mean, I didn't think that could happen. But maybe Sid could just do it over? My dad's curse won't come back all the way, will it?"

I squeeze her hand, trying to comfort her. She's been through so much with all this shit already. If the horror of what her father did to her—making her a target to attract all those men to her, taking away her control—if that comes back . . . I don't want to think about what that would mean. "He's not sure, Kara. It might not even have anything to do with the curse. It could be related to something completely separate."

"Right," she says, like she's trying to convince herself as much as me. "Because it could be something totally different than the spell. Like something I picked up on a job. It could be some kind of residual muck from that loony-bin shoot I've been working on with Jax and Connor."

"Sure, that's possible." Though I have no idea how. "Or it might be a side effect from your concussion." Connor really did go on WebDoc and read that a head injury that didn't heal correctly could cause the ears and eyes to bleed.

She's quiet for a few seconds, then she turns and looks at me intently. "I'm going to be all right."

She seems to almost be wishing it into being, like a spell.

Then she whispers, "I'm yours now, so I'll be all right," making a small sound of resignation before she's suddenly moving, leaning in, grabbing my shirt in her fist, and kissing me full on the mouth.

It takes me a second to react and get my bearings. But then she's pressing into me, deepening the connection and pushing me back onto the bed. I let her, even though it's not what I expected, even though it's not a good idea.

Since when has that mattered between us?

But this isn't the PG vibe I've been feeling recently between us. Her skin is hot to the touch, the air around her vibrating. And she's holding on to me like her life depends on it, like she did before my Awakening when our connection was a force all its own.

I'm yours seems to tickle my ears as we kiss, the odd tone in her voice.

I know I should stop, that something isn't right, but I can't help it. I've missed this. I get lost in my own need, trying to show her how much I want her in the way I grip her hips, how I pull her closer.

We move in sync as we find each other in that space where no words are needed and neither of us will ever be alone again. She's shaped against my side as my hands slide up her back and I wish that I could touch more of her skin, wish that her shirt was anywhere but between us.

I pull aside her neckline, kissing along her shoulder. She sighs and shifts her body over mine, her hair tickling my face.

The position heightens everything, including my surprise, and that sense of unease grows to a roar in my ears even as my body urges me on.

But just as I'm about to pull away, to stop the spiral, she goes still, her palms on my shoulders. She makes a sound in the back of her throat, a kind of surprised breath, and the air turns from a lustful buzz to a frigid tundra in three seconds. She looks down at me, but she's not seeing me. Her eyes are glazed over, liquid white blue like the summer sky.

A shiver runs over my skin. "Kara?"

She stares through me.

Something moves, but it's not me and it's not her. It's something more. Her energy, her soul, it cracks open, a blossom of secrets baring itself, sliding over her chest and shoulders, down her arms like water made of blue light, hypnotic and lovely. It spreads out between us, stronger than I've ever felt it.

Then it spills onto my chest.

A surge of emotions—pain, sorrow, hope—jars my senses when her energy touches me. Breathing is impossible. There's nothing inside of me but her. And I know everything. Her past horror, her weakness, her hurt, her hunger for escape. Everything. It's now my own.

Her eyes close and she sinks down to rest her head on my chest, pressing her body against mine again. She lies there, silent, and I'm still with shock until she whispers, "Something is changing inside of me, Aidan, and I don't want it to stop. I'm not afraid anymore. Of us, of this." Her fingers slide under my shirt and roam over my belly. The air's gone back to a form of normal. Her heartbeat is comfortable and steady. "I can't let anything take that away from me."

I stare wide-eyed at the ceiling, trying to catch my breath. Does she realize that a piece of her—her spirit or her soul, maybe both—went into me? I can still feel the blue energy spreading through my body, like it's in my veins now.

And it's making my chest hurt like hell.

"I want you to come to me tonight," she says, sounding tired. "I want to be with you. For real this time."

"You need to rest," I manage to say. My voice sounds far away, like it's not really mine. "We still don't know if you're okay."

"I feel better now." There's a quiet satisfaction in her voice, like she's perfectly relaxed. "All I needed was a kiss from you, a real kiss. It's like magic."

The block on the house has never been able to keep our connection hidden. From the beginning, our link's been too strong. But whatever just happened was far beyond anything else I've ever experienced. Like the subtle web that ties our souls together just became iron cables.

"You still need to rest," I say. *And I need to make sure things aren't falling apart again.*

"But I want you to be mine," she whispers. "All of you."

"I am," I say. I lean closer and kiss her forehead, my muscles protesting the movement as if I've run a hundred miles. I shift out from under her and settle her comfortably into her sheets again. "Always."

She snuggles into her pillow, breathing out in contentment, half-asleep already. "Always."

I move off the bed and go to the mirror above her dresser, taking off my shirt and looking at my reflection. My normally bronzed skin is a little dull and there are dark circles under my eyes. But that's how I've looked for several weeks now.

My gaze locks on my chest where a blue glow still pulses over my seal of Awakening.

My heart beats faster as I watch the glow sink in, melting into the burnt circular pattern I still don't understand.

I look back at Kara, her quiet form so peaceful now. I can still feel the weight of her pain, but now it's in my own skin. Her heavy energy settles into my body, as if she just transferred all her troubles to me.

I walk over to the window and look out to the perfectly blue California sky. I pull the Star of David from my pocket and grip it tightly in my fist, finding myself praying—pleading, really. *Please, let us be all right, please keep us safe, protect us, protect all of us.* Over and over. Because I can't, I just can't lose anyone else.

SIX

Rebecca

I sit on my bed and stare down at the cell phone in my lap, willing it to ring or ding with a new text from Aidan. But it just looks back at me, a black screen, silent. Why didn't he let me know he wasn't going to be at the coffee shop yesterday? Why didn't he show? It doesn't make any sense; it isn't like him not to at least call.

I need to see him. Okay, I always *feel* like I need to see him, but this time I *really need* to. Especially after that thing I drew last night . . . the cave with the skulls. All those skulls. And Aidan standing alone in the middle of it all. After I finished the drawing, I got a horrible feeling, looking at it. Something is really wrong. And I know he's the only one who'll be able to make sense of the image.

Dad thinks I'm PMSing because he saw me moping around yesterday when I got home from the non-coffee. I know it wasn't a date or anything, but it felt like I'd just been dumped. And I'm so pathetic that I actually called Samantha to complain about it. She promptly christened Aidan a dillweed and offered to fix me up with another one of her brother's friends—the last one she threw at me had a crazy obsession with feet and actually caressed my ankle at the end of the date. Um, no thanks.

I run my finger over the bumpy line on the inside of my arm. The scar is still bright pink and stings every now and then from the skin trying to twist back into place.

People think that I did this to myself, that I was trying to get attention, because of my brother, Charlie. They think I tried to kill myself because I was lonely. And sad. Which I was, but . . . I didn't slit my wrist.

There's a knock on my bedroom door. "Emery, are you going to be ready soon?"

"Come in," I say, shoving my silent phone in my bag with my clothes, like it's offended me. Because it has.

My dad opens the door a crack and peeks in, cautiously. We've spent a lot of time together lately, but he's still worried I'm on the edge. "You finished packing already?" Do I want to admit that I finished packing yesterday morning, ten minutes after he told me I was going to Samantha's? Because that's the same time I decided I was actually going to Aidan's.

Now I'm second-guessing that decision. "Maybe I should just stay home, Dad."

His wide brow scrunches up. "Alone?" He opens the door the rest of the way. "I don't like that plan. I called and worked things out specifically so you wouldn't have to be home by yourself again."

"I know, I'm just feeling unsure about staying with Samantha."

Dad leans on the doorjamb and folds his arms over his chest. He's dressed in a nice grey V-neck sweater and slacks. He just had his hair color touched up so the silver is a little less noticeable at the temples, the brown more solid and rich. He's a straightlaced guy, all business usually. Nothing like Charlie was, nothing like me. At least, I hope I'm not like him. Not that I don't love him, but he shuts himself off. He's left me feeling alone even when we're both in the same room. I never want to do that to anyone I care about.

"I thought you *wanted* to stay with her," he says. "You always have so much fun together. And she knows what you've been through. I may have to be in New York for a few weeks. I'm not comfortable with you staying here alone for that long."

"You never cared before," I mumble, then feel guilt spike my throat.

He takes a breath in and releases it. "I was wrong to leave you before. I told you that. I'm sorry, sweetie, really. If that Aidan boy hadn't been with you the day it happened—" His words cut off.

I'm sure he wouldn't talk about Aidan so nicely if he knew the real story. My dad trusts the LA Paranormal crew, in a way, because he doesn't know that I stayed at the house with them that whole week he was gone. He certainly doesn't know that a possessed boy who lived there sliced my wrist open. Or that it was apparently Aidan's fault. If my dad knew all of that, there's no way I'd be seeing Aidan again. Ever.

So, I lied. I said that I was wandering the streets after a party that night and Sid found me, took me in. He let me sleep there at the house, and the next morning—even though the people there had tried to talk to me and help me—I decided I couldn't live anymore.

I had to lie. I couldn't exactly tell him there's this whole hidden world parallel to our own, where demons roam, or that one of those demons was chasing after me. Then he'd definitely put down a deposit on a padded room.

And now I'm going to lie again. I'm going to pretend that I'm staying with Samantha and her parents, but then I'm going to take a cab to Aidan's place. Samantha's busy with summer dance competitions, and her mom is a medicated harpy. Not to mention her stepfather.

I shiver, thinking about the last time I was in touching distance of that pervert.

For now, I only have the summer program at the arts academy to keep me busy while dad is gone. At least if I'm at the LA Paranormal house, I won't be bored. I can be close to Aidan and learn more about his world. And I won't have to fend off step-pervs.

"It's okay, Dad," I say, rising from the bed and walking over to him.

We haven't been apart since the "incident," and I'm actually going to miss our quiet breakfasts and evenings watching *What Not To Wear* together while he's gone. He's learned a lot about matching versus coordinating, if I do say so myself.

I plant a kiss on his nose and wrap my arms around his neck, resting my head on his chest. I wish we could just be poor so he'd never have to go anywhere. Then maybe I wouldn't lie. Maybe we'd be a family again, like when Charlie was here. "I'm taking my anxiety medication and I'll be fine. I'll stay with Samantha, and I'll try to be cheery. You don't have to worry."

He kisses the top of my head and hugs me tighter. "I'll come back as soon as the merger's solid. I swear. I won't be gone a second longer than I have to be."

"I know."

SEVEN

Aidan

My arms are empty when I open my eyes. I spent the night lying next to Kara, worried about what might happen next. But it appears we made it through without incident.

The sun is low in the morning sky, painting the horizon orange and pink. Kara is up, looking through her closet, tossing socks and shoes and shirts behind her. A blue Doc Marten lands on the foot of the bed.

"Where the hell did I put that damn thing?" she mumbles, rising up on her toes and pulling a box off a higher shelf. She shuffles around inside it before dropping it and grabbing a second one.

I rub the sleep from my eyes and yawn. "What're you looking for?"

"Nothing. I don't know."

"Oh . . . kay." I sit up and study the closet vomit. "That's a lot of crazy for nothing." Obviously she's more energetic than she was yesterday.

"I know. It's just dumb."

I stand and step over the piles of clothes to get to her. "How're you feeling? Better?"

She smiles, still looking through the shoebox in her arms. "No bloody eyes this morning, so that's a bonus."

I wonder if she realizes something weird happened yesterday, more than the blood. It appears she's still oblivious. I have no idea what happened either, so I'm not sure how to bring it up.

"Good," I say, peeking over her shoulder. The box is full of photographs and papers. "Seriously, what are you looking for?"

She snatches up a folded piece of paper and lifts it above her head like she's found gold. "Ah-ha! Bazinga!"

"Oh goodie, a paper."

"It's my earthquake keeper."

"Your what?"

"Since forever, whenever there's been an earthquake, I've written down the date and time and stuff. Then I carry the list around with me the rest of the day for good luck." She holds out the paper, and I see a list of dates and some details like epicenter or the day's weather, each line written in different ink. "I told you: lame," she says.

What an odd thing to be looking for. "Are you expecting an earthquake in the near future or something?"

"Ha!" She points in my face, like she caught me being slow. "You didn't feel it? Happened like an hour ago."

"An earthquake?" Strange I didn't feel it. Not the first time I've slept through one, though.

"Yeah. I wonder why they always seem to happen early in the morning. Weird, huh?"

"Is this a hobby of yours? Chasing quakes?"

"I'm a California Girl. I just think it's interesting. Plus, it'd be nice to know when we're about to break off into an island."

I laugh, surprised by this goofy side of her. "You're so cute."

"Laugh it up, prophet boy who can't even feel an earthquake." She crinkles her nose. "And I'm not *cute*."

I lean close and kiss her furrowed brow. "If you say so."

"How did Kara's visit with the doctor go?" Sid asks me as he comes in the back door from his shed after lunch. I'm sitting at the kitchen table with Jax, reading the text I've written to Rebecca, not sure I should press "Send." I need to apologize for being a no-show yesterday. I have no idea what she's thinking because she never called or texted to ask where I was.

It shouldn't matter, but it does. It tastes like sawdust in my mouth when I think about hurting her.

"Kara's okay, I think," I say. The doctor came and went pretty quickly. "No more blood and he said her vitals looked good. She slept fine last night, too. He scheduled her an MRI at his clinic in a couple weeks, just in case." I need to tell Sid about the blue energy that came from her and seemed to go inside me, but that definitely isn't going to happen with Jax in the room.

"Oh, she slept good, huh?" Jax wiggles his brow up and down. "You get her nice and tuckered out?"

I roll my eyes and stand from the table, slipping my phone in my pocket without sending the message. I head toward the office and motion for Sid to follow me.

Sorry I didn't come yesterday, the message in my pocket says. *I need some time. I hope you understand.*

Understand what? That she can't be a part of my life right now? That no matter how much of a mystical connection Rebecca has with me, it makes things impossible to balance when she's in my life? She's too pure and good, and this place I live in right now is steeped in death and pain. People around me get hurt, so protecting her means keeping her far away for now. If seeing Kara bleeding from her eyes doesn't confirm that, then nothing will.

But I also know that the reason I can't seem to press "Send" is because none of that matters. I can say she needs to stay away all day long and it won't change a thing. Rebecca will still be there, standing just at the edge of my sight, a part of my future, like Ava said.

And Ava's visions were never wrong.

Once Sid and I are in the office I shut the door. "Did you find out if the curse is making Kara sick?"

He shakes his head, looking exhausted. "I still have a lot to read through, though. Maybe I'll get Connor to take me to Eric's warehouse later today. Is Kara sleeping?"

"She's heading out with Connor to check one of their cameras at that old psychiatric hospital. She isn't in the mood to sit still, and apparently there's trouble with one of the feeds."

Sid lights up a little at that. "So she's feeling better!"

"I'd say she feels *more* energetic, not less."

"How strange," he says, eyes wandering to the floor in thought.

"And there's something else," I say, not sure why I'm so hesitant to tell him. "A weird thing happened when . . . well, when she kissed me yesterday."

A frown creases his brow. "Do you mean after the blood-show? You kissed her—was that wise?"

"Do you want to know what happened, or not?" When he nods, I continue. "Her energy, her blue light, was really thick and it sort of . . . entered me. I felt it. I felt *her*."

"It actually entered your body?" His voice is tight and full of concern. "Has this ever happened before?"

"No, this is a first, as far as I know. Could it be connected to the bleeding? Why would her blue light actually go inside of me? It's only touched me before."

Sid shakes his head and studies the floor between us. "I can't know for sure. Perhaps after I figure out why she's bleeding, we'll have an answer. In my experience, the exchange of power only occurs when one half of a powerful whole is attempting to heal another—one mate trying to mend the other with their essence."

"If that's what happened, then it should've been *my* power entering *her*, not the other way around." She was the one who was sick.

"I can only think it's linked to the blood. I'll need to keep looking, but this might help in finding an answer." He sighs and turns away, walking over to the door. Before he opens it he asks, "Have you been reading Eric's journal? Any new tips on Ava?"

I'm not sure why he's asking that now. He hasn't pushed me to talk about my sister for the last two weeks or so.

"I've been reading it," I say, "but no new tips."

I've actually been reading it obsessively ever since Ava left, trying to understand my powers and figure out how to bring her back. The only possible solution I've found would be to complete the spell that the Heart-Keeper started when he slid the silver dagger into her chest. I admit, some days I miss her so much that I consider going for it and praying that she'll awaken fully herself and that the Darkness won't win. But there's no way to be sure I'd bring the pure Ava back by completing the spell. And the girl who opens her eyes on that altar needs to be *my* Ava. Plus, there's no way that I could actually cut out my sister's heart.

"Why do you ask?" I say.

"No reason," he says, red sparking in his eye.

I give him a look.

His cheeks flush as he realizes he's caught in a lie. "Old habits. I'm just . . . I'm not sure when the correct time to tell you certain things is. And as things are, with Kara—"

"You tell me as soon as you know. Don't keep stuff from me, it won't help either of us."

"Yes, very wise. My apologies."

When he just stands there, studying the surface of the table beside me, I prod. "Well?"

He grips his cane tighter and his nerves spark sharply enough I feel it through the muffled energy of the house. "I may need to show you."

I follow him as he walks out the back door to his shed. We stand beside the weathered structure and the dark magic seeping out makes an ache grow in my bones. I hate this place. It's an oil spill in the middle of a nature preserve, mucking up the air and killing life all around it.

The blood circle on the door has been freshly repainted—I don't even want to think of what furnished that. The smell of sage and anguish seems to permeate the wood.

Sid unhooks the three locks and opens the latch, but before letting me see past him, he turns and says, "Just keep this between us, please."

"Sid, get on with it."

He sighs, looking pained, and moves to the side, motioning me into the shed. My feet root to the ground, though. I won't totally immerse myself in the dark casting magic again. The weight of that power is a feeling I never want to relive. Ever.

The altar is across from the door, covered in dried wax and blood. There's a pentagram made of black yarn, and black candles stand at each point of the star—the sight of that formation makes my skin crawl even more, reminding me of my mom's casting habit and where it's brought us. And to top it all off, a cat skull is sitting to the side with the Chinese character for *sneaky* etched on its forehead. Scrolls are stuffed into the wine racks underneath, overflowing, with more of them stacked on the floor in the corner. Rows of bottles filled with mysterious objects, liquids, and powders rim the shelf above it.

Sid's bed is against the wall to my left, and at the foot sits the trunk, the prophecy stone carrying my destiny tucked inside.

It all looks the same. "What are you trying to show me, Sid?"

He pushes the door open wider, letting the light spill higher on the wall beside the bed. The symbols for *grounding* shimmer in the light, newly painted just like the one on the door. My stomach rises at the sight of so much fresh blood.

Until I see . . . something *else*. Oozing down from the ceiling like black tar.

A chill rushes over me. "What is that stuff?" Obsidian-colored liquid drips down the wall, running in thin lines, as if the wood is bleeding demon blood.

"As you know, this shed is made to be a talisman that helps me stay in this time. It mimics a doorway."

"Like the cave, you mean."

"Yes." He steps into the shed and points with his cane at the red circles on the wall. "And this is why I put these marks here, to weave the time spell into the fabric of the structure itself. But then this began early this morning." He motions to the black ooze. "It bubbled out after the ground shook under me."

"That was an earthquake, Sid. They happen all the time. This is California."

"Does that happen all the time?" He points at the tar-like substance running down to the floor.

"I don't know what the hell that *is*."

"It's a sign of crossover!" He throws his hand in the air, looking exasperated.

A crossover. A demon crossing over? "But that would leave a sigil behind."

"Only if the demon crossed over in this spot from a Veil state. And that would be a burn mark. The black blood is a sign that something crossed through the *doorway*. It manifests in all the linked sites."

"And this is linked to the dam."

"Yes. This is linked to the Devil's Gate, where I took you the day I told you about your father. That's where I came through, so that's the power I was attempting to mimic."

"So the demon could have come through that gate."

"Or it could have come through any of the linked sites."

"Like the beach cave."

He nods.

"Is there an earthquake every time a demon crosses over? This happens a lot?"

He shakes his head. "Absolutely not. The Key Keepers are angels of Light. They've guarded the doorways since right after the time of Noah. They despise demons and never knowingly let them through. So, no. No demons ever cross. Unless they've escaped."

"What do you mean, 'right after the time of Noah'? Who guarded the doorways before that?" I ask.

"No one. In the time of Noah, demons and angels walked among humans, unhidden. To my brethren and me it's always been known as the Cycle of Darkness, and it's blasphemy to speak of it—no one wants to tease the ears of the Key Keeper."

"Well, what about the demon I killed yesterday? That thing was corporeal. Didn't it get called up through a doorway or something?"

"A demon called over by a human is merely going from a Veil state to a corporeal state. They've been on this side of the doorway, behind the Veil, for eons. Some lower-level demons were given lee-way to remain here, kept in check because they reside on the other side of the Veil. The stronger and more deadly demons were locked away in the place we call Sheol."

"For good."

"For as long as the angels stand guard. When a human calls up a demon from the other side of the Veil, the creature will only get a small window of time to become molecular before slipping back across. But if a demon ever managed to break through a *doorway*, it would have no time restrictions. It would cross as a beast and would remain in a corporeal state, and have no use with being coy."

"And so, you think this goop," I point to the black ooze on the wall, "is a sign that one might've escaped." A terrifying thought by the sound of it.

Sid nods.

"But, wait a second, you started all this by mentioning my sister."

"Her link to the cave, her blood being the key to open those gates to Sheol, it's obviously a factor. Don't you imagine we should consider her as a possible reason for any new shifts in the power of the doorways?"

"Ava could have done this?" I ask, icicles creeping through my veins. "She might've let something loose?" I think about the claws I saw that night in the cave, when the gates opened for only a few minutes. Those claws belonged to some beast, trying to escape.

"If not her, then someone using her blood."

EIGHT

Aidan

I grip the steering wheel of the Camaro and try to focus on the road in front of me, not letting the frustration take over. Sid promised me that the spell he cast had hidden Ava. He said *hidden*, specifically. Like, no one should be able to find her, see her. How the hell could someone use her blood to open the doorway?

Before I left the house, I reminded him of his promise. But then *he* reminded *me* that he's not as powerful or smart as he once was. Like it's some kind of excuse for why he just *whoops!* left the key to the end of the world out in the open. It doesn't give me a lot of hope for how helpful he'll be waking Ava.

And now with Kara . . . damn, I need someone with half a brain to give me a hand here. Makes me wonder where Eric—my absent guardian angel—is for the millionth time.

I can only hope Sid is wrong about the black stuff running down the walls of his shed. Maybe a demon hasn't come through at all. Maybe it's the gross casting magic in that shed that's gooping up the walls. It's fairly thick with nasty in there.

I pull off PCH and turn down the parallel street, parking several hundred yards up the road from Mrs. O'Linn's house. I take a side path that I found last week. It's a bit of an awkward descent to the beach, but this way I can avoid seeing my great-grandma; she still isn't aware of the blood connection, and I plan on keeping it that way, so the less contact, the better.

The fog is thick, the noonday sun not warm enough to break through. It never is here. Even now, with July in full swing, this section of shoreline is always shrouded in fog. It settles on the beach, coating the water in a thick grey mist. The sound of the water pushing slowly up the shore is muffled, but I can feel the stillness of it. Everything seems to be waiting. Just like me. Waiting for Ava to wake up.

Once I've made it to the sand, I walk down the beach. The damp air is sharp in my lungs. The familiar smell of salt and sea sticks to my skin. I shiver and tell myself it's from the cold, but when I approach the cave, I know right away something's wrong. There's a strange vibration in the ground. Like the sand is transmitting some sort of pulse. I enter slowly, with my inner guard up, locked tight into place.

The walls glisten like black onyx in the shadows, highlighting the white stone of the archway inlaid in the wall on the opposite side of the room. I step closer to the altar, the pale form lying atop it a waiting sacrifice.

My sister.

I breathe a sigh of relief. She's still there, the same as yesterday morning, a fragile sleeping beauty. There are no fresh wounds on her arms or anywhere that I can see. Her blonde hair spills around her head like a halo. Her hands are folded over her chest, covering the hole the dagger left behind. Her face, her bare arms and legs, sparkle like alabaster from the flecks of sand that settle in a thin coat over her skin. Perfectly preserved. Still no decay. No change.

I will her to open her silver-blue eyes. "I'm not giving up, Ava. I won't." I know what she would say. I know she would want me to

move on and pretend like everything could be normal. But that's
all impossible now.

I close my eyes and try for the hundredth time to reach her
mind with my own, but there's only a strange stillness answering
back, as if the air is holding its breath. It's unsettling and my gut
doesn't like it. Moving closer, I touch the neck of the violin that's
on the altar, resting at Ava's feet. I pluck a string to break the energy
up a little. The note bounces off the cave walls, high and mournful.

And it's followed by a growl that rumbles around me.

I go still, all senses keying in to the feeling in the air and the
vibrations under my feet. The sound came from the wall. Or, more
accurately, the doorway. I watch the black stone and pluck the violin string again.

The growl rumbles once more. Louder.

I step back from the altar and move to the other side. My shoe
slips on something slick. I look down—

Oh, God.

I cover my mouth with the back of my hand. It's a bloody piece
of *something*. Skin? Fur? There are more pieces scattered over the
sand. Whatever the carcass is, it's totally unrecognizable. And the
pieces of torn flesh are actually organized. The limbs and organs
are set in a pattern of some kind. A triangle, with other bits laid out
in a sort of upside-down V.

Then I see the head. It's placed facing the gateway. A dog. Its
snout points straight at the center of the archway.

My stomach rises. *What the hell did this?*

No, I don't want to know. I don't want to see what made that
twisted piece of artwork, taking such care with each scrap of skin
and intestine.

A noise comes from the opening of the cave. Sand grinding
against the stone, like dragging feet. Or claws.

Scratch, scratch, scratch.

My pulse hammers against my ribs, beating inside my head so hard it's all I can hear for several seconds. And then the sound of heaving breath begins echoing off the cave walls, noises of sinus and teeth and phlegm in the throat. It's not the thing that was growling a second ago, I'm pretty sure. The noise is coming from the wrong direction, by the cave opening. Something grumbling under its breath, the sound of skidding. A shadow moves along the wall, coming closer, until the thing appears from behind the altar.

The creature is small, shorter than the stone slab my sister is lying on. It has thin, bony arms and legs, wings more like a third set of limbs, linked with webbing. It has a long, pointy nose and large bat-like ears.

And it's dragging something behind it.

Part of a human leg.

I jerk back in horror, hoping my eyes are wrong.

The tiny beast comes into full view, and I reach up to grab my amulet, reassuring myself it's still there. The demon can't see me. It can't see. I bite my lips together and try not to gasp, not to gag, not to make a sound.

A human leg.

The creature stands beside the pieces of the dog, like it's observing the demented artwork. The mark on my chest begins to burn, but I can't act, not with Ava so close and vulnerable. I argue with myself: *kill, wait, kill, wait.* Until it looks up to study the wall where the doorway is.

And that's when I see what it's really looking at. A crack about a quarter inch wide and four inches long, running across the center of the opening. How did I not see that before? That's where the growl was coming from. Black tar-like liquid oozes from the fissure. A bleeding wound.

The demon is staring at it, as if willing it to open, holding that human leg in its claw like it's a log. The toenails on the foot are painted pink with a daisy on the big toe.

A gurgle comes from the creature as it lugs the chunk of human flesh in front of the dog head, dropping it unceremoniously to rest along the base of the doorway. Then it clacks its teeth and scuttles out of the cave, into the foggy sunlight.

I gasp in air, realizing I've been holding my breath. I have to focus. On not losing it. I have to force my gaze away from the blood and the death at my feet. And make myself think. Think, I have to think. That thing could be back any second with some other horrifying object.

I study Ava more closely, worried. Because if I didn't see the crack in the wall, maybe I missed something else. But she still looks untouched. I go to the spot in the cave where I hid her things and grab her bag and dump everything out, hoping to find something useful. A half-burnt smudge, a lighter, our mom's grimoire, Ava's stuffed rabbit, Mr. Ribbons, a Rainbow Brite pencil box, a bottle of powder, and a Ziploc bag filled with what look like dried chicken feet.

Nothing. Nothing here I can use to block the entrance to the cave so the demon can't come back in. Dammit.

I open the pencil box and empty it onto the sand. Chalk!

I scramble to the cave opening and brush the inches of sand away from the threshold. I uncover the stone floor and find a small circle of embedded rocks, four of them, each one etched with a symbol for a season and its elemental pairing. Summer and water. Autumn and earth. Winter and air. Spring and fire. I'm not sure why they're here or how they're embedded so securely into the cave floor, but the formation is obviously not to dissuade demons from entering or leaving. Maybe they have something to do with how the doorways work.

I take the chalk and begin writing the names of God in Hebrew, the first three that come to mind: El Emet—The God of Truth; El Elyon—The Most High God; El Yeshuatenu—God is our Salvation. I write each one three times, all in a row, marking a line across the threshold. My instinct says that the names will burn a demon's flesh on contact. Hopefully that's right.

I cover the writing back up with a thin layer of sand, and feel that the cave is somewhat secure, at least for now. I hurry back inside to gather all of Ava's things, shoving them in her bag again. Except for the smudge. I go ahead and light that, then I set it close to the opening, so the smoke fills the entrance; it won't scare the beast off, but it'll annoy the hell out of it. I slip the bag over my shoulder and approach the bloody mess of remains. I stare down at the pieces of dog and human in horror before gritting my teeth, holding my breath, and kicking it all to scatter the bits randomly, hopefully ruining whatever spell the creature was attempting to cast.

I wish I could take Ava with me, but I know I can't. Still, just because the demon didn't seem the least bit interested in her doesn't mean another one won't be. I need to get help.

I pull out my cell and hunker down in the farthest corner of the cave, where I can still watch the opening. The line rings and rings. Sid picks up at the last minute. "Hello, LA Paranormal Investigative Agency. How can I be of service? No job is too—"

"Sid!" I hiss, trying to whisper. "I'm at the beach cave. You need to get your ass here. Now. Something's wrong with the doorway."

"Oh, my. I was correct?"

"Just get here. I don't want to leave Ava alone. There's a corporeal demon making some sort of spell in here—or it was, I don't—"

A beep sounds as he hangs up.

"Okay. Don't bother asking any questions or anything. Shit." I shove my cell back in my pocket and settle in to wait.

NINE

Aidan

A half hour passes and the little demon hasn't come back with any new parts. I listen over the rhythm of the waves, trying to hear if anyone's approaching. Every sound could be either the demon returning or Sid coming to help, and waiting here for either one is making my nerves raw.

Several horrifying questions occur to me as I wait, the smell of blood and sulfur like acid in my nostrils. Whose leg is that? And where's the rest of her? My great-grandmother lives right at the top of the rise; the leg is too young to be hers, but it could belong to her nurse, Fa'auma.

Panic sets in then.

What if I'm here, hunkered down, while my own grandma and her nurse are being ripped to shreds only yards away? My insides begin to unravel as I wait. But I can't leave Ava, I can't—

"Aidan!" Kara's voice comes from up the beach.

I scramble to my feet, to the cave entrance, panic turning to anger at the realization that Sid brought Kara here to this horror. He knows about the weird energy exchange between us, and she was bleeding from her eyes only twelve hours ago. But there she is, walking beside our slow-moving mentor.

"What the hell?" I hiss at him when they reach me. "Why did you bring her?"

"Screw you," Kara says, looking annoyed. "I came because I wanted to help. And Sid needed a driver. He's not feeling well, or haven't you noticed?"

He seems his usual self to me, wide eyes looking around, and calm as always—even though he should be freaking out. I'm freaking out.

"Don't be silly, I'm fine," Sid says, patting Kara on the arm like an old man would. Except he's twenty-four.

"You're supposed to be checking the camera feed from the hospital with Connor," I say.

She rolls her eyes. "We finished. Stop being a spaz. I can take care of myself."

I bite my tongue until I can say, "I'm sorry, Kara, but this is bad."

"Just explain what happened," Sid says.

I turn back to the cave and they follow. "The wall is cracked and the same black goop, like in your shed, is seeping out. The demon seems to be attempting to cast a spell." We go around the altar and I motion to the floor, at the sand-coated massacre.

"My God," Kara breathes. She covers her nose with her hand and points at the leg.

"Yes, that part's human," I say, my stomach rising again. "Like I said, I think it all must be for some sort of spell."

Sid sighs and runs a hand over his face. "They were probably attempting to look for the key their leader promised them. Demons are a gossipy bunch."

I stare at Ava, my throat tightening. "But why would they be looking when the key is right here?"

"They don't know that, obviously."

"They're seriously that stupid?" I ask, doubtful. "They can't figure out the thing they're looking for is right in front of them?"

"Not if they can't see her." He shrugs, like it's all so obvious. "The spell I did is still fairly solid, from what I can tell."

"The spell? Obviously the cave isn't hidden, Sid. The demon waltzed into this place like it lived here. It killed a dog and possibly some woman! Ripped it to shreds right there!" I point at the pile of remains.

"The spell is on Ava alone, not the cave, Aidan," Sid says. "No one would believe a cave suddenly just up and disappeared. It's been here far too long for a spell to trick the minds of those who know right where it is."

Relief floods through me. And annoyance. "This would have been great information to know an hour ago when I called you in a panic! My fucking grandma could be in danger, but I didn't want to leave Ava because I was worried the demon would come back."

"Well, perhaps we should check on Mrs. O'Linn, too, then."

"Ya think?" I brush past him and rush up the beach, yelling behind me, "Wait there."

———

I reach the front door of my great-grandmother's house and pause before knocking, trying to catch my breath. I can't let it show that I'm upset; the woman has no idea what's going on, and I have no plans to tell her. What was I thinking, not secretly placing wards around this place, too? I should've realized this could happen, that this area would be a hub of activity, even with Ava being invisible. Thank God she's still hidden, at least.

The door opens before I can knock and my grandma's nurse, Fa'auma, is there in the entry. Both legs intact.

"Are you just going to stand out there, sweating?" she asks. She smiles wide and in my relief to see her safe, I answer with my own goofy grin. "I can get you some lemonade, you know."

"Sorry, I was just looking for Mrs. O'Linn to ask her a question," I say, then sputter, "I found this spot in the garden, off to the side, that seems to be dying, and I just wondered if Mrs. O'Linn wanted me to take the bushes out altogether, or something . . . Maybe water it by hand?"

Fa'auma waves me inside the house. "You are just too helpful, young man. I'm going to have to try and convince her to start paying you for all your help."

I begin following her into the entry, but as I step over the threshold an odd sense of the ground tipping makes me hesitate. I know that feeling. I haven't felt it in a while, but I recognize it instantly. An angel is close.

And as I walk into the living room, I can't help saying his name in surprise. "Eric!"

Mrs. O'Linn looks up from a *TV Guide* crossword puzzle and frowns at me. "What? Did you just call me a ferret?"

I gape at Eric, who's standing right behind my great-grandmother's chair. Neither of the ladies realizes he's there.

He's in the form he was in when he came to me after I died, during my Awakening, when I discovered he's my guardian. The burns or markings or whatever they are on his upper chest and neck seem almost violet against his pale skin, as does the long scar on his scruffy jaw, which appears to have come from a knife or a fight of some kind. His hair is so golden it glints in the sunlight, making him a little blinding to look at. And he's wearing those odd clothes again, made out of something like handwoven wool, instead of his usual five-thousand-dollar Italian suit. He stares back at me, obviously seeing me in spite of my amulet. But he stays still, silent.

"Aidan wants to talk to you about a dead spot in the garden," Fa'auma says to my grandma. "You be nice now." Then she wanders off to the kitchen, likely to get me something to drink.

Mrs. O'Linn huffs and then points at the flowery couch. "Sit. You're distracting me from my crossword puzzle."

I lower myself slowly onto the overlong couch along the wall. I give Eric a questioning look, but he just shakes his head and frowns.

Annoyed, I mouth at him, *What the hell is going on?*

Before I can see his response, Fa'auma sticks a drink in my face and I have to smile and act normal. Ice clinks in the glass as I take it, my limbs still shaking from everything that happened on the beach.

"My word, boy, wake up!" my grandma barks. "Are you on some kind of gang-banger drug?"

I shake my head. "S-sorry. I was . . . I thought, um—"

"Well, spit it out!" She waves her *TV Guide* at me. "It's almost time for my show."

I clear my throat, trying to find my focus again. "I mean, um . . . I saw some dead, uh, plants is all."

Her brow goes up. "Well, you're acting as if you're about to confess to killing them."

"No, ma'am." I look over to Eric and glare at him. Where the hell's he been? And why is he suddenly showing up at my great-grandmother's house, of all places?

"Then take a break," she says, as if I've actually been working in the yard all day. "Drink your lemonade and watch my show with me; it'll be on soon, after *Judge Judy*. It's a good one; the woman kills people for a living. Quite unrealistic but she *is* spunky. I could have played that role, you know. In my younger years, I was much more adept at being spunky than most. The young these days, they just don't understand . . ." She keeps going on but I tune her out.

She does this a lot, the rambling. Most of the time I find it endearing, but right now it's like a fly buzzing around my head.

Eric seems to take her distraction as some sort of cue and walks over to me. It's oddly fascinating to watch, almost like he's in slow motion. As he moves, gold flecks catch the light, falling from his shoulders and hair, and there are small flames at his feet where he steps. He motions for me to stand and I obey, unsure if I even have a choice.

"What's happening?" my grandmother asks, sounding flustered. "Are you ill?" I must have an odd look on my face because she appears genuinely concerned, which is totally unlike her.

Before I can answer, Eric is reaching out to me, touching my temple with his gold-tipped finger. And then everything stops, the world is suddenly frozen. My grandma is stock-still, halfway to her feet; Fa'auma is standing in the entry, with a hand raised to her throat, completely immobilized. Like shocked wax statues. It'd be funny if I couldn't see the horror on their faces.

They're staring at something on the floor behind me.

I turn and look down, and see . . . *me*. My body is lying there, pale as a ghost, the limbs oddly askew. I'm staring down at myself even though I feel like I'm still standing on my feet.

Damn. It's happening again. I'm dead?

I step away, creeped out. "What the fuck did you do, Eric?!"

"You're not dead. Just asleep."

I glance back at my body and realize my head is bleeding, like I hit it on the coffee table when I went down.

"You will return to your body in a moment," he says.

I scoff, turning back to him. "I'm so relieved. I'll also have a concussion, from the look of it."

"Your new body heals quickly. You'll be well."

Yes. My new body. I look him over, his old-world clothing, his proud chin. He seems a little different than the last time I saw him—besides all the gold and angel stuff, I mean.

"Much has happened on the other side," he says, answering my unasked question. He sounds tired.

Well, I have a whole lot more to ask. "What the hell is going on, Eric? Where have you been? I have no idea what I'm doing, or how to fix anything with my sister. I'm totally lost. I need help—"

"Enough. Other things needed my attention. You were capable of taking care of yourself for a few days."

"It's been weeks," I snap. "Everything's a mess. I've been digging into everything I can to figure out how I can bring back my sister and I've found all of nothing. Now Kara's sick and I'm totally clueless. I need help with my sister, to find her and bring her back. I have no idea what—"

"Your sister is why I've come," he interrupts, his voice grave.

"What do you mean?"

"A seal has been broken and I believe your sister's soul is to blame."

"What seal?"

"A seal over the Realms. There's been a breach. Shortly after your sister was placed into her between-state by the Heart-Keeper, a cry rose from the East and there was talk of a revolt under the archangel there, Rafa'el. The spirits have become scattered among his ranks and it's causing chaos on both planes. I believe Ava's father is attempting to find her. He will soon discover she's no longer in her body, if he doesn't know this already. He's not a creature to be trifled with, and we cannot allow him to find her if he's broken ranks. Nothing good will come of it."

"Her father." Ava's angelic father, who bought time with my mother like she was a common whore. Not someone I ever want to meet. Or meet again, since I probably knew him as one of her "boyfriends" once. "Who is he?"

"One of the dominions, or *Hashmal*, a midlevel eastern spirit; his name is Jaasi'el. He is the keeper of fire, spirit, and spark in those lands under Rafa'el. Or he *was*. So much has gone wrong so quickly." His features sink with concern the more he says.

A dominion. That's really not good. I've only seen one of their kind once in my life, when I was nine, and it was more a blink than a real look. But even from that small peek I know that I never want to run into one and be on its bad side. They're huge; more than seven feet tall, and they have wings that span a good twenty feet. There are vines growing up their arms and legs like armor, and what look like thorns growing from their knuckles.

"So, you're here because of Ava's father?" By the tense look on his face, I can tell Eric knows how bad it could be to cross a dominion. But I don't see why we'd have to cross this one. What's so terrible about an *angel* finding Ava? Eric should be focusing on the Darkness. "You do realize there's also a demon down on the beach, making artwork out of the insides of a dog in front of the gateway, right?"

"Of course. I sensed a witch call it up and felt it become corporeal. It won't cause any trouble, though. It's merely a scout."

"A scout for what?"

"I don't know. Perhaps one of the generals waiting on the other side of the gateway. Or it could merely be seeking its master."

That doesn't sound good. How can Eric not be sure? And the memory of the growl I heard coming from the wall isn't making me feel any better.

"As long as one of these scouts doesn't figure out how to open the doorway, they're harmless. The smaller scouts will be drawn here and to other doorway locations by the vibrations, by the calls of their generals, but they won't find a way to complete their task as long as your sister remains hidden.

"Jaasi'el, however, is another story. He is powerful, and the Key Keepers of the gates favor him enough to help him get through into Sheol to seek Ava's soul. This is another reason I've come here to check on the protections; I wanted to be sure Jaasi'el hadn't found her body—the soul and body must be reunited if he wishes to truly have her for himself. But the protections appear to be very solid, despite your mentor's failings."

"Sid's doing the best he can." I have no clue why I'm defending the guy, but I suddenly feel annoyed, seeing Eric's obvious unhappiness with everything.

"It won't matter, he has very little time left here."

A weight settles in my chest.

"He broke the rules of nature, Aidan. He will have to pay the price eventually." His voice is hard, and I wonder why he's acting so above it all. It's not like him.

"You've turned into a bit of a dick, Eric."

"My name is Azri'el. Eric was a construct for hiding what I truly am." He kind of sounds like he's saying that more for his own benefit than mine. "My task was never to be more than a protector and a watcher."

"Eric was my friend, but whatever."

"That time has passed. Now *you're* something else as well. You're human, but not the same as those you'll save. And you'll see, it will separate you from them. They won't understand the difference; they'll fear it."

I think of the way the cat lady looked at me, the way people always seem to look at me now. But how is that any different than when I was a street kid? "I'm used to being an outcast."

He nods, then looks over to the two frozen figures in the room. "You should go back to the women now. I'll protect them if anything attempts to do harm, but you'll need to put some barriers in place around the property. I have other things that need my attention. If I can't find Jaasi'el and hold him back, then you'll have more to worry about than a lower scout. You'll have unimaginable things coming through that doorway. Things not seen by human eyes since the time of Noah."

TEN

Rebecca

The cab driver pulls up in front of the LA Paranormal house. I hand him one of the many hundred-dollar bills my dad left me—guilt always pays well. When I tell the driver to keep the change, he jumps right out to help me with my bags, obviously excited about the forty-dollar tip. I thank him and tell him I can manage on my own when he offers to walk me to the door. Then I turn and head up the brick path.

I stop at the base of the porch steps and straighten my shoulders, trying to convince myself I did the right thing coming here. Aidan didn't meet me for coffee and didn't text because he was busy. Everything is fine. It has to be.

Flowers line the porch and bright-green grass carpets the yard; they're obviously not concerned about the drought. The house looms over me a little; the three-story Victorian is like an old yellow farmhouse that doesn't seem to fit in the neighborhood. It should be cheery, but it isn't. The windows stare back at me like they know I'm intruding.

My scar tingles at the thought of going back inside there. But I take a deep breath and walk up the steps onto the wrap-around porch and face the red door. There's a wreath made of an odd mix of plants hanging on it.

I knock. When no one answers after a few seconds, I reach over and ring the bell.

The door opens quickly. It's that Jax guy, a frown of annoyance on his face. "No *Watchtower*. I'm already actualized, thanks," he says before looking at me. Then his eyes settle on my chest, trailing up to my face. "Oh, shit, hey! The sexy redhead." He winks and pushes his black-framed glasses up his nose. "How's things in rich-girl land?"

Jax is kind of cute, actually. He has a cool style and is always smiling. If only he wasn't such a chauvinistic pig.

"Is Aidan here?" I ask.

He shakes his head. "Nope. On a job, of sorts. But maybe I can help." He folds his arms across his chest and leans on the doorjamb.

I try to peek around him. "Isn't Connor here?"

He rolls his eyes and turns, yelling into the interior of the house. "Connor!" Then he motions me into the entryway. "You sure he's the one you need, Ruby? He's the grumpy one, you know. I'm the fun one."

"It's Rebecca."

"Sure, right." He glances down at my cleavage again, then back to my face with a wicked smile. "You here to hang, or what?"

I clear my throat and clutch the strap of my shoulder bag tighter. "I need a place to stay."

His face opens wide, brow going up and smile spreading. "Really. That should be interesting."

I don't know what to say to that. It's obvious I'm the butt of some joke in his head.

Connor comes from the back of the house, saving me. "Hey, what's up?"

I forgot how blond and tall he is, maybe six feet and built like a swimmer. He fills the space he stands in like he's claiming it. He's eighteen or nineteen, as I recall. Though he seems older with that shadowed look in his very blue eyes.

"Red here is wanting to crash," Jax says.

"Rebecca," I correct. I don't like being nicknamed for the color of my hair. I glare at him. "Rebecca Emery Willow McLane. But you can call me Emery."

He winks again. "Sure thing."

Connor seems confused by my paragraph of names—I don't blame him, really—but he just studies me and then says, "I'm not sure there's room for you anymore."

Oh, God, I didn't even think about the possibility of being rejected.

Jax looks at Connor with a frown. "What? Of course there's room." Then he turns back to me—or my chest, I should say. "There're plenty of beds around here that would welcome you, Red."

I cringe. "Wow."

Connor shoves Jax aside, grabbing my bag like he's trying to be helpful. But then he says, "This is a bad idea. Isn't there somewhere else you can stay?"

"No," I say through my teeth.

He slips the strap of my bag over his shoulder and then just stands there and stares at me. It's a digging stare, like he's trying to figure me out, not like how guys usually study me. And he's actually looking at my face. It makes me notice his eyes and how light his eyelashes are, almost white. Something about him reminds me of Charlie. Probably just because he smells like the ocean.

Okay, I should *not* have noticed that.

"Fine," he says at last. "You'll bunk with Holly again."

I like Holly. She's totally insane but she's easy to get along with and not judgmental in the least, unlike my other friends who pick you apart like birds fighting over roadkill.

"Fine," I say.

I follow him up the stairs, into Holly's room. He sets my bags on the spare bed. "Holly's at the college. She's taking summer classes. But she's usually home around five."

"I know," I say. "We text." I've kept in touch with her a little. "And we're Facebook friends." I sit beside my suitcase on the bed. "Where's everyone else? Are they out investigating something?"

He doesn't answer for a few seconds. He folds his arms across his chest, looking me over like I'm a problem. "It's nothing personal," he says, his serious tone unnerving me, "but you really don't belong here. Especially now. There's too much going on, and all you'll do is cause trouble."

I don't say anything, unsure how to respond to such a blunt assessment.

And if that wasn't enough, he adds, "We don't have time for any more *90210* high school bullshit."

Whoa, low blow. "Are you kidding me? Last time I was here, I got my arm sliced open and nearly died. You think I don't understand how intense things can be? I just need a freaking place to sleep for a little while."

"It's not as if you can't afford a room at the Hyatt. You came here to be close to *him*."

"It's not like that," I say, feeling like he's accusing me of a crime or something.

"Aidan isn't on the market, Rebecca."

Guilt turns to defensive anger. "I don't deserve the third degree, *Connor*," I say, mimicking his derisive tone.

He pauses at that and his posture changes, a little less aggressive. "Look, I'm sure you're a nice kid and all, but—"

"I'm not a *kid*," I say, probably with a little more heat than I need to. It's all so infuriating and mortifying. "I'm perfectly capable of minding my own business and staying out of the way. I'm sixteen, not six, so kiss my butt."

He releases a small puff of laughter and his hands go up in surrender. "I get the message. You're older than the hills and wise as an owl."

I want to throw something at his smug face. Who does he think he is, talking to me like this? I'm here, asking for help, and he's acting like I'm trying to break up the couple of the year. As if he has a say in who I can like or who can like me. What a total a-hole.

And, for the life of me, I have no sassy comeback to throw at him. Which just infuriates me more.

His smile fades a little and he moves like he's going to leave, heading for the door. When he's right beside me he pauses, only an inch away, and whispers, "I know you could probably have any guy you want. But you're not going to get this one."

He says it like an apology. But I hear it like needles in my heart.

He moves to the door and before he slips out, he says over his shoulder, "And don't think he'll be happy that you've come back."

ELEVEN

Aidan

I have to sit through two cases on *Judge Judy* before the two women let me off the couch to leave. I finally convince them that I'm fine, I was just dizzy from not eating, which made me trip and hit my head or something, I don't know. I'm so confused and distracted by everything that Eric said, I just babble until they stop clucking like flustered hens.

And to keep them from calling 911 or their concierge doctor, I eat two PB&Js and drink a glass of lemonade, a glass of milk, and then somehow manage to get down three Oreos.

I'm pretty sure I'll hurl if I move too much.

Apparently, I was only "passed out" for a few seconds. But I was with Eric for much longer than that. He talked about a whole lot of stuff he didn't actually *explain*. Ava's father is coming and he's a badass dominion angel of some kind. And he's pissed. All that was pretty clear. What wasn't clear was why Ava's dad is suddenly interested in saving his daughter who he abandoned to Darkness. He's creating a very large problem by leaving ranks, though. Now parts of the spirit world are breaking into chaos because of it. And as things begin to crumble, everything twisted and nasty on the other side of Sheol is beginning to peek through.

"Read the journal," Eric kept saying in answer to my questions about my new role. And also in answer to my questions about how I can save my sister.

After the fourth time he said it, I pretty much yelled at him that I *had* been reading the damn journal but I couldn't find any real information on anything except my new body. He just looked at me stoically and said I wasn't reading it right and that the most vital thing I needed to know for now was in the first under-passage—whatever that means. Then he touched my head and sent me back to my body before I could ask him anything else.

He's been standing behind my great-grandmother's chair ever since, his body still and his features grave. He said he's going to protect the house and the souls inside, mark it to warn any other spirits away—including other angels—until I can get the land warded. The demons are apparently going to be drawn here, to the area near the cave, now that the doorway is cracked. Eric made it fairly clear, though, that he's got better things to do than babysit and watch crime dramas, so I have to hurry. The guy's turned into a major stiff. A bossy one.

I'll need to block the cave opening with more wards, the strongest I can find. And I'll have to figure out something with Sid to protect Mrs. O'Linn's house, as well as the beach—something to keep the demons from attempting more spells with any animal carcasses. I'm going to have my work cut out for me over the next few days.

I make it to the door, the ladies following me. To soothe their worries I take a paper bag of yet more food from Fa'auma. My great-grandmother lectures me about eating better and scolds me for interrupting her "repose." In spite of her disapproving frown, I can smell her concern for me and feel her hope that I'll come back soon so she can make sure I'm okay.

"I'll see you in a day or two," I say and lean over, pecking her forehead with a kiss. Her skin is soft and smells like baby shampoo. A wave of affection rolls through me, but I know she'll hate it if I try for a hug, so I just pat her bony shoulder and step back. "Don't worry, I'm tough."

"Oh, nonsense," she huffs. "I don't worry." But she looks a little flustered from my kiss, touching her pink cheeks as I say my good-byes.

When I get down to the beach, Sid is gone, but Kara's sitting outside the cave, waiting for me.

"Sorry it took so long," I say. "I just wanted to be sure they were okay." But instead I chatted it up with my guardian angel, then was force-fed half the peanut butter and jelly in Southern California.

"Sid had to go wait in the car," she says. "The pull of the doorway was making him sick."

I nod and look down the dark corridor of the cave. The pull doesn't even feel that strong anymore. Definitely not as strong as it was before Ava went to sleep. I think of what Eric said about Sid not having much time left, and my stomach hurts.

"The leg the demon dragged in," I say. "We need to figure out who it . . . goes to."

Kara scrunches up her nose. "Ugh. That was just . . . Sid couldn't be in the cave for more than a second, so he made me check it to see if there was recent bleeding. Looks like the demon didn't get the leg off of anyone living."

That's a relief.

She holds up Ava's bag and hands it to me. "I picked everything up, so it wouldn't get lost. I thought you'd want it."

I take the worn brown leather satchel, knowing it holds the reason we're standing here talking about demons ripping off legs: my mom's grimoire. "Thanks," I say. Even though I don't really want it, I need to be sure it stays hidden, too.

"Is everyone all right up there?" she asks.

I move away from the cave and look out at the waves. "Yeah, but we have to get to work, putting wards up around this place. Eric said the demons won't stop coming."

"Eric? You saw him?" She's the only one I told about Eric being an angel. Everyone else still thinks he's been missing because he's on some expedition to find illegal loot.

"Sort of." I breathe out, feeling tired and stuffed with cookies and sandwiches. I turn and rest my hand on her upper arm, needing a connection to her. "I just have to think. And figure out how to block some of the negative stuff that's about to come rolling in."

"We just got more salt from Costco. And Connor and I can try out some of the rune magic we've been learning."

"For now, I need to get out of here." Maybe the gateway's affecting me, too, because I'm feeling overstimulated and nauseated. Or maybe it was the whole out-of-body-experience thing. Can a guy get motion sick from traveling through space and time in seconds?

Kara moves closer, reaching out to touch my face. "You don't look so hot, either." Her fingers graze my jaw.

I give her a half smile. "They fed me a few pounds of Wonder Bread and Skippy up there. My hotness may now be buried in layers of PB&J."

"Seriously?" She rolls her eyes and slips her arm in mine as we head for the car. "How did I ever fall for a guy who can't handle a few old ladies doting over him?"

I pause when we're halfway up the path. "Wait. Did you say you've fallen for me?" I wrap her in my arms, her warmth soothing my raw nerves already.

She laughs into my chest and tries to pull away, but I don't let her go. I kiss her temple and grip her by the shoulder as we continue walking.

I try to hide that I'm using her steadiness to hold me up a little.

I need to come up with a plan to get this place locked up tight, to protect my great-grandmother and Fa'auma, and Ava. And I have to hope that whatever Ava's father is planning, it won't make waking her up impossible.

———

Kara drives Sid home in the Mustang. They get back to the house before me; the sleek red classic is parked ahead of me in the driveway. I sit in the warm cab of the Camaro after I pull in behind it, not wanting to go into the house yet. I just need a few more minutes to breathe. And digest—both the six pounds of food in my gut and the fact that I'm facing some kind of possible creepy spiritual jailbreak. After I've been sitting and staring at the license plate of the Mustang for a few minutes, my phone vibrates on the seat beside me.

A text from Kara. *You need to come inside. Now.*

I sigh and pull the keys from the ignition, then slide from the car. As I walk along the path to the back of the house, I sense myself being tugged by Sid's shed, but I ignore the pull. There's nothing good yanking on me from in there. I breathe past it and walk up the back steps, through the door, into the kitchen.

"Oh, man," Jax greets me on his way out. "You're so screwed." He pats me on the shoulder as if he's consoling me.

He actually seems genuinely concerned, which is unlike him, so I pause. "What're you talking about?"

He gives me a sigh and a shake of his head, then says, "Don't let the females get you down, bro," as he goes out the back door. I get the feeling he's making an escape.

"There you are," Kara says, coming into the kitchen. She doesn't look happy.

"What the heck is going on? What's wrong with Jax?"

"Oh, he's just worried I'm going to murder you."

I study her, trying to figure out if she's kidding. She's definitely not in the same jolly mood she was in a little bit ago. "Because . . . ?"

"Because your other girlfriend is going to be living with us for a few weeks."

I step back, thrown. "Rebecca?"

She gives me a look. "The fact that you knew exactly who I was talking about isn't helping me feel better."

"She's staying *here*?" Not good. Worlds colliding.

"So you didn't know?"

"No. No way." Rebecca said she had a surprise for me when she texted about our coffee date—the coffee date I ditched her on yesterday.

"Well, she's made herself at home in Holly's room again. It's like old times." She gives me a stiff smile. I take a breath, processing the news. Kara must think the look on my face is panic because she adds, "I guess I can take Monday, Wednesday, Friday, if you're worried about writing up a new make-out schedule."

I laugh, despite the tension coming from her. She's even cuter when she's pissed. "You're hilarious." I reach out and pull her closer, planting a kiss on the top of her head. "My make-out schedule is all full up." Her skin warms a little under my palm. I rub my thumb up and down her arm, trying to soothe her, trying to decide how annoyed or worried I need to be about Rebecca joining our house again.

Talk about bad timing.

"I really don't want to be the crazy jealous girlfriend, Aidan," Kara mumbles, sounding deflated.

A spark tingles in my chest at her words. "So you're falling for me *and* I'm your boyfriend? This is moving pretty fast for me. I don't know . . ."

She half-heartedly smacks me on the chest. "Don't be cute."

"Now you're asking the impossible."

I win a small giggle and a sigh that feels like relief. "*You're* impossible."

"True."

TWELVE

Rebecca

Holly grabs my hand and pulls me out of our room to the landing. "Listen, you have to face this stuff, KWIM? It's major bad mojo to keep toxic memories all bunched up inside your head."

A second ago I was jitter-talking, and I mentioned a nightmare that I had where this thing that looked like Gollum from *The Lord of the Rings* was trying to feed me poisoned birthday cake. I thought it was kind of funny and that it would lighten the mood, but I shouldn't have opened my mouth. Apparently Holly thinks of herself as a home-brew psychologist now that she's taken three classes at the junior college.

"The dream is like a window," she says. "The 411 on your deeper self."

"So, I'm scared of *The Two Towers*? Or cake?" I know she's hinting that I'm scared of the demons and stuff—of course I am—but I'm not sure this is something I want to be digging deeper into. Not now, anyway. My stomach is all jumbled. I've been sitting around for more than an hour, waiting for Aidan to get back home.

After the Connor confrontation, and seeing the look on Kara's face when she spotted me a second ago, I'm ready to puke from nerves.

To say the emo-rocker girl didn't appear happy would be an understatement. And she's very intimidating. She seems like a dark Asian faerie or something. Her look is all edges and contrast, with black boots, dark jeans, and an off-the-shoulder *Star Wars* shirt. Her wide, innocent-looking eyes are juxtaposed against her wild, purple-tinted black hair. And she has about nine dozen piercings in one ear and only one in the other; in my experience a lopsided piercing pattern is usually the sign of not giving a damn. She's that punk-pretty that only certain girls can pull off.

Holly acted like it was no big deal when Kara's glare shot daggers at me. She just calmly explained to Kara why I'm here, as if we're all the best of friends. I think she was playing it cool on purpose—smoothing over the reintroduction of an old wrinkle.

Kara wasn't playing along, though. I recognized the look on her face. I've seen it on the faces of other girls enough to know when I'm an unwanted addition to a group; the look of a threatened diva. As if Kara doesn't know she could have Aidan worshiping at her feet if she wanted. It bothers me, more than normal jealousy. I swear, it's not just the average triangle-shaped love scenario. My life is not *Twilight*—if it was, I guess I'd be Jacob. Totally depressing.

But it's not like that. It's more complicated. More intense. My proof is that I can *feel* Aidan's emotions.

Yes. Feel them. Like I'm me, but I'm him, too. It's really strange. The first time I noticed it—when I was at the party that night on the beach, and he emerged from the darkness, so concerned about me—I felt his worry, and I thought I was losing my mind. Later, I realized that the strangeness didn't stop there: Even though I'd never met this guy before, I'd been drawing him for years. Aidan was the angel in my artwork—like I'd been envisioning the future.

It was crazy. But also comforting. It made the odd sensation of experiencing his emotions a little more tolerable.

Not that I ever enjoyed it. Especially the moments when I had to feel his need for Kara—my God, knowing his hunger for her, his desire, that was . . . disturbing. I'm really hoping I can just avoid the two of them together.

Kara's in the kitchen now, so I can breathe a little easier. Except for this psycho-testing I'm undergoing with Doctor Holly.

"Okay, so you were lying there." She points at the top of the staircase.

I nod, like I'm listening, but I'm actually trying to figure out if it was a terrible mistake, leaving Samantha's and coming here.

"Hey-loo?" Holly sings, waving at my face. "Lay down."

This is ridiculous.

She motions to the top step. "In the spot where *it* happened."

I know she won't stop babbling about all this nonsense unless I go along with it for a second, so I lie down on the landing and fold my hands over my chest. "What now?" I ask, pretending I'm into it.

"Well, you RET—replay the emotional trauma, of course."

"Of course," I mumble, closing my eyes. My stomach growls, reminding me I haven't eaten since breakfast.

And then I feel a spark of emotion in my belly, drowning out the hunger. It's shock—but not my own.

It's *his*.

My eyes fly open and I lift my head, looking toward the burst of anxiety.

He's standing at the bottom of the staircase, looking up at me like he's seeing a ghost. His bronze skin is more sallow than the last time I saw him and he looks tired, but he has that same presence, power pulsing off of him in waves. And he has this awareness in his eyes like he's sensing and seeing *everything*.

It's the same feeling every time I see him. The rush of elation and euphoria, as if I've made it home after a long journey. And the safety. Always the safety when I'm close to him.

Holly pokes her head around the bannister when she realizes I'm looking at someone. She waves at Aidan. "Don't freak. I was just showing her where it all happened. Like, re-envisionist therapy."

His shock turns to a frown. He starts up the stairs and in spite of how frustrated I am that he blew me off yesterday, I can't help the way my heartbeat quickens. His hands clench and unclench as he comes closer, as if he's touched something that makes his fingertips tingle. There's uneasiness in him, resting right beside my own.

"You relive moments and whatnot," Holly continues, like everything's fine and normal. "And then things are supposed to come clear. I'm doing a paper on it for chemical psych. I mean, this girl's gotta have baggage, right?"

He stops at the top of the landing and stares at her like she's completely crazy.

I stand and wipe my hands on my yoga pants, suddenly wishing I'd worn something less black for this re-envisionist thing. There are now smudges of dirt on my thighs. I sigh and look at Aidan to say, *Someone needs to sweep,* but when my eyes meet his, the casual words stick in my throat. Who the hell cares that I have spots on my pants? He's thinking of how he saw me nearly bleed to death right there, and his mind is racing from the shock we just gave him. The *thud, thud, thud* of his heartbeat vibrates in my temple.

So instead I say, "Sorry," and swallow because my mouth is now a desert.

He clears his throat and glances my way, but he won't really look at me. "So, you're staying here for a few weeks?" he asks.

I study his profile, the way his jaw muscle flexes. Connor was right, Aidan's really not happy that I'm here. "I'm not sure. I might just go stay with Samantha instead." I've obviously made a mistake. I try not to let the rejection sting too much.

He looks at me then and his brow creases. "You don't have to go."

I wish I could feel him wanting me to stay more than I do. "It's for the best."

"Ay dios mio," Holly says. "This is cray, children. Talk about awk*ward*. Here, I'll FIFY." She takes my hand and Aidan's, then pulls us into her room. "Now either talk it out or make out." Then she spins on her heel and leaves us, shutting the door before either of us can protest.

We both just stand there, facing each other, a bit thrown. Well, thrown and embarrassed.

I back up a step or two, not liking how being close to him makes that vulnerability in me feel so much stronger. "I'm sorry. I thought it would be a nice surprise. I didn't think . . . I shouldn't have assumed."

"It's fine, Rebecca, really." He says the words, but I can tell he doesn't mean them; me being here is making him nervous. "Don't feel bad," he adds. "Things are just nuts right now."

"I only came because my dad's out of town for work and I didn't want to be alone."

He nods his head. "What does he think about you being here?"

"He doesn't know. He arranged for me to stay with Samantha's parents, but Samantha's busy with dance competitions." And to be sure he knows I'm not a total stalker, I say, "And I'm not much of a fan of her stepfather's roaming hands." The gross stepdad isn't the only reason I wanted to stay here instead, but the main reason—wanting to be close to Aidan—seems to have flown out the window, given his reaction.

Aidan sparks with protectiveness at my words. "Why didn't you tell your dad?" he asks.

"My dad doesn't need another reason to worry. He's been through enough."

His eyes lock with mine and for a second it's like we're moving back to the way we were over the last few weeks. Comfortable. Safe. Friends. Even though I want more, the thought of losing our friendship is making it tough to breathe.

"Why didn't you call me yesterday?" I ask quietly, not sure I want to know the answer.

He blinks and guilt filters from him. "I . . . I was going to text you, but . . . I'm sorry, Rebecca. Everything's crazy right now."

"What's going on?" I want to move closer to him, but I'm not sure how.

He takes a few breaths, then goes to sit in Holly's Hello Kitty desk chair, leaning forward with his elbows on his knees, rubbing his hands over his face. His dark curls fall forward and a glint of gold shimmers on the tips as the sunlight shines through the window behind him. He looks up at me and even now, in my confusion and conflict, I'm struck by how lovely he is, how his black lashes frame his troubled hazel eyes, how that odd marking on his left arm looks almost alive with the tension in the muscles beneath.

"A lot is going on," he says. "I don't know."

"Aren't I still your friend?" I ask. "You can tell me, Aidan."

His guilt surfaces again, stronger this time. "You are," he says, staring at the floor. "You are my friend, Rebecca."

"Then why are you pulling away?" I lower myself onto the edge of the bed, facing him. "And don't tell me that you're not, because I can feel it, something's changed."

He blows out a long breath, then says, "Something has changed. I'm not sure why I didn't tell you before, why I acted like it wouldn't matter. Because it does. It was wrong of me."

"What?" My nerves turn raw as his helplessness trickles into me.

"I told you some things about me, how I can see stuff, like ghosts and demons, but what you don't know . . . you don't know that there are other things I can do. Parts of me, parts of who I am, that you won't ever know or understand."

I stare at him, confused. "Like what?"

His eyes meet mine and the intensity in them seems to suck the air from the room.

"I can see your soul," he says, his voice scratchy, like the words are difficult to say. "And I can see when you lie."

Shock numbs me to my toes. It sounds so crazy—he sees my *soul*? But, then again, I have no idea why I would be afraid of Aidan seeing into me. I feel his emotions, after all.

"But that's stuff I could always do," he continues. "Since the day I met you, I could see you were a virgin. I knew you cared about me. I knew things about you that no one would know about a stranger. So much was clear to me from the moment I met you."

He could tell I was a virgin just by *meeting* me? It's like that dream where I realize I've been walking around school naked all day. What else has he known all this time?

"It's not just you," he says in a rush. "I see everything, everyone the same. I can see Jax and Holly's souls, too. And the soul of the guy behind the counter at Starbucks."

Well, that makes me feel special. I don't know what to say. What does a soul even look like?

"We're friends, you and me," he adds, "but I know that you want more than that."

I swallow hard but don't look away. I won't deny that I care about him.

"But I think that's because we're connected in other ways, too, because of your abilities and mine. It's just . . . the thing is . . . I'm changing now. Becoming *more*—I can't explain it."

I'm connected to him in some way, he's right. And he thinks that's why I'm attracted to him?

"Something happened," he continues. "Something changed in me. I'm connected to Kara now . . . still connecting, really. It's like puzzle pieces fitting together, and it's more than just me being attracted to her. It's bigger than that. She'll be a part of me forever now. I wanted to believe I could still be your friend, even though I knew you liked me more than that. But I've realized it's not right. It's not fair to you."

My mind is lost in everything he's said. One thing is very clear, though: he loves Kara. I see it in him, feel it when he says her name. "No . . . it's not fair."

"I'm supposed to protect you, I know that now. But I'm not doing a very good job."

I don't feel protected, that's for sure. I'm a gaping wound right now. A naked soul he's been looking at, seeing all my flaws and not choosing me. It's ridiculously crushing.

"I think it's best if you're going to stay here that you know the whole truth. And I definitely think if your dad's out of town, that you should stay with us."

His concern for me is genuine; it feels like a grip on my shoulders. But if I do what he says, if I stay here, am I being weak? Am I giving into that side of me that needs affirmation? I can't tell. I can't even tell if it matters. My insides whisper that I need to stay close, that I need to listen to him, even if it hurts.

Which is crazy. And totally not the inner feminist voice I'd rather hear.

"I'll think about it," is all I can manage for now. I need to give him the drawing I have in my pocket still. I need to figure out if I'm going back to Samantha's or someone else's place. I need some sane advice, but everyone I trusted for that is gone now. Even my imaginary angel.

THIRTEEN

Aidan

I can't focus. Hurting Rebecca, seeing the torment in her eyes—torment I put there . . . it's tearing me up. And pissing me off.

"Pass the red one," Connor says, waving at a basket of USB drives at the end of the table in the office. "I was placing cameras last week, and this weird thing came up on one of the feeds. I was thinking you could help me check it out."

I pass him a drive stick.

Connor takes it, then hands it back, scoffing. "This isn't red on Earth, dude."

I look down and see it's blue. "Sorry." I put it back in the basket and find the red one.

Connor inserts it into the laptop. "What's got your neurons captive?"

"Nothing."

"Does this *nothing* have red hair?" He's got this look on his face that tells me he doesn't like any of this stuff with Rebecca.

"Something like that."

"You have to focus, Aidan. This isn't about her."

"I know." But it is. I just wish I understood how she fits.

"Rebecca may be a Light, but supposedly I am, too," Connor says. "Do you get depressed when you hurt my feelings?"

"Wait." I lean back in mock surprise. "You have feelings?"

He chuckles and opens the USB drive, searching through the folders.

Connor's right, he is a Light. And so are Finger and Jax and Holly. But I don't feel even a quarter of the connection with them that I feel with Rebecca. She's different. She always has been. I just wish I knew why. Then maybe I wouldn't have to feel so guilty every time I want to care about her.

Maybe it's time to stop thinking about that. It's not like I don't have enough stuff going on as it is. I need to throw myself into fixing the cave and waking Ava. I just hope Eric can stop her father.

"Kara says you guys have been working on learning some rune formations," I say.

He looks sideways at me like I'm accusing him of something. "Nothing kinky."

"Ha. No, I mean I may need your help with some wards for my great-grandmother's place. And the cave. I need to keep demons off the land."

He nods. "Yeah, I think between Kara and me we'd know just enough to be dangerous."

"To demons."

"Sure." He focuses on the folders in the USB, clicking on one marked *Fosters_livefeed*.

After this, maybe I should read Eric's damn journal again, get more info there. I can look for the "under-passage" Eric talked about, whatever that is. A passage within a passage, obviously. A code? Shit, I'm getting a headache.

"What's Sid say about this video feed?" I ask, trying to care about the task in front of us.

"He hasn't looked at it yet. I figured it's better to let the guy rest. He hasn't been real solid the last few days."

Eric's words come to mind again, making the ache in my gut return. "What do you mean?"

"He's tired. Really tired."

I nod and wonder why he's not elaborating more. It's obvious Sid is lowering his guard more with Kara and Connor than with me. I don't know why, but it bothers me.

"And he's okay with you taking over the decisions?" I ask.

"It's going to have to happen sooner or later, I guess. Might as well give the guy a break while he's got a chance to have one." He sighs, as if resigned to a heavy future.

The idea of Sid not being here one day, not a part of this thing he's created, feels so wrong. And even though he's a pain in the ass and sneaky as hell, the guy grows on you. I don't want to imagine how we'll get through all this without him.

Connor moves the cursor and clicks on a video file labeled *attic*, opening it in the media program. He moves the time marker to three-fourths down the timeline before letting it play. "Watch the right corner, by the small door."

I watch the still image of an empty room bathed in green night-vision tech. Like the label on the file says, it's an attic. It has a low ceiling and wood floors. There are boxes stacked on the left, a chair turned over in the middle of the space, some empty book-shelves in the shadows along the wall. Several bright green dots create a pattern on the opposite wall, likely from a laser Connor set up when he placed the camera. The dots are in a grid around the door he pointed out. The door is in the corner, about half the nor-mal size, reminding me of something from *Alice in Wonderland*. It's probably a small closet. And someone doesn't want it opened; there are three very large latches holding it closed.

"That's where the owner of the house said she felt the thing shove her," Connor adds, pointing at the tiny door. "She claimed she was trying to unlock the cupboard to clean it out. There was the smell of something dead in the house, and it was the only spot she hadn't checked yet."

"Why'd she lock it like that?"

"She didn't. Former owner."

I look more closely and notice what looks like a word carved into the wood door, near the top latch. It's difficult to see, but it almost looks like it says *dybbuk*. Yiddish for a wraith-type spirit.

"Is this family, or the former owner, Jewish?" I ask.

Connor shrugs. "Didn't ask. Why?"

"The door, there. It says something. I think it's Yiddish."

"Well, in five seconds you'll only have a hundred more questions, so watch those lights."

I focus back on the green laser points on the wall, and—

"Whoa!" I say, as the video goes black and the word scratched into the wood seems to shine, as if made of light. After about half a second, the green glow from the night vision fills the room again, and I know beyond a doubt something with mass moved past that door. Something big enough to block out all the light from the laser.

"Crazy, right?" Connor says.

"Maybe it was an animal?" Not likely, but I have to keep an open mind. Not everything is paranormal, even though in my world it feels like it is.

"I checked the room for droppings when I placed the camera but didn't see anything. And the client doesn't own any pets. Plus, do you know any possums or raccoons that move that fast?" he asks. "Or that can make something glow, like that spot on the surface of the door?"

I shake my head. "And the lady was physically touched?"

"Shoved. She told me she scratched her hand, got a gnarly splinter from the floor because of the fall."

My curiosity is definitely piqued. "When do you go back?"

"Whenever you can come with me. I'm tired of sitting around."

"Tomorrow, then. And you can help me with setting up the protections for my sister and grandma afterward."

He shuts the laptop and pulls out the pen drive, tossing it into the basket. "What are the protections for?"

I sigh and lean back in the desk chair. "A demon left a bit of a *gift* in the cave where my sister is. And supposedly things are being drawn to the site."

He makes a face, obviously realizing my request for help won't be too fun. "What kind of *gift* did the thing leave?"

"A human leg."

His eyes widen. "Are you shitting me?"

"I wish I was."

FOURTEEN

Aidan

The next morning I get up early and head downstairs to make coffee, hoping I'll be the first one up so I can get the last of the Cap'n Crunch. Jax seems to have a nose for disappearing cereal and always gobbles up the good stuff before I get any. I'm going to start hiding some in my room—it's becoming clear why Holly marks her shampoo with a skull and crossbones.

I'm opening the cupboard when Kara comes in.

"What were you and Connor up to last night?" she asks.

"Just looking over some video from the Foster place. And I was talking to him about the rune thing. I think he's gonna help me today at Mrs. O'Linn's. Do you wanna come?" I find the box of Cap'n Crunch and set it on the counter, then go to the freezer for the coffee grounds.

"Yes, get me the hell out of here." She sighs and leans on the counter next to me.

I look sideways at her. She's still annoyed about Rebecca. "Be nice."

She gives me a fake smile. "You know I'm never nice."

"Right." I scoop the coffee into the filter. "That's what you'd love everyone to think, but I know you too well, little lady." I hand her the pot and she turns to the sink to fill it, handing it back to me.

"This *little lady* can totally kick your ass, mister."

I pour the water into the back of the brewer and smile. "Yes, she can. I'm fully aware." I set the pot back in place and press the "On" button. Then I grab her hand and pull her closer. "My gut has had several opportunities to become comfortable with that idea."

She slides her palms up my chest. "I only punched you that once. And you're lucky it was your gut; you were being a very large asshole."

"But you've forgiven me."

"Maybe." She gives me a coy look and tilts her head like she's leaving it open for discussion.

But before I start kissing her again, I need to check something. After what happened the other day, I can't be too careful. "How're you feeling?"

She sighs and pulls back a little. "I'm fine. Look." She points at her face and opens her eyes wide. "No blood."

"You don't feel sick? No headache or anything?" I touch her temple gently.

She shakes her head. "Just from this conversation."

"You know that I'm going to worry. That was terrifying."

"I know." Her features turn more somber. "But really, Aidan, I'm feeling totally normal. In fact, I feel better than ever."

The idea should lift a weight off my shoulders, but instead it just raises more questions about why her energy poured into me and why the marks on her soul are blurry. When we go out today, I need to get a good look at her soul.

She continues, "I'm so much better, in fact, that I may want to finish that conversation we were having the day before yesterday." She reaches out and slides her finger like a feather over my neck. "You know, the one with the kissing." She rises onto her toes and touches her lips to my jaw. "And the touching." Then she runs her hand down to my stomach, lower, and lower—

I bite back a breath and grab her wrist. Then move so I can see her eyes.

I let a heartbeat go by. We stare at each other, her face now serious. And I see it there, the same thing that's inside of me. The need to connect. To finish what we started all those weeks ago. I don't think I've seen that in her eyes before. I felt her want me when she touched me, but it was always like her mind was somewhere else. Like we weren't really connecting anymore once we started getting closer to what she feared and all her dark memories crowded in.

We haven't gotten close to the edge of that cliff again, not since the night in the hotel, just before my Awakening. I don't think my body could've handled it if we had, anyway.

I rub my thumb across her wrist, feeling the thin bump of her scar, and I dare the question. "What's changed?"

Her brow pinches. "Nothing."

But something has. And I'm willing to bet it has to do with her bleeding eyes and the way her energy merged with mine. But does it really matter? Maybe I need to stop thinking so damn much.

I lean in and touch my lips to hers, letting myself sink into her for a second, sliding my hand up her arm and across her shoulder, to the nape of her neck. Her skin is soft under my fingertips, the feel of it making me want to touch her more. And the way she responds to my touch nearly makes me forget to stay on the safe side of the line.

A squeak comes from the hall and I pull back, my head full of how much I want her.

When I turn, there's a flash of red hair and I spot Rebecca running back up the stairs.

FIFTEEN

Aidan

Connor and Kara and I gather the supplies we need for the attic job at the Fosters' and for the wards at my great-grandmother's house and the cave. Sid is still in his shed when we're leaving; he asks Connor if he could pick up a few scrolls from Hanna at SubZero, so he can do more research about Kara's blood-show. We figure we'll head there first. Jax decides to come along, too, since Rebecca is here to help Holly with filing and other office stuff. This thrills Holly to no end, since it means she can focus on her homework today.

I feel bad leaving Rebecca there with the grunt work and consider inviting her along on the job, but she isn't even willing to look me in the eye. My guess is that the answer would've been no anyway, considering how embarrassed she seems from walking in on me and Kara.

Rebecca goes to the summer program at the arts academy three days a week, like Ava did, so she won't be stuck in the house all the time, at least. And now that everything is out in the open between us, we can be honest about where things stand.

"You're thinking about her again," Kara says. She's next to me in the backseat of the Camaro. Connor's driving and Jax is shotgun.

I turn to her. "Huh?"

She rolls her eyes, but she takes my hand and weaves her fingers through mine.

We get to SubZero and park in the back lot. It's odd being here at Eric's club without him. And I haven't seen Hanna since that last night when I tried to save Ava; I still have the alabaster box Hanna gave me, tucked under my bed where I don't have to look at it. The thing is just a reminder of how I failed to save my sister.

As we walk across the parking lot to the warehouse, I focus on Kara's skin, trying to see her soul better, now that we're away from the house.

It surfaces easily. What used to be handprints are now just greyish-brown smudges. The red print on her throat is blurry, too. And the Chinese characters on her neck from her father's curse are light silver.

Her soul is definitely changing. But what does that mean? I know it can't be good. The blood-show made that more than clear.

When we get to the warehouse, the outer door is already open. I look around but don't see Hanna in the front offices. I put aside my worries for Kara for a second and feel for Hanna's energy. It's coming from the back where the vault is—a bright warmth that smells a little like cinnamon and sugar.

The others follow me as I walk deeper into the warehouse, down a long hallway, to the thick steel door of the vault. It's wide open and Hanna is standing in the frame. She's dressed in stretch pants and a long T-shirt. It's strange to see her in such mundane clothes, instead of her usual designer blouses and skirts. I wonder if something's wrong.

Of course something's wrong. Eric is gone. And Hanna's always been beside him. They were a team.

She comes forward and surprises me by wrapping me in a hug. "Aidan, how are you? You look tired." Her scent fills my head and I let myself be comforted for a moment before she pulls back and holds her hand out to Kara. "And how are you, sweetheart? Sid told me what happened."

Kara goes stiff at the show of affection until Hanna releases her hand, and then she manages to say, "I'm fine. Really."

"Is that why you've come?" Hanna asks. "Sid had me set aside the temple scrolls so he could figure out what may be going wrong, or if the blood-show was just a fluke. I found three new pieces that Eric had hidden in his desk."

Connor says, "We're also looking for information on runes. Kara and I have been studying the differences in configurations and we're missing some of the stronger protection combinations."

"Of course," Hanna says, motioning for us to enter the vault. "I'm sure we have something. In fact, I recall a very old book on rune study that came in a shipment a week or two ago. Maybe that will be helpful. It's in old Norse, but I'm sure Aidan can translate. Oh, and since you're here, Aidan, I'd like you to look at something for me. There were some abnormalities on one of our surveillance videos, and it's a bit curious."

She smiles, but it's a sad excuse for a smile. I want to ask her how she's doing, but I don't want to upset her by talking about it. As we walk into the vault, the look of the place surprises me a little, increasing my concern. It's very different than the last time I was here. The long shelves of artifacts still run in rows down the room, like a supermarket that sells dusty pieces of history. There are statues in the right corner and glass cases full of weapons, metalwork, and preserved cloth to the left. But where things used to be in boxes and covered up, for the most part, now many of the items are lying here and there, exposed, along with papers and stacks of open books, as if someone was frantically doing research.

Jax wanders over to look at the glass case of swords.

"What are you trying to protect?" Hanna says. "If you don't mind me asking."

"My great-grandmother's place," I say. "And the cave."

She nods. "Is everything with your sister all right?"

"Yeah, I think so." I consider not saying anything else, but then decide that she deserves to at least know her boss is around. "Eric is there, watching out for everyone. For now."

Her eyes fill with so much emotion it hurts to watch. The air swirls with her feelings, making me itch to move away. Shock, fear, joy, and a fair amount of pain.

"He's back," she says quietly.

I don't know what to say now. I spilled the beans, trying to be honest, and her reaction feels stronger than a hurt friend. It almost seems like she's a jilted lover. I'd always felt how bonded they were, but that was before I knew what he was, and I had no idea things between them were so serious. Why would an angel get so deeply involved with a human? Why would he leave her with no explanation, not caring how she felt? Even a friend would've prepared us all for his inevitable departure better than Eric did.

"He told me that I need to get some wards up," I say, trying to redirect the conversation. "The doorway is attracting demons and it's a bit of a mess."

She nods again. "I see."

"And I need to dig up info about dominion angels or any other midlevel angels. There's one named Jaasi'el; maybe he's in old literature or something? He's Ava's father and he's trying to find her, which apparently isn't good." I don't say that Eric told me all that, because I'm not sure how much she knows about him, if she knows that he's an angel. "It's all so confusing. Do you know anything about how all the realms and dominions work? I'm still unclear on some of the angels' ruling structures."

Hanna seems distracted and it takes her a second to respond. "Sure. I believe I have something that could give an answer or two.

Let me check the inventory." I figure that she's going to wait to look into it, but she backs up a step and excuses herself, obviously disturbed.

Kara leans in and whispers, "You don't think that she and Eric were a *thing*, do you?"

I watch Hanna disappear into the back of the vault. "I don't know."

But I'm pretty sure that I do.

Connor leans on the desk. "I told the Fosters we'd be there at one, so we need to get this done." He pulls out his phone, checking the time. "We have fifteen minutes to collect stuff."

Jax opens the glass case and picks up one of the swords. He slices it through the air with a *whoosh*. "And I'm freaking starving."

"Hanna said she set aside the scrolls for Sid," Kara says, looking over our surroundings. "Maybe we can find them."

Connor turns to study the clutter on the desk. He opens a drawer. "Hanna doesn't look good. I guess we could come back for the stuff after the job."

"Plus, food," Jax adds.

I leave them to make my own search, heading in the same direction as Hanna. I find her at the end of a row of shelving; it looks like a section of Jewish artifacts. There are several ossuaries—or bone boxes—in various sizes, and what look like two very old Torahs wrapped in blue velvet, along with folded, aged cloth with blue stripes on the edge that could be a priest's robes.

Hanna looks up. She sniffs and wipes tears from her face. "I just needed a minute."

"I get it. I'm sorry, Hanna."

She shakes her head. "No, Aidan. Don't take this on. It's not your problem. I knew when I got mixed up in this world that it would hurt me eventually." And then she adds more quietly, "I just couldn't seem to help myself."

I study her graceful features and wonder if Eric couldn't help himself either. "I'm glad I met you, you know," I say. "You were kind to me when I needed to be reminded the human race didn't totally suck."

She smiles at that. "You were quite the scraggly kid when Eric brought you into this place." She studies me. "You've really become a man now, though. And you've come into your powers so gracefully."

What she doesn't know . . .

"My mother had the sight," she continues. "She understood what was down people's paths before they could see it for themselves. I have a little of that ability, too. Just a little. But it was enough to see how vital you are. And now I can see you're not alone in your heart anymore." She glances down the aisle of shelves to Kara, who's sitting in the desk chair. "Is she the Eve to your Adam? The other half to your soul?"

It's a blunt question and I suddenly have trouble swallowing. Because, yeah, when I look at my future, I can't seem to see happiness without Kara there. "I want her to be."

Hanna touches my shoulder. "Then she is." Her smile becomes sad again. She takes a deep breath and turns to slide one of the bone boxes closer to the edge of the shelf, like she's pointing it out. Bone boxes were used to house the bones of a Jewish man or woman once the body decayed enough. If the bones were kept together, then they'd be safe for the resurrection that some believed would eventually happen.

This box looks heavy. It's made of limestone, about two and a half feet long, tapering down to the base, twelve inches deep. There's a flat lid on this one, but some of the others on the shelf have vaulted ones. And some stand on legs while this one doesn't. It's also almost totally unmarked, while the others have designs and faded writing covering their surfaces. But this one might just be older, the decorations of death worn smooth by weather and time.

"What is this?" I ask, feeling a strange vibration from it.

"The abnormalities on the video the other day seemed to surround this box. I was hoping you could feel if there was anything going on with it."

"What was on the video?"

"I'll give you a copy of it," she says, "but the ossuary appeared to have orbs around it for approximately three hours, several dozen of them. And it started at the same time as the earthquake yesterday morning, which I would think is probably linked in some way."

The earthquake. When something shifted on the other side. The same time Eric said Ava's soul broke a seal over the barriers. It all has to mean something. "Who's in this thing?"

"The papers say that it holds the bones of a male, no mention of his origin, and the inscription is vague." She points at the side of the box where words are carved into the soft limestone surface in Chaldean. I move closer to see it more clearly. The script is faded from time, but I'm used to reading old things.

"*Leave the dead to bury the dead and find your . . .*" I have to squint to figure out the next words, "*home with the Light.*"

"I believe that's a blessing for the living," she says. "Or maybe a warning to remain pure and stay away from the dead, which would make you unclean in many cultures. But here's the person's title, or their job, and I can't make heads or tails of it." She motions to the only other markings on the box, three tiny lines of text inside a circle on the front.

"*Servant and keeper of Baal, awaken not,*" I read aloud. Most bone boxes would have names as well as titles on them, since they're used to recall the life lived, similar to a sarcophagus. But this one doesn't appear to have anything except a title and some sort of warning.

Awaken not. How would you awaken bones?

Ossuaries span from the early fifth century BCE into Roman times. From what I can see, the other boxes on the shelf are Jewish, from the Roman era. But this box looks like it's much older, at least several hundred years older, and it's obviously of Babylonian origin. It's actually pretty amazing to see it still intact.

"Eric brought this back from one of his trips to Iraq. He returned with this, the small alabaster box I gave to you after your Awakening, as well as the two amulets, one of which you're wearing." She gestures at my chest. "It's why I felt you should know about the orbs, since it all appears to be connected."

"Did Eric ever say anything about the box?"

She seems to consider this, as if she's not sure how much to tell me. "He did mention that it had something to do with his task and the reason he was here." She pauses, looking troubled. "He said it was connected to why we couldn't be together."

But what would this thing have to do with Hanna?

"Will you look deeper for me?" she asks. "It might answer questions for both of us."

I realize she means this box could answer questions she has about Eric. I wish that I could tell her what he is, that I could just say it out loud. But I have no idea what sort of reasoning Eric has for keeping his origin a secret.

So I take a deep breath and reach out, placing my hand gently on the cool surface of the limestone.

My body goes tense instantly, like my muscles have turned to stone, too. My insides are far from still, though. They spark to life in a fury of movement and then swirl in a rush as they seem to reach out for the box.

The world around me dims to black, then shifts.

When it clears again, I'm lying in a cave, looking up at vaulted stone. I'm on some sort of altar, laid out and stiff as death. There are a number of women surrounding my body, their hair covered with dark wool fabric, their dresses torn at the neck as a sign of mourning. They cry openly and wail as they set bottles on the stone slab where my body lies. Then they begin applying oils and herbs to my cold skin.

This is a memory of the man whose bones are inside the box; somehow, even in death, he felt the touch of their fingers and their salty tears.

He was old, but had expected to live much longer still. He was not meant to walk the path he did, and yet he walked it in obedience, always honoring his father and his God.

They wrap me with cloth from the waist to the thighs. They bind my feet and my hands to make it easier to collect my bones once the flesh rots from them.

Then the women do something odd: they take a stone bowl of seeds and crush them with a pestle, add a little wine from a skin, and after stirring it with a small brush, they begin painting the orange-bronze concoction onto my body in circles and lines. They continue weeping as they work, covering my whole chest in patterns.

Because I was vital. I was loved. But I have lost what was mine so long ago—

A sudden burst of power sparks from the dead man and I jerk back to the present. Heat surges through me, as if the power was my own. I clutch my hand to the mark on my chest, feeling like it's been burned, even though there's no real pain. My whole arm, up and down my mark, is lit with a dull pulse of light and then it fades away, back into my skin.

"What was that?" I ask, breathless. The smells of the vision, of hopelessness and myrrh and the earthy paint, linger and mingle with the dust of my actual surroundings.

"Your markings, Aidan, they flared to life." Hanna's voice is full of anxiety. "Did it hurt you?"

I shake my head. "No. Not really. I just saw a vision." I flex my arm, bending it at the elbow. My muscles still feel a little like stone. "There were women in mourning. They were preparing my body—this man's body—in a cave; the tomb, I guess."

"You became the man?" she asks. "Could you tell who he was?"

I shake my head. "I could feel things, some personal emotions, but they were too abstract. I would need to touch it for longer, I guess, to see more details." Not something I want to do—be a dead man. Once was enough.

She seems to consider whether or not to push me further, the tangled smell of internal conflict filtering into the air. "Eric said this was to be kept hidden. He said it would help me someday to understand why he was here, why he was watching over you, and why he and I couldn't be . . . distracted."

It makes sense that this third object would be connected to me somehow if the other objects were: the amulets, the alabaster box with the feather inside. And now an ossuary filled with ancient bones. Bones of a man who lived to a ripe old age. He was full of sorrow, a weight heavy on his shoulders, even in death. It was such a clear feeling. Familiar, actually. The weight of destiny.

"I'm sorry," I say, seeing her need for answers. "I could try again later. Maybe I'll see more." Or I could just tell her Eric's an angel and he's supposed to be guarding me. Which must be why he can't be with her—the whole angel/human thing.

Hanna lifts her chin in resignation. "Thank you." She straightens her shoulders and touches my arm again, like she's soothing me, even though it's obvious she's the one who needs the comfort. "Let's get the video, and maybe it'll show you more. And I'll find those scrolls for Sid so you kids can be on your way." Her sad smile returns as she walks away, leaving me to stare at the bone box.

It connected to my power, somehow. It connected to me. Could it have answers about Ava's father? Or help me protect my sister from him? Could it explain why I'm here to begin with? So many questions. Answers are practically extinct these days. But I don't see why that should keep me from searching for them.

I look higher on the shelf and reach out to touch the blue velvet wrapped around one of the Torahs, whispering the blessing,
"*Baruch ata Adonai, elohainu king of the universe, asher ba-char
banu mikal ha-ah-mim v'natan lanu et torahto. Blessed are you
Lord, giver of the Torah,*" wishing I could touch the mind of God
instead, then maybe I could understand what all this mess of emotions and pain is leading us to.

SIXTEEN

Rebecca

I'm pretty sure I've completely reorganized this ragtag business they have here. Being a nervous cleaner can be both a blessing and a curse. Things get clean, but only when I'm anxious or panicked. When I'm content or happy, my stuff's strewn all over the place.

Over the last several hours I've thrown myself into straightening this joke of an office, twice reorganizing the stack of pending files, creating a system for the basket of messages, rearranging the corkboard. And the paperclips. Oh, and I totally changed the filing so it's now by alphabet, category, *and* date.

That crazy system should teach them not to stick me with the crap jobs.

Holly has been texting me from up in her room every half hour or so with a smiley face. Sid peeked in on me once, but he didn't say much. The guy's looking a little pale, his shiny bald head extra shiny. I almost suggested a good vitamin D supplement since he's obviously not making it out into the sun much.

After I'm done with all the paperwork stuff I sit down at the newly tidied message table, take up a pen, and slide one of the squares of sticky notes in front of me to write on, then press "Play" on the ancient machine. It clicks and starts humming as the gears turn. The messages are scratchy and blurry—if sound can be *blurry*, old-timey tape decks have that sound quality: blurry.

The first message is a guy complaining about his neighbor's backyard marijuana habit and how it's affecting his dogs, as if LA Paranormal is a sort of PI/neighborhood watch for people who don't know how to talk to other adults. I write on the note: *Grumpy guy with grumpy dogs and herbal issues. No spooky stuff.* Then I jot down his name and return number, which is missing two digits. I don't rewind to check, because his voice is annoying and I'm already bugged that I'm doing these menial tasks at all.

The next message is from a woman for a job LA Paranormal seems to already be working on, and the third and fourth messages are from her, too. She's in a bit of a rush by the sound of it. I write down: *Spazzy lady with something dead in her attic and scratches on body issues. She's not happy.*

There are three more messages, all pretty silly, one with a toothbrush as the central complaint. Once the machine clicks to a stop, I press "Rewind" and listen to the spinning reels whir. I doodle flowers on the edge of the message tablet until a loud click sounds and the "Rewind" button pops back up.

I slide the papers away and then pause, my eyes falling on my flowery design.

Only, it's not flowers.

I frown at the one, two, three skulls connected by vines. A dagger in each hollow eye.

Great. Another drawing of skulls—that has to mean something. And skulls aren't usually a sign of rainbows ahead.

I still haven't given Aidan the drawing that came to me the other night. I don't even want to talk to him about it anymore. I don't want to talk to him about anything. I'm so crushed, so mortified—like, *killmenow*. I didn't sleep at all last night—Holly's midnight recitations of therapeutic mind techniques didn't help. And then I got a nice jolt of ick when I felt Aidan and Kara's kiss this morning. Since then, I've planned to leave this place about a hundred times, but when I start packing, I get jittery and panicked, like I'm scared to leave the house, scared to leave Aidan's side. It's ridiculous and childish. And extremely annoying.

It's my fault for lying to myself. I knew he cared about Kara in a way he doesn't care about me. But I pretended it didn't matter. And then I got a nice big shock when he told me Kara's changed him, connected to him. It felt like my head had been plunged into a bucket of ice water.

I just need to face facts. I'm officially the *other* girl. It doesn't matter how I feel inside, or how I know I'm connected to Aidan. He doesn't feel it, not in the same way.

My phone pings and I look down to see the fifth happy face of the day from Holly. I sigh and wander to the entryway of the house, leaning on the railing of the staircase. Screams and the sounds of men fighting come from the living room. I lean forward and see the large, greasy boy, Finger, staring intently at the TV, thumbs flying on an Xbox controller.

He's such an oddity. I've never heard him speak, or even acknowledge my presence at all. He just sits for hours on end, engrossed in his violent video world. I wonder who he is, or why he's here. It seems like he's just a fixture, for the most part, like a lamp. A wave of pity washes over me as I watch him. I make up a story in my head about how he ended up here, a story about his parents—immigrants, maybe—who left him here alone, thinking he'd have a better life. Which I suppose he—

Finger looks up, staring right at me, making my brain freeze. He straightens his back and lowers the controller. *He's looking at me, he's looking at me*, screams in my head, like it's a big deal, like I'm supposed to do something, but I have no idea what.

And then he smiles. Not a small smirk or a tilt of the lips, but a grin that could be considered cheesy.

"Hi," I say, with a half wave. Because I don't know how else to respond. He's looking at me like I just made his day. But I have no clue why he's so thrilled.

He blinks once, twice, and then I feel a slight twinge behind my eyes, and my chest fills with warmth. It feels like . . . like someone's giving me a hug. Did he just do that somehow?

Ugh, this house.

Finger's eyes trail back to the TV and his thumbs start moving over the controller just as the back door opens. Jax and Kara walk in; I feel like I've been caught doing something secret, but I have no clue why. Aidan isn't with them. I back up and attempt to hide behind the bannister.

But Jax spots me me. "Hey, Red. You do all my work for me?"

I glare at him.

Kara walks past us without a word. She goes into the office as Jax stands there, looking me over like I'm a page in a magazine.

Before I can tell him off, a shout comes from the office. "WHAT IN THE HELL?!"

I cringe.

Jax's eyes light up with glee.

Kara storms out of the office and glares at me. "Where the fuck are all my notes on the hospital shoot?"

Uh-oh. "I just . . . I was organizing and . . ." Crap, I hope I can find the papers she's talking about. Everything was such a mess! And I was so angry when I was straightening it all up.

"Lay off the newbie, Kara," Jax says.

Kara growls in frustration and disappears back into the office. I follow her into the room, cautiously. Kara's scary when she's mad. Her presence is overwhelming.

"I can find it," I say, sounding way more confident than I feel.

"You shouldn't have messed with any of it," she says, shoving papers aside and undoing half my work in two seconds. "You just come in here and touch shit and act like you own the place."

I lean down and start looking through some of the stuff that's landed on the floor. "There were some that said hospital—"

She yanks a paper out of my hand. "This is none of your business. You have no idea what's going on. You don't belong here at all!"

"I'm sorry, Kara, I didn't—"

"Don't you dare be nice to me. I know why you're here, sneaky little bitch."

I stare at her. "Excuse me?"

She stops shuffling through the papers and turns to me, moving closer. "I know what you've been up to. Texting him, mixing up his head. I won't let you hurt him or make him feel guilty. He doesn't need you anymore."

"What? You're crazy." Yes, I texted him, but I wasn't pushing, not really. And it was pretty obvious to me yesterday that he's not interested in me. At all.

She smiles, but it's not a nice smile. It's super creepy. "I've figured you out and I've felt your energy. I know how you can pull his strings. I know what you think you are to him, but you're wrong. I'm here now, and I won't let you screw with him."

My mind spins. "What in the heck are you even talking about?!" I so do *not* pull Aidan's strings. I can barely get him to answer my phone calls.

Kara just looks at me, like she's waiting. But whatever she's waiting for, it isn't coming, so she adds, "Just realize, when the time comes, you'll have me to deal with. I won't let you take him from us." She tosses the papers in her hand back onto the table and walks out of the room, leaving me with the oddest feeling. Like the world just turned topsy-turvy. And instead of being the heroine of my story, I'm suddenly the villain.

SEVENTEEN

Aidan

After we drop off Kara and Jax at home, Connor and I argue about where to go first, Mrs. O'Linn's or the Fosters'. The original plan was to hit the Fosters' before heading over to my great-grandmother's, but I'm dizzy and drained now—probably from reading the bone box. I'm also confused. Because as we were leaving the club Kara got quiet and insisted she be dropped off at the house instead of coming with us. And I know it was because on the way out of the vault I told her what I'd seen on her soul. She started acting weird right after that. Then when I asked what was wrong, she blew me off, claiming she was tired and wanted to lie down. Which all guys know is girl-speak for, *I don't want to talk about it.*

I just need to get the protections up around the beach cave as soon as possible, so I'll have at least one thing checked off my list.

But Connor won the argument, obviously. He's driving. So, it's the Fosters' first.

After a twenty-five-minute drive, he pulls the Camaro up to a Granada Hills home.

"We'll just check in quick," Connor says. "I swear, we'll get to your grandma's place before sundown."

"Are you going to be solid on the rune stuff without Kara?" I ask. As much as I want to keep her in my sight right now, I'm glad she's not with us just in case something goes wrong—her weakness could get her hurt.

"I'll be fine," Connor says, sounding as distracted as I am. "The rune book Hanna gave me is exactly what I needed to fill in the gap, I think. And you've got the spirit pouches to bury, since Kara did those last night. All that, plus some oils and salt, and we'll be good to go."

Let's hope it's really that easy.

The Fosters live in an old neighborhood, first established in the forties. Tall purple plum and sweetgum trees line the road, casting their lacy shadows over the various yards. The simple, single-story houses are on good-sized lots. Newspapers sit on the porches and midpriced cars are parked in the driveways. Dogs bark in the distance and birds chatter in the branches above. It's *Leave It To Beaver* land.

Connor gets out of the Camaro and walks up to the house; it even says *The Fosters* on a plaque beside the front door. I hang back and try to prepare myself for the inevitable slime ahead. If this really is a *dybbuk* hidden away in the attic, the job won't feel like collecting butterflies.

Connor knocks. I stay behind him as a woman opens the door, a screaming baby on her hip. Her hair is tied up in a tangle of brown curls and there's a frazzled look in her eyes, a smear of something green on her pink shirt, and what looks like flour on her cheek and forehead.

"Thank God, you're here!" she says. The baby's wail grows louder and the woman looks like she's about to burst into tears, too.

It's super nerve-wracking. If I had to listen to that every day, I'd definitely cry.

She walks away from the door and starts talking like we're just supposed to follow. I lock up my inner walls as tightly as I can to block out any negative energy or spirits. Then I take a deep breath and step into the house.

As soon as I pass the threshold, something presses against my senses, like it's trying to break through. But whatever it is, I'm able to block it out. I smell the rot, like something died, but I'm not going to try and sift through anything I sense yet, so I ignore it. I focus on the physical surroundings instead of the spiritual ones and listen to what the woman is saying, about not sleeping, about the smell of something dead, how her husband searched the attic and now things have gotten worse.

"Then, just before you got here, this happened!" She leads us into the kitchen. All the cupboards are open and shattered dishes cover the tile floor. She shakes her head, looking at the mess. "I don't even know how to start picking it all up. I can't put Rosa down or she cries so hard she turns purple. She was never like this before. Ever. Not until the mess in the attic started. The other kids have been staying at the neighbor's house for two days, since the smell is so bad. My oldest son was throwing up, saying his chest hurt. I was so scared that it was making him sick." She pauses, like she's getting up the nerve for something, then she whispers, "And last night . . . these came." She lifts her shirt a little on the side, revealing three long, puffy red scratches. "I don't know what to think anymore." The misery in her voice, in her energy, is palpable.

Connor studies the marks for a second, seemingly unfazed. He's got Sid's unaffected look down pat.

But we both know what those scratches mean. At least, I would hope Connor knows. If whatever is in this house scratched her, it's claimed her, and might be getting ready to possess her. Usually that would mean a demon, but with the locks and the carving of *dybbuk* on the attic door, I'm still wondering about a wraith. In rare cases, a wraith can possess a human host. It would have to be a pretty powerful one, though.

I look around the house more closely, searching for any religious symbols, something that could be agitating the spirit. There's a painting of the pope at the entrance to the hallway to my left. The glass is cracked. "You're Catholic?" I ask.

"Yes," she says. "I had to take down my crucifixes because I woke up yesterday to them all hung upside down." She shivers. "It was so disturbing, I just put them in a drawer." She points at the desk in the corner of what might have once been a dining room but is now an office.

Connor and I share a look, and I'm fairly sure we're both thinking the same thing: whatever was in the attic is now trying to take over the house.

He pulls his phone from his pocket and opens the audio app, then clicks "Record" before saying, "You mentioned the trouble was mostly in the attic."

"Not anymore," she says. "After my husband messed around up there, everything just got worse."

"Did he open the door in the attic? The smaller one that was locked?" I ask.

She gives me a questioning look. "Do you mean that cupboard? I don't know. I couldn't get it open when I tried, so I gave up."

"Can we take a look?" Connor asks. "And maybe get some video footage?"

"Yes, yes please, do whatever you need. I can't take this anymore." She sighs and the child on her hip seems to quiet a bit, hiccuping and puffing her chubby cheeks. Her big glassy eyes watch Connor and me, like she's wary of us, as she grips her mom's shirt and curls against her chest.

Connor already knows where the attic access is from when he placed the cameras. I follow him to a back bedroom of the house, which looks like the nursery, with a crib, dresser, and rocking chair. But it's dusty, like it hasn't been used in a while. And it smells like sewage and rot. I recheck my inner walls, making sure nothing can get through, as Connor switches apps on his cell phone and begins filming, getting some rough footage of the room, focusing longest on the creepy image of the dusty crib. Then he motions with a free hand to the attic access door, so I take the string and pull it down, unfolding a ladder, the camera on me now.

"You wanna go first?" he asks, like he doesn't want to go up at all.

I bark out a laugh. "Be my guest, Guillermo del Toro." I motion to the ascent.

He smirks at me from the other side of the camera and begins the climb with one hand, narrating what he's doing as he goes. Half his body is in the attic, half in the room, when he pauses, muttering, "Shit." He looks down at me. "The door's open."

My gut churns.

"This just got a lot more complicated if your whole wraith prediction was on the mark," he says.

Sometimes I hate being right.

———

We head back out to the car to collect some supplies from the trunk.

Connor puts on a crucifix and grabs a bag of salt and a bag of what look like crackers. "So, I'm thinking we trap it like we do with the demons," he says. "This thing seems to dislike anything Catholic, so we sic the sacrament on its ass." He points into the trunk at a metallic container that looks like a flask. "Wanna grab the holy water?"

"Wraiths aren't like demons." And we're not even sure it's a wraith. We're not sure about anything. I pick up the bottle of holy water and slide it in my jacket pocket. I'm pretty sure it won't help, but whatever. "It may not be something we can easily trap."

He sighs. "Well, then what's your plan? If we only cast it out it'll just go wreak havoc somewhere else."

I don't have a plan for this. I came along to get help from Connor with the protections for the beach cave, and now my head is starting to pound. My *plan* was to not get involved in any more drama if it doesn't have something to do with waking up Ava or helping Kara.

"That's what I thought," Connor says when I don't answer. He shuts the trunk. "So a trap it is."

"I just hope it sticks."

"But you can *kill* demons now, right?" he asks, like he's clarifying.

I rub my fingers together and think about the crusted demon blood that was caked on them like mud. "Yeah."

"Don't you think your talent could work for other . . . *things*?"

I consider it. "I guess that I could try and see." But we'll definitely need a backup plan.

"Okay. Just try to have a little faith, dude."

We ask Mrs. Foster if she can step outside or go to a neighbor's house for a little while. The last thing we need is for her or her kid to get attacked if the wraith fights back. She grabs a few things for the baby and then leaves, saying she'll be next door, thanking us until it becomes a little embarrassing.

Connor follows me to the back room and then sets up his phone on the tall dresser beside the bedroom door, clicking for the camera to start recording again. I get ready to open myself up to read the place so I can figure out where this thing is hanging around. I think about all the demons I've trapped over the years and tell myself that this spirit can't be worse than one of them; it certainly can't be that strong.

"You ready?" Connor asks, like we're going to battle.

The way I'm feeling right now, I'm not ready for a knock-down, drag-out fight. "Not really, but we can't exactly come back later."

Well, we could, but we'd likely return to find a woman possessed by a wraith, who murdered her own kids.

Connor steps back like he doesn't want to be too close to me when I open myself up fully.

I take a deep breath and close my eyes to fixate on the space around me, what's close, not letting my insides take in too much right away. Death is palpable in the air, but I see now it's from a long time ago, it's not recent.

I reach out a little more, looking for something, a memory in the air, in the energy, but all I feel is death. Weighty, sticky death. And then I sense something zip across the hall, out of range. The sudden movement makes me open wider as if my power is chasing it, seeking it out. My feet itch to move but I stay still, just trying to get a fix on the thing before walking toward it in the physical realm.

"What're you feeling?" Connor says.

I shake my head, not wanting to break focus to answer.

"You're lit up, you know."

I didn't know, but it's a good sign that my power thinks it can destroy this thing—

There! I open my eyes to see a shadow speed across the hall again. It seems to be centering its focus on the bedrooms, going from one to another. And a thought emerges: *a spider weaving its web to claim its home.* But it doesn't feel like the thing has totally succeeded yet. The house hasn't been claimed fully, some of the energy still feels warm and alive.

I move into the hall and Connor starts laying out the crackers on the floor—they're wafers for communion, I think. I'm not sure how something like that would work, but Connor seems to know what he's doing, placing them in the corners of the room in threes.

A black mass of tattered shadow zips past, within three feet of me, entering the room to my right. In its wake is a silver string, glistening in the golden light now spilling from my mark. Then I see more metallic threads weaving a criss-cross pattern from room to room. They coat the hall in a shimmering chaos of lines.

It's claimed the hallway. I turn and look around the nursery where Connor is standing and see even more threads. So many more. They cocoon the crib, the rocking chair, and even cover the window, dimming the light. This room is obviously its favorite space.

"Can you see anything peculiar?" I ask Connor. "Like webs?"

He lifts his head from placing salt and looks around, caution tensing his muscles. "No."

I have to be sure which side I'm seeing, the physical or the spiritual one. I turn back to the hall just as the wraith disappears into the farthest bedroom to my left.

My power pulses brighter along my arm and my insides push me to act. When the wraith is about to cross my path again, I lunge.

And I catch it by its billowy cloak.

It jerks back with an air-rending screech and a bony claw scrapes across my chest. The heat sears through me as my shirt rips in four long tatters, my blood now speckling the doorjamb.

Rage bursts to life inside me to replace the pain, and I swing, my fist hitting the shadow where its head should be. It feels like I've plunged my hand into a bucket of ice, just as tangible, and just as cold. The black shadow shifts, flickering into human form, legs, arms, head appearing like a hologram with a bad signal.

Let go, it says without sound. Its ghost lips move but the words come to me through my chest, instead of my ears.

It is a *he*. A man with thick-rimmed glasses and oily hair slicked to the side. From the 1940s, I'd say, by the style of his clothes. I try to feel his story, sense the energy of how he became this thing, but it's as if he's blocking me, keeping it a closely held secret, even in death.

Release me, he mouths, *or I will tear your lungs from your chest.* His form grows wispy again, features sinking in, becoming a hollow emptiness, hands morphing into claws.

Behind me, Connor begins saying a benediction about light breaking through and about God's promise to protect.

I ignore the wraith's threats and yank on the dark cloak, tugging it into the room where Connor has the trap set up.

It screeches again, a sharp-edged sound that cuts at the inside of my skull. The form flies up, over my head, the shadow fabric wrapping around me. I keep my grip, even as it tries to get into the attic. It scrapes at the air, yanking, desperate to escape me, to escape before I imprison it again, like it was before.

As I feel its fear billow out, my own fear fades. My power surges, my mark coming fully to life. Flames flicker over my skin, and whatever confusion I had earlier about my life washes away. "*HaShem Eloheiynu,*" I say, scripture flashing into my mind. "*HaShem Eloheiynu* will go before me as a consuming *eish.*" I yank as a rush of energy courses through me with the word *fire—eish—* and force the shadow down into the salt circle with a whoosh of air. "He will consume you, *dybbuk.* He will destroy you, He will drive you out." And as it hits the ground, my fire travels to the tattered edges of the wraith's cloak, beginning to consume the darkness. But before more than a few inches can be devoured, the flames are snuffed out by the creature's movement. It writhes, pushing at the salt boundary with its bony, clawed fingers.

Release me, it cries, its visage flickering back to human for a moment.

"We have it trapped," I say through my gasping breath. Fatigue falls on me as I watch it fight against the salt barrier. My power feels completely sapped from that simple struggle.

Connor moves along the outer edge of the salt circle. "Holy water," he says.

I pull the flask from my pocket and hand it to him, still not sure it will have any effect.

Connor unscrews the lid and flicks the bottle in the direction of the circle, water drops flying out and sprinkling the floor. The wraith hisses and lunges to the side, trying to get away.

"A little more to the left," I say, directing him to where the shadow is. "What're you doing?"

"Hoping." He flicks more and it hits across the shadow's legs. Steam rises up with a fiery sizzle. I can barely believe my eyes.

"It's doing something," I say. But how? Holy water is just . . . well, water. But then I smell myrrh and frankincense with a tinge of cedar. "What is that stuff?"

"Holy water. With a nice spike of altar oil mixture added for good measure." He flicks it again and hits the wraith right in the face.

The shadow writhes and wails, coughing up black tar, its form melting a little.

"Do it again," I say. "It's working."

He tosses more and more of the mixture onto the circle, hitting the form again and again until it's barely a shadow, malformed and crackling, like a piece of ice placed in the hot sun, sinking, sinking into the floor until it's a small puddle of silver mercury. The webs puff into smoke around us, dissipating. Light beams brighter into the room, cutting across the circle to reveal what's left of the wraith. And then that puddle bursts into smoke, threading up, up, up in grey strands, through the attic door.

"It's gone," I whisper, amazed. I guess I don't have to worry if I can kill it or not.

"Gone?" Connor sounds unsure. "Like, it left?"

"No, it melted."

"Holy shit." He holds up the flask of holy water. "This stuff's badass." He laughs and slips it into his back pocket, then frowns in my direction. "You're bleeding pretty bad there."

I glance down but can only see my tattered shirt stuck to my stomach. I pull it over my head and wipe the blood from my chest and abs with what's left of the red cotton. More blood trickles out, trailing down my stomach in thin lines.

I wait, watching the bleeding wounds. But nothing happens. They don't heal. They bleed, they sting like a motherfucker, and they aren't closing up like they should.

EIGHTEEN

Aidan

There's a first-aid kit in the trunk and a clean shirt. After Connor helps me bandage up, I slip on the spare white T-shirt and try not to think about why I needed first aid at all. At least everything at the Fosters' is done now. I really wish I understood how some oils could destroy a wraith. It nags at me because it doesn't fit with the knowledge in my DNA, but I watched it with my own eyes. So it must be possible.

Connor gave Mrs. Foster two of the spirit pouches that Kara made, telling her to keep them wherever she and the baby slept. With the wraith gone, she should have the peace of mind she needs to settle her spirit, though.

We pull up to my great-grandmother's at six thirty, just as the sun is beginning to sink lower over the water. Before I do anything else I climb down the rocks to check on Ava. As I descend I have to grit my teeth and try to ignore the stinging in my muscles and this damn headache that won't quit. Connor starts the rune placements around the house, working from the outside in. In the car, he explained that he'd write symbols on rocks and organize them in different patterns to create a muting, similar to the blocks at the LA Paranormal house, along with other patterns that will sting demons a little, like an invisible electric fence. Finally, he'll place a couple rune stones that will create confusion spells. It's going to make one hell of a cocktail when he's done.

When I get to the cave, the place feels quiet. There's no change since yesterday. Ava's pale silhouette appears silver grey as twilight settles within the stone walls, and her body remains locked in that strange sleep. The pieces of the dog carcass are gone. Hopefully Eric came in and cleaned it up, otherwise I'm not sure how it all disappeared.

I stand by the altar for a second and do what I always do—what I've been doing every day for weeks: I reach out with my mind, looking for her. I find nothing but stillness. She's not dead, but she's not here, either. It's like staring into an empty room. I want to shake her, to scream, *Come back!* But I shove the torrent down and turn and walk up the beach to the house.

I look around the yard, trying to figure out where to start. I might need to get into the house and hide some of these spirit pouches if this is going to work, but I don't want to bother my grandma and Fa'auma unless I really have to, so I'll leave that until later. The pattern I'm going to use out here is a sort of *keep out* sign. I'll create a triangle north to south with the third point directing the energy west, toward the sunset.

I try to ignore the burning of my sliced-up midsection as I grip my bag of pouches, feeling the weight of the spells inside the sack, each one filled with sacred dirt, rye, salt, and a small piece of rowan wood with a balancing number sequence written on it—*333*, most likely—wrapped in a hundred percent cotton fabric that's stamped with a circled Star of David. If all that doesn't do the trick to keep the demons away, I have no idea what will.

Just as I get ready to place the first pouch, I feel something come up on my right, quick and silent.

I spin, backing away in a defensive posture before I realize who it is.

"Eric," I say, pain sparking across my torso from the quick movement. "What the hell?"

"I've come to help."

"I thought you were already here."

"I mean, I've crossed over." He holds up a hand, showing me he's flesh. I didn't even notice he looked different because of the surprise of seeing him, plus the sun is turning to dusk over the water behind him, shining in my eyes.

He's wearing jeans and a white T-shirt, his hair a light brown instead of blinding gold. He's Eric again.

"Wow, so you're really here."

"I am."

"Should I be worried?" What sort of bad development could've made him come back? He was so adamant that he'd be staying on the other side.

"No, there are just some things I can only fix in this form. And I've decided to make myself available to you while I can."

"We can use all the help we can get." I hold the bag open for him to take some of the pouches.

He takes one and walks toward the rock ledge, then turns back to me. "Will this do, to begin?"

"Sure," I say as I move to a spot beside him and bend down to tuck a pouch into a gopher hole beside his foot. I grit my teeth as I stand and he leans closer, like he's curious.

"Are you feeling unwell?" he asks, studying my face, my shaking hands. "You seem . . . depleted. And I smell blood." He sniffs at the air like a hound. "Why do I smell blood?"

Well, I did just destroy a wraith, and my wounds aren't healing. But I felt exhausted before that, too, and this headache is making my vision blur. "I'm fine," I say as I move to another spot a few feet away. "I just came from a job and didn't get a chance to clean up good."

Eric seems to accept the answer. He looks over the cliff down to the water beating against the rocks far below.

"Hanna's worried about you," I say. I probably shouldn't butt into this whole thing between Eric and Hanna. It's not like I understand cross-world romance. But I can't seem to help myself. "You should let her know you're okay."

He doesn't react or speak. He just takes another pouch from the bag I'm holding and then bends down to tuck it inside a rock crevice, just under the lip of the ledge.

"Do you even care that she's wrecked?" I ask, wondering if he's really as cold and indifferent to Hanna as he seems.

His eyes snap to mine. "Of course."

"Then why are you hiding out here? Why aren't you letting her know you're okay? If you can be fleshy for me, you could at least call her."

"This isn't a movie, Aidan. Flesh and infatuation are temporal. There are more vital things that need my attention right now. It is the end of the world, after all."

"Don't be so dramatic," I say, feeling like he's making excuses. And nothing's over until it's over. "The woman loves you like crazy. And angel or not, you're being an ass."

He just stares at me, blinking like I spoke Farsi.

"Or not." I sigh and walk to the next spot that needs a ward, closer to the path that leads down to the beach.

He follows me, looking out at the violet and orange sky. "You think that's true? She cares about . . ." he glances to his open palms in front of him, like he's studying something strange, " . . . me?"

"I'm pretty positive she *loves* you." I lean down, gritting my teeth again to hold in a hiss of pain, and find a spot to bury the pouch.

"She doesn't know me like she thinks."

I make a small hole for the ward, then place some rocks over it. "Just trust me, Eric. Hanna cares about you."

He releases a long breath, like he's resigning himself. "It doesn't matter. The Brethren don't think like that. We're not entitled to."

I give him a disbelieving look. "Sounds like you think like that, at least a little."

He pauses, taking in my words, and then he comes closer, asking quickly, "How does it feel, this human love? Aren't you afraid of it? It seems so . . . powerful and dangerous."

He's right—it is scary. Terrifying, really, opening myself up, only to be torn to shreds if something goes wrong. And if Kara's taken from me like everyone else I've cared about . . . But it's too late now. I'm consumed by her already.

"This isn't about me or Kara. This is about a woman who's been good to you, good to me—a punk kid—and you haven't given her the respect she deserves. You didn't prepare her at all, you just left, and I'm fairly sure she would cross oceans to be with your lame ass."

He frowns, like I hit a nerve. "I never promised her anything. There are things she might never know or understand."

"So she doesn't know you're an angel?"

He shakes his head. "She believes I'm something *more*, but she isn't sure what I am. I can't speak the truth aloud to anyone unless I've been released to, as I was with you. It's forbidden. And so is attachment. Especially of the sort between a man and woman."

"It's a bit late for that," I say, wondering how a guy that can read minds in the spirit realm can't see the truth of what's right in front of him in the flesh. "Just call her. It's not huge. Just a word, so she'll know you haven't totally left her for good." I start walking down the path that descends to the beach, looking for another spot.

"But I have left her for good."

I turn back around. "Wow."

"I have to follow the Law, Aidan. My attachment to her became too strong, so I felt it was time to move on. I've left myself vulnerable to discovery and let my flesh grow too strong. I have new sympathy for the Watchers of old."

"For a guy so determined to keep your angelic self a secret, it seems to me like you've been leaving her crumbs everywhere. What about that ossuary you showed her?" I ask. "The one you got in Iraq? She said it held answers about why you were here."

He goes perfectly still and stares at me, tension in every molecule. "She told you about the bone box?" As if it were some state secret.

I hesitate before answering, "She asked me to read it. And the stuff I saw—"

He comes at me, taking me by the arm, stopping my words. Panic bursts from him in a sudden explosion. "You touched it? Did your power spark? Did you link to the energy?" Every question seems more urgent than the one before.

I stutter, "Just for a second. Nothing bad happened, Eric."

The frenzy of emotions bouncing between us seems to grow more frantic with each passing second as he stares, studies me, searching for something, his green eyes wide and panicked.

"How much—how much energy did you feel?" he asks, gripping my shoulder tighter, each syllable underlined with a jerk of my body. "What did you see?"

I hold up a hand. "Okay, calm down. Nothing happened. Really. All I saw were some women preparing him for burial. That's all."

"How were you seeing?" he asks quickly.

I don't want to answer. Whatever he's worried about, it's bad. Very bad, by the feel and look of him. But I say it anyway. "It was like I was inside his body."

A chill fills the space around us and he releases me like I'm tainted. "Adonai, help us," he whispers.

I stumble back. "Holy hell, what the fuck's the problem?!"

"I should have never shown her. It's too soon for this to happen."

"Who? Hanna? What in the hell is in that box, Eric? You're freaking me out."

He shakes his head, his misery a bitter tang in the air. "It's the Harbinger of this world's end."

"In a bone box?" That makes no sense.

"You've linked to him, reminded him of his humanity." Eric's helplessness is so thick around us, it's tough to breathe.

"Who?! Who the hell did I just connect with?"

He looks over to me, weighty desperation in his eyes, as he whispers two words, "Your father."

NINETEEN

Aidan

All the air leaves my lungs like I've been punched in the gut. "What?" I must've heard wrong. *My father?*

"Your father is in that box."

"D-Daniel . . . Daniel the *prophet*? You mean he's, like, going to time-travel back again?" My headache grows, my pulse a hammer in my skull now. "He's coming back?"

"No, not like that, Aidan. He never traveled again after his punishment. He died an old man, well known and well loved in the court of magicians."

"Then . . . I don't understand."

"His resurrection, among others, was prophesied after your birth. And his return was said to be the first Harbinger."

"But . . . how—he's human, right? How can he be resurrected?" It doesn't make any sense. And the idea is terrifying.

"This is what I was supposed to prepare you for, eventually. Much later down the road. You were meant to learn to harness your power in order to raise him up and bring forth the first seal. But it appears you were already strong enough and began the process by accident. It's all happening too soon."

"How are you so sure? How're you so sure that I did a resurrection thing on the ancient bones of this guy in the box?" I can't think of him as a father, I just can't. He's a far-off Bible story in my mind. And I have no father.

Eric seems to consider my doubt, and I try to muster up a spark of hope.

Maybe he's wrong. I mean, shouldn't it be harder than just touching an old box to bring someone back to life? Especially someone whose bones have probably turned to dust over the centuries?

"You are his son," Eric says, like he's reasoning it through. "You're meant to be the one to do this; the prophecies are clear. And you're the only one with the resurrection powers."

"But you can't be sure I woke anyone up from the dead."

"I suppose we would be sure if we looked in the box."

"Wonderful. You do that. I'm going to focus on one thing at a time; for now, it's these protections. We need to be sure the demons being called here don't find Ava's body. You can take care of the guy in the box." He's not my father, I can't think like that. He's just a man. And the last thing I want right now is to face that part of me. "Ava's father is the one making trouble right now, anyway. We should be fixing that first. The dead guy can wait."

"Yes," Eric says, sounding distracted. "Jaasi'el is also a dilemma."

"What could the dominion want? It's not like he cared about Ava all these years when I was trying to protect her from the demons." Something I failed to do.

"I assume he feels the need to stop the demons from controlling her," he says absently, his mind obviously still on the last subject. "She must be neutral or on the side of Heaven. Otherwise, he could possibly see her as a threat and destroy her, if he cannot save her."

"Are you serious? Now an angel wants to control her?"

"Of course. Either side would wish to control her. She's a key." But then his features shift, like something is beginning to dawn on him. "Why did Hanna want you to read the box when you were there?" he asks.

"She said there were orbs around it in the security feed."

"The earthquake," he says under his breath.

"Yeah, the morning of the earthquake. It's connected?"

"I have to go," he says in a rush, beginning to walk away.

"Wait, what the hell?" I yell after him. "What am I supposed to do?"

"Like you said, keep focused on protecting your sister's body for now," he says over his shoulder. "And read the journal; you should find the under-passage now that things are shifting again. It will tell you everything you need to know."

I growl in frustration, wondering why the hell he can't just show me this mystery passage. But before I can ask, he leaps over the edge of the cliff, falling into thin air.

I'm jerked out of my shock by Connor's voice coming from behind me. "Hey, are you almost done?"

I look away from the cliff where Eric disappeared—what the hell kind of exit was that? Connor is standing at the top of the path. I motion to the half-full bag in my hand. "I still have to complete the pattern." But the bomb Eric just dropped is turning my gut numb. These protections feel useless considering everything that's going on.

Connor walks toward me. "All the rune combos are in place. How can I help?"

"I just have to finish the house and then we can work on the cave entrance," I say, unfocused. I have to pretend like I'm still the same Aidan from this afternoon. Before I was told I might have resurrected my ancient father from a twenty-six-hundred-year-old pile of dust in a box. My *father*. How could Eric be right? How could I have done something so monumental and not have realized it? It feels even more impossible than anything I could've imagined. But I know it's not. Not in my world. Nothing is impossible in my world.

When we get home, I sit in the car and call Hanna to ask if I can come back for a few more things tomorrow. I tell her I need sacred dirt and a demon bowl or box for a job, even though that's a lie. I know that I told Eric he could handle my . . . father, that I wasn't able to deal with it, but on the way back to the house my curiosity and fear got the better of me. I have to make sure that the box hasn't birthed something horrible; I can only hope Eric's wrong or overreacting.

Hanna seems perfectly fine on the phone. I hear the clinking of glass and the hum of a vacuum in the background, so I figure she's getting ready to open the club for the night. Always a good sign. It wouldn't be business as usual if everything had gone to hell, spiritually speaking. She tells me how to open the outer door and the inner vault, giving me the code keys to memorize, telling me not to write them down. I'm supposed to text when we're on our way; she'll help out if things in the club aren't too busy. I kind of want to look at everything alone, though. Just in case.

I hang up the phone and head through the backyard. Sid is sitting on the back porch swing, looking off into nowhere.

"Hey, where have you been?" I ask, trying to sound light-hearted as I walk up the steps. But as I study him, my heart sinks. He seems thinner and paler than even yesterday. Is that possible?

He turns to me and smiles. "Just resting. I hear from Connor that things are going well, that you even saw Eric. I'm glad he's home safe from his travels. And the Foster job sounded like a nice challenge. I would have loved to have gone and been a part of the process."

I sit beside him on the swing. "How're you feeling?" I don't want to talk about a job like nothing else is going wrong; not when he seems to be fading away suddenly, as if his time here with us is slipping away more quickly, right before my eyes. The way Kara explained it, I thought we'd have longer to figure things out, make a plan to help him, before he got sick from his time traveling. But it's obvious the consequences of those broken rules are showing up to take their pound of flesh.

He keeps smiling at me, like he's memorizing my face, before he says, "I'm very thankful that I've been a part of your life, son. Truly. Your father would be so proud of you."

My chest aches at the mention of Daniel. I wonder what Sid would say if I told him I might have begun the resurrection of his old mentor? I don't want to say the words out loud, though. I can barely allow them in my head without feeling like I might lose it.

"What was he like?" I ask quietly.

Sid turns to stare out at the overgrown grass again, his smile becoming listless. "Oh, much like you. He was young and devoted. Strong and stubborn when it came to those he loved. I miss him."

Part of me wants to meet him, just to feel his energy, to *see* him like I can see other people, inside. But another part of me has always been terrified at the idea. In the Ketuvim he was shown as a man who was strong in faith, but the stories only say what he did, not who he was.

"Someday you will meet him, face to face," Sid says.

My nerves jump. "What?"

"In the afterlife," he says, his voice trailing away, like he's only half in this world and half somewhere else entirely. For a moment there I thought he knew about the box, but clearly he doesn't.

I stare at his profile, the sunken look of his eyes. I can see the pulse in his neck now, the slow and weak rhythm. His frame is starting to shrink severely, his skin like a shirt that doesn't fit right, the muscle practically gone. It hurts more than I thought it would, seeing him like this. Fading away. I haven't known him long, but he's the closest thing I have to family right now. And I've found myself caring about him, in spite of how I've tried to keep my distance. He's a stable point. The idea of him leaving us is more than a little unsettling, with the world around me falling apart more every day.

"What's going on with you, Sid?" I ask. "Talk to me."

He sighs and leans his head back against the porch swing. "I thought I'd have more time, but since the earthquakes began, I'm feeling . . . stretched thin. I think I'll be leaving soon. More quickly than I thought I would."

There it is. Out loud. A stab of pain in my throat follows the realization that I'm about to lose someone else. "We can fix this, Sid," I say, my voice tight.

"No. Not this. I've felt the day coming for a while and I pretended I was invincible, that I could play God with time. But I was foolish."

"You can't just give up," I say, urgency filling me. He sounds so resigned. Like it's all done already. "Connor, Kara, and I, we can fix this. We can figure out how to keep you here, to heal you."

He closes his eyes and a smile fills his face again, like he's sitting and enjoying the warmth of the sun on his skin even though it's night. After several seconds of silence pass, he whispers, "I am more than blessed. More than filled. Thank you."

But he's not talking to me. He's not thanking me for anything. He's thanking God.

And I envy him that assurance. That peace. I want to find that kind of surrender, that kind of faith. But this weight on my shoulders refuses to allow me to feel anything but urgency and pain about what I can't change.

"We're all hurtling toward it, you know, son," he says, a tear slipping from the corner of his eye. "When you see it, you'll understand. The destination is that moment of becoming whole again, but it's not the destination that matters in the end. It's the journey along the way. And I have had one amazing journey."

TWENTY

Rebecca

I'm sitting at the kitchen table, flipping through my *Cosmo* magazine, not really digesting any of it. Something about the feeling of the shiny pages on my fingers, the sight of the lovely people who smile as if they don't have a care in the world . . . I know they're just acting for the cameras, but it's a reminder that there are smiles out there. There are happy people, somewhere.

I'm also sneaking glances at Aidan through the paned glass of the back door. He's sitting next to Sid and they both look somber, talking and watching the empty yard.

When Aidan stands from the swing, I focus back on the magazine. But as he comes in the door, I can't help looking up in alarm. Emotions follow him in like a storm—anger, sorrow, guilt, and a hundred others that speed through me so fast, I barely recognize them.

At first I bite my lips shut, but then the tornado starts to make me dizzy, so I ask, "Are you okay?"

He stops on the other side of the table, staring down at the faded kitchen tiles. I study him for a second, his hunched shoulders, the corners of his mouth drawn down. It's horrible. I blink back tears, my throat going tight even though I have no idea why. Everything he's feeling is getting mixed up in my head with my own emotions. I look back down at the magazine, my vision blurring.

"I shouldn't exist," he says.

My head snaps back up. "What?"

"I'm not supposed to be here. It's all gone wrong. I've made everything wrong." A dark feeling billows from him, a cloud of loss. "My sister wouldn't have even been born. The world wouldn't be in danger. Sid would be home safe. And Lester . . ."

Okay, now I'm scared. What could've happened? I push the magazine away and stand, moving toward him. "Aidan, what're you talking about?"

"He's dying because of me."

I freeze halfway across the room. "Who?"

"Sid. I may as well have killed him. My life has made his impossible."

What's he talking about? Sid does look sick, but . . . dying? And how could that possibly be Aidan's fault?

He turns to me. "You think you know me, but you don't. You don't know anything. I'm only good at fucking everything up. Everything I touch dies or ends up hurting someone."

I close the distance between us and grab him by the arm. "Stop it! That's enough. It's all lies, Aidan. All of it."

"Didn't you hear me? I'm killing him." His misery is palpable; I feel like I'm choking on it.

"Yes, I heard you," I whisper, moving my hand over his shoulder, trying to sooth him. "But you're upset. You aren't thinking straight."

"I can't watch Kara die, too. And you."

"Aidan . . ." I stop talking and rise up, wrapping my arms around him, unable to hold myself back. I don't know what else to do except clutch him to me, trying to make his pain stop, as if my touch can keep him from hurting.

"Please don't," I whisper. "Don't be so sad." My voice cracks and my insides ache with his sorrow. He's so close—the smell of his skin, the feel of his solid form—and all I can think of is how badly I wish he were mine. All mine. Because I know that if he were, I could fix this; I could make the storm inside of him stop. All of it.

At the thought, something in me cracks open and the dam breaks, emotions spilling out of me. Tears wet my cheeks as one wave after another hits me, making me shiver. It's sorrow, it's loss, but it's not mine, it's Aidan's. It's his heartache I'm feeling—I know it is. And I'm taking it on as my own, carrying it for him.

It burns in me, the ache in my chest becoming like a fire.

Through my closed eyelids, I see a light flash, and I open them. To actual fire.

I gasp, jerking back.

Golden flames flicker over Aidan's shoulders, then trail onto my arms. His mark is a light all its own, the power warming the air around him. But he doesn't seem to notice his own skin. He's gaping at mine.

I look down to see those gold flames coating my palms. I raise my hands in front of my face, stunned and terrified. I feel nothing, no burns, no heat. My hands aren't even warm.

I open my mouth to scream but nothing comes from my throat except a choking sound.

Then the world dims, tipping, before it all goes black.

TWENTY-ONE

Aidan

I watch Rebecca's hands in horror as she backs away. They're coated in flames. My flames.

Panic races through me as my power slithers up and down my mark, lighting up my shoulder and chest. The glow of her hands casts itself over her face in a yellow dance, reflected in her wide eyes. Eyes that now seem made of their own fire.

She opens her mouth, like she's screaming, but no sound emerges.

And then her eyes roll to white. Her head snaps back. And her body goes limp, crumpling to the linoleum like a puppet whose strings were just cut.

I jolt from my shock and crouch at her side, grabbing her by a limp wrist, taking her head and pulling it onto my lap. "Rebecca!" I yell. It feels like a yell. It comes out like I'm drowning.

A second ago I was tormented. I was lost and confused because of what Sid had said, what's happening to him, what could be happening with my father. Then Rebecca wrapped me in a tight hug and all I could feel was her warmth, her breath on my neck . . .

She held me and a fleeting memory passed through me, of that moment in the club when I first met her and she smiled at me, when she touched me that very first time and I wanted to kiss her. But I kissed Kara instead.

With that memory, my energy came to life, spilling from my shoulders, my chest, but before I could react, Rebecca and I were both on fire. My power was reaching out for her.

I shake her, saying her name again. "Please, Rebecca! Wake up!"

Kara is suddenly beside me on the floor. Holly and Jax and Connor are hovering, and Sid is coming in through the back door.

"What happened?" he asks, panic in his voice.

Then Kara says, "Did she faint?"

"She . . . she was on fire. She had fire in her hands," is all I'm able to get out. And it doesn't make sense. It's crazy. "What did I do to her? Did I hurt her?"

"Fire?" Sid says, lifting Rebecca's hands and studying them. "There are no burns, Aidan. She isn't hurt. Are you sure—?"

"Yes!" I say, too loud. "It was real fire. I think it came from me, from my power, when she hugged me. I think my mark did this."

"Hmm . . ." Sid's face falls in a frown. He reaches out and touches Rebecca's cheek, running a fingertip under her right eye, then he rubs his thumb and forefinger together, studying them before he holds them up to show us. "Gold flakes."

The kitchen light catches on his hands, and sure enough, speckles reflect gold.

"Whoa," Jax breathes.

"What does that mean?" Connor asks.

"Couldn't it just be glitter from eye shadow or something?" Holly says.

Sid shakes his head. "It smells like roses. And it seems to be in her tears." He glances sideways at Kara and the two of them exchange the oddest look. Kara shakes her head, like she doesn't want Sid to say anything.

"What!?" I bark. "Stop hiding. What do you know?"

"I know she's going to be fine," Sid says, like there's no secret. "We should take her up to her bed, though, since it may be a while before she awakens."

"So, you know what this is," I say.

He looks over to Kara again. "Yes. I believe so."

"As long as she's fine," Connor says. But the troubled look on his face doesn't reflect the mellow words.

"Help Aidan take her upstairs," Sid says to Connor as he stands straight, moving back to lean on the kitchen counter for support.

As I help Connor pick her up, I say over my shoulder to Sid, "You're going to tell me what the hell just happened after I get her settled."

Sid nods. He exchanges another look with Kara.

Anger fills me. Definitely more secrets. Dammit, I thought that part of my life in this house was over.

Connor and I get Rebecca settled in the bed. He sits beside her on the edge and tucks the blanket in around her. "She's so cold." He touches her forehead. "Like ice."

"What the hell? How is this happening?"

"It's always insanity, man," he says, resigned. "End of days and shit. Who knows?"

"She's supposed to be safe here," I mumble, staring down at her pale face, her fiery hair spilling over the pillow. She's so pure, so normal. So uninvolved in all this. It's horrible that my own screwed-up life is infecting her now. "I should've sent her to Samantha's. This wouldn't have happened."

"You don't know that. Right now you need to find out what's going on. I'll watch her."

"Yeah." I stand there for a second in the doorway, before adding, "I'll be back." Like I need to say it. Like I need her to hear me.

When I get to the kitchen, Sid and Kara are walking out the back door.

"Sid needs to be in the shed," Kara says to me. She takes his hand like she's helping an old man. "He can't do this without some stable ground."

More like he needs dark magic. But I know it helps his body stay in this time, as creepy as that is.

I wait just outside the shed door as Kara gets Sid settled on the bed. He sits with his feet on the trunk, walking stick on his lap.

The smell of dried blood and sorrow spilling from the shed is strong enough to knock me over, but I hold fast. I just need to put up with it long enough to get some answers.

When Kara steps out, she doesn't come to stand beside me. She folds her arms over her chest and leans on the wall beside the door, looking out at the yard. Then she says in a matter-of-fact way, "Rebecca is the girl you were supposed to be awakened by."

I blink as the shock hits me. "What?"

"When my headaches started last week, I realized something was wrong. But I didn't want to tell you before I was sure. I was finally positive about it today, when you told me that my curse was turning silver." Her voice is void of emotion as she touches her nape. "That's why I had to talk to Sid. I had to find out if it could be true."

"If what could be true?" I ask. It's suddenly hard to breathe.

"I was made to be your other half by the spell Sid did on me to reverse my father's curse, but Rebecca is your *true* soul mate, made from birth to be yours. It was always supposed to be her that woke your powers. Not me." Her voice catches a little, sending a sharp pain through my chest. "It was never supposed to be me."

"What are you saying? How . . . ?" I don't understand.

"Every soul is looking for its mate," Sid says, "though not every soul finds it. I assumed once your soul linked with Kara that everything would set itself right, as it should've. But I didn't take into account that your true soul match would be close by. I thought when your destiny changed, so would hers. It never occurred to me that she would be one of your Lights. That she would have already been hurtling toward you." He sighs. "I believe what happened in the kitchen a moment ago was your power finally recognizing her, so it physically *touched* her."

"And this is the first I'm hearing about this soul mate thing, why?" I ask, overwhelmed by what they're saying.

Could it be true? It would explain so much. Like why I felt so protective and drawn to Rebecca even while I was falling for Kara. It would explain why I didn't feel the same way about the other Lights. And why I can't seem to let Rebecca go, even when I try.

"I didn't know it was possible, Aidan," Kara says, her voice now tinged with desperation. "My headaches started right after your Awakening. I assumed they were from my concussion, but when I went to see an old friend who's a witch, and she read my cards, something she said made me realize it was all connected." When she sees my face shift at the mention of a witch, she adds, "I needed to know our fate. I knew you wouldn't approve. And I knew you would've insisted I tell you everything that I was feeling, but I was scared. I wanted to wait until *after* I was sure."

Helplessness filters into me, not understanding why she didn't let me know what she was struggling with. "What did the witch say?"

"She said I was suffering because there are consequences when you try to fight destiny. She said that a punishment was coming because I'd stolen another woman's mate." Kara hesitates for a second and then says, "And something else changed the day I started bleeding." She lifts the bottom of her shirt a little, then she turns to show me. Her tattoo. It's faded, now only a pale version of the violets and lilies that were the sign she was meant to be mine. "Sid's spell is definitely failing, which is why you saw my father's curse turning silver. It's returning."

A chill works over me. "The blood-show, *this,*"—I motion to her now pastel tattoo, my throat tight—"it's all some kind of a punishment?"

"Yes and no," Sid says. "I believe the witch was sensing something, but she read it wrong."

"What's the truth then?" I ask.

"We aren't sure," Kara says, quietly. "But I think it's all because you're meant to be with Rebecca, not me. It all seems to come back to that."

Agitated, I run a hand through my hair. "This is crazy."

"Fate is a difficult taskmaster," Sid says with a shake of his head.

I want to punch a hole through his damn magic shed. What the hell kind of answer is that?

Kara pushes off the wall, facing me. "I'm sorry that I didn't tell you everything, what I was thinking the last few days. I knew if I did that you might blame yourself or feel you needed to fix it. And I need you to be able to focus on your destiny, Aidan. That's why we've fought so hard." Her voice is weak and small. She steps closer, her eyes locked on mine, pleading. "I want you to be mine, but there's so much more to this than just you and me." She reaches out to touch my chest, pressing her palm against my brand.

"I get it, Kara," I say, covering her hand with mine. "I do. But . . . it all feels corrupted. And *wrong.* I need *you,* just as much as anything else. And it's not because of some spell or some magical link, not anymore. It's because it's real, and it's my choice. *Our* choice." Fuck fate; the guy's a bastard. "So, we'll figure this out," I say, "together, okay? Don't keep your fear from me. Not anymore."

She settles into my arms, wrapping herself around my middle. "I can't lose you, Aidan," she says into my chest. "I think it might kill me."

I kiss the top of her head and whisper into her hair, "Yeah." I want to say, *Me too.* Because with all the mess in my life, this here in my arms, this girl, she's the only thing that keeps me standing when I want to give up.

Her arms tighten around me and she buries herself in my chest even more.

Sid clears his throat. "Well, this is all lovely, but perhaps we should get to work on finding a way to fix it."

TWENTY-TWO

Rebecca

I wake with a jerk, sitting up straight, a hundred thoughts and feelings and strange memories rolling over me.

But it's all jumbled. It's all wrong. I never kissed Aidan. I never held hands with him, sitting on a tree branch high above the ground, or kissed his bare shoulder beside a river. We never made love in tall grass with limbs tangled together, my skin, his skin. No. Definitely not. I can't—

Someone touches my arm, stopping my thought rampage. "It's all right. You're okay," a voice says, deep and soothing.

My surroundings come into focus and so do my memories of reality. The hug. The fire on his shoulders. "Aidan! Is Aidan okay?" I ask, as I look over and see Connor sitting on the side of the bed, his face in shadow. I blink at him, surprised. "What are *you* doing here?" That came out way snarkier than I intended.

His brow goes up. "You're welcome?"

"What happened? Where's Aidan? There was fire. He was on fire!" Ohmygod, I sound like a loon. But I can't seem to help it. "There was fire on me, on him. Gold fire. There was fire on my hands." I hold up a hand and it looks perfectly normal.

Connor takes my wrist and settles my hand back in my lap. "Like I said, everything's fine."

"But, Aidan . . ."

"Yes, Aidan does light up sometimes with fire. It's kind of a thing."

"*Thing?*" Like a defect? A talent?

"A power," he attempts to clarify.

But it's still not very clear. "Like how he sees souls?"

Connor hesitates. "Sort of. Sure."

I deflate back onto the pillow and put a hand to my forehead. "I just . . . I'm so confused."

He nudges me over to make more room on the bed. "Yes, it's confusing," is all he says.

He settles in, slipping off his flip-flops and putting his legs up on the mattress parallel to mine.

"But it is what it is," he adds. Like that helps at all.

I sit up slowly and lean on the wall beside him. "Aidan has powers. And that golden fire, or whatever, is part of that." I wonder why it latched on to me.

"Yeah." His head falls back against the wall. "He's got all these things he can do, and it's basically so he can kill demons and save the world."

I laugh. Connor turns to me and raises a brow, making me choke on my laughter. "Seriously?" I ask. "Save the world."

"Yep." He looks forward again.

"Well . . . okay." I don't even know what to say to that.

"Don't worry, you don't have to understand it. You just have to accept it."

"Okay." I hug myself and shiver from the weight of it all.

He seems to think it's a sign that I'm cold; he pulls the blanket from beneath him and tucks it around me like I'm a kid.

When he's finished, he leans against the wall again.

I stare at his profile for a second, taken off guard by his nurturing touch. "So Aidan is supposed to save the world," I repeat. It sounds even weirder when I say it out loud.

"Supposedly."

"And he kills demons with his gold fire."

"No, he stabs them."

I scrunch up my face. "Sounds messy."

He shrugs. "Haven't seen him do it." Then he adds, "Well, I did see him trap a demon once. Sort of. And I saw him catch a wraith, which was pretty bloody. But it was his own blood."

I try and imagine Aidan caging a demon like someone would cage a hungry lion. "And you help him?"

He smiles, like that's funny. "No. Not really."

"What is it *you* do, then?"

He sighs, sounding tired. "Survive."

TWENTY-THREE

Aidan

The house is dark and quiet now that night has settled in. Connor's still in the room with Rebecca. Jax is downstairs in the office watching YouTube with Holly and arguing about some new promotional ideas for LA Paranormal. I showered and changed my bandages—still no healing happening as far as I can tell. I wonder if I should get someone to stitch me up, but I can't think of who. I could call Sid's doctor, but then Sid would know, and he has enough to worry about. Plus, it's not like I want to announce my new weakness. So, I just wrap myself back up and plead with my power to fix the mess.

Kara is sleeping in her bed a few feet away from me. I'm sitting in her chair getting ready to open Eric's journal for the bazillionth time, to look for that "under-passage."

Eric said that I should be able to find it now. I guess because I've—what?—linked to my dead father's bones?

The thought sends a shiver through me.

Just as I'm running my hand over the leather binding, getting ready to open it again, someone knocks on the door.

"Hey, it's Connor."

"Yeah," I say, quietly, not wanting to wake Kara. "You can come in."

Connor opens the door and I lean forward.

"What's up?" I ask. "Is Rebecca okay?"

"She's awake. She's fine."

Some of the tension leaves my muscles.

"I should probably talk to her," I say, more to myself. She needs to know what's happening. The secrets aren't helping at all. But how do I tell her something like *this*? I barely understand it all myself. And I really don't want it to be true, that my soul would've rather chosen Rebecca instead of Kara.

"What'd Sid have to say?" Connor asks.

I blow out a puff of air. "Oh, you know, the usual. A bunch of stuff I wish I'd known two months ago."

"About your power? Did all this with Rebecca happen today because of it?"

"Yes. And no. It happened because of both of us, I guess."

"You mean, Rebecca has powers like yours?"

"No. Not like mine." I pause. "It's just that she's the one who was supposed to awaken my powers, not Kara. They think Rebecca's my real soul mate, the one chosen for me by fate or some shit. And that could have something to do with Kara being sick." My throat closes, not wanting to follow that thread any further with Connor. The guilt is a hundred boulders on my back.

"But Sid did the spell. And you feel everything with her, so . . . strong—"

I shake my head. "No. The fact that I care about her now is just human stuff."

"Wow, that's . . ."

"Yup."

A troubled look paints a shadow over his features and he turns to look at Kara's sleeping form. "So, you're supposed to be with Rebecca now? Not Kara."

"That's not going to happen."

He nods slowly, looking a little relieved, but still doubtful. "So what happens to Rebecca? Could all this hurt her in some way?"

"I don't know. There are still a lot of questions." Loads more questions than answers.

"Kara must be wrecked." His brotherly worry shows in his eyes.

"She's suspected for a few days, but she was too scared to tell me."

"Yeah, that sounds like her," he says, like he's seeing it all clearly. He's known Kara a lot longer than I have and probably understands her far better.

As Connor starts to leave, I say, "Hey, I might be going by the club tomorrow to check on a few things. Make sure Rebecca and Kara are okay, will you?"

He hesitates. "What's going on at the club?"

"Nothing."

By the look on his face, it's obvious he doesn't believe me, but he agrees before heading out of the room. "Sure. No problem." And then he closes the door, leaving me with thoughts about the mess of fate.

———

I sit for several minutes, staring at Kara, before I open the journal to the first page.

Eric's familiar words cover the surface in his tidy handwriting. I flip through the book, not really seeing any of it; it's all the same information I've been looking at for a month. First it explains my Awakening, how the change worked, how my powers rose. It explains demon lore, outlining their limits and my strengths. It says a hundred things that I already know about my mission to kill them. But right now, it's all completely useless. I grip the edges of the journal in my hands, trying to decide whether to rip it in half or throw it out the window.

"Just show me, dammit!"

Something pricks my thumbs, as if the pages are suddenly filled with tiny needles. And I can't let go. I can only watch as a wash of red seeps across the parchment in thread-like waves. I stare in shock, no longer feeling the sting on my thumbs as my blood actually becomes a part of the paper's weave. And then my blood is the ink, curling itself into crimson text, right in the center of the page, in a language I've never seen. But I understand the terrifying words perfectly.

You will touch death with fire and bring it into life once more. What you awaken shall usher in the world's end. The Cycle of Darkness has begun.

I stare at the blood script and try to make sense of it. Dread fills me. I awakened someone already, according to Eric. I awakened Daniel, my father. And Eric called him the first Harbinger.

Shit. I need to check the ossuary. Now. I need to see for myself whether Eric was right. I close the journal and grab my jacket, then head downstairs.

I'm rushing through the kitchen when a soft voice whispers from behind me.

"Hey." Something tugs my shirt.

I jerk back, then see it's just Rebecca. "You trying to give me a heart attack?" The house is totally silent. It's past midnight and everyone's asleep now. Everyone except the two of us, I guess.

"Where you going?" she asks.

"Out. But you should be resting."

"I feel fine." She tilts her head, like she's thinking. "Actually, I'm super antsy. I need to get out of here."

"It's late."

"*You're* going somewhere. So I can, too."

"You aren't going anywhere right now," I say, trying to be intimidating. "You need to rest and this isn't resting."

But I'm obviously not intimidating enough, because she shoots back, "You're not the boss of me, Aidan."

I sigh. "Are we six now?"

"I'll wake up Holly and Jax and Kara—" She points at my face when I raise my brow. "Yes, I said Kara. She won't like you going anywhere at this time of night."

"She's not a part of this."

Rebecca looks dubious. "I thought she was a part of everything."

As I stare at her, my bastard of a mind replays Kara's words: *Rebecca was meant to be the one . . .* She's wearing tight blue jeans, tall brown boots with heels, and a very tight pink T-shirt that hugs her waist and breasts. She's sexy as hell. And I'm definitely not going anywhere with her alone.

"Are you seriously going to push this?" I ask through my teeth. She nods. "Absolutely."

"Fine. Wait here." I point at her like it'll stick her to the spot, then I go upstairs to wake Connor.

———

Connor glares at me in the rearview mirror from the backseat of the Camaro, arms folded over his chest, hood up. Rebecca is sitting shotgun, her fingers tapping on her denim-clad knees, looking content.

"You should've just tied her up," Connor grumbles. "A little duct tape. All fixed. I'd have untied her in the morning."

Rebecca watches the city go by as we make our way down Wilshire. "I don't see why Blondie-Boy had to come at all. It's not like I've never gone to a club."

Does she want me to remind her of the last time she was at this club? Not that I would. And it's not like that horror was her fault, anyway.

I'm also not going to mention the fact that I brought Connor along because I didn't want to be alone with her. So, instead, I throw out, "Connor can just hang around and make sure you're okay while I get the supplies from Hanna."

She turns and makes a show of looking Connor over. "He's kind of big to be a babysitter."

"I'm in no mood, woman," he grunts.

Rebecca giggles and turns back around, apparently having a grand time. She has no idea how torn up I am inside, sitting next to her, thinking about how the two of us being together like this would hurt Kara. "Just please stay out of trouble." I say it a little too forcefully, and she cocks an eyebrow at me. "And don't drink anything."

"Holly was right," she says. "You *are* a buzzkill."

We get to the club and I attempt to convince Rebecca to stay in the car; Connor's almost asleep again and he seems reluctant to get out. But she won't have any of it. She leaps out, sauntering toward the alley, heading for the entrance before I can stop her. She's half dancing, half walking to the loud music that spills from the walls of the club.

Connor drags himself out of the Camaro and groans, "I've got her." He follows, hunched over, looking miserable.

After I see he's caught up, I turn and head across the parking lot to the warehouse. I don't call Hanna, deciding I'd rather do this alone. I move through the main building and type in the code for the inner vault per her instructions. The thick door thuds and hisses open.

Once inside, I close it and punch in the code to lock things back up. The thud sounds again and the lights flicker on, one by one, going down the rows of shelving. The place is still in a state of confusion, unpacked boxes and randomly stacked books and papers everywhere. As I walk down the aisle, I try to hold on to the hope that Eric's wrong about whose bones might be inside that ossuary, and what might have happened when I touched it.

But a chill works over me as I get closer to the box. Chunks of tan limestone are scattered across the shiny white floor, and smaller bits begin crunching under my feet as I approach. Not good. I scan the shelf, hoping maybe one of the other boxes just got knocked over, but don't see the ossuary I touched yesterday.

Probably because I'm stepping on what's left of it.

I lean down and pick up a large piece of the limestone, running my thumb over the smooth surface.

An image flashes behind my eyes as I fall into the vision. I'm outside the dead man's body this time, an observer, taking on the vantage point of the stone box instead. I see a scattering of bones where they fell. The pieces vibrate on the linoleum, flesh regrowing like a time-lapse video. Blood appears in red beads that roll together, joining along the bones to become the vessels. Bronze skin stretches over calf and thigh, over fingers, neck, and face, hair sprouting in dark curls.

The body rises to its feet, naked, shimmering flakes of light and heat circling the male form. He takes a moment to steady himself, looking around. Then he moves. Walks down the aisle a few steps before disappearing into a burst of white light.

The stone I was holding drops from my hand, thudding back onto the floor as I return to the present. If that *was* the prophet Daniel, he's now very much alive.

TWENTY-FOUR

Rebecca

As soon as I get in the club—thanks to Connor, who seems to know everybody working here—I make a beeline for the dance floor to wash away all the crazy going on inside me with loud music. I let the vibrations fill my skin like a living thing, soaking it all in: the smells and colors and pulsing air. It's real and urgent. I love to dance. It takes my mind off the madness of my life. I don't have to think about what's happened, or why. I don't have to think about what I saw or felt.

Thinking about it only makes me more confused. No matter what Connor says about Aidan being a magical demon-killer who'll save the world, I still have no clue what his power has to do with me, or why it would affect me like that. Is something *wrong* with me? Am I evil? Is that why his fire seemed to want me? Is that why I dreamed those weird things afterward? The things I felt in the dream, with all those tastes and smells surrounding me as I touched him and kissed him . . . they seemed so real. It felt like he was the other half of my heart.

But that can*not* be in my head right now. It wasn't real. It was all just some freaky vision. And I have no right to feel anything even remotely steamy toward the guy. He's practically married to Kara.

When I couldn't fall asleep, I tried to draw, hoping to find answers, but nothing came to me. My mind was blank, except for a buzzing; a sort of white noise left over from Aidan's fire touching my skin. It was time to get out of that house.

And now, in this loud world, I can forget. I can forget that my brother died, that my heart is broken, that I'm alone.

I'm not alone in this moment. I'm surrounded by beauty, by close bodies and smiles, and that fake life, full of plastic people, where no one feels anything real.

I get lost in the rhythm of wild beats, the rustle of excited breath. The crowd moves like a living thing, each of us a piece of something larger, a joint celebration of life. Hands graze my arms, my waist. I dance until sweat collects on my brow, wets my hair, and runs down my temple, down my lower back, dampening my shirt. Until I feel like I've connected with everyone on the dance floor, one partner after another, getting to know each one without words, just movement.

I feel Connor's eyes watching me from the edge of the floor. And sure enough, when I glance over to where I left him, I spot him through the crowd. The lights pulse behind him, turning his hair dark, making it so I can't see his face. But he's definitely staring at me. Like, *really* staring.

I frown as the world tips a little, a wave of dizziness washing over me. I blink and just shake it off, then go back to dancing. But even after another song, he's there, in the same place. Except, wait . . . he's sliding into the crowd.

I decide to follow, to get him to dance with me—if he's going to be babysitting anyway, he may as well join the fun. I make my way to the spot where he stood, then look over the cocktail area. I thought that I was right behind him, but I don't see him anymore.

I wander over to the bar and an older guy instantly accosts me, asking if I want a drink. He leans over all skeezy and bearded, telling me I'm too beautiful to be thirsty. I say thanks, but no thanks, even though I'd love a stiff drink right now. A little Jack and Coke would wipe my busy mind for a good few hours. But the last time I hid my confusion and pain in a bottle, I found myself woken up by a gorgeous guy, who would eventually ditch me.

I find Connor on a couch in a dark corner, his hoodie up, head bowed, arms folded over his chest. I walk up and stand over him, waiting. When he doesn't move I kick his flip-flop with my boot.

"Hey, sleepy. Don't you wanna dance with me?"

He grunts and his head falls back. "Hush, child."

I plop next to him and tap his shoulder, like an annoying little sister. "Pretty please, Connor."

He grunts again and puts an arm over his eyes.

"Oh, stop being a drama queen," I say with a laugh, bumping his side. "I know you're faking it. You were spying on me a second ago."

His arm falls and he sits up straighter, leaning in like he didn't hear me. "What?"

"You're a big faker. I saw you watching me."

His face scrunches in confusion and he shakes his head.

I point to the spot on the edge of the dance floor where he'd been standing. "Right there." But now I'm suddenly doubting that it was Connor. I hesitate and look back at his face and realize he's serious. He wasn't watching me.

I shrug like it's no big deal, but I start to feel queasy. "*Someone* was gawking."

"Well, you're pretty," he says, like it's obvious.

I blink at him. Is he just being nice to me again? I find myself not able to look in his eyes. They're not flirty like I'm used to from guys. They're honest, and I don't know what to do with that right now. "Oh . . . kay."

He leans in closer. "Come on. You're fully aware of how gorgeous you are."

I'm half-flattered, half-offended. But my stress pushes me over the edge of offense. "Seriously? I'm *that* girl to you?"

"You telling me you're not aware?"

I have no words. Because, yes, I know how guys look at me. But it's not my freaking fault. "There's nothing wrong with knowing I'm seen in a certain way. I am *not* stuck up."

"Of course not." But he smirks and his arms fold back over his chest.

Smug jerk. I growl and find my feet, heading for the bathroom.

My fit of frustration is put on pause, though, when I find myself in a very long line. Kind of takes the wind out of my sails. And it makes me feel ridiculous, because I don't actually have to pee. I stay in line for a second, though, because I don't want to give in right away.

Which is totally sad.

I deflate and wander back over to the bar, leaning on the end near a swinging door that says *Employees Only*. Standing here keeps me on the edge of the crowd, and I'm out of sight of the old guys hungry for a take-home gal.

I can't see Connor from here, but I can picture him, sitting all hooded-up and stuffy in his high tower of perfection. Grumpy old man. He's got no right to judge me, anyway, with that tan skin of his, all warm against his light hair. And those muscles. And those glorious eyelashes! He's freaking perfect himself, self-righteous little—

Rebecca.

I freeze. Was that someone saying my name? It whispered over the pulse and noise of the bar, a soft hum in my ears.

It comes again: *Rebecca.*

I look around, but everyone seems caught up in their own drama, chatting with possible dates or ordering drinks.

Rebecca. This time it sounds like it's coming from behind me. I turn to the swinging employee door and push it open a crack to peek. It leads to an empty, dimly lit hall. There's someone down there in the shadows.

Rebecca . . .

I jerk away, letting the door swing shut, and bite back a squeal. The figure definitely just said my name.

Don't be afraid.

I shouldn't be able to hear him over all the crazy noise in the club. And something about him feels familiar. A distant piece of me recognizes him.

I push open the swinging door again and step into the hall. My legs shake as I look at the man in the shadows ten feet away.

"Thank you for hearing me," he says. I search my memory for a face to match the voice, feeling like it's just out of reach.

"Do I know you?" I ask, stepping closer. He moves out of the shadow and my breath catches in my throat. "Aidan!" It's Aidan. But no, that can't be him. This guy's, like, thirty. "Who are you?" I ask, voice weak. He looks exactly like Aidan—the same high cheekbones, dark lashes, the same full lips. And the heavy curls combined with those hazel eyes, like shimmery green glass.

"My name isn't important," he says. "I've come to bring a message and you'll be the one to help me."

"Me?" What does he mean? I should be terrified right now, talking to a strange man in a dark hallway, but I'm not. In fact, I'm totally relaxed, as if I'm looking at an old friend. I can't seem to muster up any real concern or fear like a sensible person.

"Yes, you and others. But for now, I'll speak only to the keeper of his heart."

I blink at him. "Whose heart?"

"The Fire Bringer. He will need to be ready, but I cannot prepare him myself."

His words shouldn't make any sense, but somehow I recognize who he's talking about. "Uh, you mean, Aidan? You may have the wrong girl. I'm not anywhere near his heart at the moment."

The man's lips curl up in a sad sort of grin and he tilts his head. "But you wear his soul mark over your own heart." He motions to his ribcage and I wonder if he means my butterfly tattoo—but how in the name of heaven would he be able to see that? "You are meant to be his," he adds when I still look at him doubtfully.

What makes this guy think he knows *anything* about my heart or Aidan's? "Maybe you should be looking for Aidan. He's around here somewhere." I point behind me.

"I know where he is," he says, moving closer. "I wish to give him time to settle into his place before I speak to him. For now, you will be my connection."

This is just so weird. "Who are you?" I ask again, this time trying to put more force behind my words.

"I am no one of significance."

"Well, I won't pass on any messages to him if I don't know who's sending them."

"You will tell him that he cannot stop what's to come," he says, ignoring my stubbornness. "He should be ready. He must hold tight to the hem of Grace and the tattered remnants of Forgiveness."

I feel myself giving in, listening intently, but I protest like I'm not. "I'm not going to tell him anything. I don't know you. You might want to hurt him—he has lots of things trying to hurt him, you know." As I say this, I'm pointing at the man and moving closer, like by getting in his face, he'll buy my objections more.

He steps forward in a rush of movement, his body coming within inches of mine, faster than I could've blinked. My heart stops in my chest, then skips sideways.

"You are brave," he whispers, raising his hand to touch his fingers to my forehead, as if he's placing something on my brow. "But you must realize, this clay vessel is set to crumble; your fragile flesh will be tested in ways you cannot imagine." He closes his eyes and cocks his head as if listening hard to some voice I can't hear. "You are the mother of many but your womb is empty." He says these words with surprise in his voice. "You will lose your anointing, your heart, your soul. You will pass on this blessing and bear no life within you, though you were meant to give birth to a whole world."

He opens his eyes again, searching my face, looking pained. "You are correct; you do not belong to him as you should. That was stolen from you, and the path has changed once more. I am so sorry, child." Tears glisten in his eyes and my throat goes tight, feeling as if he's broken my heart, and yet I'm not sure why. "Tell him what I've spoken of," he says quietly. "And then make your journey. Though it wasn't the one set in blood among the stars, and this shift may cause pain for so many, it will be well with you, and you will find your way to Peace."

His hand falls back to his side and he steps away from me, his features lined with misery. It hits me like it's my own hurt, like I have some reason to be as tormented as he looks.

Then he bows his head and disappears.

Poof!

Gone. Right. Before. My eyes.

One moment he's there and the next he's just . . . not. And the air seems to sizzle with heat where he stood.

I reach up to feel my brow where he touched me, and my fingers come away slick, like he had oil on his hand. I look at my fingertips, slide them together as the scent of night jasmine fills my head.

An image of my mother comes to my mind, a memory of a photograph my father kept beside his bed for many years before it was placed in a drawer and forgotten, just like her. Charlie always said she smelled like jasmine and summer. The loss of her, of any memory of her, becomes a deep sorrow. How could I not have ever known her? How could she have chosen to leave? And Charlie . . . My chest aches with it, my eyes sting.

And then the weight of it all hits me, my body shaking under the heavy reality of what my heart suddenly takes on. The truth. I've lost so much. I've lost my hope. I've lost Aidan. I'm alone. And it's useless to pretend otherwise.

TWENTY-FIVE

Aidan

I leave the vault and hurry across the parking lot, my mind full of questions about what my vision of Daniel could mean. My father is back. Wandering the city of Los Angeles. Because of me and my power. The idea is just . . . it doesn't fit in my head. I need to find Connor and Rebecca and get out of here. I need to talk to Sid.

The club is loud and full of that familiar buzz of a hundred different energies mingling together like a blend of putrid oils. It saturates my skin, trying to sink in, and I don't bother fighting it off or blocking it out as I search the crowd.

I'm relieved to find Connor quickly, near the bar, talking to a guy and motioning with his hands. I come up and hear him describing Rebecca. "—boots, a pink shirt and jeans. And really red hair." The guy he's talking to points at the bathroom and Connor shakes his head. "Already checked there—" He sees me and moves away from the guy. "Aidan. Shit, man. I can't find her." His voice is steady as he yells to be heard over the thunder of the music, but the look on his face is harnessed panic. "She walked off because she was pissed at me. I thought I'd give her a second, but when I went after her, I couldn't find her anywhere."

I scan the crowd quickly, the urge to get out of this place grow-ing; the music beats at my aching head. I barely hear Connor's words as I search for Rebecca's red hair. It's really packed in here now—I'm not sure if we'd see her even if she were three feet away. "You check that side, I'll check this side, if we—"

Someone taps my shoulder and I turn. The guy is large, like a football player, his neck thick and his shoulders like mountains. He leans in and says loudly, "You lookin' for the redhead?" I nod and the guy points toward the end of the bar, to the door that leads to the break room and the employee bathrooms. "She's with one of the bussers in the back. They were just asking if anyone knew—"

But neither Connor or I hear any more, both of us making a beeline for the swinging door. I can't let my mind go to where it wants to go, to the last time I found her passed out in this place. Connor pushes through first, and I grumble, "You were supposed to watch her."

He doesn't turn around. "I didn't think she'd actually drink anything! She kept saying no to the guys who offered." He sounds miserable, so I don't let any more of my frustration or worry loose. Whatever happened, it wasn't Connor's fault. He's not her keeper.

I am.

We enter the break room in a rush. There's a guy sitting on the couch beside a dazed Rebecca with a phone to his ear. He star-tles at our entrance and jumps up, backing away, almost climb-ing behind the furniture. "Whoa," he says in a stoner voice. Then he says to whoever's on the other line, "No, dude, these guys just totally crashed in like there's a freakin' fire." Then he releases a ner-vous laugh. Connor snatches the phone from him and the guy's laugh turns to a choke. "Hey, what the hell?"

Connor looks at the screen—probably to make sure it's not 911—then hands it back to the guy. "Sorry. Just checking."

Stoner Guy says into the phone, "Hey, man, I gotta jet. Crazy happenings," then hangs up.

I move to Rebecca's side; she actually looks okay. Her head is cradled in her hands, though, so I can't see her face. "Rebecca, what's going on? What are you doing back here?" I turn to glare at Stoner Guy. "Did you see what happened?"

"Slow down," he says, holding up his hands. "I found the girl back here crying, is all. I was just making sure she was chill, right?"

I take a deep breath and ask Rebecca again, "What is it? What's wrong?" But she's still not looking at me.

"She's all cut up about some dude," Stoner Guy explains. "She just needs a beat is all."

Connor frowns at her, then kneels down, facing her, touching her knee gently. "Hey, you okay?" he asks, quietly, like he's trying to calm a troubled child. It's odd. Definitely not Connor's normal style.

He actually gets a head-shake from her, though. More of a response than I got.

"Hey, can you give us a sec?" I ask Stoner Guy.

He blinks slowly at me and then says, "Totally, dude. Most definitely. I'll be behind the bar if you need anything."

"Great, thanks." I give him a stiff smile as he leaves the room, then I turn back to Rebecca and squat down beside Connor. "Okay, what's going on, Rebecca? Come on."

"Hey," Connor snaps. "Let her take her time."

"We don't have time," I grind out.

"Why? You have an appointment to be somewhere at one in the morning?"

"No, I just need to get back home." I need to get back to Kara, to figure out what the hell is going on with my resurrected father. I need to talk to Sid.

Rebecca's voice is muffled through her hands. "He said that I was your soul mate, Aidan."

Connor looks at her with wide eyes.

My awareness keys on her as the words hit me. "Who said that?"

"The guy," she whispers.

"What guy?" Connor asks, voice tight.

"He looked just like you, Aidan," she looks up and stares right at me, then, her eyes full of shock, "if you were, like, thirty. And he said I was your soul mate, that I was supposed to have been yours, but something about my path changed or is changing—I have no idea. He knew me. But I can't see how. And he was just so sad." She sniffs and takes my hand in hers, gripping it. "What did he mean? I feel like he ripped out my heart."

The guy . . . she talked to some guy. Who knew her story, her truth. A man who looked just like me? A chill works over every inch of my skin, the hair prickling along my arms. Could Daniel— my father?—the bones I watched re-form in a vision—could he have come in here and found *Rebecca*? Why would he do that? Why would he speak to her and not me?

When neither Connor nor I respond to her questions, she adds, "I need to know who he was." She keeps looking at me with glistening eyes, like she's unable to turn away. "His words felt so . . . true and important. Like he was seeing right through me. And Aidan, he knew you and he said I needed to give you a message."

It's suddenly tough to breathe. "What message?" And why didn't he give it to me himself? If he could find Rebecca, he could find me. His supposed *son*. Instead he's telling Rebecca, he's telling her she should've been mine. Just like Kara said. "What exactly did he say?"

She glances away and releases my hand, then rubs her palms over her knees. "He said I was supposed to be his connection to you, because I was your soul mate. But then when he touched me, he said something had gone wrong, that things had changed from what was written in the stars."

"Rebecca," I say, trying to figure out how to explain. "There's no way to know for sure."

"He knew. I felt it in his words when he spoke, it was the truth." She looks at me again. "And you knew. Didn't you? That I was supposed to be with you, not Kara."

"He just found out today, Rebecca," Connor says.

My throat swells as all the emotions collide inside of me. I can only shake my head in answer.

"Who was he?" she asks me. "You know him. You're afraid and confused."

"It was my father," I manage, not sure how she could know what I'm feeling.

Connor's head jerks back in surprise. "What?"

"I need you to tell me the message, Rebecca," I say, ignoring his shock. Connor will have to wait to ask his questions. "Whatever he told you, it's very important."

"I know," she says. She stands and walks over to the opposite wall.

Connor and I both rise to our feet, the expectation in the room thickening with each second that passes. Rebecca stares at the floor, pacing a few times back and forth. Then she goes still and begins to whisper in an odd voice, almost like she's speaking as someone else. "You can't stop what's coming. You should be ready; hold tight to the hem of Grace and the tattered remnants of Forgiveness."

It's silent for what feels like several years as we all take in the words. I can't stop what's coming? Does he mean the angel that's coming for Ava? Or is he repeating what the hidden under-passage in Eric's journal said: *What you will awaken shall bring the world's end*?

Daniel was a prophet, so if it was really him, then I can assume the words are true. More than that, though, I *feel* their truth. Deep in my core. And now that I've heard them, I'm accountable to them.

I've been warned.

Be ready.

But I have no clue what to be ready for. "We need to get back,"
I finally say. It's time to find answers, instead of always stumbling
over questions. Sid will have them. And Eric.

Rebecca grabs my arm before I can turn to the door. "What did
he mean, Aidan?" Her brow is pinched; she smells like sharp torment and loss. The energy in her grip is frantic. "What's coming?"

"I wish that I knew," I say, not pulling away from her, letting
her hold on to me. I need to feel her pain. My fate being fucked
up is fucking up everyone else's, and I need to not hide from that
anymore. "I'm sorry this is happening to you."

"None of this is your fault, Aidan," she says. "You need to stop
believing that it is." The lost look in her eyes is physically painful to
see, and it makes me want to accept her words, to believe that her
hurt isn't because of me. But that's not my reality right now.

She reaches into her back pocket and pulls out a folded piece
of paper, then holds it out to me. "Here, take this. I was going to
give it to you the other day at our coffee, but . . . well, here."

I take it from her and unfold it, opening what looks like a
drawing in charcoal pencil. It's smudged in several spots from
being carried around, but I can still see the image clearly. Skulls.
Loads and loads of skulls. Off in the distance is the cave. And there
I am in the middle of the carnage, standing in the field of death.
I stare up at a sky that's roiling with lightning. My dagger is on
the ground, resting against a small skull by my foot. The skull of a
child?

You cannot stop what's coming . . .

The Cycle of Darkness has begun . . .

I shiver, digesting the image for only a second before I fold
it back up and shove it in my pocket. I'd burn it if I thought that
would do any good. But this is just paper, just a blurry glimpse of

the future that Rebecca saw; there's no way to burn the future. It's coming, one way or another.

TWENTY-SIX

Aidan

We all walk through the club, Connor holding Rebecca's hand so she doesn't get caught up by the crowd. I trail behind them, watching how he moves beside her, like he's parting the waters. I wonder if she's noticed that he's being chivalrous for her, or if she thinks that's just how he is. I got a whiff of his attraction to her as we were leaving the house earlier tonight, and now I see it might be more than that. Looks like it won't just be her heart getting broken because of this mess.

I come up beside Connor and lean in so he can hear. "I'll meet you guys at the car. Gonna go tell Hanna that I got what I needed."

He nods and disappears down the hall with Rebecca as I head up the office stairs. A bouncer stands on the landing in front of the door. Frank, I think.

He holds up a hand. "She's with an employee."

"I need to give her something and get home. Can I slip in for just a sec, Frank?" He looks me over, then seems to recognize me. He moves aside, giving me a nod.

"Thanks."

I open the door and step inside, staring into the dark room as I shut the door behind me. I try to blink back the shadows a little as something odd slinks over me, uneasiness stirring in my gut. The room looks empty.

But several out-of-place smells begin to hit me—brine and the sea, the crisp spring breeze of new green life. And then I realize it's all masking a deeper scent. Something sinister and putrid just under the surface.

Death.

"Hanna?" I say, my voice hoarse from surfacing fear.

A low growl emerges from my right, behind the couch. A growl that turns into a sinister chuckle as a form emerges from the shadows. "A young, fleshy boy," the thing—whatever it is—says. But the words come out made of crunching glass and clacking stones. "So yummy and young and spry. I know you, fleshy boy. I smell your oils and sweats."

I stand frozen as I watch the six-foot hunched thing slink forward to perch on the back of the purple couch. It's looking in the wrong spot because it can't see me while I'm wearing the amulet, but apparently it's still extremely aware of my presence. Bony knees point at the ceiling and two sets of claws, on feet and hands, dig into the soft fabric with a *pop* that releases puffs of white cotton stuffing from the couch. Its oily skin is the color of pitch, with shimmery black feathers covering its shoulders and upper thighs to the waist. Its odd-shaped mouth is like a purple beak, but when it speaks, the beak is clearly soft and pliable. Two holes sit just under its bulging, sideways blinking eyes.

And then I realize: its purple beak is splotched with a shiny liquid.

The creature reaches back to pick something up from behind the couch and then holds out whatever it retrieved with a three-pronged claw as if inspecting a find. It looks like ... oh, God, is that a human organ?

"Tasty, fleshy female. Then crunchy, fleshy boy." A forked lizard tongue springs from its mouth, licking the chunk of flesh where fresh blood is dripping onto the couch.

Hanna.

I want to shout her name, but I can't seem to move or get my voice to work. I'm in a frozen panic, my heart crushing to dust in my chest. Sorrow and horror threaten to drag me under, even as rage and bright need fills me. The need to kill. My mark doesn't spark right off, but I almost want it to this time. I want to grab this thing and cut it into ribbons. I want to tear its throat out with my bare hands. It killed Hanna.

Hanna.

No demons are supposed to be able to enter this place. Eric put up protections—he made sure it was safe.

But the wards apparently don't work anymore.

The demon tilts its head, looking perturbed. "No, no. I smell frown-frown, fleshy. You'll sour the meat."

It killed her. It killed Hanna. It's the only thing I can think. I picture her gentle smile, her kind eyes. "I'm going to eviscerate you, *dever.*" I manage to say.

"I do what I must, what I'm twisted to do, fleshy boy. No threat-threats if you can't follow with action now."

This thing's corporeal. It's as much flesh as I am. Another demon that's managed to make it across the Veil, but one that didn't bother to disguise itself much at all, other than a small amount of glamour on its face. A horror movie come to life. Not hesitant to kill. And even though it can't see me, there are more than two hundred people downstairs in the club that it *can* see, all of them potential meals.

The demon seems to be listening for my movement as I side-step to block the door. I hold fast to my power; it stings under my skin, beginning to burn, but not as much as it should. I need to focus it. I want it to be as strong as it can be. I can't be weak. Not now.

I start to reach for my dagger, but before I can pull it free, the creature springs forward, coming at me, swiping a claw at my center. It rips off my amulet, leaving two long slashes down my chest to join the ones I got from the wraith. My shirt and my bandages tear. My whole body burns with the pain of new wounds.

I curl in on myself, stumbling to the floor, and scramble away as my feeble power flickers back to almost nothing, still too weak. The raven demon rumbles its low chuckle again and prowls down the arm of the couch, to the floor, and then perches on the edge of the desk.

I wasn't prepared for this. I wasn't ready. But I pull out my dagger anyway and begin the words, *"The light of Elohim surrounds me—"*

It interrupts me with a clacking of its teeth. "No, no. You don't believe these things. These words are empty in your mouth, fleshy boy. Your bones are faithless." It looks right at me, seeing me now with my amulet across the room. "So faithless and weak." Its bulging eyes turn from black to silver as it keys in on me and smiles.

Then it springs again.

I scramble to the left, slashing at it with my blade, but it lands on my side, front talons digging deep into my arms, holding them tight. The back claws sink into my waist, piercing through my gut.

A scream rips from my chest.

The creature yanks with its hind claws, tearing me open.

"Die, fleshy. Pour your blood out for me."

My body convulses. Every limb aches, weakening, making it too much to even hold my dagger as the blood spills out with each waning beat of my heart.

The demon keeps babbling as everything blurs from the shock of what's happening. "Master Hunger brought me through the door when the earth shook. Master needs you out of the way, needs you with the worms where you belong, and he gives me the honors. He is here, yes. Helped me make my way from Sheol, calling me through. He tells me your fleshy flesh is mine if I want it." It grins with its misshaped lips and hisses through its sharp teeth.

Oh, God, the demon Hunger? Could that horrifying beast somehow have found its way back from wherever Ava sent it? If that's true, then it won't just be searching for me—

Rebecca.

"No," I say as the fire rises again inside me. My useless dagger hand sparks to life, my mark flickering through my torn shirt on my chest.

The demon spots the golden river rolling over my skin.

It screeches and releases me, flying backward through the air, landing on the arm of the couch. Then its scream turns into a mew as it shrinks down like it's trying to look smaller. "It's all right, boy of earth," it says in a sly tone. "Calm your fire. You will meet your filthy god soon."

I try to lift my head, to move, but my muscles are made of lead. *"The love, the light of Elohim enfolds me,"* I whisper. *"He enfolds me."* I manage to get a tighter grip on my dagger hilt. *"He enfolds me . . . His light enfolds me."*

The demon sneers down at me from its perch on the couch, looking disgusted. "Pathetic creatures. The filth of Grace may enfold you, but you will still watch me eat your heart." And then its face begins to shift, its violet mouth elongating, hardening into a foot-long razor sharp black beak. And it's horrifying.

My power surges in my torn gut and my heavy limbs react, moving me as far away as I can go. My body shakes, my blood slicking everything around me. I press my back into the one-way glass, feeling cold, so cold. The damp tatters of my bloody shirt chill my skin. My power grows, and the light roiling over my arm brightens. I feel my broken body begin to heal, one molecule weaving back together at a time.

But it's too slow for the damage to be undone.

The lights of the dance floor pulse behind me through the glass, sending blues and purples over the oily feathers on the demon's shoulders as it slinks closer, seemingly unafraid of my dagger or my power now. It's almost beautiful in its size and shape, man and bird and beast, magical and petrifying.

And then it's over me, looking sideways at my blade. It screeches at me, the light from my power reflecting in its eyes.

In a rush of air it lunges, razor beak slicing deep into my lower torso before I can defend myself.

No pain comes. No shock. I am numb. Cold.

My arm rises up. And I slide my blade into the demon's neck, slow and deliberate.

Before it can pull away, I yank down, releasing a river of black.

The beak opens, its dark tongue flicking out as I manage another gouge right at the base of the jaw, locking its mouth open in a silent gape with the tip of my dagger.

"*The love of Elohim enfolds me,*" I gasp as my power surges into the body of the creature. When I see the black eyes fill with my fire, I pull my dagger free.

The light flickers inside its open beak, and screeches rise as its body bursts to flames. Then it crumples in on itself, becoming ash and dust.

I stare at the dark pile. Even turning it to ash doesn't seem like enough. It killed Hanna.

Hanna.

The weight of exhaustion and sorrow falls over me in a rush. My head tips back against the cool glass. The vibrations of the music on the other side enter my skin, a pulse so much faster than my slowing heartbeat. I look down at my torso and don't know how to digest what I'm seeing. My shirt is in tatters—or is that my skin hanging there? I can't tell one from the other with all the blood; everything is shiny and crimson. Except for a spot of white. A bone—that's a rib, bare of flesh.

The pressure, pain, and grief mount as if my chest is holding in a storm. I cough, sputtering red.

And more. And again.

I'm not healing at all. The broken pieces of me are too far gone.

My limbs won't move. The air around me thickens, becomes impossible to get into my lungs. I failed Hanna. How could I have made such a horrible miscalculation? She's gone now—truly gone. And I'm swiftly following after her. My mother—I'll see my mother now. I'll chase her in the sand, my steps too small to catch up, but I'll run faster, and she'll be up ahead, waiting for me patiently.

Somehow, with my last breath, I manage to call out to her.

TWENTY-SEVEN

Aidan

I open my eyes to a frozen world. I'm looking through glass, down at a crowd of people on a dance floor below me. People are caught in their movement like statues, as if someone hit the pause button. Then I shift my gaze and see it. My body, to my right. It's sitting on the carpet, leaning against the glass. My neck is limp, head tipped to the side. Blood smears my neck, my face . . . everything seems to be painted in red. It leaks from my lips, shimmers on my torn belly, and pools under me, creating a crimson mirror.

I look around for Eric, but somehow my spirit knows I'm not here to chat with anyone. I'm not here to be warned or instructed. This is nothing like that. I look up at the ceiling and realize the building has no roof. Above me is a huge expanse of the sky, scattered with more stars than I can ever remember seeing over the City of Angels. I watch them gleam as a blue-green light appears in a slow, steady bleed across the sky. Part of me wants to follow its path, to reach out and touch the light, feel its warmth.

But something tugs at me, holds me here, something at my feet.

My attention wanders back to my torn and broken body. And I remember I'm dead. Very. Dead.

But . . . this isn't how it was supposed to happen. I'm not destined to be killed by some demon in the club. After everything. How can it end here? It can't.

My cold, torn flesh seems to disagree.

I forget the sky and move closer to my mangled body. The air around me is like a living thing, pushing me back, pressing in on me from all sides. But I ignore its insistence, needing to understand.

"Who are you?" a soft, curious voice asks from behind me.

I turn and see a young woman standing on the other side of the couch. Her form is pale; I can almost make out the bookshelves on the opposite wall through her body. A ghost?

"I'm Aidan," I say, not sure why the sight of her isn't bothering me.

And then I realize where she's standing: the same place the body was, the body that the demon was eating. *Hanna*. Wasn't that Hanna?

I move around the couch and look down.

The young woman's gaze follows mine. "Who's that?" she asks.

It's not Hanna. The body isn't Hanna's. Relief fills me in a rush, but then realization quickly follows in a bitter wave as I look down on what remains of this other young woman, her brown hair tied in a bun, face untouched and perfect, while her work uniform is torn apart just like her body.

"That's you," I say numbly.

She blinks down at herself, then over at my dead body. "And that's you?" she asks, like a child might.

An emotion pricks inside of me for just a second: frustration. "It wasn't supposed to happen this way."

With a sigh, she says, "No."

"No," I echo. And then the anger trickles in, beginning to wash away the numbness. Slow at first, but soon a swell of it floods me. It's not just anger, though—it's more than that. It's as if my power is sparking back to life a little, stirring in my insides that I no longer own. My body calls me back.

You will touch death with fire and bring it into life once more the journal said. *You will touch death with fire and bring it into life once more. What you will awaken shall usher in the world's end. The Cycle of Darkness has begun.*

"No," I say again. "It wasn't supposed to happen like this. And we're not going to let it."

She gives me a look of surprise. "We're not?"

"What's your name?" I ask, letting my soul be led.

"Miranda," she says, but it's almost a question, like she's not sure.

"I need you to trust me, Miranda."

You will touch death with fire and bring it into life once more.

She nods slowly, her translucent form solidifying a little more. "All right."

What is death? What do I touch? My eyes travel to her ravaged body . . . *bring it into life once more.* I kneel beside the shell of what once was a woman: Miranda. Something stirs in me as I get closer, it moves through my bones like a whisper, and when I reach out I see the mark on my hand, dark against my ghostly skin. The mark moves over my arm. It curls and uncurls, over and over, and when I make contact with Miranda's dead body, my fingers grazing the blood-speckled skin, a part of the mark slides away, onto the lifeless arm, transferring from me to her.

"I can hear it," she says. "Someone's saying my name. Someone's calling me." She tips her head, listening. And then she flickers and disappears.

I turn and look down on her mangled body.

But it's not mangled anymore. And all the blood is gone. Her clothes are still torn and her skin is pale, but the gouges and tears are all healed. She's no longer a mutilated corpse, but she still appears to be a corpse.

Maybe it didn't really work? Not all the way. I look at my ghost arm and see that the line on my mark that went onto her skin is still missing.

And then I see where it went, onto her soul. It's wrapped around her bicep, just above her elbow, delicate and barely noticeable.

What does it mean? Did a part of my power go into her? And if it did, does that mean that I have less?

What am I thinking? It doesn't matter anymore. I'm dead.

I stand and walk back to my own body, feeling alone now in this silent world. I lift my eyes back to the stars overhead and wonder what the hell God's thinking. "Really?" I ask the blue-green light still flowing across the expansive sky. "What do you want from me, then? What's all this about?"

The light seems to brighten in answer. And then it moves closer, pulsing like a heartbeat. Closer. Closer. So large it fills my vision, blinding me. The heat of it begins to sting my skin, warmer and warmer. It fills every piece of me, overwhelming everything else. Until I'm branded by it, seared.

Sealed.

Then the heat seeps away, the light gone, and all I see is darkness.

Someone's saying my name far away, calling me in a frantic voice. I turn to see who it is, but I'm suddenly made of stone. My muscles protest and my chest burns. I can't breathe.

"Aidan!" a male voice says, worried. "Are you sure that's his name?"

"Yes—I mean, I think so." That voice is familiar, female. I heard it a long time ago, when I was dead.

The man speaks again, a deep, gravely voice. "I thought he was here to talk to Hanna. Where is she?"

"She got a phone call and stepped out the side door a few minutes ago. I was just waiting for her when . . . gosh, I don't remember."

I crack open my eyes. A hand grips my arm, the smell of relief and panic mingling in the room, creating a bittersweet cocktail of emotions.

"Hey!" the male voice says, giving my arm a shake. "What happened? Did you pass out, kid?"

"I told you we didn't need to call 911," the young woman says.

I open my lead eyelids wider, wide enough to see a blur of black suit and brown hair.

"How'd you both get your clothes all torn to pieces?" the man asks, sounding dubious. "Did you do that to each other?"

"No! Jeez, Frank! I think I'd remember that."

Frank comes into view first, his face hovering over mine. "Well, maybe you hit your head and don't remember." He's so close I notice a twisted scar just under his left eye.

"Don't be a dope." The woman comes into view next. I see that it's Miranda, the dead girl, holding her white uniform shirt closed with her fist. There's no blood on her at all. Not one drop.

I manage to move my head and look down at my own tattered torso. But there's no blood, no lacerations, no claw marks left from the wraith's attack earlier, not even the impossible hole from the demon's beak. There's nothing but thick white scars to prove that anything happened at all.

The only thing in tatters now is my blue T-shirt.

TWENTY-EIGHT

Aidan

Frank has asked me what feels like two hundred questions, and he still won't let me leave to find Rebecca and Connor. I barely hear him over the words thundering in my head.

Dead.

I was dead.

And where's Hanna? Miranda said she'd stepped out to take a call, but where did she go? I need to be sure she's okay.

Instead of Hanna, it was this woman, Miranda, who was dead. But now she's not. She's fine. Because I brought her back? My God, that's just . . . that's crazy. But . . . if it's true that I resurrected the Biblical prophet Daniel from bones and dust, if I could do that, it makes a crazy sort of sense that I could bring back someone who'd just been dead a few minutes.

The under-passages in Eric's journal still ring in my ears: *You will touch death with fire and bring it into life once more. What you will awaken shall usher in the world's end.*

I stare up at Miranda as Frank asks his questions. My mark is still there, on her arm, just like it was when I watched it slide its way from my soul onto hers. Clearly, though, she can't see it, and doesn't remember anything that happened. Thank God.

I look down at my own mark and see the piece is still missing. I can only assume I gave her some of my power in the resurrection. I'm not sure how to feel about that.

Frank finally lets me go, despite the fact that Miranda and I can't give any good answers. As I make my way to the car, I pull out my cell and I punch in Hanna's number. I listen to the rings, praying, "Please pick up. Be okay, please be—"

"Hello, Aidan? Are you here yet?"

I release the breath I was holding. "You're okay?"

She pauses. "Yes, why?"

"Where are you? I went up to your office and you weren't there."

"I'm fine, Aidan." She pauses again and I hear a male voice say something.

"Who is that you're talking to?" I ask.

"It's Eric."

"I need to speak to him," I say, a second wave of relief passing through me. He must've listened to me and reconnected with her. Which is crazy. But I'm so glad he did.

"He says he'll call you," she says. "Are you all right?"

No. "Yeah, I guess. Tell him I really need to talk." I decide not to push, to just take the win: Hanna's safe, she's with Eric, and I can ask my million questions when I don't feel like I've been torn to bloody bits and then taped back together. Which I guess I sort of was.

————

"What took you so long?" Connor asks when I slide into the backseat of the Camaro.

Rebecca turns around in her seat, her eyes squinting to focus on me. "What happened? What's wrong?"

"Nothing," I mutter. I stole someone's shirt from the break room, so it's not like she's looking at my tattered one. Second shirt ruined in two days.

"I know there's something," she says. "You're . . . different."

I sigh, really not aware enough to explain. "Listen, I'm still processing. I'm all right, though, okay?"

She seems to be considering whether or not to push more. "Okay," she says, quietly.

Connor starts the car and heads out onto the main road.

After we drive for a while in silence, it comes back at me in a burst of memory. "Hunger!" I say the name louder than I'd meant it to. How could I have almost forgotten?

Rebecca looks at me and asks with a frown, "You're hungry?"

I grip my retrieved amulet in my fist. I'm relieved to see she's wearing hers, too. "Hunger, the demon. The one that was after you before. It may be back."

Rebecca leans away from me, like she's trying to get away from my words. "I thought you killed it."

"No, my sister exiled it, or I thought she did. The day Lester hurt you—I watched the demon go."

"Why do you think it's back?" Connor asks, glancing over to Rebecca.

I shake my head and find myself at a loss for words again. So instead of explaining, I opt to stay focused on what the demon's return means for Rebecca. "If you keep your amulet on and I keep mine, it won't be able to find us."

If Hunger is back, it's a complication, but as long as the beast focuses on me, then it'll be fine. All I'll need to do is sneak up on it with a nice sharp blade . . .

Just thinking about gutting the thing thrills me. I would so love to get my hands on the beast that killed Rebecca's brother. And at the moment, I feel like I have nothing to lose.

I died. I was dead. Again.

My throat stings at the memory of it all, the visceral echo of the agony from the claws tearing open my stomach, from the demon's beak stabbing through my chest. A strange helplessness fills me as I realize . . . I'm stuck. Not even being ripped to shreds by a demon can save me from this path I'm on. Not even a horrifying death can help me find an escape. For some reason, I'm trapped here, in the madness that my existence created. I'm caged in the flesh, unable to stop what's coming . . . *The Cycle of Darkness has now begun.*

TWENTY-NINE

Aidan

I head upstairs to my bedroom, exhaustion and confusion a lead blanket on my shoulders. I need sleep. A lot of it.

But I find myself pushing open Kara's door instead of my own.

Her blinds are closed, keeping the streetlights out. I hear her steady breathing, see the shape of her body on the bed. I want to climb into the sheets beside her, even if it's not right. She's the only one who can quiet this storm inside of me. She's the only one who makes me feel like I have a choice in all this mess. It's selfish as hell but I need her.

So I close the door behind me and sit down on the wood floor, leaning against the wall beside her bed. The darkness coats me and I close my eyes, listening to her sleep, trying to feel for her energy.

After a few minutes her body shifts and I hear the sound of sliding sheets. "Aidan?"

"Sorry," I say. "I'll leave in a minute. Just sleep."

"What's wrong?" She sits up and climbs out of bed, coming to stand over me. "Are you okay?"

The soft tone of her voice, the concern in it, breaks my resolve to not burden her with any of it tonight. "I don't know," I whisper.

She kneels in front of me and reaches over to turn on the lamp beside the bed. The soft light reveals her worried expression. "What happened?"

I have to say it. I have to make it real. "I died."

The air goes still with fear. "What?" she breathes.

"A demon, it . . ." I shake my head, not able to find the words for the memory, "but I came back."

She looks me over, her eyes wide and full of emotions. "Where?"

"What?"

"Where were you hurt? I don't see any new cuts or anything."

I pull my shirt over my head and set it on the floor. Then I shift so the light shines on my side where the demon's claw dug the deepest.

"Oh, Aidan—" Her hand covers her mouth, tears glistening in her eyes.

"They're just scars."

She nods, a tear sliding down her cheek.

"I'm fine, Kara." I feel the need to say it out loud even though it's not really true. "I'm okay."

"Your poor body," she says, touching my healed wounds, her fingers gentle. "The scars are so big. There are so many of them . . . What kind of demon did this?"

"A corporeal one. Midlevel. Huge."

"My God." She comes closer, her side leaning on mine as she touches her lips to my shoulder, warming my chilled skin.

I soak in her touch as she traces her fingers over my hair. "There's no blood."

"I woke up and it was all just . . . gone." My voice sounds casual, but when the memory of talons and tearing flesh flashes, the stark violence of the event jars me again and I shiver.

She moves around to study my face, my neck, my arms, like she's searching for more scars. Her face is so lovely, so real, her scent like honey and warmth. She's only in a tank top and under-wear, so much of her skin ready to touch mine, ready to heal my heart, my soul.

I reach out and slide my fingers up her leg to her hip. "I need you, Kara," I whisper, like a confession. As much as I don't under-stand my life, my world right now . . . this, Kara and me, when we're together, I get it.

She answers with her own touch, running her palm up my arm, then trailing her fingers over my clavicle. "I'm sorry," she says. "I'm sorry that things are so mixed up right now. I should've told you what I've been dealing with right away, but I was scared that—"

I stop her repentance with my lips.

She releases a small sound of surprise as I let her feel my greed. But then she's surrendering, pressing into me.

So I take more, pulling her closer, dragging her onto my lap. She wraps herself around me and I grip her hips. I trace the curve of her waist, kissing her until my death doesn't matter, nothing does—not even breathing—if she's not with me. I'm completely lost in the sensations of her, her smell, her sounds, and I know she's following me into the chaos, into the swirl of need and hunger and desperation.

She holds on to me like a raft in a storm. I close my eyes and taste my fear on her lips. I feel my pain in her skin as she pulls it from me, as she seals my inner wounds with her hands, sliding them over my face, down my chest and scarred sides. I think about her blue light, how it poured into me, wondering if this is how she felt, released, unburdened. Or if I was actually hurting her, stealing something from her, taking parts of her I wasn't meant to have.

The chill of her sweet energy weaves over us as she envelops me. And I know that if I open my eyes right now, I would see it, twisting around our bodies. But I don't open my eyes, I don't let myself think about what we're doing, what it could mean, or how I shouldn't let this happen before I understand everything.

I don't care. I only need. I bury the worries, the reality of what I don't know.

I pull her down to the rug, clutching her to me as the barriers fall, as we shed our clothes, shed our inhibitions. My mind tells me to slow down, my heart tells me not to hurt her, and I ready myself to pull away before she shrinks back in fear.

But she doesn't waver. She kisses my scarred skin. She tells me she needs me. And nothing in her hesitates. Her breath, her flush of desperation echoes her words, like a voice far off, calling out for me to save her.

So I stare over the edge and let myself fall.

———

I watch the wave curl and crash in a white rush. It sprays salt and sand outward, then slides its way up the beach, closer and closer, until it touches my toes and wraps around my ankles, rising to my thighs in a surge. The chill of the water stings at my legs; the sand under my feet shifts as the tide stops and begins its return to the sea. My jeans stick to my skin. The salt tingles in my nostrils.

But the water doesn't return. I stand, damp and cold, watching the fog, waiting for the ocean to rise again. To come back to me. Same as before. Over and over. The rhythm of back and forth, the song of always.

Instead, the beats of my heart count the time, and nothing happens.

Until the fog shifts, gathering, forming into something. Someone. The smell of brine turning into the scent of death, becoming rot and ruin and flesh decaying into earth.

And there. The fog becomes a living thing. Becomes my sin.

Lester.

He stands where the waves should be. A white form of the boy he once was. Only a memory now.

He lifts a smoky arm and points to something behind me. His mouth opens in a silent scream that vibrates the ground beneath my feet. But I feel the meaning, the message, as I turn to look, knees shaking. I see the cave opening. See it growing, wider and wider, until the darkness of it becomes everything, swallowing my whole world.

A skull rolls from the cave, coming to stop beside my foot. And then another and another, until they're spilling from the opening like a river of death.

"Look what you've done!" he screams over the clacking of bone. "Look what you've done!"

THIRTY

Rebecca

There's no way to process or understand it all. There just isn't. Does that man—Aidan's father—really know my future? And now Aidan says that demon from before is somewhere close again. What did he call the thing? Hunger? Shivers roll over me and I hug my legs to my chest, snuggling deeper into my blankets.

I'm lying here, watching Connor sleep sitting up, as I try to sort everything out in my mind. But order isn't exactly happening. Nothing's going into its proper place. Nothing fits. My head aches from trying. There's been a strange pain behind my eyes since Aidan's father touched my forehead with oil, and it just keeps getting more horrible the longer I lie here, thinking about everything. I consider taking one of the little blue pills that the psychiatrist prescribed for my "depression" and "anxiety," but I hate how they make me feel. Or not feel, I should say.

I just need food. Or a run. I need something.

Holly was up a while ago, off to summer school, so I can't convince her to distract me. She wasn't happy about our intruder, Connor, but I convinced her to leave him in his awkward position and let him sleep. Of course, Connor would probably prefer his bed to the way he's "sleeping" right now, on Holly's Hello Kitty desk chair with his feet propped up on the foot of my bed. He's being a horrible watchdog, in this state.

And I'm sick of lying here, thinking the same things over and over.

"Hey." I sit up and tap his foot. He has really long toes.

He grunts, annoyed.

"Take me somewhere."

His eyes open halfway and he gives me a *what is wrong with you?* look.

"Don't you have class today?" he asks. "At some rich-kid music academy?"

"There's no way I can pretend I'm normal after last night."

He just looks at me like he's not sure what to do with me.

"I know. I'm a hilarious mess. Can you please take me out? If not now, later, after you get some sleep? Maybe to the mall or something?"

He rolls his eyes.

"Or the beach, maybe?"

He tilts his head like he might actually be considering that request.

"Yes!" I say, feeling like I hit the right note. "You can surf. We both can!"

His eyes widen. "You surf?"

"Don't look so shocked, Bodyguard. I'm a CaliGirl."

He's still looking at me like he's not buying it.

"Okay, fine, I surf a *little*."

"Enough to kill yourself, probably."

"You can teach me, then. Charlie was—" I stop, my throat clogging up. I try to force it all deep down again, shaking myself back into focus. "I mean, I just need a refresher."

He's studying me like he does, with those honest eyes. "Okay, we can go for a little while. But I have to be back this afternoon to check on a job."

I smile in victory, feeling thrilled to be doing something totally normal and familiar in the midst of all the crazy.

"You shower. And I'll find a bathing suit in Holly's closet."

"Calm down, CaliGirl," he says, trying to hide a smile as he stands up, stretching. "It's just some saltwater and sand." He's even taller as he reaches up like a cat in the sun. I try not to notice the small strip of flesh that shows at his belly.

I move to Holly's closet in case I blush. "I can get ready quick, so don't be a diva in the shower."

"I'm getting in the ocean. I don't need a shower."

I turn back to him, giving him a look that says I disagree. "After being at the club last night? Aren't you feeling sticky?"

He shrugs.

"Well, I'm showering." I turn back to the closet, opening a drawer to start my search. "Last night was just too . . . ick." Between sweating on the dance floor, then having my head anointed by some mysterious Aidan-double, I feel like I'll need to turn inside out to get clean.

"There's a drought, you know. It's polite to try saving water."

I spot polka dots and pull a bikini top from a tangle of underwear. "It's also polite not to smell like a dead rat." I hold up the top and wave it at him. "Now leave so I can do girl things."

Connor's gaze averts and he looks uncomfortable. He slips on his flip-flops, mumbling, "Right," before turning to leave the room. "I'll load up the Jeep."

THIRTY-ONE

Aidan

I wake in a rush, my skin chilled and damp, as if I really was standing in the tide a moment ago, like it wasn't a dream.

Lester . . . the sight of him like that, tortured, lost . . . It makes everything in me shake. The vision replays over and over in my mind.

Look what you've done!

It echoes, making the brands on my soul burn. Memories circle me like a beast ready to devour me again. My dagger sliding into Lester's neck, my palms coated in his blood. Ava's blood on my hands as I pull the blade from her tiny chest. My mother's blood, a dark shadow spreading over my life. So much blood. So many things gone wrong.

I turn over and look at Kara, making sure last night wasn't a dream. The bad memories begin to fade as I study her.

She's facing away from me, the curves of her body outlined by the sheet. Perfection I can hold in my hands. I want to touch her but I don't want to wake her. There are too many emotions inside me right now. Wonder and remorse, amazement and guilt; it's all jumbled, thinking of what we did.

What I want to do again.

What we never should've done in the first place.

Afterward, there was a moment when I thought she was going to cry, but she just clung to me and kissed me, and all I could do was hold her in amazement. The terrified girl I kissed that night a month ago seemed to have disappeared entirely. She was all warmth and hunger beside me in the darkness. The only sorrow and pain in that bed was my own. I don't know why or how, but this time it was Kara comforting me. Her heart seemed unburdened, even as I handed her my own troubles, telling her what had happened, every detail I've been obsessing over, everything that's taken me captive. I even told her about the way her energy spilled into my chest. She listened and kissed me and told me not to worry, that things aren't always what they seem.

She kissed me until I was falling into her all over again. This time I tried not to rush, I wanted to make each touch count, each breath mean something, until I drifted off to sleep, entwined in her arms. And as I sank into dreams, I released the weight of my past that I've held tight. The need to hide myself faded a little more.

That was last night. And it was amazing. But now the sun is rising and I'm opening my eyes to the stark reality of what I've done. How I've made a promise, even if I didn't mean to. I've claimed Kara for myself now, in more ways than spiritual ones. And she's claimed me.

We've challenged Fate again.

But I want the weight of our choice not to matter. I want to press forward with her, be with her. Again and again. And yet, I know that can't happen. Not until we figure out what's going on with her—what's going on with both of us.

I shift closer, touching her shoulder, my chest tightening as I realize I've surrendered my heart to her, more than she'll ever know. My lips follow my fingers along her skin, and I try to think of how to show her what I'm feeling, *really* show her.

She sighs and scoots back against me. I brush her hair from her neck, kissing the small birthmark at her nape. "Kara," I whisper, reaching around to slide my palm over her belly and hug her against me. "Are you awake?"

She sighs again and then her breath catches as her body jerks, like she's in pain.

I back away a little. "What's wrong?"

She rolls over. Blood leaks from the corner of her eye to stain the pillow.

All the air leaves my lungs.

Another drop spills from her ear.

"My head," she says, her words muddy. "It's . . ." She lifts her hand to her temple. "God, it's pounding."

I stare in disbelief and horror; it's happening again.

"Ah, God . . ." She hisses air through her teeth, and both hands go to her head. Pain creases her features, pinches her mouth. And more blood leaks from her ear.

"Kara," I reach out, not knowing what to do.

I grip her shoulder as she shivers and presses into my chest with a whimper. "It hurts."

Dread rises up and beats at the inside of my chest. I press my palm into her back, my mind spinning, horrifying thoughts roiling inside me. How could I . . . how could I have let my guard down for even a second?

After a few torturous moments of her trembling against me, her skin chills under my touch and she begins to still.

And then she goes totally limp in my arms.

My heart stops. I shift back, trying to see her face. It physically hurts to look at her; the blood spilling onto her cheeks from her eyes; her slack mouth. But I can feel her pulse in her neck.

Don't you dare leave me, Kara.

I settle her into the bed before running to get Sid.

———

She's still passed out when Sid and I get back to the room. I have some myrrh oil in my pocket; I'm hoping it'll help her spirit feel safe. Holly comes in with a rag to wash Kara's face. Jax just leans on the doorjamb, looking more serious than I've ever seen him.

I consider calling Connor, who's apparently off surfing, but decide to wait and see what happens. There's nothing he can do. Last time, she woke up fine. And if he's with Rebecca, having a simple day . . . those are so few and far between for all of us. After what went down last night, I can give him a few more hours to be normal and blissfully unaware.

"What happened?" Sid asks, frowning at Kara's naked shoulders. The sheet covers her body, but he's probably aware that's all she has covering her right now.

Holly glares at him like he's thick in the head. "You know what happened, Sid."

He glances over at me, studying my bare chest—I only put on pants before running to get him, but not a shirt—then he locks eyes with me. I look at the floor like a coward.

"So you had sex," he says, sounding miserable. "I assumed that wasn't going to happen."

"They're not monks," Holly says, beginning to clean Kara's ears and hair of blood.

He nods like he's conceding his foolishness. "Yes." He sighs deeply and pulls an amulet from his pocket. He places it on Kara's forehead and then leans over, kissing it, muttering something quietly, like he's saying good-bye.

My chest aches, watching, wishing I could act, wishing there was something I could do.

Sid stands and clears his throat like he's swallowing sorrow.

"What's happening?" I ask. "Is it because of the curse, the counter spell, or the whole Rebecca thing—what?"

"I'm afraid that it's everything." His eyes are heavy with emotion. "And it is you."

I stare at him, unable to breathe. "Me." I did this? I hurt her? Oh, God . . .

"Yes, I just was hoping . . ." He pulls me away from the bed, turning me toward the window. "If what my reading has led me to is correct, then she can't withstand what your powers are doing to her. And, as we now know, she wasn't meant to."

"How—" My voice cracks. "How are you sure it's my power? How do you know?"

"The scrolls Hanna gave you, the ones I used years ago for the spell, they had warnings. Most didn't apply and others seemed far-reaching. I read them in the beginning, considered them, but believed none would manifest if you both followed the path with a pure heart."

Pure. I am in no way pure at this point. If I ever was to begin with. "What were the warnings?"

"The spell I did on Kara had two parts. One would reverse the curse her father placed on her, the second would allow for her to be a vessel to attract you and specifically harvest your power so that it could be awakened. In its simplest form, it would mimic what some would call a soul mate. Normally, this kind of spell wouldn't affect either party in any way other than to allow them to feel closely linked. Once she awoke your power, the secondary spell should have fallen away, or at least deadened."

And if that second part of the spell had faded, it would explain why my physical connection to Kara hasn't been as strong. "That's happened already," I say.

"Yes." He looks over to Kara. Her skin is so pale. Holly is taking the bloody pillow out from under her, and she doesn't even stir.

Sid rubs his bald head, looking miserable. "I was a fool. I should've told you as soon as I realized that your power might be healing her soul, and at the same time undoing the spell I placed on her, reversing it, and bringing back the curse. I just didn't think this," he motions to my bare chest, "was a possibility right now because of her past."

"I don't understand. Her bleeding this time is because we . . ." I don't know why, but I can't say it. Had sex. I had sex with Kara.

"No," he says, like he's trying to reassure me. "It would've happened eventually anyway, the more time you spent with her. But this could have sped the process up, made things worse. Since the Awakening, your power is more than she can handle, and as it heals her soul, it's also killing her flesh."

Realization fills me and dread quickly follows. I needed her. I needed her last night and I took what I needed, damn the consequences. This is all completely my fault. I did this to her. I should've known this was a possibility after the first time she had the blood-show. I should've known I needed to slow down. God, I'm a fool.

"We need to take a step back and reevaluate things," Sid says. "You need to consider whether you should pull away completely. Perhaps attempt to pair with Rebecca instead. Maybe that would heal some of this. Since she's the one you're supposed to be with, there may—"

I push off the edge of the window. "No. Don't even go there. That's not happening."

"You can't be with Kara anymore, Aidan. Look at her."

I do, and my chest constricts with agony. How could I let this happen? "I can't let her go, Sid. I just can't. She's a part of me now. I wouldn't even know how to take it back if I could."

"I know, son. I see that you care about her deeply." He releases a long sigh. "We'll try to make it right. But if it's not possible . . . you may need to prepare yourself to let go. Otherwise you could lose her forever."

THIRTY-TWO

Rebecca

There are a hundred reasons for me to be panicked or overwhelmed by confusion right now, but as Connor leads me out into the waves, both of us dolled up in wetsuits, I'm completely at ease. He has this way about him. Like even when everything's chaotic, he's solid in the storm.

And he looks amazing in a wetsuit.

I, however, am wearing Jax's old suit, and while the kid's body is a straight stick, mine is definitely not. Moving and breathing in this thing is a challenge.

Connor brought his longboard for me to ride, a yellow-and-black number with a wave decal on the nose. It's so bright I could find it in a hurricane; nine feet long, but thinner and lightweight for the length. I'm pretty sure I'll be able to stand up on this monster of a thing. If this wetsuit doesn't strangle me to death before I get past the break, that is.

The water is a warm sixty-eight degrees and the swell is a clean three-to-five feet. There's no wind. No clouds. You can see the islands out there like dark sea monsters on the horizon. Then it's blue all the way to Hawaii. A perfect day.

I sense Charlie in the briny smell of the water, the taste of salt in the air . . . He's so close it's like I could turn and see him coming up behind us, his crown of auburn hair dampened to dark copper, a smirk tipping his mouth because he just told a joke about my freckles eating me if I don't get my lily face out of the sun. Then he'd pass me with that blue Maverick board under his arm and slide into the waves like they were where he was born.

Instead of where he died.

"Hey." Connor kicks water onto my board to get my attention.

I blink away the past and squint at him through the sunlight bouncing off the water.

"You good to go?" he asks.

I nod. My leash is on my ankle, the massive board is under my arm. Sort of. And I'm dying to wash away the madness of my life in the Pacific.

"Okay." He eyes me warily, then directs me to look to the right, where the shore curves out and becomes a rocky cliff. "We'll paddle straight out from here, but the break—that's the place we'll want to catch a wave—is over there. So we'll just paddle parallel to the shore once we get outside—see the part that's past the waves where that guy is bobbing—"

"Yes. I know where the outside is," I interrupt, feeling like he must think I'm from Kansas or something. "And I know what a break is. What a duck dive is. A left, a right, or a barrel. So you can save me the lingo lesson. I've been out here my whole life."

He just stares at me, his mouth open a little.

"What I need is practice," I say. Then I add, "Please," to soften the sass.

"Okay." He gives me a short nod, looking me over again, like he's seeing me for the first time. "Just wave if you need me."

"Perfect." I give him a curt smile and then start walking farther out into the waves, wondering if it was smart to paint myself as some kind of North Shore ripper, when I'm really just a beach bunny who listens to cute surfers talk about themselves a lot.

He pats my shoulder like a chum and takes off, running past me, through the break until the water is mid-thigh. Then he's leaping forward to slide his short, swift board into the waves. He goes over them, one, two, three, then dives under the next few, until he's past the break, outside, all in what felt like a minute.

As I get deeper—and as the waves begin knocking me over—I realize that this board is freaking ginormous. It wouldn't be so bad if the swell was half this size, or the ground under my feet wasn't suddenly becoming rocky, cutting into my soles. I drop the board and push it with my hand, guiding it over the waves. I'll get this thing outside the break if it kills me.

Determination fills me and I finally start swimming, towing the massive board behind me. The waves yank me back again and again, but eventually I triumph over the current's insistence and make it to the calmer water. As I get myself positioned on the board and begin to paddle, Connor glides up beside me.

"You made it," he says, like he wasn't sure I would.

My bluster is long gone and he knows it. When the ocean kicks your butt, you have no choice but to be humbled. "Okay, so it's been a while."

He just laughs and paddles beside me as we make our way to a good spot. I know he could go a lot faster but he's being nice.

When we get to the break, he settles in, sitting up on his board.

This is the part I was always best at, the waiting. I slide up, straddling my board, balancing easily.

Connor watches me for a second, his gaze searching, like he's trying to figure me out. But then he seems to give up without a word, looking out to the break. He strikes his usual pose, crossing his arms over his chest and hunching, as he watches the distant swell like a psychic reading the future. I study his profile, the strong cut of his jaw, his regal brow, and I wonder again who this guy is. And why he's sitting here with me.

But soon the sun warms me to the bone and I'm too relaxed to care. My legs swish back and forth in the cool water as I watch the kelp float by. The rocking of the swells and the sound of the crashing waves on the shore behind us lull me into a state of perfect peace.

"Last night," Connor says. "I'm sorry I was a jerk."

He's apologizing about last night in the club? I release a small breath of laughter.

"I know I can be . . . unfun," he adds.

I can't help smiling. "You mean uptight?"

His features relax into a comfortable smirk when he sees I'm not upset. "Something like that."

"Thanks for bringing me here."

He nods.

"You might not be too horrible," I add.

His smirk turns a little more deadly. "You too, Surfer Girl." And then he slides down to his belly again, paddling away, toward an approaching swell in a graceful glide over the water.

———

We set our boards in the back of the Jeep, and I contemplate my saltiness. Connor pulls out two gallons of water, hands me one, and motions for me to dump it on my head. As he rolls his wetsuit down to his waist and begins washing himself off, I realize we haven't spoken two words to each other since getting out of the water. He's just comfortable being quiet and it's nice.

"Thanks," I say. "For distracting me for a while."

He lowers the half-empty gallon to look at me, hair slicked to his forehead, water dripping down his face and chest.

"Sure." He sets the jug down and picks up a towel, doing a rough dry of his short hair. "You still have that look on your face, though."

I frown. "What look?"

"The one that you've had since yesterday. Pinched." He imitates a furrowed brow and a tight mouth.

I sigh and begin peeling off my wetsuit to the waist. "Well, it's how I feel, so that makes sense. Pinched in the fingers of life, like a trapped bug."

"Yeah, I get it." He wraps the towel around his waist and begins pulling the wetsuit down his legs.

I have to turn my gaze away, trying to pretend I don't feel totally awkward, knowing he's naked as a jaybird under there. When we got suited up earlier, I was too busy squeezing myself into my own straitjacket to notice him changing. Now I'm standing three feet away, facing him.

He pulls on his shorts under the towel, seemingly oblivious to my embarrassment. "I like your tattoo," he says, setting the towel aside. He motions to my body.

I look down and realize he means my monarch, on my ribcage. "Oh, yeah. I got it after my brother, um, died." God, I can't even say it and it's been almost a year.

He stands up straighter. "Your brother?"

My throat tightens, but I want to answer. I want to talk about him. Especially here, in his sacred place. My dad never will; he always changes the subject when I bring him up. It's like Charlie was never a part of us and it just feels wrong. "Yeah. He's the one who taught me to surf. Well, sort of." I laugh past my sadness, remembering how he used to tow me out and then tease me about seeing sharks as he showed off for the girls on the beach. Not much learning, but a lot of laughter.

"I'm sorry."

Everyone always says that. "Yeah." But I know there's nothing else to say. Words don't help. "He was a total beach bum, always ditching school to surf. My dad was livid because Charlie had totally blown off college applications and he missed his window for Stanford prelaw. Charlie would've never gone anyway. No matter how much money Dad threw at him. He was determined to stay free." I look out at the water. "And I guess he is."

"It's nice that you guys were close." There's a longing in his voice that makes me curious.

"I think every little girl needs a big brother," I say. "Mine was the best, though."

A smile forms on Connor's face, but it doesn't reach his eyes.

My curiosity grows, so I dare to ask, "What's your family like?"

The fake smile vanishes.

I hurry to add, "Sorry, you don't have to answer that."

He looks away, to the passing cars on the highway. He stands there for so long I'm not sure what to do, and I can't tell if he's mad or sad or something else, because I can't see his face.

I clear my throat, feeling totally lame for blowing the good mood, and then I figure it's best to just move on. So I peel the wetsuit the rest of the way down my legs, leaving myself in only the bikini I borrowed from Holly, skin covered in goose bumps. I dump the gallon of water on my head, sighing as the sun-warmed contents of it soothe my chilled skin. Then I towel off, put my yellow sundress on, and slip into my white sandals.

Now Connor is looking past me at the waves like he wishes he were out there again.

"So . . ." I say, because the silence is becoming strange, "time to head back." I comb my fingers through my hair, attempting to untangle it as I watch him stare.

He nods but doesn't move. "I wish I'd never known them, you know?"

His confession startles me, even though I don't exactly know what he means. "Who?"

"My parents."

"Oh."

"They were addicts. Nothing about them was good."

"I'm sorry," I say, returning the useless words.

"Nothing about me was good, either, though. Not until recently."

I frown, unable to see him as anything but steady Connor.

He turns to me, his features hard. "I hated them for a long time. Sometimes I still do. For what they put themselves through and what they put me through. I was just in their way. And I was the jerk kid who thought his parents gave a fuck. I didn't even realize how much they hated me until I woke up in a gutter one morning after they'd dumped me there." He watches me so intently, and when my eyes widen in question, he adds, "I'd passed out from drugs *they* had given me—drugs they'd given me more than once to be sure I left them alone to do their partying. I was twelve."

I move closer, not able to stop myself.

He steps back but then settles, like he didn't mean to. "I don't know what a real family is. Sid and Kara, everyone in the house, they're my family now." And then he says, quietly, "And you, I guess, if you want."

He's staring right into me with those honest eyes.

"Me?"

He gives me a sad smile. "Every girl needs an older brother."

Warmth fills my chest, replacing the ache of hearing his painful confession. "Yes. They do."

He just keeps looking at me, studying my face as I study him. Something passes over his features and he starts to reach out, almost like he's going to touch me.

But then his features harden again and the moment's gone.

THIRTY-THREE

Rebecca

The house is silent when Connor and I get back. Finger's not even in the living room playing Xbox.

"I need a shower," I say as we come to the bottom of the stairs. "A bottle pour isn't gonna cut it."

"Arrowhead would be insulted," Connor says with a smile in his voice.

I grin back. "Thanks for today."

"Anytime," he says, his voice soft.

We both stand there, staring at each other, and I want to say something so the connection between us won't end. But before I can speak, Jax comes out of the office, making a beeline for Connor.

"Man, thank God you're home. Things went south with Kara." He looks genuinely worried.

"What is it?" Connor asks, suddenly focused and tense again.

Jax glances at me, like he's not sure he should say anything with me around.

"Rebecca's fine," Connor says. "Spit it out."

"It's the bleeding. She and Aidan had a conjugal and now she's not waking up. Her eyes, nose, everything, man, all leaking blood."

Oh, God. "Kara?" I ask. "She's bleeding from her *eyes*?" Wait, did he just say *conjugal*?

That means Aidan and Kara . . . oh. Oh, wow. I did *not* want to know that.

"She's bad," Jax says. And my heart breaks because Jax—Jax of all people—sounds like he's in pain, too. "Sid isn't sure—"

Connor doesn't wait for the rest, he just bolts around the bannister, past me, and takes the stairs two at a time. I follow, coming up behind him as he crashes into Kara's room.

Aidan's sitting cross-legged at the end of the bed, near Kara's feet, head in his hands. He looks up when Connor enters in a rush.

I stumble and have to grab the doorway to steady myself. The emotions roiling around Aidan are seething and desperate. Almost violent. I whisper his name under my breath in my shock. He was so raw and lost last night, after whatever happened at the club. And now the tension in him feels like a band ready to snap and destroy the whole world.

"What happened?" Connor asks.

Aidan just shakes his head.

"She'll wake up," Connor says, like he's trying to convince himself as much as Aidan. "She did last time."

Aidan rests his head in his hands again. Beside the bed there's a stack of books and rolls of paper that look like ancient scrolls from a movie.

There's a chair off to the side. Connor slides it closer to the bed and sits in it. I can only stand in the doorway, holding on to the wall. My insides stir with a million emotions as I watch Aidan, his hunched shoulders, his fingers gripping his hair.

He lifts his gaze to look at Kara, his misery stinging my skin. "I'm hurting her. Somehow. Because of my powers." His voice is shaking. "We get close and it somehow changes her, makes her sick."

Oh my God, that's just . . . horrifying. "And you didn't know?" I ask.

"It happened once before," Connor says.

"But it didn't seem linked to anything," Aidan says, like he's trying to find a way to lighten the weight of it all.

"You'd never hurt her on purpose," I say.

He looks up at me. "But I did. I hurt her."

"We'll figure it out." I move into the room and stand beside the bed. "There's a way to fix this and we'll figure it out."

I can barely believe I'm saying it. I know that he should've been with me, that he should've been mine, and that's what I wanted more than anything else. But it's not what I want now. Now, more than anything, I want Aidan to be complete and whole. I want him to keep feeling the love he has for Kara, the love I can sense so big in the room it hurts. Because it's pure and good and right. And I'm not about to be the bitch who ruins it.

THIRTY-FOUR

Aidan

I sit in a chair at Kara's bedside and watch for signs of her waking as I pore over several stacks of books and piles of scrolls. She hasn't moved. Not once. I keep checking her pulse, because the longer I look at her, the more I panic, thinking she's on the verge of leaving me.

It's been five or six hours since she fell asleep. Dusk is filling the summer sky. I've read over most of the books, the marked passages Sid's been poking around in for months now. The scrolls took a little more effort, since I had to piece together passages that have worn away over time.

Sid was right, according to every warning pertaining to the spell he put on Kara, something—obviously me—is making that spell slip. But if it slips enough that the curse her father put on her returns . . . what will that mean? That curse almost destroyed her before Sid saved her from it. And now something in me is reversing all of those protections.

Something in me is killing her.

There has to be a way to fix it.

Night falls and darkness fills the room. Eventually the house goes silent. No one comes in to check on me, no one knocks. It's like they know I don't want to talk.

I find myself drifting off, barely noticing when the book I was staring at slides from my hands, hitting the floor. But as my mind gives up and my body sinks into sleep, a fleeting image of the beach cave comes to me, reminding me of my sister and what I owe to her as well, what I owe to so many who sacrificed, thinking they would save me. And just as I'm muttering out a prayer for protection over Kara, over Ava, over everyone I care about, darkness takes me into a dream where I can be numb to it all.

———

The sound of water crashes behind me, followed by the repeated clack, clack, clack *of smaller rocks tumbling in the tide as it retreats. A damp breeze comes up, chilling me, sticking the smell of salt and ocean to my skin.*

Kara stands only a few feet away from the entrance of the cave, facing me. She's wearing underwear and a thin tank top again. Her legs and arms are covered in goose bumps. Her bare toes curl in the moist sand.

Even in the dark, her face is so full of light, so lovely, her skin bright porcelain against the backdrop of the silver-black shadow of the cave.

A knowing smile tilts her lips, highlighting the dimple in her left cheek. The blue of her eyes brightens as she casually brushes the hair from her shoulder.

She's so close. My body needs to go to her, to feel her in my hands. But I can't touch her. I'm not supposed to.

Her head tilts, and she motions for me to come closer, her smile growing.

I push back at the voice inside of me that tells me no, and I step forward. She bites the side of her bottom lip and reaches out to touch me as I approach.

But then her face changes. Her smile fades and her hand goes to her neck. Her features twist. Pain marks lines in her brow, and a choking sound leaves her throat.

Something sharp and silver glints in her chest.

In horror, I watch a red blossom grow around it until it becomes a deep crimson shimmer, spilling over her breasts, coating her belly, then sliding in thin lines down her thighs.

She stares at me, eyes terrified, mouth open in a silent scream as the blade tip disappears into her sternum.

And then she crumples to the sand.

Ava stands behind her, a stark white form against the cave entrance. Her silver hair swirls in the wind, curling around her like it's alive. She's holding a dagger. Blood runs from the blade onto her fist in a thick glistening coat, drip, drip, dripping into Kara's pool of black hair.

The sand at her feet soaks up the life, then seems to take on the shape of skulls, so many of them, bleached white from the sun. The ground crunches as Ava steps forward, bone grinding against bone. She stares at me, anger turning down her mouth and narrowing her eyes.

"Look what you've done," she says, through her teeth. "Look what you've done."

———

Something touches my head and my heavy lids open. I squint at a pale face and dark hair hovering in front of me. A smile grows across the face and a dimple appears.

"Kara!" I croak out, grabbing her, pulling her to me. "Oh my God." She settles on my lap as I hug her. Every cell in my body sighs with relief. She's awake. She's alive.

"Ugh, you're killing me," she grunts as I squeeze her. "My eyeballs are gonna pop out."

Her words bring back the possibility of the horrors ahead; they bring back the dream, the vision of Ava's hands coated in Kara's blood. I loosen my grip but I don't let go.

She kisses my forehead. "How long have you been sitting here in this pile of books?"

"I don't know." Feels like forever. And I still don't have any answers. None that I want.

But she's okay. I squeeze her arm to remind my skin she's really here.

"So, it happened again, didn't it?" She sounds like she's preparing for the worst. She moves from my lap to the bed and my hands feel empty. "The last thing I remember is that rager of a headache."

Before I say anything, she sees my fear and lays back on the bed, pressing her palms into her forehead. "Shit. What now?"

Misery bites hard into my chest. I whisper, "I'm hurting you."

Her arms fall to her sides and she stares at the ceiling. "Are you sure?"

"Yeah." I need it not to be true, but it is.

She sits up and looks at me. She doesn't seem surprised.

"Did you know this could happen?" I ask, a chill working over me.

She looks down at her hands.

"Kara." I lean forward in the chair. "Please tell me you didn't know this might happen."

She shakes her head. "I'm yours, that should've protected me."

"What are you saying?"

"I mean, I'm not a Light, so your power might affect me differently, but I thought since I was yours, in your heart—if I kept being yours—it wouldn't matter."

"Wait, Sid said this blood stuff was happening because of your curse and because I'm not your soul mate, or whatever."

"That's true," she says, sounding like she's trying to defend him, in case I think he's lying to me or something.

"Kara. We had sex. How could you not tell me that you thought I was making you sick?"

She shakes her head and scoots to the edge of the bed, leaning forward and gripping my knees. "No, Aidan, it's not like that. I still don't buy that this is bad."

"You were bleeding from your eyes!"

She looks at me with a small, ironic smile, and I'm stunned by her reaction to all of it. What is there to smile about?

"I had sex with you, Aidan," she says. "Don't you get it? Ask yourself: How in the hell did I go from terror at the thought of intimacy like that, to peace with it in a matter of weeks?" She gives me a pointed look. "You're cute and all, but you're no magician. Well, you are, but you know what I mean."

"No, I really don't."

"Before I met you, I *lived* fear. I walked in it like sludge. I felt it on my skin. I had no idea what it felt like to be normal or have safety. It was a vague memory, if that memory was even real or just imagined. And then you came into my world. Everything shifted sideways. You kissed me and I felt it: light in my skin, breaking off the pain. By the time we woke up the morning after the Awakening, I was so sure. I can't explain it, but I knew that you could save me." She reaches out and touches my chest. "And you have."

I rise from the chair. "Kara, I'm killing you, not saving you."

"No," she says, matter-of-fact. No red spark in her eye—she believes it, whether it's true or not. "You're saving me."

Her soul is changing, that's obvious from the blurring hand-prints, which could be why she's less fearful. But it's also obvious her body isn't accepting any of it as an improvement. And the Chinese characters on her neck from the childhood curse her father placed on her . . .

"The counter spell is failing," I say. "Sid says the warnings make it very clear. They say the blood-show is a sign that your protection against the original curse is weakening."

She stares at me, her mouth open a little, like she has no idea what to say.

"I'm breaking it, Kara. My power. It's tearing away the magic, undoing everything Sid did to you. It might be healing you, but it's also leaving you helpless again. I know you want me, but do you really want *that*?"

"It doesn't matter," she says, standing and coming closer, her voice tight. "I'm better, Aidan. So much better. I can breathe and not ache. I can touch you and feel free. I can't lose that."

"And so what do we do?" I say. "We stay close and just hope it doesn't kill you, or bring back the curse so you go crazy?"

"We have faith," she says, grabbing my hand. She brings it to her jaw and closes the last foot of space between us. "Love me and have faith that that's enough to save me."

There's a storm inside of me as I watch her. She's so calm. But I feel like screaming. She's not going to let me keep her safe. I should say something horrible, shove her back, do something to make her hate me. But that's never going to happen. I can't even imagine doing anything except holding her closer.

So I don't really have a choice.

I shake my head and touch her cheek, her hair . . . memorize every curve of her face, every shade of cream in her skin, so that I'll have something to take with me when I go.

THIRTY-FIVE

Aidan

The house is silent as I make my way down the stairs in the middle of the night. I left all the books on Kara's bedroom floor except for Eric's journal. I grabbed a few things to wear and my toothbrush, shoving them in the small duffel bag, along with the alabaster box and Ava's bag of secrets. But I left my cell phone on the dresser. I can get a new number from Hanna later. I don't want anyone to be able to get ahold of me too easily.

I couldn't kiss Kara good-bye; there was no way. As the day passed yesterday, I acted like everything was fine, playing off my lack of affection as fatigue—even though she probably saw right through me.

By the time night came around again, everyone seemed to be buying that things were back to normal. Yes, Holly was watching Kara like a hawk at dinner, and Jax didn't seem to have it in him to crack any of his usual jokes. But there were moments of ease, and Finger even blinked a bit in Rebecca's direction. Rebecca studied me during the whole meal. I knew she was sensing my detachment and getting worried about what I was going to do. But it doesn't matter. I'm pretty sure she won't tell anyone.

And as Kara settled into bed, I sat beside her, pretending to read, pretending I wasn't studying her as she fell asleep, and praying that I didn't lose my will to leave.

I'm not going too far; I can still watch out for her. But there's no way in hell I can take the chance that my power could kill her. I need to learn more about how my abilities affect others, and I need to be sure she's safe. That they're all safe.

I walk toward the bus stop, feeling the familiar weight of the LA streets settle on my shoulders again, as if welcoming me home. I could go to the abandoned warehouse I slept in before I came to LA Paranormal. Or I could find a new spot to hunker down in. The idea is horrifying, actually. I never thought I'd be back out here. And this time I know what I'm missing. I know how alone I am.

I board the bus heading in the direction of Eric's club. I'm sure there's a spot there to sleep for one night; it'll keep me in familiar territory. I'll figure the rest out when the sun comes up.

———

I don't sleep. It's too cold and my body isn't used to being out in the elements all night anymore. I've gone soft, apparently. So I just tuck my dagger at my side and watch the mouth of the alley, closing my eyes every now and then to pretend like I might actually get rest. I'm not sure what time it is when the sound of someone clearing their throat rises over the pulse of passing traffic in the distance.

My nerves jump, and I grip my dagger tighter as my eyes spring open.

It's Hanna. I hadn't even heard her walking down the alley. She's standing over me, holding what looks like a cup of coffee and a white paper bag. She's dressed like she just came into work for the day, her clothes clean and pressed.

"What are you thinking, Aidan?" she asks, her brow furrowing. Her concern presses at me.

The cold morning air sends shivers through me now that sleep's not making me numb, and the only response I can manage is chattering teeth. I hug myself and press into the brick wall behind me. I'm curled on a pallet in the corner of the alley behind the club, my hoodie on backward, knees tucked under to keep warm. LA can get cold once the sun goes down.

"Why are you out here?" she asks, looking around at the alley with disgust. "One of the bussers saw you when he brought out the trash and almost called the police. You're lucky he came and got me first."

It was Stoner Guy from the other night. I don't think he recognized me, but I was fairly sure he wasn't going to call the cops.

"Morning," I say.

"Come inside, for heaven's sake. You need to clean up."

I manage to move my stiff limbs and follow her around to the other side of the club, in through the back door. "Go sit in the break room and I'll meet you in there," she says. "There should be coffee."

Then she heads up the stairs to the office and I head for that caffeine.

I warm up pretty quickly once I get settled on the couch with a nice hot mug in my hand. Now all I need is a shower.

Hanna comes in and gives me the paper bag she was carrying. "Eat this and then shower in the apartment behind the warehouse. After you wash the alley off you, you'll come into the office and tell me what's going on and why you were sleeping outside." I open my mouth to protest, but she interrupts before I can get a word out. "And if you argue, or give me a hard time about it, I'll call Sid."

I shut my mouth.

"My guess is you don't want him to know you're here," she says.

"No," I say.

She sighs. "Eat and we'll talk in my office a bit later." And then she leaves me to my breakfast: an egg, smoked salmon, and spinach wrap from the deli down the street.

As I eat, I consider what's next. If Hanna knows about Daniel being my time-traveling dad, and possibly knows that Eric is an angel, that would mean it's all out on the table. I'll be able to explain everything honestly—the whole story, including what's happening with Kara—so she'll see why I had to leave the house and can't go back. Not until I figure things out.

Right now, I need to make a decision about how to actually do that. I could focus on Ava and her father. But I'm pretty sure I won't be any help to Eric against some badass dominion angel. The best I can do is block it from coming anywhere near Ava's body, and I've pretty much done that already.

I could try and figure out how I'm raising people from the dead. Maybe that will help me heal Kara, and possibly bring back Ava? And if things go in an unthinkable direction . . .

It would mean learning as much about my powers as I can, figuring out everything I'm able to do and *why* I can do it. Daniel said that I should prepare for this inevitable thing that I can't stop. But the *how* is definitely unclear. It feels like I can't stop anything. And stewing about it all certainly isn't doing anything to help. So, I scarf down the last of the breakfast sandwich and pour a warmer for my coffee. Then I head out to find that much-needed shower.

THIRTY-SIX

Rebecca

I'm not even remotely surprised when I wake up and everyone's talking about Aidan being gone. Well, Kara's not talking, she's growling. I was so relieved when she was all right yesterday that I almost forgot that I don't like her. She was glued to Aidan's side the whole day, but I could feel his anxiety reach astronomical levels, and I knew he was about to do something big.

He believes he's hurting her, even though I'm not sure that's right. He loves her. Really loves her. So why would his power hurt her? It doesn't make sense to me.

Anyway, it is clear why he left—to protect her—but everyone's in freak-out mode. Even the ever-calm Sid seems panicked, rambling on about plans and fate and "How will we be sure it all falls into place?" He, Connor, and Kara huddle in the office first thing in the morning, apparently planning how to be sure things *fall into place*. I don't know. I'm staying out of it.

If Aidan wants to tell them how he feels, then he will.

Eventually I get hungry and head for the kitchen to see if there's anything good to eat in the pantry. This house is junk food central and I'm desperate for steel-cut oats and strawberries, with hand-whipped cream like our housekeeper, Marguerite, used to make me. Or homemade bread with rosemary butter and fresh squeezed OJ. It looks like I'll have to settle for *Snap, Crackle, Pop!* and a cinnamon-apple Pop-Tart again, though.

I pour the milk over the small rice puffs and eat in silence. A few bites in, Kara comes through the back door and heads straight for the table, taking the chair across from me. She sits and watches me eat, not saying a word for several minutes. My snaps, crackles, and pops lose their zing, getting soggy because I can't eat with her staring at me like that.

I start to speak, like, three times, but can't figure out what to say. We've barely said two words to each other since the moment we met, and those two words were basically Kara saying, "Fuck off."

At last she leans back and says, "You know, right? About me and Aidan."

I'm not sure what she means—is she asking if I know they had sex? Uh . . . weird.

"I know he wants to be with you," I say.

"You do, huh?" She gives a short, skeptical laugh. "Well, that's not what I meant. I was under the impression that he told you about that predicament the three of us are in."

Oh. "Um, yep."

"Good. So you're aware of why I hate you being here."

"Yep."

"Nice. Okay, then I don't have to threaten you again out loud?"

"Nope."

"Perfect." She gets up from the table and starts to leave the room, then turns back like she just remembered something. "Do you wanna tell me why you're not freaking out that Aidan's gone?"

Nope.

When I don't answer right away she comes back to stand next to my chair. "Do you know something you're not telling us?"

I clear my throat and decide the only way I'll make it another day in this house without losing what's left of my dignity is to claim my space. So, I drop the spoon in my bowl with a clatter and stand to put myself at eye level with her. "Yes, Kara, there is something I know that I'm not telling you." I clear my throat again. "I'm not telling you how worried Aidan is about his sister, or how worried he is about you—and basically the whole freaking world. I'm also not telling you that he's pretty sure he's killing you, and he can't stand to look at himself in the mirror because of it."

When she steps back a little, her eyes growing, I add, "And would you like to know how I'm aware of all these things? Well, I can sense every damn emotion he has. Like, I can sense how every time he looks at you he's wishing he could kiss you and touch you, how he adores you and can't stand it when you're not around. How he counts the minutes until he sees you again, and how the club reminds him of the first time you kissed. Oh, and I can also sense that he doesn't feel any of that for me. That help at all?"

She just stares at me, her eyes glistening.

And now I feel like a total bitch. I soften my voice and say, "I'm not freaking out about him being gone because I know beyond a doubt that he's going to come back as soon as he can. He'll always come back for you, Kara."

She looks at her boots, then says quietly, "You care about him. I know you do."

I release a long sigh. "He doesn't feel the same for me. He just doesn't. So you don't have to worry about me taking him or tricking him or manipulating him. I wouldn't ever do that."

She folds her arms across her chest like she's trying to protect herself. "Sorry I was a bitch to you."

"Let's just say we start over."

She nods and stands there for a second like she's trying to decide whether to say something else. Finally she comes closer, leaning in, in a conspiratorial way. "So, do you maybe want to help me and come along for a little adventure tomorrow night?"

Her request knocks me off guard, striking me speechless.

"Never mind," she says, backing up as I stare at her. "It was a lame idea."

"No," I say, quickly. "I'll go."

She relaxes a little again. "Great."

"Can I ask where this adventure will take us?"

She smirks. "The mystery is half the fun."

"You mean keeping me in the dark is half the fun."

Her smirk turns into a smile. "Something like that." She heads for the back door, but before she shuts it behind her, she turns and asks, "If you knew where he was, would you tell me?"

I consider that and then answer honestly. "No, I wouldn't. He'll do what he has to do, and then he'll be back."

"You sound so sure. Don't people ever disappoint you?"

I lean back in my chair and sigh. "Constantly."

———

I get bored watching Finger play some zombie game for an hour, and go look for Connor. I head up to his room and spot him through the half-open door. "There you are," I say, pushing it open the rest of the way.

He stands in a rush from the bed, looking caught. "What?" he says as he slides something into his pocket.

Weird. "I was bored. What're you up to?"

Connor steps back like he's trying to get space. "I'm just thinking about this job we're going to do at the old mental hospital." He seems distracted, cagey.

"What's going on with you?" I ask.

"Nothing," he says, too quickly.

He's all tension and knots. Why can I only read Aidan? It would really be great to see into other people, too. Especially Connor—Connor with those serious eyes and settled ways.

He's not settled now, though. That's pretty obvious.

"You're a bad liar," I say under my breath, looking around the room. It's smaller than the other rooms, about a third of the size, actually. The walls are bare except for the three surfboards resting in a rack on the far side. The bed is neat. Who knew guys actually made their beds? Charlie never did. The room doesn't have a closet, but there's a small dresser beside the bed that also serves as an end table. I guess everything else he owns is in there. Which obviously isn't much. He's the epitome of moderation.

When he doesn't say anything, I ask, "How old are you?"

"Nineteen," he says. "I think."

My gaze skips to his. "You don't know?"

He shakes his head. "It doesn't really matter."

But . . . not knowing how old you are, when you were born exactly, that's just . . . wrong. "How do you ever have a birthday party?"

He releases a small laugh. "Hasn't really ever been a concern."

It's like we were raised on different planets. I live in a totally separate world from the people in this house. Or I used to, anyway. Now I don't know where I belong.

"I'm a sham," I say. Because I think I always knew something about me was different: the dreams, the drawings . . . I always blew it off as my artsy side and tried to hide it. But, underneath, something about my "regular" world didn't feel real. I let myself be wrapped in the facade. Happily, even. Until fate took Charlie from me. Then I couldn't pretend anymore. "I have no idea what's going on inside me."

"We'll find him," Connor says, like he's trying to console me.

For a second, I'm so distracted by the path my thoughts have taken, I'm not sure who he means. "Aidan," I say when I remember. "He's fine."

Connor raises his brow.

"But *you* don't seem fine," I add.

"I'm not really your concern," he says, sounding confused.

"Sure you are." I walk over and sit on his bed. "I thought we were family now."

He just keeps frowning and picking at his thumb like I'm making him nervous.

When it becomes obvious my line of inquiry isn't going anywhere, I stand again. "Listen, Connor," I say. I've only known him a few months, and only actually talked to him a couple times over the last few days, but I feel comfortable around him. I want him to be okay, and for him to know he's helping me through all this strangeness. "I'm sorry if I'm driving you nuts. You've been really nice. And I know I can be annoying."

I decide to throw caution to the wind and close the distance between us. Then I rise to my toes and press my lips to his cheek in a quick peck.

It's meant to be sisterly and sweet, but I find myself lingering for a breath longer, taking in the warmth of his skin, feeling the beginnings of scruff at his jaw.

I'm lost in it for a second, surprised by how good he feels up close.

Then I lower myself back down and study him, his strained expression, his rigid shoulders. My fingers slide down his arm and I step away, swallowing hard. Is he angry? Did I ruin everything because of my need to connect? This is what I did with Aidan, and it seemed to push him away.

What is wrong with me? I am seriously mental and in need of—

My thoughts freeze as Connor takes my upper arm and tugs me back into his chest. His other hand grips the nape of my neck, gently drawing me up, closer to his face. I gasp from the sudden intimacy, his mouth half an inch from mine, his steady breath brushing at my cheek. His scent fills my head, salt and heat. But he doesn't kiss me. He doesn't do anything except breathe and look tortured.

So I rise up that last centimeter and touch my lips to his.

His grip on the back of my neck tightens. His chest tenses under my palms. But his mouth is delicate, a feather against my skin, kissing me like no boy's ever kissed me before.

Reverent—that's the only word to describe it. A moment of worship. His lips slide over mine, unsure at first, then more urgent as each breath quickens, and my insides melt into a puddle from the feel of him.

But then he's stepping back. He keeps his hand resting at my nape for an extra second. His thumb caresses my skin and all I can do is stand there in stunned silence, gaping up at him.

He leaves a warm tingle in his wake as he releases me completely. "I shouldn't have done that," he says.

I'm so bewildered, it takes me a second to realize what he said.

Then the familiar bitter taste of rejection fills my mouth. "Why?"

He looks right at me. "I don't want to be second in line for anyone."

That's not what I expected. He's afraid of being rejected, too? "Connor, that's not what's happening here."

"Isn't it? You want Aidan, but he's chosen someone else."

"Well, yes, but . . ." But what? He's right and there is no *however*. "You're just lonely."

His words sting; they feel like an accusation. "You don't need to be a jerk. You kissed me, too, you know. And I can tell that you . . . have feelings for me." Whatever happened at the beach, there was something between us. And he's the one who just pulled me into his space, begging me to kiss him.

"You're too damn beautiful," he says.

Thanks? Frustration turns to anger and my cheeks turn hot. "This again? Seriously?"

Like a forced confession, he says, "I like you. All right? But it just won't work."

I close my eyes, my insides turning sour as I sink back to the bed. What a mess.

"I'm an ass," he says, "I know. But I can't be your man of the hour, Rebecca. I've known girls like you before. I can be your friend if you need me, but that's it."

Of course. My friend. "You've known girls like me? I'm that common, am I?" My words come out sounding defeated. I would normally hide how hurt I am, but I'm too tired. And I'm done. I'm finished with this game.

"That's not what I mean. You're special. Of course you're special."

"And stuck up, don't forget that gem."

"Rebecca—"

I hold up a hand to stop him from hitting me with any more daggers. "Please, call me Emery. It's what my *friends* call me. And since you're just a friend, and that's all you can be, just stick with that, okay?" I stand, exhausted.

He runs a hand through his hair, agitation tightening his muscles. "Dammit. I'm just fucking this up."

"Yes, you are, but I'm used to it now. That's one bonus of having others in line before you. You don't have to be the first one to step on my heart." I walk past him and out the door before he can stop me, before he can say anything else about friendship and distance and la-de-da girls like me.

I think about what Aidan's father said in the hall at the club, how my destiny is changing, how it's heartbreak and emptiness now, and I believe it. I wholeheartedly believe it. I am walking rejection. I'm the one who everyone will befriend but never love. I'm the girl on the fringe, looking in the window and wishing for warmth.

Maybe it's time to go back to the plastic world where I belong— the world of shopping and bitchy gossip and alcohol-fueled parties—where no one feels anything real.

THIRTY-SEVEN

Aidan

Hanna and I talk for several hours after my shower. Well, I talk and she listens, as I spill my guts about Kara and everything else, about how helpless I feel.

She knows about Eric now—that becomes clear quickly. Apparently, he decided to tell her everything the other night. He obviously cares about her, and if the constant awkward pauses in our conversation about their reunion are any indication, the making up included more than just *talk*.

I want to ask her how she can love a guy who's so crusty, but I guess Hanna has a soft enough heart for both of them. And now that Eric's come clean, she understands my role and why he watches over me. Which means I've gained another ally, and at this point I desperately need one.

After I refuse to crash in the warehouse's back apartment, Hanna insists I sleep in the warehouse itself. She loans that apartment out to clients sometimes, and I'm not about to take a free ride while also hurting business. So she sets up a cot in the back of the vault and gives me keys to the bathrooms on the other side of the building. It's a much sweeter setup than I ever had before—before LA Paranormal, anyway.

She says she can give me a couple days before she calls Sid, but she reminds me that he's my legal guardian, and he deserves to know where I am. Which he does, he's earned that. So I promise her that I'll call him and let him know that I'm all right.

Meanwhile, it's past time to really start figuring out my power, to see how far I can take it. I know that I can resurrect people, but I also know that doing so depletes my abilities. Maybe there's a more efficient way to harness the power and make it go further. I'll definitely need to conserve it if I'm going to find Ava's soul and awaken her, all while fighting off some possessive dominion angel.

There's a spot west of Sunset that's a nice thick feeding ground for demons. Hookers, addicts, and loads of twisted energy to draw in the other side. So I start making my way to that area. A few bus changes and a couple blocks later, and I'm almost to where the energy starts to thicken and it's tougher to breathe without tasting waste on my tongue. Depression and fear are palpable in the bodies that walk past or hide in the shadows of storefronts and doorways.

I see two ghosts along the way—not what I'm looking for, though. I pass a demon that's chained to a guy who's handing out flyers for something that looks like a church that worships snakes. Or maybe worms—the artwork is pretty bad. I don't want to mess with bound demons, though—a demon that's owned by a human. Or possessing demons, for that matter. I pass two females— arguing over a guy—who are practically leaking sulfur they're so full of demons. I need a creature that'll follow me, a feeder or a lurker. Easy prey.

I come around a corner and see the perfect specimen, across the street from a strip club entrance.

Its skin is an odd pale blue, with dark veins visible through the surface. The head is small and thin, tiny feelers poking out from under the chin and what would be the hairline—if it had hair. The eyes are slits, three of them stacked low on the forehead, just above the over-large nose. The creature is only about three feet tall, with transparent, fly-like wings hanging from its back. It's fairly mundane as demons go, even though I'm pretty sure it has a nice maw of sharp silver teeth behind those pale lips. Still, it'll be good practice.

My seal burns on my chest as I walk closer, studying it. I pull out my dagger and make my way across the street, to the left of the demon's human target, so the guy won't see my blade. The demon isn't attached to the young man's skin or chained to him, so it's a free agent for now. Or it could be working for a higher-up demon.

The guy is about my age, and his life hasn't been kind. His soul is wrecked. He's got a ton of handprints covering it, several of them red around his neck. There's a black onyx mark that reads *slave* in demon tongue on his forehead. And as I move closer, I smell the energy of a junkie.

He's shaking a little, fidgeting with his too-tight shirt, like he's trying to show off more of his thin, pale chest. When he sees me, his features shift, trying to hide the fear in his skin, but I feel it, prickling around me. Strong.

"Hey," he says, his voice high and light. "You seem lonely." The blue demon bug turns to see where the guy's looking, but its eyes go this way and that, not seeing me.

"Hi," I say, coming up to stand a few feet from the demon, who's now making a face that could be a frown. "What's your name?" I ask the guy.

He bites his lips; they have gloss on them. "I'm Scarlet." He's wearing a red shirt—a woman's blouse.

"Hey, Scarlet. Do you maybe want to get something to eat?" I motion behind me to where I think there's a twenty-four-hour diner.

He eyes me, cautiously. "I don't wanna lose my spot. What's your poison?"

Poison? I'm not sure if he's trying to sell me drugs or himself. I just want to get him away from the demon. "I'll pay," I say, holding up a twenty. The dagger is still tucked away at my other side where he can't see it. Hopefully.

"I only do one hand-off for that." He doesn't seem pleased but he's not walking away.

My gut sinks, thinking of how this kid's night probably goes, normally. Give a john his body for an hour, then go buy a few rocks of meth to turn numb, lather, rinse, repeat. He's probably only sixteen or so, by the look of him up close. He isn't going to live past twenty out here.

I decide to be honest. "Listen, Scarlet. You're about to see something very weird, but don't be scared, okay?"

His shadowed eyes widen.

I pull my amulet necklace over my head and hand it to him. "Can you just hold this for a second?"

The blue demon bug hisses and flies back as I appear two feet away.

"Don't run off, okay?" I say to Scarlet. "I need that back."

He just nods slowly, watching me walk toward what appears, to him, to be nothing.

"Okay, sparky," I say to the demon. "Let's see what you can do."

The familiar urge to kill seeps into my blood as I watch the creature round its back like it's trying to look bigger. Steam rises from my arm, and my chest aches with the burn of my seal, but I clench my insides and try to keep my mark from sparking to life.

My powers seem as hungry and awake as ever at the moment. Maybe even more so, as if my resurrection rebooted them. But I need to hold the fire in as long as possible. I need to figure out how it feels to control it and how I can conserve it better so I don't end up depleted halfway through a fight.

At the moment, it feels like I'm holding back a freight train.

The demon flutters up, flying high enough to face me. Its buzzing wings press air into me that smells like rot and stings my skin like needles. And then I realize there are actual needles pricking my skin. Red dots appear all over me, like bleeding pox. Thin silver splinters fall away, *tink*ing onto the ground once they hit their mark.

Scarlet must feel it, too, because he squirms and starts itching at the track marks running up his arm.

I hold my hand out to protect my eyes, the jabs sparking all over my body as the tiny darts hit harder and deeper. Time to stop holding the freight train in.

I let go of my insides, releasing the power. It surges into my muscles, my skin, and steals the breath from my lungs.

Something pops at the air and sends Scarlet tumbling back, ass to concrete, just as my mark surges to life with a *whoosh* of heated air, shoving the demon back in a rush.

I grab it by the ankle before it gets out of range and yank. The wings fold up, stopping their onslaught. The body arches and thuds into the ground, the skull hitting the sidewalk. It barely stuns the creature, but it gives me the perfect angle.

I raise the silver dagger, its light casting over the demon's blue skin, turning it green. A fleeting urge to rip the bastard's wings off zips through me, but instead, I slide the blade right into its middle eye slit.

Black ooze gushes out before the body bursts into flames, then disappears in another *pop*.

I glance over at Scarlet, trying to catch my breath. He's gaping at the ground where my dagger blade is half-buried in the cement.

He gets back up on his feet, unsteady, and turns his eyes to me and my bloody skin. "Fuck ten elephants, what the hell am I on?"

I start wiping the blood off my face and arms with the bottom of my T-shirt. "Told you it'd be nuts." I pull out the dagger from the cement, then slap the blade against my leg to break off the rest of the black clay that was the demon's blood. "You wanna get that meal now?"

Scarlet blinks at me as I slide the sort-of clean knife into my back pocket. He doesn't speak but he doesn't run, either. When I walk over to him, holding my hand out for my amulet, he backs up a step and presses it to his chest. "What are you?"

I lower my hand and look at him. "I'm Aidan. And I'm dying for a soda. Do you want one or what? I think there's a diner a few blocks from here."

He licks his lips and seems to consider. Then he holds out my necklace. "Can I have some Jack in mine? I think I need it."

I laugh and slip the amulet back over my head. "How about a little ice cream instead?"

"Big spender, huh? Can the lady have a cherry, too?"

"The lady can buy whatever she'd like."

He raises his brow. "How much do you cost, handsome?"

"I'm not for sale," I say, starting to walk down the street, heading for the diner. *I'm taken.* His question makes the weight of not being near Kara settle back on my shoulders. Panic grips me as I think of how my absence is probably hurting her. I can't forget why I'm out here on this cold night, instead of home beside her.

"Priceless, then," he says in a dreamy voice as he comes up next to me and brushes dirt from my shoulder, knocking off a chunk of blackened demon too, even though he can't see it.

I give him a sideways smile and we walk the rest of the way in silence.

———

Scarlet's actual name is Raul. As we walk into the brightly lit diner, he confesses that he uses a new name every night, depending on where he's hanging around and what shirt he's wearing. We sit and he eats a double-bacon cheeseburger and fries and I sip my soda. He's actually great company, talking a lot so I don't have to. He tells me about his family—mother, five sisters, and grandmother in Guatemala. They sent him with a coyote ten years ago, when he was six, and he hasn't heard from them since. But he tells me about each of them in detail. He spends about an hour weaving tales about his pet parrot and bemoaning how much he misses it.

For a guy with so many red handprints on his neck and track marks up his arm, he seems fairly chipper. Maybe he's just glad to be filling his stomach; at the speed he's ingesting his burger, I'd say he doesn't chomp down double-bacon anything very often.

He takes a sip from his drink as he studies my markings. After he swallows, he asks, "So, you're like magical or something?"

I'm surprised he didn't ask about it sooner. But how do I explain what I am? I don't even know. "I'm just me."

He cocks his eyebrow. "You were a lit-up bastard back there."

I decide honesty's worked so far, so I just say, "I don't really know what I am."

He nods, like he's accepting the answer, and pops a fry into his mouth.

"So, where're you crashing?" I ask, trying to sound like I'm being casual. Really, I want to find out if he's going to be all right; I'm not sure why that demon was with him.

He eats the last three fries on his plate and pushes it away before answering. "Listen, I'm not someone you'd be wantin' in your life, sweetie."

"Really, why's that?" I lean back in the booth, folding my arms across my chest.

He laughs. "Oh honey, you're too slick to know what's good for you." He waves out the window at the city streets. "The less time your lovely ass spends in this town, the better."

I smile at him, totally floored that he thinks I'm some kind of uptown boy. "I used to crash near the tracks."

He looks at me like he doesn't believe me.

"I set up in an empty warehouse for a while; it had a nice loft," I continue. "The owner came around, though, and I almost got caught, so I split. And then there was the alley behind the flower shop." I smile, watching his face turn from incredulity to amazement.

"What sorta gig you got that took you from alleys to designer cotton?" He nods to my Abercrombie & Fitch T-shirt. Sid is insanely fond of shopping and buys stuff way higher on the scale than he needs to. Fruit of the Loom would've been fine. Especially considering the way I've been going through clothes lately.

"I fell into a gig," I say. "They pay in clothes." And trouble. Raul seems interested and opens his mouth to ask another question, but I stand up before he can get it out. The less he knows about me, the better. "I've gotta jet, but I'll be around. You can find me at SubZero if you ever need anything."

He blinks up at me as I take the check and hold out a hand to shake. He hesitates but takes it after a second.

A flash of red eyes and the sound of running feet and gasping breath bursts into my consciousness before he pulls back.

"You've got quite the grip," he says, shaking out his hand and sitting back in the booth.

I just give him a stiff smile and try to keep myself from noticeably shivering. But because I can't help myself, before I walk away I say, "I can help you, you know. If you need it."

His mouth curves up but his eyes look sad. "You bought me bacon. No other help needed, friend."

And so I nod and walk away. But I'm fully aware that what I saw was his soul running from some demon. Owner or captor, whatever. And from the rising up of my insides, I'm pretty sure my power wants to do something about it. Unfortunately, Raul will have to get in line.

THIRTY-EIGHT

Rebecca

I'm sitting in art theory class only half listening. I can't believe I'm here, in the real world; I shouldn't have come. I mean, I thought I could pretend—I've been doing it for so long—but I just can't anymore. I had to get out of that house, though. With Sid all sick and creaky, Aidan gone, Kara not sure about me, and Connor wanting to be "just friends," I can't stay there and remain sane. So I called the car service before anyone was awake and left.

First, I sat at Starbucks with the driver. Weird, I know. I bought him coffee and an egg sandwich and we sat reading the paper. A nice guy, Larry. He seemed happy.

Now I'm at school and I'm totally out of it. I can't stop thinking about that conversation with Connor yesterday. Or his hand on my neck. Or his lips. My God, his lips.

Shut up, brain!

The weirdest part is, it wasn't Aidan. And I'm okay with that.

The teacher's voice cuts through my fog.

"I'd like you to incorporate these elements into your final summer project." He points at the overhead screen, which is sectioned off into four images. "There's extra credit for those who can incorporate all of them."

Elements? Project? Oh great. What did I miss?

He continues, "If you'll turn to page three hundred and five you'll see more examples. The images might feel disjointed, but each one is like a puzzle of the artist's mind. I need you to choose one and write a fifteen-hundred-word analysis, along with a visual response in the medium of your choice."

What, what, what?! I want to bang my head on my desk, but that's not exactly the action of a sane person, and I'm supposed to be pretending. I just don't have the mental power or capacity right now to write a paper or do some pointless school project.

The teacher puts an image of another painting on the overhead and begins picking it apart. I should be at the beach instead of here, hanging out with Charlie's memory and the dolphins. Charlie would know what I should do right now.

". . . if Miss Emery can find her way back to us."

My head snaps up at the sound of my name. I was doodling on my notebook—more skulls from the look of it, *great*—while I was at the beach with Charlie in my head.

"Sorry?" I ask.

He walks toward my desk and glances down at my doodles. "I assume, since you've decided to work on something else, that you're already aware of what the artist was thinking?"

I shake my head. "No, Mr. Hicks."

He points his pen at my notebook and my skulls. "André Leclair's *Within The Reaches of Angels* is what we are discussing, Miss Emery. Not pirates."

This time, the skulls are attached to full skeletons, three of them. "Yes, sir."

"So," he turns back to the front of the room and motions to the overhead, "would you please tell us what you believe Mr. Leclair was trying to portray here?"

I look at the image on the screen, trying not to visibly cringe. It's basically how I've always visualized hell. There's a skinless figure in the center being eaten from the belly by what looks like a huge viper with sharp fangs. Fire rises at the feet of the figure, and the background is made up of twisted green vines weaving in and out of a wall of . . . skulls.

Suddenly, those hollow eyes of death seem to be staring right back at me. I begin to see smaller creatures in the tongues of the flames, in the eyes of the viper, tiny beasts hiding in the layers of horror. I see the vines attempting to break the wall of death, and I wonder if this troubled artist had the ability to draw the hidden story of the future, like I do.

I put on my deep-thinking face for the benefit of Mr. Hicks and say what I decide he'd like to hear, "I think Mr. Leclair was struggling between his need for religious approval and his realization that he's been corrupted by impurity and sin. This is obviously an image of the agony and injustice the artist felt."

Mr. Hicks is properly impressed, and clearly a bit annoyed that I was able to sound smart so easily. "That's an interesting thought. We know that much of Leclair's surreal work was seen as overly erotic for the day. Would you like to delve into that further, Miss Fallon?" He points to Loretta Fallon and soon forgets about me. Yes, leave it to Loretta. She's all about the overly erotic; some of her party activities would make even the liege lords of ancient Rome blush.

Loretta starts theorizing about how society has made men the keepers of the sexual and I half listen, sort of agreeing with her, but not caring enough to add to the discussion at the moment. I'm just glad that I'm not the center of attention anymore.

When class is over, Samantha's waiting for me outside the door, hugging her music notebook to her chest. "I don't have anything for an hour because Mr. Smythe got the chlam from sucking face with Mrs. Florence last week."

"That's not how chlamydia works, Samantha," I say. "And Mr. Smythe's father just passed away, so that's probably why he's not here."

She shrugs. "Well, Loretta said she saw Mrs. Florence making out with him in the green room backstage after the encore performance of *Pippin* last week. In any case, I'm bored and Apple is skipping to go to her mom's shop on Rodeo because the assistant called and they got next year's line in early from France. I think we should celebrate and ditch, too. I miss you." She side-hugs me. "Plus, you owe me for all the acrobatic lying I've been doing for you to my mom and your overprotective father." Then she starts babbling about purses and why this new line is *so* much better than the last one because of something to do with the texture patterns they're going with this year . . . I have no idea. And I really don't care. Fashion isn't my thing, even if it is everything to Samantha. The only real reason Samantha and I have stayed friends all these years is because when you peel back the silk and satin, she's a lioness. She'd never hurt me, and she'd defend me to the death if anyone else tried—socially speaking, anyway.

I agree to tag along because I can't take school anymore. And if I go to Rodeo with Apple and Samantha, I won't have to go back to the LA Paranormal house yet and confront Connor. I'm wondering if I should just collect my things from there and head home with Samantha. Then I won't have to be in a house filled with tension, and I won't be lying to my dad anymore, either. Every time he calls, I feel more guilty.

We climb into Apple's Audi and are soon stuck in traffic on Santa Monica Boulevard. The two girls up front are gabbing about the fall shows they're planning on going to and trading gossip about some of the designers. Apple's mom is a queen in the LA fashion community and she always knows everything about everyone: movie stars, politicians, designers, you name it. Apple is always happy to share her dirt.

I look out the window and suddenly wish I'd applied for one of those art residencies abroad like my aunt suggested after Charlie died. Dad certainly has the money. It would've given me a goal, and maybe I wouldn't have felt so disconnected from my life. And I wouldn't have met Aidan or had my heart broken. And then broken again.

"Some guy in a trash heap with wheels is waving at you, Emery," Apple says, looking in her rearview mirror. "He's been following us since we got off the 405."

I spin around and gasp when I spot the familiar mangy Jeep in our blind spot on the right. Holy crap. Connor? He sees me looking at him and waves for us to pull over. Is he high?

I hold up a finger, mouthing, *Just a second!* Then I turn back to Apple, growling under my breath as I ask, "Can you pull over?"

She laughs and snaps her gum. "Seriously?"

"Yes, seriously."

She turns onto Avenue of the Stars and pulls into a hotel valet area. Connor pulls in behind us, brakes squeaking.

I slide out of the backseat and ask Apple to wait, saying I'll only be a second. Then I stomp my way to the rear of the car as Connor rushes toward me. "What the hell?" I say.

"You left—you can't *just leave.*"

"Actually, I can. It's this weird thing called, *you're not my father and it's a free country.*"

He gives me a look, then shakes his head and leans closer. "It's not safe right now, Rebecca."

"Emery!" I say louder than I mean to. I hear whispering and turn to see that Apple and Samantha have gotten out of the Audi and are sharing a cigarette and pretending not to eavesdrop. Perfect. "Call me Emery," I say more quietly.

"Just get in the Jeep," he orders.

I set my jaw and turn back to the Audi, going for the door handle. He grabs my wrist from behind and spins me around, getting so close his heat mingles with mine as he puts his lips to my ear and whispers harshly, "You want me to say it so they can hear? You want them to know that the demon that wants you dead might be back?"

My pulse skips at the word *demon*. And it dawns on me what he means. The demon Hunger. Aidan said it might be back, but why would that mean Connor needed to stalk and kidnap me?

I pull away a little so he's not so close. "I'm wearing my amulet."

He shakes his head, then glances behind me, probably to the other two girls who've gone totally silent. "Can you please just come with me?" His voice has a desperate edge to it now.

"You could've just texted me, you know," I say, backing away.

"I did. You didn't answer."

I give him a disbelieving look, pulling my phone from my pocket. I press the button to turn on the screen and nothing happens. "Battery's dead."

"Hey," comes a sly voice on my left. Apple. "You trying to steal our girl?"

Connor keeps his eyes locked on me.

"Who's this, Emery?" Sam asks; she comes to stand beside me, taking a protective pose.

"He's hot," Apple adds, raking her eyes over Connor's muscular form. "Way cuter than the Valley reject you invited to my party last month."

Heat rises on my cheeks. "This is Connor. Connor, this is Apple and Sam."

Connor really looks at them now. "Apple. That's your name?"

She giggles her high-pitched flirt-giggle and touches her long blonde hair—she is so typical when it comes to boys. And designer bags, for that matter. "You always follow girls into hotel parking lots, Connor?" she asks.

"I just need to talk to Rebecca here, and then you can get back to shopping."

Samantha is giving him an assessing look, like she's making sure he's safe. "Why do you keep calling her Rebecca?"

"Yeah, only her brother called her that," Apple says, totally clueless as to how her words just stabbed me in the heart.

Samantha glances sideways at me, a pained look in her eyes.

"And you might be cute," Apple adds, "but you're no Charlie."

I want to curl in a ball and block out the sudden pain. How could Apple be so clueless? Yes, she's a bitch, but not usually this much. She must really think Connor's cute.

He looks away from them and back to me, his eyes gentle. "Come on, I'll explain everything, I swear." He holds out a hand in offering, a lifeline as the storm rises inside me.

So I take it and let him pull me to the Jeep, ignoring Apple's chatter behind me. I mouth to Samantha, *I'm okay*, as I get into the passenger side.

She motions back for me to text her before we pull past them in the roundabout.

I don't let myself cry as we head down the familiar streets and Connor doesn't say anything, not until we're pulling off the freeway again and entering his neighborhood.

"I'm sorry," he says finally. "I was a total jackass to you yesterday. I should've thought before I said anything. I—"

"Don't worry about it." I just want to forget our kiss and his subsequent rejection of me. Definitely not wanting to talk about it. "Can you tell me now why you needed to kidnap me, though?"

He blows out a puff of air. "Your amulet won't protect you against this thing if it gets one of its minions into a human host. Once a demon's possessing someone, the human eyes will see you and the thing will be able to do whatever it needs to do for its master."

A wave of icy air washes over me as I realize how vulnerable I was all day at Starbucks and then school.

"And I can't see demons like Aidan can," he adds, "so if it's close to you, I'll have no idea. We just need to be careful, Rebec—I mean . . . damn."

"It's all right," I say, exhausted from it all. "Call me whatever you want." Then I turn to him and add, "And thanks for coming to make sure I'm safe."

"Aidan left me a note," he says quickly, like he's confessing it to me.

"He did?"

"It's what I was reading when you came into my room yesterday. He reminded me about the demon and told me to be sure and watch out for you."

Of course he did. "Oh," is all I can manage. Because it wasn't Connor wanting to protect me. Again, it was Aidan.

"I was the ass who didn't even think of it."

"Well, I'm not your problem," I say, looking out the window, trying not to be disappointed yet again. I'm not Aidan's responsibility anymore, either. I guess it's time for me to learn to take care of myself.

And with that thought comes a feeling of steadiness. It is time for me to stand on my own. *Past* time. I guess I've sort of been doing it already, but I need to get over my fear of being alone.

Connor swerves the Jeep, shocking me as he pulls off to the side of the road and jerks to a stop, putting it in park. He sits there for several seconds in silence, gripping the steering wheel.

"What's wrong?" I ask, when I can't take the silence anymore.

"The reason I came after you," he finally says, "is that just thinking about you being hurt or tormented by any*one* or any*thing* makes me nuts. I came because I can't stand the thought that I hurt you, because I'm a prick and a coward and all I can think about is how much I want to kiss you again. From the second I saw you standing in the house two months ago, right after you met Aidan, my gut's been in knots. I go to sleep trying to erase your smell from my head, wake up needing to erase you from my dreams before I go crazy."

"Connor," I whisper, "I—"

But he turns to me and moves closer, so close, sticking the words in my throat.

He lifts his fingers and brushes my cheek. "I know you care about Aidan. Maybe it'll always be Aidan, I don't know—with this fate shit, no one knows. But I won't pretend I don't care if that's going to push you away and hurt you. I thought it was the right thing to do, but I can't, I just can't let you believe I don't care." His eyes settle on my lips. "Because I do. So much, it feels like a punishment."

I stare at him in stunned silence, unable to formulate a response. His touch slides down to my jaw, and his thumb and finger take my chin, tipping my head.

"I want to kiss you again," he says quietly. "This time I won't pretend to regret it."

I wait, holding my breath, until he closes the distance between us and my eyes shut, a sigh of relief leaving my chest. His lips brush mine, so gently it's like a whisper, but it sends a rush of heat over my skin. His hand moves to my shoulder, gripping me, like he's straining to hold back. With each touch my heart beats faster, and as the kiss deepens I feel myself getting lost in the moment of breathless tension.

And then he pulls away, and I open my heavy eyelids. His features are pinched like he's in pain, and I'm not sure what he's feeling.

"Don't," I whisper. "Whatever you're thinking, just stop. It was perfect."

"I'm not a good guy, Rebecca."

"You are to me," I say.

He shakes his head but he doesn't say anything else. He just breathes deep, in and out, and then squeezes my hand before letting go, like he's trying to reassure me. I can only sit back in the seat and watch him pull onto the road again. I try to hold in a sigh, as the feeling of this moment soaks in, deeper and deeper, into my skin, my heart, to a place inside where whatever happens after right now, that perfect memory won't ever be stolen from me.

THIRTY-NINE

Rebecca

Kara peeks her head into Holly's room around eight o'clock. "Do you still want to come?" she asks me. Her voice is tight, but there's vulnerability in her eyes.

I have no idea where she's taking me or what we're going to be doing, but I feel like it's important that I at least try to be her friend. Even though I'm pretty sure that's never going to happen. I mean, she's Kara. She hates me.

The weird thing is, I don't hate her anymore. If I ever did. I just don't trust her. Aidan trusts her, though, and I trust Aidan, so I'm going to see where this open door leads.

"I've just gotta get my boots on," I say, grabbing them off the closet floor.

Holly looks up from her book. "Where are you *amigas* going?" She's sitting in bed, trying to get through *The Jungle*, by Upton Sinclair, for some English class she's taking. She has to keep setting her alarm for thirty-minute intervals to stay awake. I already told her that Kara's taking me on some mystery adventure tonight, and hinted that maybe she could come along, but Holly was pretty adamant that she's staying out of all adventures for a while, since the ones she took with Ava got Lester killed.

Kara opens the door a little wider when she answers. "I just need to check something."

Holly glances over to me, looking like she's trying to send me a message: *Don't go*, maybe?

I zip up my second boot and stand, straightening my sundress. "Well, I'm ready for whatever." I grab my pink cardigan off the foot of the bed.

Holly snorts. "Don't say that. A dead lady came to me last night in my dream. She'd kicked the proverbial bucket while bungee jumping. Those were probably her last words before the bungee snapped."

"God," I say.

"Yeah, she wants me to find her fiancé and hit him in the balls with a socket wrench—apparently he was some sort of car mechanic, I don't know . . . but he cheated on her with her sister. Yikes." She sighs, like she's gossiping about an actual friend. "Anyway, I told her she should just AMF and move on."

"Are we seriously talking about this right now?" Kara asks.

I slide on my cardigan. "What's AMF?"

Kara groans. "Does it matter?"

"Adios, mother effer—but, like, with an *ucker* at the end." Holly winks.

Kara throws her head back. "So lame. I'm leaving. Good-bye." And she turns, heading for the stairs.

"You better consider this," Holly says as I'm rushing to follow.

I pause and give her a questioning look.

"Kara's in a bad place right now, friend. You want to be careful. Her claws sting when they come out."

"I know." I've felt them dig in. "But I need to try and make this right."

Holly frowns. "Why?"

I shake my head, not knowing the answer myself. It just feels important. "Please don't tell Connor, okay?" I don't need him chasing after me again. If that demon, Hunger, and its minions really are out there looking for me, they'll find me eventually. And I can't hide in this house forever. Time to take my freedom back a little—from boys, from fear.

When I hurry out the back door, Kara's sitting on the porch step, waiting for me. "You finally ready?" She stands and starts walking through the yard, to the garage. I follow, deciding silence is my best bet for now.

We climb into the Camaro. She starts the engine then pushes something, making music fill the cab. It's a man singing, and the thing she pushed—which looks like a smaller version of a VHS tape from the '80s or something—says *Simon & Garfunkel* on the side. It sounds nice, melodic and relaxing. I wouldn't have expected Kara to like something like this, though.

"What kind of music player is that?" I ask in fascination. I can hear a whirring sound just underneath the notes.

She laughs. "Haven't you ever seen an eight-track?"

Uh, that would be no. "Does it play video, too?" Didn't VHS play video? I look around for a screen but I don't see one.

She laughs harder. "Oh my God, you are hilarious. Wow."

Okay, I'm going back to being quiet.

After a good half hour we're pulling off the freeway, into what appears to be a not-so-nice neighborhood. I stare at the people walking down the street, the graffiti and dilapidated buildings, wondering if we should really be in an area like this at night. "Where are we?"

"I think this is Lynwood or Watts. Around there." She looks sideways at me when we stop at a light. "You scared?"

My heart speeds up. "I'm just not sure we should be out here at night."

"Where we're going isn't that bad," she says. "Better than the place in Chinatown where I grew up. Some of the walls in our building were made of cardboard and pieces of furniture. The old lady who ran the complex was crazy as shit. Tossed a kid's dog off the roof when it peed in the hall."

I don't even know how to comment on that.

"Just don't look anyone in the eye," she says, turning down a residential street.

I grip the edge of my cardigan.

She smirks. "I'm kidding. Relax."

"We're in the projects. At night."

"People actually live here, you know. They don't just shoot each other and steal each other's cars. There's, like, kids and grandmas and stuff."

"I know." She's making me feel like a prissy rich girl from *The Hills* or something. God, I better not come off as prissy.

She parks under a streetlight, in front of several rows of apartment buildings. We get out of the car and I move to walk close beside her, trying not to think about all the movies and TV shows I've seen where there were stabbings and shootings in places that looked just like this.

Kara points the key fob at the Camaro and clicks the alarm on as we make our way down the path between the two buildings.

"She's right up here," Kara says, pointing to the second building down on our right.

"*She*, who?"

"The witch."

Not liking the sound of that. I try not to look at the group of six huge guys standing by an apartment door on our left. "Why're we here?" I ask, but she doesn't answer.

A whistle comes from the group of young men and someone catcalls, "Don't go, Ginger. You're breakin' my heart."

We finally stop in front of a door and Kara knocks. There's a strange symbol above the peephole. A few seconds pass when all I can hear is the clinking of chains and sliding of locks, then the door opens.

"Kara, child," the woman says, with a warm smile on her face. "You surprise me, I thought you'd be done with all this."

Not a super good reader of the future, then.

She's pretty, in a safe, grandmotherly sort of way. She's a round African-American woman with silver-grey hair, tied with a scarf. Her dark eyes seem to carry a lot of mischief in them. Her grin shows her teeth, and several are covered in gold. Her clothes are colorful and flowy, and about a dozen necklaces clatter at her chest; several dozen bracelets clack as she moves in for a hug.

She squeezes Kara—who pats the woman's back awkwardly—then turns to me and grabs me for a hug. I don't have time to respond before she's holding me out in front of her by the shoulders, looking me over. "Oh, girl, you're goin' down a rough road." And she makes a sound in her throat like an underline of the statement. "Poor thing."

"This is Rebecca, Miss Mae."

"Lovely." She squeezes my upper arms. "She's just lovely. Look at that hair! Pretty as a sunset."

I give her a stiff smile. "Thanks?"

Miss Mae laughs heartily and waves us in.

"Who's coming to visit, Aunt Mae?" Someone asks from behind me.

We all stop and turn. A young African-American man stands outside on the porch with a group of guys—the ones that hooted at us when we walked by.

"You reading people's futures again?" he asks. "Inviting the riff-raff back into the hood?"

"Don't be nosy, now, Tray." She waves her hands like she's shooing a stray dog.

He looks the same age as Connor, maybe a year or so younger, but there's a hard edge to his eyes that makes me think he's seen too much pain. He's dressed in baggy jeans and a large white T-shirt, and he has gauges in his ears and an intricate tattoo on his neck. He smiles and his gaze skims over me, then Kara. He seems to recognize her. "Back again? How's my brother?"

"Jax is fine," Kara says. "Better now that he's not living with his dad."

Tray nods and then looks over to me again. "You a new recruit to the house of crazies?"

I shake my head.

"She's a friend of the new guy, Aidan," Kara says.

He smirks at her. "I thought you were that Aidan guy's *friend*."

I expect her to be annoyed, but she just smirks back and punches him in the shoulder. "I'll tell Jax you said hey. But you should come by one of these days. Things have been tough since Lester."

Tray nods. "I'll find time." Then he reaches out, touching her cheek in this very endearing way that makes me wonder. "You taking care of yourself?"

"Always."

"You let us work, now," Miss Mae says to them. She takes me gently by the arm. "Come on now, sweetheart. Let's get that lily skin inside before the wolves pounce. Those boys're crafty. They'll have your doe eyes full'a stars before you know it."

A couple of the guys laugh and Tray smiles at me, and I see what she means. He's got the same smile as Jax, slick and handsome, but he seems much more dangerous. Mostly because he's being a gentleman.

"Nice to meet you, friend of Aidan's," he says.

"Rebecca," I say, as Miss Mae pulls me farther into the apartment, shutting the door.

The place is small but tidy. I can see she's tried to cover the water stains on the walls with paintings and quilts, and the stained carpet with rugs. The kitchen, living room, and eating area are all in one room and there's a door beside the kitchen—probably leading to a bedroom and bathroom. The space is dimly lit, with only one lamp. I expected to see a lot of black, with skulls and pentagrams everywhere, but instead everything is full of color, with images of animals and nature settings in paintings, photos, and fabrics.

"So things still aren't ironed out, then?" Miss Mae asks Kara as she settles at the yellow kitchen table. She motions for me to sit in a chair across from her.

Kara sits on the sheet-covered couch a few feet away. "No, it's gotten a little more complicated."

"But this is the one?" Miss Mae points at me.

I look between the two of them. Why are they talking about me like I'm not here? "*The one*, what?" I ask.

Miss Mae doesn't answer, she just picks up a large deck of cards and sets it in front of me. "Shuffle these, child."

I stare at the deck. Tarot cards, I'm fairly sure. "I'm here so you can read my tarot?"

"I asked if you wanted to help," Kara says. "This is how you can help."

I feel tricked. She didn't want to tell me where we were going because she needed me to be here. I'm the reason we came in the first place.

"How's this supposed to help?" I ask.

"Our Kara here is very sick," Miss Mae says. "That's due to how she stole your destiny. If you could see your way to let me read you more closely, maybe answers can be found."

I turn to Kara. "Aidan said that you're sick because his power is hurting you."

"Because magic was used to change me, and make me link with his powers. I wasn't born to be the one," she says. "That was you."

Kara stole my destiny, as Aidan's father said. But the how or why don't matter anymore. We've come to the *what now?*

I take the cards and shuffle as the two of them watch.

"Think about the boy, Aidan," Miss Mae says. "Think about what he feels like, how he smells, think all the things you can't say out loud about him. First, I'll read the cards, which will be our foundation for the soul map."

I'm not sure I want to know what a soul map is. I feel Kara staring at me but I close my eyes and do what Miss Mae told me to. As the cards sift through my hands, I let myself think of Aidan, how he makes me feel safe, how lovely he is, his amazing body, his eyes so full of depth, how my heart ached when I felt him wanting Kara and not me, and how much I wanted him to be mine. And then I open my eyes and place the newly shuffled deck on the table.

Miss Mae begins laying out the cards in a pattern, face down, and when she's done she looks them over, like she's considering. She turns the first one face up. "The Lovers, reversed. Yes, I expected this." The card looks hand painted: a man and a woman who could be Adam and Eve, standing together under a bright sun. It's numbered with a *VI* and says *The Lovers* at the bottom. It's upside down.

"Lovers imbalanced," she says. "You love him but he doesn't love you." She turns the next card. "The Emperor. You see Aidan as your authority." She turns the card underneath and sets it on top. "The Knight, reversed. But he's disappointed you."

My chest stings. Is this just going to be a rehashing of all the old wounds?

She moves to the two next cards and flips the first. "Death, reversed, hmm."

Death?

"You're resisting a change that's attempting to make itself known." She turns the next. "High Priestess. You're very intuitive. Listen to your heart. This is where the answers lie."

Well, that's a little helpful, I guess.

"Now . . ." She takes a rolled-up square of white velvet from beside her and hands it to me. "This is where we begin the mapping. Lay this out in front of you and place your hands on it, palms up."

My heart beats a little faster as I take the soft fabric and unroll it on the table. It's embroidered with a golden circle around a double star with six points. I set my hands on it, palms up, and wait.

She places a clear crystal between my hands and then takes a small bottle and sprinkles the contents on my palms; it smells like a forest. She mutters something and suddenly I begin to feel tingling in my fingertips, a slight buzzing, like my hands are falling asleep. I can't tell what she's saying; it sounds like another language.

"Don't be afraid," she says. "But this next part might sting a little." And I realize she has a small silver dagger in her hand. "It takes your blood now. Are you willing to allow this?"

I stare at her, at the blade, then shift to look at Kara. She's watching everything with obvious pain in her eyes.

"You don't have to," she says.

"Doesn't Aidan hate this witch stuff?" I ask her. "Why're we doing this?"

"Not all witches cast darkness, and I need to do this my own way. Mae is a friend and she's willing to help, if you're willing to participate. The soul map will show us what piece of the puzzle you have that I don't. She already did mine."

"And it'll tell us how to fix this?" I ask Miss Mae.

She shakes her head. "No way to know for sure, but it should show what's gone wrong on the underside of things, where human eyes can't normally see."

It was *my* destiny that was messed up here, but somehow we're trying to fix Kara's instead of mine? It feels so upside down when I think about it all. And yet, it's the right thing to do. She's not some girl stealing my boyfriend; she's a girl who's in love and she could die from that love.

"Okay," I say, turning back to Miss Mae. "I'm good. Let's finish."

Miss Mae gives me a sympathetic smile. "Good heart, child. Such a lovely heart." And then she takes a hold of my hand, slicing into my left palm. At first, it's a sharp pain, but then it begins to burn. And burn.

I grit my teeth and squeeze my eyes shut for a moment as she makes a second cut along my right palm. The two wounds aren't deep, but it's like there was salt water on the knife or something. The heavy ache bites through my nerves and travels up my arms.

The blood flows quickly as Miss Mae turns my hands over and presses my palms down onto the white velvet. I watch the stain spread from under my hands; it begins to create a shape over the fabric's weave as she whispers more words I can't understand. The fire in the cuts rises and rises. My breath quickens and tears sting my throat, filling my eyes.

But I can't let myself cry, no way, not in front of Kara.

Finally, Miss Mae lifts my hands off the velvet and Kara stands, looking at the shape left behind.

"Oh my," Miss Mae says, staring at the fabric. "There it is."

"Is it angelic, though?" Kara asks.

I don't look at the patterns left on the velvet yet. I'm too busy staring at my palms, which have no cuts on them. The only sign of what just happened is traces of blood.

"How did I heal so fast?" I ask.

"It's a part of the spell," Kara says. "That's why it burns. You were pretty tough, though. I know how much that hurts."

Miss Mae hands me a damp towel to clean the blood off. "So, it looks like your blood is somehow blessed. Perhaps this blessing was placed on your mother while you were in her womb?"

"I never knew my mother," I say.

"Did she die in childbirth?" she asks.

"My dad said she ran off."

Miss Mae looks back at the dark-red shapes inside the white velvet circle. "Hmm . . . well, then we can't be sure of this." She points at a part of the stain that looks like any random bloodstain to me. "For now though, we can definitely be sure of this." She moves her finger lower down in the stain. "This is your unique bond to Aidan. It's a Heavenly mark, an anointing for protection."

"So, does that help?" I ask.

Miss Mae looks over to Kara, who rolls up my soul map and hands it to me. "It doesn't yet. But at least now we know."

I put the soul map in my purse, unsure why I'd want a piece of fabric covered in my blood. "What do we know?"

Miss Mae sighs. "Oh honey, Kara's soul was damaged and broken even before she met this Aidan boy. As his power grows, it's trying to heal her deepest parts. But in that healing, a lot of power needs to be used, and that much power isn't meant to be held inside a normal human body. Kara's body is breaking down from it all, even as her soul heals."

"But, maybe there's a way to hold the power back," I say, wishing I didn't sound so pathetic.

Miss Mae takes Kara's hand, like she's trying to comfort her. "If there is, Kara hasn't found it."

I search Kara's desperate eyes. "Then what's going to happen?"

She doesn't look away when she answers. "If I stay with him, I'm going to die. Soon. It might already be inevitable."

FORTY

Aidan

Sleep hit me hard after I got back from my demon-hunting excursion; my body was exhausted from the crazy encounter. I dreamed about Raul, and woke up wondering if I should've done more for him. His spirit was surprisingly strong, considering his soul was so weak.

I sit up on the cot, putting my feet to the cold floor of the vault. The lack of windows in here makes it impossible to know what time it is. I could've slept the day away for all I know. And I don't have time to do that.

I grab my bag and lift it to my lap, then reach in and scrounge around inside it, looking for my toothbrush.

All of a sudden, something shocks me, making me jerk back my arm and jump to my feet. It felt like something bit my fingers, zapping an electrical current up my arm.

The contents of the bag scatter across the floor and I realize I grabbed Ava's bag by mistake. The pencil box, my sister's stuffed bunny, Mr. Ribbons . . . all of it's lying there.

Along with my mom's grimoire. That must have been what shocked me.

I flex my fingers, trying to shake off the feeling. And that's when I see the corner of a pink piece of paper sticking out of the grimoire's worn pages. Pink paper with a pattern of musical notes printed into the background.

I stare at it, knowing it's not my mom's, knowing it's Ava's, not sure what to do. Does it matter? Do I want to see what it says? It was likely written when she was losing her grip.

But it could also be an answer. And I definitely need one of those right now.

I bend over and gently take it by the edge. A smaller zap hits me, running up my arm. I pull back quickly with the paper in my hand and the sizzle stops. I unfold it and see a note. To me. Written in purple ink in Ava's familiar bubble script.

Hey Demon Dork,

I know that you're reading this and feeling betrayed. A sister isn't supposed to hurt her brother like I'm about to hurt you.

You know now what I am—you know that my humanity isn't real. Your determination, your goodness, isn't going to save me. But that's not your fault. Hopefully, by giving myself to them I can at least save one of us for a little while. Maybe wherever I am now I can stand in the doorway and hold them back. But you need to hear me. Don't come find me! Don't try and save me anymore. It's too late.

The Darkness knows you're in the wrong place, the wrong time. It'll do whatever it needs to make you surrender to them.

But that can't happen. You can't be brave, Aidan.

I will see you again, I will, but for now this letter will be my voice, my way of telling you what's next. Don't throw it

away. Don't, for any reason, burn it. I'll find a way to write
again.

Soon,
Ava

The paper trembles in my grip. My pulse hammers in my head
as my vision of the words blur.

Ava . . . She was preparing to leave me that whole time. She'd
always planned to give herself to them. I knew that, but feeling it
again, after everything . . . it's like it happened moments ago.

I rub my thumb against the edge of the paper and start to fold
it back up. But then I spot another line of script, below the signa-
ture, different than the rest. It's quick and sloppy, scrawled in black
letters, but not ink. It's more like it's singed onto the page.

Find me, you'll stop the pain if you find me.

A shiver trails down the back of my neck, the hair on my arms
rising. I could swear that line wasn't there a second ago. It just
appeared. As if Ava was sending me a message. Right this moment.
I look back up to the end of the letter and read, *I'll find a way to*
write again.

Could she really have just added those new words from . . .
wherever she is?

I look around the vault and reach out with my insides, feeling
for her, for anything. It's a jumble of history and decay, the energy
around me dusty, like all the old objects.

Ava? I whisper with my mind, trying to find her like I used to.
Nothing.

Then everything starts to rattle, items rocking on the steel
shelves around me. It's quick—over after only a few seconds.
Another earthquake.

I wait for a moment to be sure nothing else happens, heart racing. I try again to sense or see Ava's spirit. But she's not here. Whatever it was, she isn't close by.

I fold up the note, slide it into my back pocket, and head out of the vault. It's obvious where I need to go.

———

There is something strange when I get to the cave: the strong smell of burnt sage. When I walk into the shadows, I see that the crack in the doorway is three times larger, which explains the earthquake. Demon blood spills from the fissure, down the wall, and the sand beneath is coated in the black ooze. It trails out like oily fingers, making its way to the altar.

Whatever Ava's father is doing, it's getting worse. And if that demon in Hanna's office wasn't lying, there's more than just black ooze coming through that crack. I don't even want to think about what might have just slipped across. The image that Rebecca drew of me comes to mind, the one of me standing in front of the cave opening, on top of the mound of skulls. And the dream I had of Ava stabbing Kara—there were skulls in that, too. The two things that link it all together are the skulls and this cave.

This crack has probably already brought death; the waitress at the club was ripped to shreds by a demon that crossed here. I may have killed the demon and brought Miranda back, but God only knows how many more victims there have been that I haven't been around to resurrect.

I step up to the altar and stare at my sister. I reach out to her with my mind, begging for something, anything, to show me how to fix this. Fix any part of this. I'm tired of the silence, tired of the air that's empty of her. I need to be sure she's all right, that she'll come back to me—

My back pocket suddenly pulses hot against my skin. The note. I pull it out and unfold it just as new words appear in that same burnt script.

It's time. You'll find me soon. The secrets like spiders will whisper in your ear.

Soon. Not sure about the spiders, but as long as I'll be getting those secrets, that's all that matters to me.

"Thank you, Ava," I say to the air that doesn't feel quite as empty anymore.

Satisfied for now, I leave the cave and run up the pathway, back to the waiting car and driver from the club that Hanna let me use to come here. I consider knocking on Mrs. O'Linn's door to say hi to the two ladies, but I'm not sure my brain or stomach are prepared for a visit. As I round the top of the rise, something flickers at the edge of my sight. I turn.

Down on the beach a figure stands, facing the water. How did I not see him when I was down there? He's not that far from the cave entrance.

His dark hair ruffles in the ocean breeze as he stares out at the horizon. He's wearing cream pants and a cream shirt that contrast with his bronze skin, and he looks so out of place, like a man displaced from his homeland, but—

The figure turns, looking up to the rise where I'm standing.

Even from here I know who and what he is.

Daniel.

His mouth moves and I know he's saying my name. I feel it, inside my chest. But he doesn't say the Irish name, Aidan. He says a Chaldean name with the same meaning: *flame.*

My feet take me back down the path to the beach, slowly. And with each step the feelings of dread and curiosity twist more and more inside me, like a blade carving out my insides. He stands on the shore, waiting, watching me with something mysterious in his eyes. As I come closer I see sorrow. I see a fear that mirrors my own. And I suddenly realize I'm not just looking at some story or icon, I'm looking at a man.

Two yards away, I stop, not able to move any closer.

"You are so much like her," he says, his voice a pained whisper.

"No," I say. "I'm not." Is he not looking at me? Is he blind?

"Your heart," he says. "Gentle, like hers."

It dawns on me that he's *reading* me, looking through me, into my soul and my inner self, like I see people. "I barely knew her," I say, feeling the sorrow of it all spill out.

But what I just said isn't true. I understood her better than I understand myself.

He just smiles sadly, like he knows perfectly well what I'm not saying.

"I left you here," he says, like a confession, "left both of you, alone."

"Yes."

"You've done well."

I stare at him in disbelief, my eyes stinging with rising tears. How could he say that? It feels like the words I've longed to hear my whole life, but they're a total lie. "Why are you here now?" I ask, my throat raw.

He turns and looks to the water again. "This is where I lived my heart-life. In this place. It was like a dream, a parallel world where I could believe in the goodness of human nature, believe in innocence. And then I was kept away, I was told of my sin, and I knew I could never enter this world again." He stares at an approaching wave, watching it curl and push up the beach and then return before he speaks again, his voice more sure. "This journey is not for myself, though. It is as a messenger. I come to warn you and speak to your future and this world's downfall."

"You're a Harbinger," I say.

"The first that will come. The next will also be brought back to this world by you."

"Me? No way. No more waking up the dead."

"It is your path."

"I have things I need to be taking care of right now that don't include the end of the world." At least, I hope not.

"You worry for your sister, the tainted one."

Anger sparks to life in my gut. What did he just call her? "Her name is Ava. And she's not *tainted*."

"Her blood, that is what I'm referring to. Not her soul. But you must leave that alone, Aidan. Your mother's sin cannot become your own."

"Sin? My sister is not a *sin*. Her life is not a sin. She's a human girl who deserves a chance at a normal life, which she's never had because her mother was so strung out on casting magic that she went bat-shit crazy and then sacrificed herself to save that *sin* that you want me to leave behind."

"You misunderstand me. I mean the sin your mother committed by believing she was a god. Her life should have been one of peace and joy with you, but she spent it casting out, trying to change her fate through manipulation. Love is the only way to truly change things. And love does not harm, it only heals. I know your mother was in pain, but she chose poorly."

The words are honest and harsh, cutting through me like a knife.

"I hear in your voice what you yearn to do," he continues, "but you need to leave that behind. Don't bring her back, Aidan. You mustn't."

"I have to." My throat goes tight. "I made a promise."

He nods slowly. "I understand. Then I will say what I must and go. These are the words HaShem has spoken: *Forgive the father of your flesh, or you will be cast among the ashes. Acquit the mother of your blood, or you will drown in her sorrow. Release the sister of your soul, or you will find your hands holding her heart's blood."*

He stands silent for several seconds and I take it all in, breathless. *Let go,* he seems to be saying. Let go of this road I'm on, this path to save Ava. How can I? Leaving her to her fate . . . that's impossible.

"I know these things aren't what you wanted for the future, but we don't control life, we merely live it, searching for Grace. You've been given a large weight on your shoulders, but it's meant to be there, for the glory of HaShem. Not for your own devices. So know that your powers will only bring back human life that your own existence caused to be snuffed out; it will only fix that which you've broken in your birth. And each time you resurrect another, you give of your own life. Nothing is free. The life that was taken for a purpose cannot be saved by you. That soul will rise to paradise and wait to be made whole again."

I stare at him, realizing that means my power has the potential to fix what my own existence has broken, as much as it's meant to fight Darkness. All these things I've messed up with my life, with my birth, there's a way to mend some of it.

Which means there's still a way for me to save Ava and help Kara.

"Good-bye," he whispers at last, his voice full of unspoken things. "There is much I wish we could speak of, but for now I must obey. Know that I see you, that I am not ashamed to call you my son, Fire Bringer. Know that my heart is heavy with yours. Forgive me if you can."

And then he begins to fade, his body turning ghostly and translucent, until he disappears entirely. I can only watch the empty spot on the shore where he's been standing. My father. The man who I resurrected from dust. And I know I've already failed him. Because I can't do what he wants. I can't leave Ava to her fate, I can't let go. I have to try and save her.

FORTY-ONE

Aidan

Just as I'm walking back through my great-grandmother's yard, a vehicle turns off PCH and heads up the road toward the house. A green Jeep.

Connor?

He speeds up when he spots me and pulls over along the road, slamming on his brakes with a loud squeak. Then he jumps out and comes at me with his arms up in surrender, like he's worried I'm going to run away.

"I walk forward to meet him. "What're you doing here?" I ask. "I'm not going back to the house."

"I need your help with that job in the Valley."

"The wraith?" I ask. "But we took care of it."

He shakes his head. "Mrs. Foster just called a half hour ago. It yanked her son into the attic."

Oh, shit.

After telling Hanna's driver I don't need him, I get in the Jeep with Connor. We head south, taking the myriad of freeways to the 118, working our way inland to the Valley, getting off on Balboa. It isn't until we're sitting at the Chatsworth intersection that Connor speaks. The silence allows the emotions from from the encounter with my father to roil through me. I keep seeing him, his face a mirror of my own, his presence so demanding yet so still. My father. The man I've both feared and wondered about for so long. And I still have no idea who or what he really is. I should have read his soul, I should have asked a million questions I didn't ask. I keep hearing his words, his prophecy about me, I hear his voice and it's almost like I should recognize it from somewhere else—I'm grateful when reality breaks back in.

"Listen." Connor sounds hesitant. "This thing happened—I guess it was a moment—and . . . well, I kissed Rebecca. Twice."

My gut flips over, but my brain fills with relief. It's like half of me is angry at his words and the other half wants to hug him. *What the fuck is wrong with me?* I don't know what to say. "You and Rebecca kissed?"

He just looks ahead at the road. "You're pissed."

Why would I be pissed? Why *am* I pissed? I love Kara. I breathe for Kara. I'd bleed for Kara. "No," I say. But I need to be honest. This is Connor. "Maybe it's the damn fated souls thing, but . . . I feel a little like you just told me you made out with my girlfriend."

"Shit."

"Yeah."

He pulls onto the street and parks in front of the house, then eyes me like he's waiting for me to freak out.

"Do you like her?" I ask.

"I kissed her. Yeah, I like her."

"No, I mean, do you *care* about her?" Because I have to wonder if he even knows her. She's been hanging around less than a week. Of course, they have been thrown together a lot while everything's been going to hell the last few days.

"Yeah," he says quietly. "I think I might. She's so . . . ridiculous. But there's something about her, you know. She's got me all messed in the head."

"Yeah." Girls tend to do that.

"I'm just not sure."

"Of Rebecca?"

"I'm not sure if I've got the balls to share her."

The words seem to hover around us before they disappear into the air. I hate how tangled up it's all gotten. I have to believe that my heart isn't a bastard, that it's not lying to me. Because if there's one thing in my fucked-up life that I'm sure of, it's how I feel about Kara.

I follow Connor up the street to the neighbor's house where Mrs. Foster's been waiting for us. She must've been watching out the window, because she comes out into the yard to meet us halfway up the walk. "Thank you so much," she says, her voice strained as tears fill her eyes.

"Is your son all right?" Connor asks.

"He's got a bruised-up arm, but he's good. Just scared. We all are—terrified, really. I just can't stand this anymore, I can't. My poor little Jeffrey."

"We'll do everything we can." Connor says. "I promise. Just sit tight."

Mrs. Foster gives a jerky nod.

Even before we get to the door of the house, I smell it again. It's sticking to the air, like rotting insides. Death is now owner of this land.

"How could this have happened?" Connor asks. "I thought we got it. Didn't you see it die?"

"I thought I did." Maybe I'm getting rusty. After reading the damn ossuary, and resurrecting my father, I was definitely off.

"I have rowan ash." I pull out the glass bottle from my pocket and hand it to him. "Rub it on your face to confuse the thing."

He unscrews the lid and dumps a small amount of the black powder into his palm. "And then what, we have tea and cake?" He rubs the ash on his cheeks, under his eyes. "We need to figure out what went wrong last time."

"Let's just see what the hell is going on before we leap to any conclusions."

I shore up my inner walls as we walk into the house, my ears ringing. The first thing that hits me is the smell, putrid and sharp, even stronger than before. Then the ringing in my ears gets louder, making me squint from the irritation in my skull. I feel like I'm in a plane, under high pressure.

"Whoa," Connor says as he comes in behind me.

The front room is disgusting. There are food containers spilled across the carpet, substances on every surface: cottage cheese, mustard, Cheerios . . . like the contents of the kitchen had an orgy.

"This thing's been busy," I say.

He puts the back of his hand under his nose. "That smell. It's everywhere now."

"Whatever it owns, it marks."

He groans. "I'm about to mark a few things with last night's dinner if we don't hurry."

I reach into my pocket and pull out my Star of David. "Here, put this on. It'll balance you out a little."

He takes it. "It's time for some hands-on Aidan action, man. My holy water mixture obviously isn't going to do the trick."

A crash sounds from the back room, glass shattering.

"I think it heard you," I mumble.

We walk toward the hall, heading for where the noise came from. "We need to learn more, get a peek at where it was locked up." I haven't felt anything yet about this thing's state of mind or its history, but I'm waiting for the knowledge to fill me any second. A wraith is a person's ghost, after all. Even if it is a twisted one.

I get three steps down the hall and the light from the bedroom window blacks out, as if the sun disappeared. The temperature drops in a rush, tiny icicles forming along the edge of the ceiling.

Another crash sounds. Before I can make it to the nursery ahead, something flies from the bedroom to my left, cracking against the opposite wall. A million shards of blue glass spray out. The slivers hit—arm, cheek, neck—and the heat of blood and pain rises to the surface of my skin.

"Enough!" I yell as I ignore the sting.

The sunlight comes back with a *pop*, the temperature suddenly back to normal. I steady myself and walk the rest of the way into the nursery. The wraith isn't gone—the smell of it still burns in my nostrils.

Connor comes into the room behind me. He glances at my face and arm. "You're bleeding."

"I know."

The room is covered in those silver ghost webs again, even more of them than before. Whatever we did last time definitely didn't work.

Connor pulls on the string hanging from the attic's trapdoor, bringing it down, then unfolds the ladder. He starts to head up, but I stop him with a hand on his arm. "Wait." Blood rolls down my thumb onto his shirt. "Let me go first, just in case."

He relents and I go up, feeling like I'm climbing into the belly of the beast. I gag on the dank air, choking a little, before I can shove my stomach back down my throat.

"You okay?" Connor asks from below.

I give him a thumbs-up and climb in the rest of the way, holding my breath.

Connor's head pokes up from the hole and then disappears in a flash, the sounds of his coughing and gagging rising up instead. "Ah, dude, that's rank shit up there."

I can't stand up all the way in this section of the large space, so I stay on hands and knees, crawling over the creaking floor, wondering why anyone would come up here, ever. The surroundings stick to my skin, thick and full of energy and supercharged molecules. I feel the spirits of dead animals, tiny ones, in the crevices and dark corners, their tiny carcasses like warnings to whoever might enter. All these years, decades, half a century. And he's been trapped; trapped in wood and stone and mortar; caged, just as he was in life.

And I realize, I'm finally feeling him, the ghost that's now the wraith.

He worked hard, he worked and worked and drew blood for them, he took life to save his soul from the light, he hated the light. It stung his skin, it reminded him of things he couldn't look at, things he didn't want to feel. Bits and pieces, that's all he was.

The awareness, it pours through me, like a dark river of fractured images and thoughts. Sanity is nowhere to be found in the shards of misery and demented logic of the twisted consciousness left here. The shadow side of who he was. A keeper of bones. Hands that drew blood. Teeth that tore flesh. Because it was the only thing that would stem the pain of what was broken inside of him. The tiny lives he took patched his soul back together. His dark, dark soul.

A little girl, her braids tied with bright-pink bows.

He loved darkness.

She looks up at him, takes his hand.

He wanted to become darkness.

He feels her tiny fingers in his and can't wait to show her the doll he bought her.

He was darkness.

I jerk from the flood of knowledge and release my held breath through clenched teeth. I close my eyes, locking up my inner walls as tightly as they'll go, and beg God to let me get my hands on this bastard. Then I wait a second as I let the air back into my lungs a little at a time. I shiver deep in my bones, despite the thick heat of my surroundings. I don't want to feel anything else from this thing. No more.

The air is full of blood and decay. It fills my chest, congealing as I cough again. I fight it as I make my way to the door of the compartment, where the wraith was locked in. It's wide open. I close it enough to see the front, with the three locks and the carved word I saw in the video: *dybbuk*.

And then I spot a flash of white inside the small space. Along the far side. I pull my phone from my pocket and tap the flashlight app.

The light reveals the brick wall, the wood floor scratched and splintered, and then it falls on the white shape. A doll of some kind, its glass eyes wide.

Next to it lies a pile of white sticks.

No, those aren't sticks. They're bones. And I see a skull where the head would be. Small. Next to the doll. A child's skull.

My stomach rises, but for a whole different reason than the smell. My heart squeezes tightly in my chest.

"Oh, God," I breathe.

"What's wrong?" Connor asks, still hanging back by the trapdoor.

I can only shake my head as I realize what all those memories and thoughts meant. He was a kidnapper, a murderer. This is one of his victims.

The image of the little girl with the bright-pink bows in her hair comes back to me. *There was something about her . . .*

Connor is suddenly behind me. "What's going on?" He's holding a rag over his mouth, muffling his voice.

"There are bones in there." I motion to the cupboard.

"The guy's body?"

The ache inside sharpens as the words emerge: "A little girl." But her spirit isn't here. Whatever happened to her, her soul's at peace.

"Shit."

I crawl closer and reach inside, gritting my teeth as I move aside a bone to grab the doll.

"What the hell are you doing?"

"I need to know how they trapped this wraith in here, so we can do it again." I take the doll by a leg and bring it into the light. Its clothes are dusty and faded with age. Its porcelain cheek is smudged with filth. The pale-pink lips are cracked down to the chin, eyelids bobbing lazily up and down over the blue glass eyes with the movement of its head. Damn, this thing's creepy as shit.

"Yikes," Connor says.

I let myself open up to read the energy, the memories of the object. The consciousness of the wraith spills back into me in a rush, images of blood and fingers and small blue eyes, and I have to clench my muscles and lock my insides down to make it stop. "Fuck."

"What's wrong?"

"I need you to read this," I say, holding it out to him.

He stares at it but doesn't take it.

"I can't read it without feeling everything else," I say. "It's too much."

He reaches out and takes the arm of the doll. "You might have to help me," he says through the rag over his nose.

I nod, unsure what he means, but figuring I'll know in a second.

He closes his eyes then, the hand that's holding the rag lowering to his knee. His eyelids start to shiver. His fingers tighten on the doll's limb. He sits for several seconds before his skin begins to turn pale and go slick with sweat. His lips are violet now and his teeth chatter. As the beats tick by, he shakes harder and harder, and my nerves turn raw.

I tap him on the arm. "Connor, hey."

His head tips back, dark circles appearing around his eyes. He's still shivering, still locked in.

My pulse picks up, realizing now what he meant when he said I'd have to help him. He's not coming out of it. I grasp harder, shaking his arm. It's rigid as steel. "Connor!" I yell.

Still no response.

I grip his chin, pulling his head forward. And slap him as hard as I can.

"Shit!" he gasps, dropping the doll and bringing his palm to his pink cheek.

"Sorry," I say. "You didn't respond to a tap."

He works his jaw. "Damn, this job sucks."

I look to the cupboard, thinking of the girl's bones inside. "Yeah."

"The memories in that thing are rank."

"What'd you see?"

He shakes his head and runs a hand down his face. "It's not worth repeating." His fatigue is palpable. Those shadows around his eyes make him appear ten years older. His cheeks are even sunken in. "I'll just say that the wraith's spirit was once in the doll, and that's how the previous owner got it in there—must've had an exorcist help them or something. Except they didn't seem to know the bones were in there, too—poetic justice, I guess, the guy's soul having to be imprisoned with the remains of his last victim. They put the doll in the cupboard and locked it in there, which also locked the wraith in there."

"How long ago was it locked up?"

"Eighties, maybe? I'm not sure. But the spirit guy, the shadow, he died alone in this house in the forties. He'd keep his victims in the room below." He points at the trapdoor opening. The nursery. "And then, after he . . . killed," he swallows, his eyes pained, "he'd bring the victims up here to hide their bodies until he could find a place to bury them. He died before he could bury this girl." He looks at the cupboard. "It was a heart attack while he was watching TV."

"The doll was the anchor, then. I wonder how it got out." A simple possessed doll would've been so much easier; burn the doll and sprinkle lavender on the fire, catching the smoke in a jar with a pentagram on the lid, then bury the damn thing as deep as you can. Now the wraith is attached to the whole freaking house. Can't exactly burn that. "I'll have to just try and kill it."

"I wish that I could gut the bastard myself."

"Hopefully I can." I pick up the doll and put it back into the cupboard. "But you might not want to be here for this."

"I'm not leaving you to do this alone. What first?"

"I'm thinking that—"

But my words, my plans, are cut short as the temperature drops in a rush and Connor flies back, lifted up and tossed into the far corner of the attic. An avalanche of boxes and furniture falls on him.

I start to lunge for him. "Connor!"

Before I can move more than a foot, I'm shoved toward the trapdoor. I stumble, arm smacking the wood floor with a *crack* before I tumble through the hole. I land hard, feeling something snap as I hit the ground, my leg twisting at an odd angle. My head bounces off the floor and everything throbs, spins, my vision blurring.

A growl comes from behind the dresser to my left. A shadowy form moves along the wall in a thick black mass, red eyes keyed on me.

I try to scramble away but my limbs don't cooperate; my leg screams with a deep throb. I'm sure it's broken. And my arm maybe, too.

The shadow takes form, the shape of a man, all swirling darkness and bloody eyes. It crawls along the wall, gravity not a problem. Its body is made of smoke and shadow, wispy threads of black trailing from it. "You come to kill," it says in a gravely voice.

Shivers race over me and I begin to feel myself heal, the bone in my leg fusing together again painfully. I bite the ache back and focus on the wraith, the wicked spirit of a man who should be in the pit of Sheol, being tormented for all eternity, not here creating hell for an innocent family.

"Time for you to leave," I say.

Its shape is almost complete now, a middle-aged man, balding. He'd look pretty harmless, if I didn't know any better.

"No more," I say. "No more tormenting this place or the people in it."

"You have no power here," he says. "Your misplaced life belongs to the demon realms. This is the realm of the dead. And I know who you are."

I stare at the man, trying to remind myself that this isn't a demon, even though he's acting like one, with all those threats and lies. But he's human. He has the weaknesses of a human, even if he's become twisted into a wraith.

He growls as he slinks down to all fours again, now eye level with me. His irises turn blue then back to a deep, bloody red. "I am king here. I am God. And your sister isn't going to save you this time."

My body goes cold. My sister? It can't know her. Can it? "I won't listen to your lies," I say.

He rumbles out a low, scraping laugh. "We call her the white witch, little innocent bird that she is. Ava bird. I haven't been allowed to touch her yet—her captors are strong and keep their watch. But I see her. I know her connection to this terra, to you . . . sssseer."

Everything in me shakes. How can this thing know about Ava? How? Is her soul close? Could it really be that she hasn't been in Sheol this whole time? She's been here, just on the other side of the Veil? I can't help asking, "Who are these captors?"

"Bright Ones hold her," he says, his voice changing pitch oddly, now high and childlike. "They chained her up because they fear the little bird she is. Wise to fear the little bird."

Hope filters into my bones, realizing he means angels hold her soul. *Bright Ones* must be angels. "If you tell me where she is, I won't kill you," I say, realizing I can move my fingers, my toes; my bones are healed, or near enough. But I stay bent and awkward.

The wraith moves closer, his red eyes hollowing out into deep, bottomless pits. "Promisssssse?"

"Yeah."

He stares at me with those hollow eyes. Then he opens his mouth wide.

And a spider crawls out.

My stomach rises as it skitters over his chin, then slides down on a silver web, landing to make its way across the floor to me. "My secrets," he says, watching the spider crawl up my arm to my shoulder. "My secrets hide down deep, seer. My secrets wove me back together after you and your friend tried to destroy me."

Terror creeps up my skin with the arachnid's prickly legs, and the air freezes to ice shards in my lungs. I want to get away, get it off me, to smash my palm on the thing—the secret—but I need to know. I have to know where Ava is.

The creature makes it to my ear and the wraith man looks on with his fathomless eyes, a slow smile creeping up his pale features. And then the spider bites me just at the base of the skull, behind the ear.

A surge of white-hot fire spills into me, blinding me, fighting to take me over. Until my power easily pushes it back. And all that's left is awareness.

I know. I know where Ava's soul is.

I blink away the throbbing pain of the bite as the remains of the spider fall like dust down my chest. "Thank you," I say to the wraith. And then I reach out, grabbing him by the neck as I let my power loose with a surge of air and heat, pulling out my dagger with my other hand. I raise the blade and plunge it into the dark man's soul.

His eyes widen in terror and shock. "You promissssed," he gasps, "I am king here."

"I lied." And then I push my power out hard, as hard as I can manage, praying it'll destroy the wraith for real this time.

The gold light washes into the shadow as its scream fills the room, shaking my bones, until the dark wraith breaks apart into nothing, ceasing to exist at all. No ash remains, no smoke. The webs covering the room around me puff into nothing, the air taking on the scent of pine instead of death. I look around me and feel like it's not enough. This man's soul should've been eviscerated, boiled, burned over and over, for what he did to those kids. Without mercy, without relief. Agony should be his fate for eternity.

At least this time, even his secrets can't bring him back.

"Connor!" I yell up into the attic. "Are you okay?"

A grunt. "I got my leg stuck when I landed. If you're done killing that bastard I could use a little help."

I climb up and stick my head into the opening.

He points at his leg, which is hidden under a piece of furniture. "A bookshelf or something," he says. "Can't budge it on my own."

I crawl the rest of the way in and help him get unstuck. His leg is pretty banged up and bleeding, but he doesn't complain. "Let's get this shit cleaned up and get the hell out of this crazy place," he says. "You better have killed that thing good, because after what I saw in that fucking doll, I'm not planning on ever setting foot in this house again."

FORTY-TWO

Rebecca

Apple is making me nuts. She's been texting me every half hour since yesterday.

```
Did you lick his abs yet? Yum.
Time to cash in the V-card, Em.
If you don't want him, I'll take him.
```

And on. And on. And on. But everything with Connor became a distant memory after all the stuff at Miss Mae's. I finally shove my phone between my mattresses so I don't have to hear the vibration that accompanies each inane comment. Then I try and keep myself busy so I can stop thinking about everything that happened last night, and what it might mean. Once we left Miss Mae's place, Kara refused to talk about any of it. I was at a loss for words, too, so I wasn't surprised. I just wish there was something more I could do to help. For Aidan's sake. If Kara dies, it could destroy him.

I try to keep myself busy, but I can't seem to muffle the ache in my chest from all the worry. I spend time in the office, writing down the messages from the geriatric answering machine; I bring Sid tea for his aching bones—that shed smells like moldy bread and feet. I watch Finger play Xbox and I take a quiz in *Vogue* regarding my "preferred first date" and what that might mean on a deeper level. I even do the dishes.

I am officially losing my mind with anxiety. I actually tried talking to Sid when I brought him the tea, but he grumbled a thank-you and then leaned back against the shed wall and closed his eyes, obviously in a lot of pain. Maybe I should find a way to go back and see Miss Mae, ask her again whether there's anything I can do.

Of course, according to Connor, I shouldn't leave the house at all. He's been gone since early this morning, out on an important job. When I saw him, briefly, it was clear he didn't know about last night. He'd be furious if he did.

Kara stays in the office most of the day, watching hours and hours of video and listening to audio files she calls EMPs or something. She's trying to keep moving, to distract herself, like I am. I get it. But I kind of wish she'd talk to me about everything.

I'm relieved when I see her come to the surface again. She wanders through the entry and into the kitchen, fills a glass of water at the filtered tap, and then shuffles over to sit at the table. After staring off into no-man's-land for about five minutes, she slowly lowers her forehead to the table.

I pretend to be looking for salad fixings in the fridge before I say anything. (The choices are wilted lettuce or droopy lettuce.)

"Are you feeling all right, Kara?" I finally ask.

She grunts in response.

"Maybe you shouldn't be doing so much."

"Whatever, Mother," she mutters.

"Is the job you're working on important? Maybe I can help."

She sits up and squints at me. "You are hilarious."

"I'm not completely useless. Anyway, what's so hard about sitting and listening to EMPs all day long?"

She tightens her lips together, trying to hide a smile but failing. "What?"

"They're called EVPs; Electronic Voice Phenomena."

I sigh and plop down in the chair across the table. "I'm so stressed about all this mess with you and me. I need *something* to do. Something besides the dishes. And I can only make Sid so much tea before he floats away."

She laughs. "What do you normally do?"

I consider the question. What *do* I normally do?

Nothing. It just feels like something. But it's not. "I shop. Or go to the Santa Monica pier and hang out."

"So, basically you live in the *90210* TV show."

I roll my eyes. That's exactly what Connor said. "The guys are far more stuck up in my life than they are on that show."

"The guys, huh? You go out with a lot of *guys*?"

I give her a sideways look, wondering what she's trying to get at. "No, Kara."

"You know, I went to that beach party your friend threw a few weeks back. It was, um, as Holly would say, TMI with a lot of T and A."

I hide my face in my hands and try not to laugh. "Ugh. My friend Apple really likes to throw crazy parties."

"Well, it was very informative as to how the upper crust live."

"God, that's sad."

"Learning is good." She gives me a half smile.

And then I remember. "But didn't some guy hurt you or something?"

She seems taken off guard by my personal tone. She clears her throat and looks away from me. "Yeah, well . . . it happens."

"But Aidan beat him up."

"Wish I'd had the energy to do it myself."

I study her—the defensive set of her chin, her fingers picking at her shirt—and I realize she's embarrassed or intimidated or something. This tough girl doesn't seem like she'd be intimidated by anything. But it's obvious that she's still not sure about me.

After yesterday, it seems silly for there to be a wall between us. Maybe if I open up more, she'll do the same.

"I have a confession to make," I say.

Her eyes skip to mine, nervous.

"I kissed Connor."

She gasps. She actually gasps. "What?!" She leans back in the chair. "What do you mean? When?" It's like she can't believe it. Like I just told her I saw the ghost of Elvis flying past the window.

"I have no idea what happened," I say, shaking my head.

A frown replaces her smile. "You're not going to fuck with his head, are you?"

I laugh. "He's too busy messing with mine."

"Connor?" She scrunches her face in a way that tells me she's not buying it.

"He kissed me and then said he shouldn't have done it."

She rolls her eyes. "That sounds like him."

"Then he kissed me again the next day and told me all this big-overture-love-theme-music stuff. I'm not sure what to think."

"Just don't break him. I've never seen him with a girl, not for three years. I was actually beginning to wonder if he was gay."

"Not gay," I say. Not if that last kiss was any indication. He melted my insides all over the cab of the Jeep. Since Kara's more relaxed, I decide to move the conversation back to last night. "So, that Tray guy is Jax's brother?" I ask. Seems like a safe question.

"Yeah, half brother. They have different dads. Tray has gifts, like Jax, but he didn't want to live here. He takes care of their mom."

"What's Jax's gift again?" I ask.

"He reads clouds. It started out as being able to tell if there'd be rain or a drought."

"So, he's like a meteorologist?" I say, kidding but also confused.

Kara grins. "No, he predicts the possible future through reading clouds. Sid says he should be able to get signs about other things, eventually. You know, more important predictions."

"From the outside, he doesn't seem like he'd be sensitive enough . . . I mean, he's such a . . ."

"Jackass?"

I laugh in surprise. "I was going to say chauvinistic pig."

"You wouldn't think he has depth, I know," she says. "But he does. You just have to dig a little."

"His brother seems nice."

She gives me a coy look. "Oh yeah? Is Connor going to have competition?"

"Oh, sheesh. I think I have enough going on with this love triangle or square or whatever. We don't need to make it an octagon."

"I think that would be a pentagon if Tray joined the party."

"God, help us—"

A throat clears and both of us turn to see Finger standing in the archway, watching us. Smiling.

I gulp in surprise.

"Hey, Finger," Kara says, not sounding the least bit worried. "Did you need something?"

He just blinks at us and smiles. Then he turns and walks away, disappearing into a closet under the stairs like Harry Potter.

"Who *is* that guy?" I ask, staring at the closet door as it closes behind him.

"Finger." She laughs like my question is funny.

"But what does he *do*?"

"Sid said he was important, but I have no idea. He just stays out of the way."

"And never speaks. No one sees this as weird?"

"Finger has his own way. I guess you get used to it."

He seems nice enough, but the sneaky thing . . . and the random smiles. So weird.

I turn back to Kara. And freeze.

A bloody tear is sliding down her left cheek. "Kara," I whisper. She doesn't even notice it. "What's wrong?" The other eye pools pink, and a thick red drop falls from the corner.

"Your eyes, they're—"

Her jaw goes tight as she realizes what I'm saying. Her hand swipes at her cheek. She looks at her bloodstained palm. "It's happening again." Her voice is cold when she says it.

I jump up to get a rag, and by the time I turn back around she's slumping over, then tumbling to the floor.

"Kara!" I yell, rushing to kneel beside her. I brush the hair from her face as more blood spills from her closed eyes, the side of her mouth, and . . . oh, God, her ears. Her ears are bleeding. That can't be good. "Kara!"

"What's all the yelling?" Jax's voice comes from upstairs.

"Jax!" I scream. "Something's wrong with Kara!"

Footsteps pound down the stairs, and in two seconds, Jax is sliding to the floor. "No, no, no, this was supposed to stop when the asshole left." He touches her cheek, then scrambles up and runs out the back door, calling out for Sid.

———

Once we get her in bed, Jax, Sid, and I just stand there staring, none of us sure what to do. Connor isn't back yet from that emergency job he's been at all day. Holly isn't home from school. Not that either of them would know better than us. Should we call Aidan? No, he left his phone here. And supposedly it's his power that's causing this.

"We just have to wait," Sid says, like he's reading my thoughts. He moves his thin, birdlike body with difficulty, over to the chair in the corner.

"Maybe if we do a spell to break her bond with Aidan," Jax says hopefully.

"That's horrible," I say. And from what Miss Mae said, it would probably be useless.

"There's no such spell," Sid says. "Not that I've ever heard of. In any event, spells of the heart and soul are dangerous. As we see here before us."

"There has to be something we can do to fix this," Jax says through his teeth. He pounds on the wall with his fist. "Something."

"Maybe it just takes time," I say. Because I can't stand to believe that it's too late.

Sid shakes his head, looking doubtful, and then echoes my fear out loud. "It may be too far gone now for any help. I just wish that I understood better what's going on."

My chest constricts. I can't bear to think of what Aidan would feel if he were standing here. "This isn't right."

"It's not," Sid says. "It's what happens when you meddle with Fate."

"It should be me lying there, sick."

"No," he says sounding upset that I'd even mention it. "It shouldn't be either of you."

"Miss Mae said I had some sort of angelic blessing on me," I say. "But Kara doesn't have it. And that could be why she's dying."

Sid sits forward slowly in the chair. "You went with Kara to see Mae? When was this?"

"Last night." I lower myself to the edge of the bed and look down on Kara's still form. "She said that Kara's soul is damaged and as Aidan's energy tries to heal it, it's killing her body. And there's something unique about me, a blessing or something, that would have protected my body from the full force of Aidan's power. Kara doesn't have that protection."

My mind flashes to the oil Aidan's father dotted on my head, to the smell of summer it brought, and the way it hit me at my core. Like it was more than just a touch or a substance. He said my blessing would be given to another.

"Is there a way to just do the same angelic blessing on Kara?" I ask. "To give her the same protection I have?"

Sid shakes his head, "An angelic blessing is beyond any human to bestow. And an angel doesn't just go around blessing people. The anointing would've been on your mother while she carried you, or you would have had to receive it at birth. It's too late once the person is an adult, or even a child. Once they've experienced this world, the corruption of the flesh would fight back against the blessing and it would fail."

The thing that Aidan's father said comes to mind again, that my blessing will pass to another. So an angel can't solve this, but maybe I can. "Can the protection maybe be transferred, though? From human to human?"

FORTY-THREE

Aidan

Connor drops me off in the SubZero parking lot, telling me he'll reach me through Hanna if he needs more help while I *figure my shit out*, as he calls it.

I stand in the middle of the lot, trying to process everything. I know where Ava's soul is. And I'm pretty sure that I could use my resurrection power to wake her up, if I could get her soul and her body in the same place. The only thing I don't know is why Daniel said I shouldn't do it.

The possibility of causing more problems does make me pause, but at the same time, there's really no choice. Of course I have to try and bring her back. Why do prophecies have to be so vague? If only there was a warning label: *Don't screw with this or your hair will all fall out and you'll grow warts the size of Canada on your forehead.*

Instead, I get: *Don't screw with your dead sister or . . .* what? Bad shit will happen. Bad shit's already happening.

The secret spider showed me her soul being guarded by two angels, two Bright Ones, near Mugu Rock. Hopefully the presence of the angels means she's safe, but the vision was more of a fleeting impression than a complete picture of what's happening there. At least I know that if her father finds her and wants to use her, he'll be in for a fight.

I head into the club, looking for Hanna. I need someone's help, but I don't want to involve anyone at the house. Getting a young girl's corpse to Mugu Rock will take some finagling.

It seems like a ridiculous spot for angels to be watching over Ava's soul, considering how many car commercials have been filmed there. But spiritual events, portholes, crossroads, are all strongest in the places where there's water—I think it helps disguise the energy. Like the beach cave, and the doorway Sid came through by the dam. So maybe the spot near Mugu is charged, as well.

I find Hanna in her office, talking on the phone. She holds up a finger for me to wait. The conversation seems to be about a paper order, napkins and stuff, and it takes a few choice words from her to get whoever's on the other end of the line to cooperate. Who knew napkins could be so combative?

She hangs up with a satisfied smile on her face and turns to me. "How's it going, Aidan? Day three, any luck figuring things out?"

I'm not sure how I'm going to approach this, so I opt for quick honesty. "I need to find Eric to get his help. Do you know how to contact him?"

Her eyes widen. "I see. What sort of help do you need?"

"I'd prefer to discuss that with him." I'm pretty sure Hanna isn't going to want to be involved in moving my sister's body.

"Is this about Kara? He asked me to only contact him if it had something to do with you and your sister."

"It's my sister," I say.

She studies me, like she's checking to see if I'm lying. "Are you sure I can't help?"

"You won't want to be a part of this." Because if we get caught wandering around with a little girl's perfectly preserved corpse—with a stab wound in the chest—that won't be a good scene for anyone. "Just tell him that if I do this myself, he'll probably end up having to rescue me anyway, so he may as well join in the fun."

She smirks. "Okay, I'll contact him."

"Thanks." I start to leave and then pause, turning back. "So, are you and he . . . like, together?"

The scent of embarrassment fills the air. "How is that your business, young man?"

"I was under the impression that angels and humans weren't supposed to, uh, fraternize."

She clears her throat. "We aren't," she says quietly. "Eric is a good soldier." She doesn't seem thrilled about the last comment, but I'm sort of relieved, even though I'm rooting for them. I just don't want Eric to be punished or fired or something. I'm not sure what happens to angels when they disobey, but I'm guessing it's not good.

"Well, I'm glad he's back," I say. "With you."

"Yes." She shoos me out with a smile on her face that she can't fully hide, telling me to let her work.

I wait. Sitting in the vault, pacing in the vault, and grunting a lot while pacing in the vault, for several hours before he finally gets there.

"Jeez, I thought you'd decided to go on vacation again," I say. "What took you so long?"

"You are very impatient." Eric leans against a shelf. "What is going on with your sister?"

"Have you had any news or anything about her father, Jaasi'el, or whatever?"

He shakes his head. "Only hints that he's close. Rumors. He's very capable of remaining hidden, even from my kind."

"The crack in the doorway is growing and there are demons escaping. I encountered one. Here at the club, in Hanna's office."

"Yes, I'm aware. I heard about the resurrection. I've fixed the wards here, strengthened them."

"Heard?"

"It was written in the annals once it was done. Your father's resurrection, as well."

"What annals?"

"I believe it's called the Book of Life here. It records the movement of souls. You've caused a lot of movement lately."

Yes, more than I'd like. I wonder if my own soul movement is recorded in there. "Well, I didn't have much of a choice with the woman."

"You did the right thing, Aidan," he says in a calming voice.

I suppose if I'd messed up, I'd have heard from him. Seems to be the pattern. "Listen," I say, lowering my voice. "I know where Ava's soul is. It's not in Sheol. It's close, on our side of the gate."

He pushes off the shelf. "How do you know this?"

"She's been seen. Apparently wraiths gossip."

"A wraith saw her? That seems unlikely. Are you sure it wasn't lying? They are much like demons, you know."

"Yeah, I'm sure. It wasn't a lie. I know right where she is, being guarded by two angels—the wraith called them Bright Ones."

"It used the term Bright Ones?"

I nod.

"That would mean she's being guarded by Powers." He doesn't sound like he believes that.

I know that Powers are an order of angelic beings that rarely take form or show their faces. They are, basically, harnessed power. Light and Good and Truth.

"Why would such beings be guarding her soul on *this* side?" Eric asks, more to himself. "I assumed she'd be in Sheol. As did her father."

"Well, apparently not. But that's good, right? Because now I can put her soul back in her body and resurrect her. Then all this mess with the door can stop. There must be a way to heal the rift—"

Eric's face turns stern. "Your gifts aren't meant for bringing back anyone on a whim. They're only meant to return the Harbingers."

As if Ava is just *anyone*. "Daniel said the gift would also right the wrong of my birth. If a death occurred because of me, then I would have the ability to change that."

"You spoke with him?" He steps back, almost like the idea frightens him.

"He came to me and gave me a message."

"What message?"

"That doesn't matter." I'm not going to tell Eric what Daniel said about Ava, that's for sure. "I just need to do what I can to bring Ava back and then try to find a way to help Kara."

"Yes, Hanna spoke of what's happening with Kara. I'm sorry that I wasn't more aware of Rebecca. I assumed your soul mate's destiny would shift when yours did. That is what usually occurs."

"Yeah, well, it didn't." The worry for Kara surges back, but I make myself hold it in. For now. "About Ava, I'm thinking we should bring her body to the spot, so that I can have her soul and body in one location. Then I can do the resurrection."

His brow pinches. "That will be difficult, Aidan. We don't know what we'll find when we reach her. And a resurrection will take a lot from you. You still aren't fully aware of the price."

"I'm aware enough. And for Ava, it's worth it." I know the price is power and I seem to have plenty of that. And what good is power if it can't save the people I love?

"I will help you, because I'm fully aware that you'll do this with or without me, and I'm your guard. Though, my role will end if Heaven is involved in any of this; I cannot fight my own brethren, even for you. And Bright Ones watching your sister is no small thing."

"I know. Let's just take it one step at a time." I go to my bag and pull out the alabaster box. "Will I need this?"

"Does it call to you? Or open for you?"

I try to lift off the intricately carved lid, but it doesn't budge. "No."

"I'm not surprised. It's only meant for things that link to your calling."

So this event ahead of us isn't a part of the order of things that connect to my destiny. I'm not sure how to digest that.

Eric releases a sigh, obviously having reached the same conclusion. "You're positive this is something you want to do? It doesn't appear to be the correct path right now."

"I need to try."

"Very well." He steps toward me, coming up to my side. "This may sting a little," he says. Then he puts his hand to my shoulder and I'm torn in two.

FORTY-FOUR

Aidan

My vision blurs, my skin burns as I'm pulled apart, turned inside out, and before I can even register the pain, the movement, I'm collapsing onto the sand. I fall to my hands and knees and my stomach rebels, releasing its contents as spots dance in front of my eyes.

"It may take a moment to steady yourself," Eric says from beside me. "But we need to hurry. Ears everywhere. Once we move her, she won't be hidden any longer." His voice echoes off stone walls, and I realize we're in the beach cave.

I attempt to catch my breath, trying not to gag again as my stomach roils. It feels like it's still catching up with the rest of me. "Okay." I breathe in through my nose, out through my mouth—once, twice—then I get to my feet and lean on the altar. "I'm not sure I can carry her." Not if I feel this way when we make the next trip. I might drop her halfway to Mugu Rock. Not sure how the whole teleportation thing works, but I'm guessing humans aren't supposed to do it.

But then I remember Daniel seemed to disappear right before my eyes. "Is that travel *poof* thing something that prophets can do?" I ask.

"Of course," he says, sounding distracted. He points at the doorway. "I see what you mean about the rift."

The crack is all the way across now, stretching from one side of the archway to the other.

"We better go," he says. "Quickly. We need to remedy this now. Once Ava's returned to her flesh, perhaps Jaasi'el will feel it and stop this madness, so the rift can be healed." He gathers Ava gently in his arms, her small form limp as he settles her head against his chest. "Hold on to my shoulder."

I reach out and as soon as I touch his skin the world is swirling once more. My entire body flashes with agony, as if I'm being stretched out for miles. We land on the edge of a cliff, rocks and dirt flying as I skid to the ground. Eric is standing gracefully, like he just stepped off a curb. Ava is tucked gently against his chest, her sandaled feet dangling.

I look around us; we're on the ocean side of the rock, behind the fence that blocks access to the weak ledge. This is where the old highway used to be, until tide and time washed most of it into the sea. Now it's just a broken memory of concrete and asphalt above the waves. The small mountain they call a "rock" is behind us, and in front of us is the blue horizon of the Pacific.

"How will I know where the Powers are?" I ask. I saw them in the vision from the spider bite, but it was very vague. First I saw Mugu Rock, then the rocky shore far below.

"I should be able to feel them if they're here," Eric says, walking along the edge of the broken road. "I sense many ghost souls, and they seem to be clouding the energy, as is the water. Just give me a moment."

Ghost energies. I let my walls down a little and immediately feel them. I don't see anything but—

Wait, there's a girl. Maybe a little younger than me. She's standing just off to the side, near a spot you might be able to begin climbing down to the water. Her eyes are hollowed-out holes. I focus my energy on her and realize she's not a wraith. Just a ghost. Her eyes were cut out when she was killed.

I shiver and shore up my walls again. But I can still see her standing on the worn rocks, the wind from long ago whipping at her torn dress. A poor girl's dress. Maybe more than a hundred years old. She just stares at us with those sightless eyes.

"I feel the energy of the Powers," Eric says. "But we'll need to go down, closer to the water." He begins to walk toward the spot where the ghost is.

"We've got to climb down?" I ask.

"Don't mind the young woman. She appears to be a deterrent, but she won't bother us."

I grit my teeth as we begin the precarious climb down the rocks. I lock my walls up tighter, tight as I can, when we pass the ghost. She doesn't move except to follow us with her sightless gaze.

"She will, however, warn the guardians that we're here," Eric says over the growing sound of the waves.

When we finally make it to the lower shore, there's a small strip of rocky outcropping uncovered by the low, swirling tide that we begin to work our way across, trying to avoid stepping in the small tide pools. "I don't see anything weird." Or smell anything, or feel anything.

"There." He moves closer to a large rock that's jutting from the churning tide ahead just in front of us, and points past it, out at the horizon.

I follow his direction and think I've accidentally looked into the sinking sun over the water. I squint, blinded for a second, before my vision clears and I see the outlines of three figures in the air. The two on the ends are like oval balls of light. I can just barely make out the shapes of wings and faces within their bright glow.

The figure between them is a grey mist, hair like smoke curling around a tilted head, arms held out, wrists shackled with heavy chains.

Shackled. Ava's soul is shackled.

"These Powers aren't guarding her to protect her, Aidan."

"She's imprisoned," I whisper.

Eric kneels on the rocks, the white foam of a crashing wave spraying him; Ava's body is still curled in his arms. He yells over the tide, greeting the bright lights. "Oh, holy ones. We have come to bring this soul back into its earthly form."

The two lights pulse in unison. They don't speak, but I hear in their sound: *She is to be held until the day of judgment.*

I step forward, legs trembling. "I'm her brother and I need to bring her back. Her life was taken before her time."

Not safe, they sing.

"She'll be safe with me," I say.

"And I am his guardian," Eric says. "I watch him for our Lord. I will speak on his behalf."

The light forms pulse more strongly, more insistent: *Not safe.*

Eric turns to me and says under his breath, "This feels wrong, Aidan. They aren't usually sent to guard just anyone."

"Are you giving up already? We just got here."

"They aren't willing, and I have no authority over them. Only you have that. If you won't let this go, then you have to order them."

I gape at him. "What?"

"The only way for you to resurrect your sister is to force their hand. They will have to obey you, as Powers will yield only to prophets."

I turn back to the bright lights, clenching my fists at my sides to try and stop the shaking inside of me. So much energy surrounds them, so much power. The idea of forcing the will of these creatures feels . . . terrifying. "I order you to release that soul."

Their hum intensifies: *In whose name do you speak this?*

The answer comes to me as the question is still being asked. "In the name of Go'el Haddam, Kinsman Redeemer and Redeemer of Blood."

This time, I don't understand any meaning in the escalating hum and the pulses of the ever-brightening lights, I just feel heat and overwhelming power. I cover my eyes with my hand as the radiance surges one last time and the pitch reaches glass-breaking levels, sending me to my knees beside Eric.

Then it's silent. Still. Both of the Powers blink out. And all that remains is Ava's silver ghost, suspended over the water.

"Ava!" I call out.

Her soul doesn't move or seem to hear me.

I stumble over the few rocks between Eric and me. "I need to touch her to pull her soul back into her body, I think."

He holds out Ava's limp form, resting her legs over a larger rock. A wave crashes, water spraying over us in a salty mist. I kneel beside her and take her hand, gripping it as hard as I can. "Come back to me, Ava," I say. "Please!"

I hold my breath and plead with my power to work, but nothing happens.

"Your energy is too locked down right now, Aidan."

"I know, I know." Urgency fills me but I don't have a clue what I'm doing, I'm not sure how—

The air beside me flickers and suddenly the ghost woman with no eyes is an inch from me, her form a translucent presence against the backdrop of the water.

Her story floods over me, the violence of her death, the man whose hands choked her, stabbed her, murdered her in the most horrible way, foul beast that he was, foul man of gold and status . . .

My insides jump to life, the power surging through my mark in a painful rush of heat. The fire licks down my arm into my hand and spreads over Ava's shoulder and chest before sinking in. A section of my mark begins to slide down my hand and wrap around her arm. When I look up and over the water, I see that her soul begins to fade out and I realize it's working.

"The wound on her chest is healing," Eric says, his voice anxious.

A crack sounds at the air, and Eric and I startle, turning toward it, losing our focus on Ava. A large figure is careening our way at rocket speed. It lands with a heavy thud on the shore, no more than ten feet away, shaking the ground beneath us, sending the tide into fits as the water tries to decide where to go. Loose rocks tumble from the ledge above with sharp clacking sounds, before splashing into the frantic tide.

The creature stands to full height, rising, rising, until it's more than twelve feet at least, dark-brown wings spread wide, immeasurable. My gut turns liquid. A dominion angel, I recognize its armor, the scent of the power. "You will not have her," it says, voice booming with authority.

My throat closes and I can't breathe. I can't move. I'm frozen, staring as its dark skin shimmers with gold dust. It steps closer. Its bare chest is covered in scars that seem more like burns, in circles and lines that are ordered—not the chaotic markings of battle. Red-orange hair licks over its head and neck like tongues of fire. Its features are vaguely human, but also entirely alien—brow too prominent, green eyes too large. It wears a simple loincloth, and from its wrist and forearm grow thorny green vines that form finger-less gauntlets.

I know I've met the creature before—I recognize its scent. But for the life of me I can't remember which face it wore when it came to my mother.

I stumble back, letting go of Ava's hand as it moves closer, each step making the tide roll back and the rocks shake. It looks down on my sister's still body. And back at her silver ghost that's halfway home.

Then the creature turns to me. "You will not do this thing."

"I have to," I breathe out.

Jaasi'el looks at Eric. "What is your authority here?"

"I am the prophet's guardian."

"Since he led me here to my daughter," Jaasi'el says, "I will release him. But take him away from this place or I will do what I must to you both." Then he turns, finished with talking. He reaches his large palm out to Ava's silver ghost, and a command fills the stone, the water, every molecule within reach. Not a verbal command, but still a command: *Come!* And Ava's soul begins to float closer to his hand.

I led him here? My stomach rises, thinking of my foolishness. "You can't have her!" I shout, my will sparking in my skin, brightening my mark. "You won't use her!"

His thorny gauntlets slide over her ghostly throat as it enters his grip. "No, I will not use her corrupted soul. I will destroy it. I should never have allowed it to come this far."

"You've broken the Law by creating her," Eric says, "and now you seek redemption in her destruction?"

"No," Jaasi'el says, sounding resigned. "I am already Falling because of my folly. That cannot be mended. But I can right the wrong and hold back the tide of destruction just a little longer."

He begins to squeeze her soul, and my body reacts as if it were happening to me. "No!" I yell, hoarse from the pain. "Stop!"

I lunge, grabbing her body's wrist just as my power surges again, filling my vision with white light. Ava's energy links with mine, through our connection, that special link I've been looking for. It's there. Bonding us in spirit and soul and body. And I feel the fist on her soul, the burning, the agony of slowly becoming nothing.

Come back to me, Ava! I scream.

The air snaps, a surge of electrical energy breaking free with a loud *crack!* against every surface around us. I'm blown back, my power flickering out as I land ten feet from where I was. Eric flies back into the tide on the opposite side. Between us is Ava's body, hovering over the rocks, just as her soul had been. But now . . .

Her white-blonde hair blows around her head. It moves back and forth with the water below her. And her mouth opens to take in a gasping breath.

Jaasi'el turns to me, growling in rage. "What have you done?"

I hear Ava's mind spark to life. *Aidan! Where are you? I hear you.*

I'm here, I answer. *Open your eyes.*

He moves toward me like a predator ready to pounce. "Now it will be on your head." And before I can move, the creature has me by the chin, lifting me from the ground. Its thorny armor digs into my skin, the prongs growing as they enter, weaving agony into my skull. "Prophet." He spits on the rocks at his feet. "Curse you and your wicked soul. I should rip out your throat."

My mind goes blank from the pain. I flail, trying to find purchase on his large shoulders, trying to attack him with my fire. I spark and fade and flicker out, my breath locked in the vault of my lungs. And just as the world seems a million miles away, I'm tossed through the air. I land in the rocky tide with a splash and a crack. My head hits hard against stone, my skin shreds over the rough surface.

A scream rises around me, a banshee tearing at the air. And then someone is picking me up. I'm yanked through the pain and darkness as Eric's voice fills my ear. "Hold on," he says. "Hold on."

FORTY-FIVE

Rebecca

I sit by Kara the rest of the day until night falls and Connor gets home. He doesn't say anything when he comes into the room, just settles in against the wall beside the bed and closes his eyes, like he's praying.

"I want to fix this," I say quietly. "Will you help me?"

He turns to me. "What do you mean? How are you going to fix any of this?"

I shrug. "I don't know, but I feel like I'm the only one who can."

He looks back at Kara lying in the bed, so peaceful. "You mean, because of the whole Aidan thing?"

"Kara and I went and saw this lady, Miss Mae, and she said that I've got some sort of blessing or something, and that's what would've protected me from Aidan's power."

He leans forward. "You went into the city?"

"That's hardly the point, Connor." I move to sit by him on the floor. "Aidan's father said that my blessing would be given to another. Wouldn't you think that's supposed to be Kara?"

He sighs and runs a hand over his face, looking lost. "I don't know . . ."

"Connor, what if whatever's in me, whatever would have made it safe for me to link with Aidan, what if it's something that can be transferred?" I so desperately want it to be true. "Sid thinks it might be possible. And if I can maybe save her, well, then shouldn't I do that?"

"This is what Sid does," Connor says. "He gets these plans and tries to fix things, and when all the spells are done and the smoke clears everything is all fucked up and people I care about get hurt."

"This is me, Connor, not Sid. I want this."

He shakes his head. "I get it. I want to save her, I do. But what if it hurts you, Rebecca? What if transferring this blessing or whatever, instead of healing Kara, it kills *you*, too?"

"I don't know." For some reason, I'm not concerned about that. I guess some might say that's insane. Or at the very least, suicidal. "I want to try."

"We don't even know where to start."

"Oil," I say, thinking of the slick stuff Aidan's father put on my forehead.

"Huh?"

"We should get oil. And I'll pray or chant or something—maybe Sid will have found another idea—and then I'll just . . . give her what's mine." It sounds so simple, but we're not children playing a game of magic. This is real. And if it fails, someone could die. "I just want to try. It'll keep me from feeling so helpless."

He releases a growl. "Fine. But please, don't get your hopes up."

———

Sid settles in the chair beside the bed, holding a smoking stick. Connor hovers next to me, both of us standing over Kara. Jax paces by the door. Holly is helping Sid look for passages on blessings—he's having trouble seeing, he said. She reads out loud a story about Jacob, who stole his brother's blessing. It's not super helpful, detail-wise, but her voice is soothing. It calms my nerves a little.

I wish Aidan were here. I feel like he'd know exactly what to do. I, however, am completely clueless. Connor doesn't like that we're doing any of it, but he's trying to be supportive.

My head hurts.

I look down on Kara's body. It's damp with sweat, her skin glistening. The white sheets are tinged red in spots from the blood leaking from her eyes and ears every now and then. She's so pale. I can't remember—did she look this bad the other day when she passed out?

"Okay, what now?" Connor asks when Holly finishes her reading.

"Well," I say, picking up the small vial of oil from the box Sid brought up, "I think we should start by placing some of this on the center of her forehead?" I glance at Sid, looking for guidance.

He nods. "This is how a blessing would normally be done. And that is rose oil, so it's very positive in what it transmits. After placing the oil, you should whisper the blessing while still touching her."

I open the small vial and tip it over onto my finger, then I step closer to Kara, touching my slick finger to her forehead like Aidan's father did to me. Then I lean over and close my eyes, whispering, "I give you my protection, it's yours now." I open my eyes, leaving my fingers on her head.

I don't feel anything. I don't see any change. The smell of rose petals and sweat mingle in the air, and disappointment filters into my chest.

"I want you and Aidan to be happy, Kara. So take whatever you need from me, okay? I can't watch this happen to you anymore, and I know you love Aidan. You know how sad he would be if he saw you right now? You can't leave him, you just can't do that to him, so take the blessing or destiny from me, or whatever it is that his soul mate is supposed to have. Keep yourself safe."

I stare at her and remove my hand from her forehead. I still don't feel anything.

Of course this wasn't going to work. It was silly. Silly to think that something so simple would have any effect.

"That was lovely," Sid says.

He has tears in his eyes. And when I look to Connor, he's turned a little away.

"It was," Jax says quietly from the doorway. "Real nice." He sniffs and looks forlorn.

There's movement behind him, and suddenly Finger is standing next to him.

No one reacts to the appearance of the strange boy. No one but me. I stare, openmouthed. I don't think I've ever seen him upstairs. No, never. Not once.

"What is it, Finger?" Holly asks.

Finger makes a noise deep in his chest, like a grunt, then he steps into the room and comes around Connor to stand beside me, looking down at Kara. He towers over me by at least a foot. His greasy hair falls across his forehead and he grips the front of his food-stained shirt with a meaty fist, like he's trying to hold his heart. His brow scrunches in pain as he studies her.

I have to tense my leg muscles so I don't step away in response to him being so close. Because it's not just that he's physically close. Something about him fills the room.

I glance over at Connor; he's watching Finger with what looks like hope on his face.

Something wraps around my hand. It's Finger's, swallowing my own.

I step back then, fear lacing through me. What is he doing?

He smiles down at me, that same knowing smile. Then he pulls my hand closer to Kara's and weaves her lifeless fingers through mine. He plants his palm over Kara's forehead, cups his other over mine. And then . . .

Oh my God, I feel something. The inner part of me, the place I recognize as *me*, shifts. And I *feel* my self. Rebecca. The girl who loves her father, even when he's unlovable; who misses her brother with an ache that could swallow worlds; the girl who wants—no, needs—to make things right if she can.

Then the sensation deepens, and I feel something reach in— *into* me. Like an invisible finger, hooking my soul. My whole being shakes, moves, my insides bursting open in a rush. I'm pulled for- ward, I'm pulled back, I'm stretching until I'll break. I feel myself everywhere, surrounding the whole world.

And then a searing pain rips through my core and I hear a scream as a piece of me is torn off. Lost. Stolen. It slips into this boy in front of me, this *thing*, this beast, splintering my soul. And I can't—I can't breathe, I . . .

I go limp, crumpling to the floor. And when things inside set- tle again, finally going still, I open my eyes. The boy—Finger—he's still smiling down on me with that same knowing look. He nods at me like he's pleased and then turns and walks past me, out of the room.

"Rebecca." Connor crouches at my side.

Jax rushes in to check on Kara.

"What happened?" Connor looks up at Sid with accusation in his eyes. "What the fuck just happened?"

Sid shakes his head, obviously shocked. "I believe Finger just pulled the blessing from Rebecca and placed it into Kara."

"Really?" Holly says, leaning over to touch my arm.

Jax is looking in awe at Kara's quiet form. "That's nuts."

"How is that even possible?" Connor asks. "I thought Finger just manipulated emotions." He helps me into a sitting position but I can barely hold myself up.

"He reads emotions and changes them by pushing his own energy into others," Sid says. "I knew it might have other expressions but I never could have imagined . . . this."

"How will we know it worked?" Holly asks.

"Or know how this could affect Rebecca?" Connor adds, sounding concerned.

"The only way to know will be to watch it play out," Sid says. "Logically it shouldn't change anything for Rebecca since she wasn't the one who needed the blessing anymore."

After the way that all just felt, something inside me doesn't agree with that assessment, but I keep my thoughts to myself. I wanted this. I asked for this. I wanted to help and hopefully I did, hopefully this makes things better for everyone, and my part in this can pass on to Kara and no more pain will have to happen, Aidan can have peace, and I can . . . I don't know. What can I do? However this affects me, I'll just deal with it.

I'm able to feel my limbs better now. They're still weak, but I can breathe easily again, and the odd pain inside me has faded to a dull throb.

"I'm fine," I say, patting Connor's arm with the little energy I can muster, and smiling up at Holly in reassurance. "Just—I think I need to rest for a second." Connor helps me up onto my wobbly legs and lets me lean on him as he walks me to my room.

Once he gets me to the bed, I collapse with a sigh.

"Why did you have to push this?" He starts pacing back and forth. "Trying to fix shit always just makes it worse."

"Connor, what if that whole weird thing just saved Kara? Don't be ridiculous—of course you'd want me to try."

"What I want is for you to not also be sick, so I don't lose both of you."

"That's not going to happen." I scoot back in the bed and get into the sheets. "Don't be such a Gloomy Gus."

"Have you not been paying attention to the shit that goes down here?"

I yawn and sink into the mattress. "I'm fine. I'll sleep and wake up still me, you'll see."

He grunts and sits on the edge of the bed. "You scared me to death, Rebecca."

"I'm fine." I lazily pat him on the arm. "See." I point at my face and give him a toothy grin.

He rolls his eyes. "I'm so tired of everything falling apart."

"Then don't let it." I slide my fingers through his and hold his hand.

He looks down at our connection and squeezes back. "You are amazing, you know that?"

I just smile and close my eyes. But the last thought that crosses my mind is of Aidan, and my heart sparks with fear. Something isn't right. But I can't seem to open my eyes to tell Connor or ask him to check. I can only sink quickly, further and further into darkness, hearing a lone violin playing a mournful tune somewhere far away.

FORTY-SIX

Aidan

I surface to the memory of Ava playing the violin. But it doesn't feel like a memory, it feels real, the vibrations of the notes thrumming in the sand beneath me.

Sand? Where am I?

"He's waking up," she says.

Ava.

I hear you, Aidan. Her relief surrounds me as she pushes an image of the two of us playing chess on the floor of her old room from last year. *You won again.*

I open my eyes to her standing over me. She's lovely and alive, her eyes sparkling silver blue. The familiar cave walls surround us. The altar is behind her, the gateway just three feet to my left.

Eric is sitting beside me. His muscles are tense as Ava kisses my cheek, and he doesn't relax them until she moves away again, tucking her violin under her chin, drawing the bow over the strings.

"Oh, I missed this so much," she says over the instrument's sighing.

"Are you all right?" Eric whispers to me.

I can breathe, but when I try to speak my throat closes and I choke, coughing.

"We can't stay here," he says close to my ear. "She's not right, Aidan, something isn't—"

The violin stops and Eric swallows his words. A spark of fear lights around us. Eric is afraid? Of Ava?

She steps closer, studying my throat, then leans down. "You're not healing," she says, sounding distraught.

I manage to say, "Resurrection, it—" but then I break into a fit of coughs, my throat swollen and seared. What did that angel do to me? And how did we get away? I push all my questions into the air.

She sets the violin on the altar and kneels beside me. "We're okay. You're going to heal—won't you heal?"

I have no idea.

"I brought us back here," Ava says, giving a sideways glance at Eric. "Your guard was being a big baby and wouldn't do it."

Eric begins, "Please, Ava, don't—"

She clucks her tongue and holds up a finger, stopping his words. "No, no. You're just causing trouble. I won't rip you to shreds like I did that other angel—you've saved my brother many times, after all—but I will rip out your tongue just to watch you grow it back."

Dread works its cold fingers inside my chest. What did she just say?

"Oh, don't be a spoilsport, Aidan." She opens her hand, her palm facing Eric. "All I want is to be together, just us. He's a big downer." She moves her hand up and Eric rises in the air, hovering higher and higher. "Balloon angel." She giggles and then closes her fingers tight in a fist. Something *pops*, and Eric's gone with a suck of air.

I stare at her, stunned. *What've you done to him!?* What's wrong with her?

She turns back to the altar and picks up her violin, then plays a long high note. "I know you like him but he's really just a stick-in-the-mud. He doesn't tell you anything. And you deserve to know things. You and I deserve to know what our purpose is and why. Don't you think?" She draws out several more notes before adding, "He's fine, though. I just sent him to Egypt. He'll wink his way back here in no time."

The notes spilling from the violin slide up and down, carrying the song into a rhythmic lull as I take in what she's said, what she's done.

I don't understand. I don't know what to feel or think, everything is an ache or a bruise inside of me, in my heart and on my skin.

"Yes, I know," she says, sighing. "You expected a different sister to come back to you. The sweet, wide-eyed child. But I'm not that sister, am I? I sort of thought I would be, but I'm not." She shrugs. *Oh, well.*

Who are you, then?

I am the future, she answers with a swell of pride. She closes her eyes, and her body moves as the music's tempo picks up and she makes it a part of herself. *I am the key to the next cycle.*

She pulls the bow hard with a final sharp note and opens her eyes.

I gasp.

They're colorless. No sparkling blue at all. Her irises are white as snow.

I press hard into the rock wall at my back. Every nerve catches fire with the agony of what I'm seeing. *Ava.* I heave breath into my lungs, and tears cloud my vision of her. She's broken. She's wrong. She's not *my* Ava.

No, I am, she says. *Completed and whole.*

I sense movement to my right and turn. Several forms are approaching from the beach, through the shadows of the cave entrance. Sulfur billows into the space, suffocating me even more. Demons. At least a dozen of them.

I try to move, try to push myself along the wall to get away as they come closer. They don't seem to even notice me, though, and that's when I remember my amulet. Ava smiles at them, as if they were little children come to ask for candy. My stomach churns.

One claw rises over the rest, touching the hem of her shirt. And I can barely believe my eyes; it's the small demon from the day after the earthquake. The one who ripped the dog to shreds and tried to do a spell by arranging the pieces of its body.

Ava looks up at me, like she hears my horrified thoughts.

"Isn't he wonderful?" she asks. "A bit of a brutal thing, but he's so loyal." She reaches out and pats his head. "He tried so hard to bring me back. I met him after I crossed the Veil and he was so helpful, guiding me to the right beings. Do you know how slow time passes on the other side, where the ghosts live? A second lasts an eternity. But it allowed me to learn a lot before those Powers got ahold of me, telling me I was corrupted. I knew this little guy would come through."

She moves to the gateway, studying the crack and the black tar leaking from it. "They're anxious to escape Sheol, see? A few have crossed already."

A demon in the group pipes up, rattling off a bunch of noises that I don't understand at first, because my power is so weak. But after a moment I make sense of it: "He destroyed one. He is Destroyer. Fire and Pain."

"Yes, yes, I know," she says to them as they all grumble their agreements. "But he's off-limits." She holds out a palm to them. "Okay, who wants to do the honors?"

The dog-spell demon twitches a wing emphatically. She moves her hand closer to it.

It slices across her palm with a long talon, releasing a line of dripping red.

Don't do this Ava! I scream at her, knowing what horror she's about to let loose. I manage to lift myself, sliding my back up the wall. My power stirs to life from my panic and I find my feet. *This isn't you!*

Yes, it is.

You have a choice.

So do you. Do this with me, Aidan. We could fix everything.

Fix it? With carnage and death?

"Oh, Aidan, you still believe this mess can be saved. That was always your problem. But this world . . . it's just not worth it. It's certainly not worth your blood."

I won't let you do this.

"And how are you going to stop me? Are you going to kill me?" She tilts her head like she's actually curious to see if I would. Then she holds out her bloody palm, almost touching the gateway, like she's teasing me.

The demons around her chatter their teeth and click their talons together, cheering her on.

"Don't worry, the great-grams and her house will be protected," she says, like she's trying to make peace. "Your wards made sure of that. I can feel how strong they are. Nice job."

I feel for my power but it's barely a hum. My blade is in my back pocket—*I can't*—no. But I need to stop her—how can I stop her? My sister isn't supposed to be this thing. This isn't her. *This isn't you, Ava!*

"No matter how many times you say it, it won't make it true." She gives me a sad smile and reaches for the wall.

I lunge, knocking three demons out of the way, and grab her by the arm, yanking her back. We land with a spray of sand, my grip on her arm solid. She releases a giggle, like she used to do when she was close to getting caught in hide-and-seek.

And then I see why: a bloody smear just below the rift.

"Too late," she sings. "You should've used the knife on me."

I watch helplessly as the streak of blood becomes a second crack, sinking the wall in at that spot with a heavy *thud*, shaking the cave, jolting the ground beneath us. Fissures grow from the carved-out spot and join the first cracks, more black ooze appearing as the rock collapses inwards again and again.

Ava kisses her palm where it's cut and then blows the kiss at the wall.

Wind and silver threads whoosh around us in a shimmering tornado; they dance for a few seconds, like glinting faerie lights. And then they all collect together and spray toward the doorway, hitting the stone in a rush. A grinding of rock, and the wall gives way, bits flying into swirling darkness. Into nothingness. An empty expanse looks back from the other side, as if we're sitting on the edge of the world.

I look into the void, stunned. The dark wind rushes around us, the pull of its gravity a roar in my ears.

Ava leans against me, putting her head on my shoulder. "Isn't it lovely?"

It's lovely and horrifying and wrong. And a piece of me dies, watching the ash and silver storm churn. My mother gave herself to save her children, the two of us, sitting beside each other at the end of the world: Ava, the daughter who began it, and me, the son who failed to stop it.

"They're coming," she whispers conspiratorially. "I can hear them. Don't be afraid." She rubs my back in comfort. "You can share this with me. It's how it should be. Remember, I said everything would be all right in the end."

Oh, God.

The first beast that emerges is half bear, half man, with teeth six inches long and cloven feet. Another comes, a bug-like creature with long tentacles and a clacking jaw. Two more, with horns and spikes growing from their blue skin. The next several seem to mesh together, a mass of claws and teeth and saliva, the space crowding with their stench.

I gasp for clean air, unable to look away, unable to move to run. Ava rises and pats me on the head before walking right into the mass of shadow and talons, her white form disappearing among it all. They part slowly, moving aside to make way for her.

She stands in front of the doorway. The charcoal and black storm behind her grasps for her, and whips her hair around her face, which is filled with contentment. I watch her, realizing I need to run for her, to shove us both into the void and let it be over. But my cowardly limbs hesitate and Ava places her hand over the empty space. The gateway returns with a growl and grind of stone, the walls shivering from the impact.

Ava moves among her subjects, touching them and studying them, one by one. She seems to be speaking without saying anything; they grunt as if responding, and move as if following directions.

When she has greeted each one, she motions toward the beach. One by one, the creatures of all shapes and sizes slip past me and out the cave entrance, escaping into the world, a dark army of madness and death. All the while Ava smiles, her white eyes watching what she has unleashed. "This should be interesting, right?" she says. And then she winks at me and disappears with a pop of air.

I sit in the sand and stare for so long at the dried bloody print left behind on the gateway that my eyes water and my head begins to ache. I'm not sure how long it is before I can make myself move. I get to my feet, leaning on the altar before stumbling out of the cave and onto the beach. There are no demons here that I can see. The sun is setting over the horizon, but the sky above seems darker than it should. Distant shadows creep over the blanket of violet and orange on the horizon, swallowing up the colors and the sun.

I fall to my knees and find my voice at last, screaming into the air. I shove my rage, my remorse, my sorrow and brokenness up, up, up as far as they'll go. Crying out to the heavens. But the heavens only stare back in silence.

I make my way back to the club. I start by walking, keep walking for several miles, finally catch a bus, then another. It gives me time to think, which turns out to be very bad. Because I find no solutions. Only questions. Always the questions. Where is Eric? What happened to Jaasi'el? Did Ava really kill him?

But most importantly, where did Ava go, and what happened to her horde of demons?

My God, what did I just witness?

I find myself standing in the parking lot of the club, staring into the alley, numb, inside and out.

Someone taps me on the arm. "Aidan, I have a message. Come inside."

I shake my head. No messages.

"Eric is safe." It's Hanna. She heard from Eric. Eric who trusted me. "He'll find you again soon, but he's going to stay on the other side of the Veil until he can gather reinforcements and receive orders."

Ava told me she ripped the dominion angel to shreds—her own father. What good will reinforcements do against that sort of evil?

"Aidan," a soft voice says.

I turn, unable to believe what I'm hearing. "Kara," I say, breathless.

She's standing next to Hanna, her dark hair framing her face, her light eyes full of sorrow, her familiar sweet energy spilling out around her. So much of it. More than ever before. It curls against her fingers, her shoulders, a lovely summer-sky blue. It's so bright. Brighter than I've seen it. With all that energy, if I didn't know any better I'd say she was an angel.

"I'll leave you two alone," Hanna says.

Once Hanna has walked back toward the club, Kara comes closer, concern etched into her features. "What happened? You're so sad."

"My God, Kara," I whisper. "Ava . . ."

But it's like I don't have to say anything else, she hears me. She steps forward and touches her fingers to my chest, just over my mark.

The blue light of her energy slinks up her fingers and soaks in, every inch of my skin going warm in a rush. Peace fills me— awareness, and hope. Kara's peace, Kara's hope.

"You're not sick," I say, my throat tightening from the tenderness of it all, a balm to my crushed spirit.

She shakes her head and then slides her hands up my chest, resting against me. I wrap her in my embrace, clutching her to me, burying my face in her hair. "I love you," I whisper. "God, I love you."

She holds me tighter and rises up to kiss my jaw. "I know," she says, sounding amazed. "I can feel it."

"How did this happen? How are you not sick?"

She moves to see my face. "Rebecca healed me."

I stare at her in stunned silence.

"I know, it's crazy," she says. "But she sort of passed on her blessing to me, the one that linked her to you."

"How is that even possible?"

"Sid said that it was Finger who did the transfer. But it was all Rebecca's idea." She shakes her head like she can hardly believe it. "The girl is . . . she's so not normal. And it's weird, but I feel like a part of her is in me now. Like, I feel different."

I pull back and look at her more closely.

She laughs and pats my chest. "It's all good things, Aidan. Don't get scrunchy face. You're worried and nothing's happened."

"Something always happens."

She sighs and leans against me again. "Can't we just enjoy the win?"

"Yeah." I run my fingers over her hair, and try to soak in the feel of her, try not to think about what could happen. Or about Ava.

After a second of standing there in each other's arms, she says, "You're still worrying."

"How would you know?" I squeeze her tighter into my chest, loving how she fits perfectly against me, reveling in her smell, the way she fills the holes in me.

She giggles.

"What?"

She steps out of my arms and there's a huge grin on her face. "You are a *total* sap, aren't you? A big mush."

"Excuse me?"

She just smiles at me and takes my hand. "Oh, this is going to be fun."

"Okay, weirdo."

She tugs on my arm and pulls me toward the warehouse. "Let's go pack your stuff."

I let her lead me inside and back to the vault, and watch as she takes over and starts tossing my few possessions into my duffel. I lean on the wall and study her as she moves around me, focusing on her soul. But as I look over her arms, her neck, I can't see anything. No silver mark from the curse on her nape, no red handprint around her throat. I try opening myself up more, but there's nothing on her skin. Either I've lost my ability or Kara's soul is—

Wait. I can see a golden light on her back, at the base of her neck.

A handprint.

Is that really the only thing on her soul? A *golden* handprint.

My hand.

FORTY-SEVEN

Rebecca

Connor walks me out to the cab that's waiting in front of the house. I'm heading to Samantha's, since my dad will be home in a few days. I figured it was time to get some space, anyway. Since the transfer two days ago, there's this odd ache inside me. Like whatever I gave to Kara was carved out with a very dull knife. It might take some time for the pain to fade. I really hope it fades.

Aidan offered to walk me out, an offer I normally would have jumped at. But I declined. I don't feel like I need him anymore—one of the effects of the transfer, I guess. I can't sense his emotions anymore, either. That ability passed on to Kara, too. I have to wonder what else did.

I haven't tried to draw yet. I'm having trouble reconciling that I may have given that ability away, also. It's too painful to think that I could really be that . . . empty.

The one good thing that may have come of it—besides saving Kara, of course—is that I no longer have to worry about that demon. Sid and Aidan both agreed that I won't even be a blip on its radar anymore, since the vital part of me that it was trying to destroy isn't a part of me now. So I can go live my life.

Free.

I wish it felt like that. I keep thinking through it all, trying to figure out if I did something wrong. I knew when I gave away whatever was in me to save Kara, I knew that it was going to be a sacrifice. I knew, I just . . . I wasn't expecting this . . . vacancy.

Connor matches my pace down the path, not touching me. "I'm glad you're okay," he says as he opens the door to the cab.

"Yeah," I say, absently. I toss my bag onto the backseat and then turn to face him.

"Rebecca," he says, a frown creasing his brow. "What is it? You've been distant all day. You know we'll still see you, right?"

"We?"

"Well, yeah, all of us."

"What about you?" Have I lost that, too? Even though it was small, it was becoming something.

He reaches out and touches my arm. "Of course." He moves closer. "Rebecca, what's going on?"

I shake my head. "What if I gave everything I am, or was, to Kara? What if I'm no one now?"

"What?" He grips my arm and pulls me away from the cab, motioning for the driver to wait. "What do you mean? You aren't all right, are you?"

"I don't know what I am anymore."

"Rebecca . . ." He takes me in his arms, hugging me to him. "Then let me tell you. You're the kindest, most selfless person I know. You challenge me. You give me something to believe in."

The phrase sounds so odd coming from his lips about me, I can't help releasing a small laugh.

"You're laughing at me," he says.

"I was imagining that you were about to break into song."

He pulls back and acts offended. "Hey, I can sing."

I smile at his fake consternation.

"You know what else you are?" he says, tipping his head in a sly way. "Impossible to resist."

Before I can argue or even process his words, his hands are in my hair and his lips are on mine. He kisses me with so much delicate urgency my body goes limp and I have to lean against him to keep from falling over. For a hundred years, we stand entwined on the front lawn, not caring if the whole neighborhood sees. And a small piece of me is reborn as I feel myself finding solid ground again. I sense those small sparks deep down that are all *me*: the piece that loved Charlie, the sliver that misses my dad's lame jokes. And the new speck that's falling for this guy whose arms I'm in. I'm not empty, I'm not broken, not really. I'm just finding my way like everyone else. And I won't let myself be afraid of that.

Eventually Connor separates us enough to say, "Don't be shocked when I pick you up from school tomorrow. We're going surfing."

Somehow I find my voice. "Like any good stalker, you know my schedule."

"Of course," he says finding my lips again.

FORTY-EIGHT

Aidan

Raul—who I'll always think of as Scarlet—holds up another shirt against my chest and studies me with serious focus. "Try this one, I think it makes your eyes stand out more." He turns to Kara, who's sitting on a jeans display. "Don't you think, Kara? The green is better, right?"

Kara just stares at him in annoyance, totally not into the shopping spree.

Raul is in heaven, though. Sid insisted we get him a few new things to wear if he might be helping LA Paranormal now and then. From what I've told Sid about Raul, he thinks the kid might be a Light. He's not sure, though, so he wants me to keep the connection for a while. I'm supposed to see if he has any gifts and figure out if we should invite him into the house. For now, he's staying at a shelter for boys, which sucks, but it's better than drugs, prostitution, and living on the street. A little at a time.

It's been a week since I brought Ava back. A week of total silence—I haven't seen her or heard from her, and I can't seem to reach her with my mind; she's doing a really good job of blocking me out. Eric believes that she's gone behind the Veil, and I can't even begin to guess what she's planning. Whatever it is, it can't be good. She released about two dozen powerful demons from Sheol the day I resurrected her. Demons that are ready to do her bidding.

Eric and I went to the cave the next day and blocked it—the Devil's Gate dam, too—hoping to stop her from getting to the gateway and releasing more. But I worry that she'll still find a way.

I put the shirt back on the stack with ten others that Raul's brought me. "We're supposed to be shopping for you, not me, Raul," I say.

"It's more fun to shop for someone else." He sighs and wanders off into the forest of racks.

I go sit by Kara. "Stop having so much fun."

She gives me a sideways smile. "I hate shopping. With a passion."

"You've just never been shopping with me." I stand and tug her up, leading her to a rack with some dresses on it. I hold up a green one with white daises in front of me. "Too much? It'll go with my eyes."

Raul reappears. "Yes, it will," he sings.

Kara laughs and reaches for the rack beside me, pulling out a pink blouse. She holds it up and her smile fades. Black goop drips from the hem. "Ew, what the hell?"

"Drop it," I snap. "And get away from there." She lets the blouse fall and backs up a few steps.

No sulfur smell, no demon, but there's black ooze dripping from the rack and leaking over the clothes, like a demon was just perched there a second ago.

"Raul," I say, "we gotta go."

I turn to him. He's frozen, staring at a woman across the store who's sifting through a stack of pants. *"Dios mio,"* he whispers.

I follow his gaze. "What?" Nothing about the woman he's looking at seems alarming.

He takes a step back, eyes panicked. "No, no, no, this can't be happening again."

"What is it?" Kara asks, squinting in the same direction as me and Raul.

I don't see or sense anything. What the hell? I concentrate on the woman and realize that I can't even see her soul. "Something is very wrong," I say, pulling off my amulet and handing it to Kara.

She shoves it back at me. "What're you doing? Put that back on!"

"That lady is going to die," Raul says. He makes the sign of the cross over his chest.

"How do you know that?" I ask.

"Blood," he says in a hushed voice. "On her face."

I don't see any blood. Could he be on something right now? He told me he was clean, but—

A large black talon bursts from the woman's chest, blood spraying up onto her face.

Screams erupt all over the store and people scatter, racks tipping over, glass doors banging open.

Kara shoves my amulet back at me. "I'll get the new kid," she says, and then she grabs Raul, yanking him toward the exit, blending into the fleeing crowd.

The woman is slumped over the display of khakis, her vacant eyes staring off into the void, blood turning the merchandise under her dark brown. Her body jerks and a small demon scuttles up her back, then moves to rest on her head.

The creature is lopsided; most of the body is the size of a low-demon's, but its right claw is huge and misshapen. It clacks two of the large talons together like it's a crab and then leaps onto a rack about fifteen feet to my left.

My mind is still trying to compute what I just saw: a woman killed in broad daylight by a corporeal demon. In the Gap Outlet.

I drop my amulet and pull my dagger from the waist of my jeans. I take a few steps closer to the demon as the familiar spark of my power flicks on inside me. My hand catches fire, light trailing up my arm, into my chest. The store is empty now. A loud alarm is blaring through the space. Hopefully I can kill the demon quickly before the cops or ambulance get here. Before it's able to kill anyone else.

The demon leaps onto a closer rack, its squinty eyes following the flames sparking up and down my arm. And then it starts to make odd, whispery noises in the back of its throat, like it's talking to itself.

"You are very dead," I say to the thing, still moving closer. It's about five feet away now, black goop beginning to drip from its mouth and . . . from a hole in its chest? It's wounded. But how would it be—

It leaps, latching on to my arm with its smaller claw as it screeches and tries to stab me with the huge talon that it used to spear the dead woman.

I lunge forward, pinning it between my body and the jeans display, and then I stab it in the throat.

My fire surges into the thing, the power eating it from the inside out, turning it to ash.

I step back, the ashes crumbling to the floor. My blood drips down my arm, then joins the pile.

I hear Kara yelling at someone and turn to see her arguing with a security guard who's standing in front of the closed doors of the store, not letting her in. I pick up my amulet and start walking over, asking myself what the fuck just happened and wondering what the hell I'm going to tell that guard.

My back pocket heats in a quick burst.

The note Ava left me.

I pull it out and stare at the folded piece of paper. I've carried it with me everywhere this week, hoping she would contact me again. Hoping it was all a mistake and that she'd come to her senses.

But something tells me this is not going to be that kind of message.

I unfold the paper and scan down to the new line of writing. My gut drops as I read the burnt script in Ava's twelve-year-old hand:

Game on, Demon Dork.

ACKNOWLEDGMENTS

I have come to discover that writing the second book in a series is like being told you can fly seconds before someone tosses you off a cliff. You sit down to write and squeeze your eyes shut as you dive in, hoping and praying that you and your little book don't end up as a pile of unrecognizable squish at the base of the mountain. I want to thank all those who kept me sane through the process and made sure I didn't literally jump from any ledges.

To my agent, Miss Rossner: As always, you are Superwoman. I don't know how I'd walk this publishing road without your awesome spunkiness and kick-butt attitude. To Courtney Miller, who is always cheering me on and making me feel like I can actually accomplish this professional writing thing: I feel so blessed that you picked my books out of the pile and said yes! To Marianna Baer, who is always so encouraging: your notes and letters somehow energize me and empower me when I read them, and you always help me see more clearly how I can grow. And to the whole Skyscape team, who made my debut year so much fun and very stress-free: so many thank-yous!

Critique partners are a writer's salvation, and all my critter peeps are TheBomb.com for shiz. A million thanks to my peeps at Codex, who magically seem able to make me feel less insane than I am and give me that extra dose of Can-Do attitude I need to finish the race—we have nearly taken over, gang! To my Society of Children's Book Writers and Illustrators (SCBWI) roomie gals, Cheri and Catherine, who put up with my constant crazy: there's no way LA was the same without us last year. And to my LBs: You know who you are. You ladies are my backbone, my safe place; I'm so glad you still put up with me after all these years. And to my core peeps, Merrie, Rebecca, Paul, and Mike: We're still rolling, guys! Panera Productions strikes yet again.

To my adopted family, the amazing souls who understand when I have to hide or cry or complain (that's you Cayse and Dave!): thanks for reading stuff over and over, and thank you so much for putting up with me and taking me on vacations when I need it.

Thanks to my mom, a.k.a. Grandma of the Year! My kids would be eating stale bread crumbs and freezer-burnt chicken nuggets if it wasn't for you. And they'd also never get anywhere on time. You rock!

To my kids: There are no words in this world to convey how grateful I am to God for you. You four munchkins have been my inspiration and my world for the best parts of my life. You give me a reason to smile when joy seems so far out of reach. And when the clouds come rolling in, you allow me to still feel the sun on my face. There isn't a mom in the world as blessed as I am.

To my husband, my soul mate, my best self, my heart: I am yours and you are mine. I can't fathom how I was so blessed to be your partner in this crazy journey of life. My cup overflows.

And always, all gratefulness and love to *Elohim Emet*, the keeper of my soul.

ABOUT THE AUTHOR

Rachel A. Marks is an award-winning writer, a professional artist, and a cancer survivor. She is the author of the novels *Darkness Brutal* and *Darkness Fair*, parts one and two of The Dark Cycle series, and the novella *Winter Rose*. Her art can be found on the covers of several *New York Times* and *USA Today* bestselling novels. She lives in Southern California with her husband, four kids, six rabbits, two ducks, and a cat.

You can find out more about her weird life on her website: www.RachelAnneMarks.com.

ABOUT THE AUTHOR